"Well done, Mildred!"

Mystery Camp, Page 156

B. Ladler

BLACKIE'S
GIRL GUIDE STORY
OMNIBUS

Mystery Camp
With the Speedwell Patrol
The Island Camp

FRONTISPIECE BY BETTY LADLER

BLACKIE & SON LIMITED
LONDON AND GLASGOW

Printed in Great Britain by Blackie & Son, Ltd., Glasgow

Mystery   Camp
by
Violet   Methley

ABOUT THIS STORY

Disappointed of a promised camping site, the patrol finds itself unexpectedly allowed the freedom of the grounds surrounding the empty mansion of Favour Royal. Almost at once mysterious events arouse the Guides' curiosity. Why is the temporary tenant of the boat-house on the river so extremely unpleasant and suspicious of strangers? Whose is the savage dark face which so scared a Guide in the garden? These are but two of the problems which disturb the routine of the camp, and which the girls—an amusing and resourceful lot—set out to solve. Even if Favour Royal's legendary ghost is only a myth, the Guides manage to provide the place with some strange apparitions while they are there! In one particular this patrol is surely unique; its capacity for stilt-walking not only providing entertainment, but, when the great flood comes, proving highly useful. The flood, and its destruction of the railway embankment, brings the story to a climax and leads to a most unexpected solution of the mystery which has afforded the camp an almost uninterrupted series of thrills.

Contents

MYSTERY CAMP

CHAPTER I

Off and On

" I *never* knew how long your real names were before." Mildred Lord, the newest and youngest and tallest recruit to the 7th Knutsbridge Company of Guides, gazed in an almost awestruck way, out of round, pale blue eyes, down from her beanstalk height.

The object of her contemplation was a kit-bag upon which the three names of its three owners were painted, Geraldine, Katharine, and Christine Guthrie. And those three names took up almost all the available space of canvas.

" Well, you couldn't put Gerry, Kathy and Chrissy on a kit-bag," the eldest-by-a-minute protested. For the three were triplets of fourteen and a bit and took themselves, on the whole, rather seriously.

" We always rather wish we'd been called

Faith, Hope and Charity: those three names fit
so well together," Kathy said.

"Or Jemima, Kezia and Keren-happuch,"
Chrissy added dreamily. "They were the three
daughters of Job, don't you know—and the
fairest women in all the land as well. That's
really all it says about them."

"And so you think those names would have
been particularly suitable! Well, I must say,
Chrissy, you've a good opinion of yourselves!"
Pollie Rayner, one of the Patrol Leaders said,
and the rest of the Company laughed.

Except the triplets themselves; they had
seated themselves without a smile, side by side,
on their sausage-shaped and well-stuffed kit-bag,
exactly alike in size, in features, in dress, short
and slim and solemn-looking. But there the
likeness ended. As Peggy Wright said, they
were what drapers' advertisements called "The
same Model in Different Shades".

Gerry's hair and eyes were nearly black,
Kathy's bright brown, whilst Chrissy's eyes
were grey, and her hair—which, with all three,
was straight and close-cropped—was very fair,
a pale, gleaming gold.

This being so there was not the slightest fear
of mixing the three up, which was really rather
a comfort. Identical triplets would have been

too much of a good thing, although 7th Knutsbridge were very proud of possessing them in any shape at all. Twins are comparatively common, but how many Guide Companies can go one better than that? Very few, 7th Knutsbridge considered, and boasted loudly and long of the privilege.

Perhaps this is a good opportunity to introduce the rest of the Company, who were standing or sitting amongst piles of camp gear, waiting for the lorry which was to take them, bag and baggage, down to the New Forest for a whole August three weeks.

Their Captain was already at Ford's Hill, having gone down in advance; the Company was to travel in charge of the Lieutenant, Katherine Cree, usually known as " Loot ", and she had not yet appeared at the rendezvous although the lorry was due in less than five minutes. It was a gorgeous morning after weeks of rain, and altogether everyone rather agreed with Pam Wright when she gazed from the cloudless sky to a large picnic basket, and exclaimed rapturously:

" *And* Mother's made the most gorgeous egg sandwiches for lunch on the way! Isn't everything heavenly?"

Pam was Margaret's younger sister; both

were pretty, both were plump, and probably the two most popular girls in the Company. Mollie Rayner and Dina Perrett were joint quartermasters, and tremendously keen on their job. Pollie Rayner was Mollie's cousin, and her inseparable companion. Letty Lawson had red hair and a temper to match; Prue Quayle was as peaceful and gentle as her name, and Dora Harling always said of herself that she had nothing particular to distinguish her except the largest feet in the Company. The fourteenth and last of the lorry party, counting Lieutenant Katherine Cree as thirteenth, was Byrde van Buren, and she, as all the rest privately felt, was rather an unknown quantity at present.

Byrde was American born and bred, and she had only lately come to live with her rich, old, English grandparents at Knutsbridge. She was pale and dark-haired, with brown eyes always hidden behind horn-rimmed spectacles, and she was invariably beautifully dressed. Even her Guide uniform looked as if it had come off a wax model representing the ideal Guide. Somehow the Company feared that Byrde would need a good deal of living up to, for her manners were as superior as her dress, and her nails carefully manicured.

" Captain says that she'll shake down in camp and find her feet and her level," Pollie confided to Mollie. " But what I'm afraid of is that her level may be too frightfully high for the rest of us. Still, we ought to be able to keep her in her place—fourteen to one."

" Unless her place is as high as her level," Mollie pointed out, and Pollie agreed that this was unfortunately possible, as they surveyed Byrde seated primly upon an immaculate navy-blue suitcase, with navy-blue rug and sleeping bag neatly strapped and rolled beside her, and a second navy-blue case which contained a portable wireless given to her lately by her grandparents.

" She's a what-d'you-call 'em far too bright and good for—oh! you know!—whoever-it-is's daily food," Pollie concluded. " Oh, thank goodness! There's Loot at last! Now we've only the lorry to wait for."

Kitty Cree came racing down the road, but she did not wave back with her usual cheery shout in answer to the girls' greetings. She ran in silence, and her round, rosy face was so grave and troubled that everyone knew something was amiss even before she reached their group, leant breathlessly against the wall behind them, and panted out:

" Girls! Camp's off!"

For a few moments the whole assembled Company were too stunned to speak. Then Mildred, who was still very young for her height and size, burst into sudden tears and wailed:

" Oh!—it *can't* be! We *must* go!"

And there followed a buzz of exclamations and questions from everybody.

" I'm afraid it's only too true." Loot had recovered her breath by now, and subsided upon a pile of bedding. " I've just heard from Captain and she's had an accident. . . . It happened yesterday."

" Oh, she's not hurt badly?"

" How did she do it?"

" What's the matter?"

" Oh, Loot *darling*, say she isn't *dead*!"

The chorus which rose showed Alison Moore's popularity with her Company; for the moment even the girls' own disappointment was forgotten, as they waited anxiously to hear what had happened to their beloved Captain.

" No, no, of *course* not!" Kitty hurriedly reassured Pam, the last speaker. " It's nothing dangerous. But she's broken her leg rather badly, and she's in hospital. Of course, that means that she'll be in bed for weeks and weeks.

So we can't go to Ford's Hill; that site—it's in a park, you know—was especially lent to us on condition that Captain herself was there; it's not an ordinary camping place and the owners are very particular."

" Couldn't we go somewhere else, then?" Mildred choked back her sobs to inquire, but Loot shook her head decisively if sadly.

" I'm not qualified to take charge of a whole camp myself, even if we had a place to go to— I'm only nineteen, you know," she said. " And although Captain's thought and *thought*, there's no one else available at such short notice. No, I'm afraid there's nothing for it but to give up camp for this year."

" Oh! it *can't* be that we've just got to go . . . g-go home now to d-dinner, like every day!" Mildred wailed; and the others were all too much upset themselves even to smile at her rather babyish way of putting it. For it *was* a dreary idea—to go back to their homes this lovely day, to an ordinary, commonplace meal.

Yet most of them saw pretty plainly that their Lieutenant was right. There was nothing else to be done; when the lorry came it must drop each girl and her belongings at the different houses in the small, quiet country town where they belonged for all the rest of the year.

" I don't know really what Pam and I are to do," Margaret Wright spoke suddenly. " Mother and Father have gone abroad, thinking *we* were both comfortably got rid of, and the house is shut up."

" Oh! Margaret, that does make it difficult!" Poor Loot looked round despairingly. " But we shall have to manage something for you, somehow."

" Look here, couldn't we just camp somewhere quite close, in a field, perhaps, near the town," Dina Perrett, who was always a practical person, suggested. " Then if it was within reach of our own people, they needn't be anxious; we could always go straight home, if necessary. And it wouldn't be so bad as giving up the camp altogether."

" Oh! no, it wouldn't!"

" Yes, couldn't we do that?"

" *Darling* Loot, do say we can—do think of it!"

The excited, eager chorus rose again, but still Kitty shook her head despondently at the circle round her.

" There isn't any suitable site, you know; they are all apt to be damp just round here," she said. " It's such a low-lying sort of district, and we couldn't go anywhere that wasn't passed by the Camp Inspector."

" If we only camped in a *garden*, it would be better than nothing, better than going home," Mildred said forlornly; and at her words a curious expression suddenly crossed Kitty Cree's face, and she gave a little exclamation under her breath.

" I wonder! . . . could we possibly . . . ? It might be worth while. . . . Girls!" She sprang up and spoke in a quick, decisive way. " I'm going over to ' The Grey Mare ' to do some telephoning; when the lorry comes it must just wait. I may be ages and ages—it's impossible to say. And it may be no good at all. . . ."

She was gone, darting across the road. She vanished into the little, whitewashed inn, and the amazed Company were left to stare at each other and wonder what their Lieutenant's strange conduct could possibly mean.

" I do wish she wouldn't talk in hieroglyphics, or whatever you call them," Pollie sighed. " It leaves one in such suspense, not knowing what's happening."

" Well, that's better than going straight home to dinner," Mildred remarked hopefully, in spite of her tear-stained cheeks and red eyes and the small, wet handkerchief clutched in one hand.

The lorry arrived and was told to wait, as

Kitty had ordered. The minutes passed, dragging on into a quarter-hour—half-hour—hour. And it was still another fifteen minutes before the absentee appeared in the doorway of The Grey Mare.

" Oh! Loot, what ages you've been!" Pam cried, but Loot answered briskly and cheerfully:

" You wouldn't say so if you knew how much I've done in the time; *I* consider I've been very quick. And . . . I've been successful. No, don't talk all together! Just keep quiet and let me tell you what I've settled, and then you can say whether you all agree to the plan. And if you *do*, well, we'll pack into the lorry and go there at once, bag and baggage!"

" Go *where*?" Letty burst out, and Kitty Cree answered calmly:

" Favour Royal!"

CHAPTER II

Favour Royal

There was a simultaneous gasp from all the Guides, as Loot had intended there should be. For every one of them knew Favour Royal; it was *the* big place of the district, about three miles from Knutsbridge, a red-brick house surrounded by red trees—copper beeches, which were crimson-brown in spring, and ordinary beeches, which flamed red-gold in autumn.

Byrde spoke just in the voice which, though very American, was too soft to be as ugly as some of the voices in films.

" It's the Earl of Lorimer's house, isn't it?" she asked, sounding unusually excited.

" Yes—but he's not really rich enough to live there, poor thing!" Kitty answered. " He's a cousin of mine, though I haven't seen him since he was a little boy; that's why I had cheek enough to ask him . . . and by a big stroke of luck he was at the address which I knew *might* find him in London, and I caught him on the

phone. He says that we may certainly camp at
Favour Royal in or outside the house. There
isn't any furniture, but the rooms are all kept
dry and clean by the woman who lives at the
lodge, in case anybody wants to buy the place.
After I'd got Ralph's permission I rang up the
Camp Inspector. *She's* quite willing on condition that we sleep in the house if it's wet,
and that I pack anyone off home by the bus that
passes the gate who's the least tiny bit ill.
And then I rang up Captain, and *she* was
delighted. What an oration I've made! Hold
up your hands if you agree—if you'd like to
carry on and make a camp at Favour Royal."

In their enthusiasm, the thrust-up hands and
arms of the 7th Knutsbridge Company resembled a forest. Kitty Cree laughed.

" Well then, we won't keep the lorry waiting
any longer. Pack in!"

Chattering like a cageful of budgerigars, they
obeyed. Once started, questions and exclamations burst out again.

" Where shall we camp, Loot?"

" In our tents on the terrace just outside the
house, if it's fine, I think; in the big hall if it's
wet. And anyhow, we shall cook in the kitchens;
it won't do to make fires all over the place."

" I've never been inside those big iron gates

at Favour Royal, but Mother always told me the grounds are lovely," Prue said. " She went there when she was little."

" They *were*, but they're not kept up now; Ralph can't afford to have gardeners," Loot answered. " They're just a howling wilderness, he says, but we may use any fruit and vegetables we find growing wild. Oh! and there's a most important thing we've got to remember—we can't roam about *everywhere*. The grassy part of the park has been hired by a local farmer for grazing, so that we must stick to the footpaths there; and the river is let to a syndicate for fishing and is very strictly preserved, both banks. We must keep away from that part altogether. Fishing people are so frightfully particular. I had to promise faithfully not to trespass—so all of you must do the same."

" We promise!" the Company chorused, but Dora added anxiously:

" But the swimming pool—I know there's a really good one — have we promised not to go there?"

" No—the pool's not near the river; we can bathe there," Kitty said, and Dora sighed contentedly.

" Anyhow, what does it matter when we've got the house, *and* the gardens, *and* all the country

round—it's very pretty beyond Favour Royal,"
Margaret said, and the others entirely agreed.

Very soon the lorry was rolling through the
big iron gates and up the moss-covered, grass-
grown drive to deposit its load of girls and gear
at the foot of the flight of steps which led up to
the terrace in front of the house.

The house itself seemed to be staring at them
out of all the blank, uncurtained window-eyes
in its long, red-brick front.

" It looks somehow surprised," Pam said,
staring back. " But then, I don't suppose it's
ever seen Guides before, and p'raps we shock it
a bit. Loot dear, aren't you feeling just a little
bit *empty*? We had such an early breakfast, and
I was much too excited to eat it."

As Pam had put the feelings of most of the
Company into words, it was settled that they
would picnic there and then upon the terrace,
since they had everything ready in the way of
sandwiches, fruit, and thermos flasks for the
meal during the journey south, which they had
expected. So there in the sun they sat in a row
upon the low parapet, and looked at the view as
they picnicked. For the house was built on
a little rise in the low country round, so that
they could see for quite a fair distance beyond
the grounds, where the river went winding

away across the flats towards the big railway embankment.

Here and there gleaming patches of water showed where floods were out, for it had been a very wet summer.

"But even if it rains again, we shall be all right here," Kitty said. "With the house to back us up, we're safe, whatever happens; it's not as though we had only the tents."

"It's *much* more exciting than an ordinary camp, we think," Gerry said, speaking as usual for herself and her triplets. "Rather like having a desert island to explore, and a wreck too —that's the house. We don't know what we may find in either."

"Well, according to my cousin, ' desert ' is rather the name for both," Loot said, laughing. "Now, if everyone has finished, we'd better pitch the tents and get things all shipshape."

"Oh dear! I feel dreadfully sluggish," Pam complained. "I wonder why one always eats more than one ought when it's sandwiches! Margaret, you'll unpack for both of us, won't you, there's a darling?"

"I most certainly shan't!" her sister answered promptly. "I'm not going to encourage you to make a little pig of yourself. And you'll feel better if you run about."

" Run!" Pam groaned, but was soon busy with the rest, for the 7th Knutsbridge prided themselves upon being very efficient campers indeed.

The wide gravelled terrace, overgrown in places with grass and moss, was soon a tiny village of bell tents, six in all, including those for stores and hospital, each with the proper equipment. The cooking gear was all arranged in one of the big kitchens; Loot had interviewed the woman caretaker at the Lodge, and learnt that there was a good store of wood and some coal on the premises for immediate needs, which they could replace afterwards.

It was decided that they would use the dixies and other camp pots and pans on the open brick fireplace, not the big kitchen range, and the cooking patrol was already busy investigating hooks and chains, discovering a funny, low oven underneath the hearth, and promising to bake scones therein for tea.

Kitty Cree sat down on the terrace parapet with pad and pencil to scribble off a letter to Captain describing their arrival and installation, whilst some of the girls finished unpacking and the others scattered to explore the garden.

Mollie and Dina were amongst those last, but, like good quartermasters, they were bent on business and had determined to find if there were really any useable vegetables or fruit to add to the commissariat. Byrde was with them, neat and precise as usual, but with very observant eyes behind her horn-rimmed spectacles.

This the other two soon discovered when they reached a large walled garden, which had evidently once been given up to vegetables and fruit. Now beds and borders and even the paths were overgrown with a tangle of weeds— or at least that was what Dina and Mollie called them until corrected by Byrde.

" But they're *not*, only just perfectly good plants run wild a bit," she protested. " These feathery leaves are carrots—look!"

She gave a little tug and the root came up easily, the root which was an undoubted carrot, all ready for a stew.

" And those with the smart white flowers are onions." Byrde was looking round keenly. " *These* are turnips; even if the roots shouldn't be much the leaves are good to eat."

" I know—turnip-tops!" Dina was determined to show that she was not quite an ignoramus. " And those are potatoes with the purply blossoms."

" Sure!" Byrde drawled in her slow way.

" And the blue flowers are chicory—that makes a dandy salad, *and* endive too. . . . Oh! I'll show you! I'm real good at salads, and you can make them of 'most anything . . . dandelion leaves—and nasturtium seeds."

" Why, Byrde, you're quite excited! . . . I didn't know you ever were!" Mollie burst out bluntly, and the American girl grew rather pink.

" 'Pends if I'm int'rested," she said. " See here! I bet I'll find you enough vegetables in this garden to last all the time we're here."

" Potatoes too? We eat a fearful lot of potatoes in camp!" The experienced Mollie shook her head wisely, and Byrde contemplated the purple-flowered plants.

" W—ell no, perhaps not potatoes," she said. " Those have run to seed and they mayn't be too good. But there's fruit too. I can see lots of berries on the raspberry vines over there, though vurry likely the early birds have been at them before *this* Byrde came—we'll soon find out."

As she spoke, Byrde was walking down the grass-grown path towards the tangle of raspberry canes and prickly gooseberry bushes, caught together by trails of bramble-like logans. The other two girls were close behind her, and heard what she heard, saw what she saw.

For suddenly from the thicket came a most unearthly and hideous yell, a kind of wailing howl, almost like that of a wolf or some other wild beast. And at the same moment a face was thrust forward through the tangle, fiercely, threateningly, a dark face surrounded by straggling, oily, black hair.

CHAPTER III

Someone in the Walled Garden

Byrde's hand had been stretched out towards a ripe dangling raspberry, but at that sight and sound she started back with a cry of fear.

And next instant all three Guides were running down the path, out of the walled garden, back to the terrace where Kitty still sat writing, to stammer out a story which seemed to her at first as incoherent as it was incredible.

" But, my dear girls, it seems so absolutely and utterly impossible!" She looked from one to the other of the three Guides as they stood round her, breathless, with flushed, scared faces. " How *could* there be anyone of that sort here?"

" I can't help it, it was an Indian—a Red Indian," Byrde said doggedly. " I've seen them before, Loot, in America; I went with my poppa to a Reservation where they lived, some of the Red Indians that are left. And they

looked exactly like this one, sort of coppery brown, with long black hair, and they did some dances and yelled as he did—it was the war whoop."

" A Red Indian war-whooping at Favour Royal! Oh! it's absurd!" Kitty tried to laugh again, but broke off, for there was no doubt about the seriousness of the three girls.

" It wasn't only Byrde—we all saw him and heard him, Loot, just as she says," Dina protested.

" He was a Red Indian," Byrde repeated. " And mad, too."

" Mad!" Kitty stared in consternation. " But how could you know? . . ."

" Angry, I mean."

" Yes, he looked horribly fierce and angry; that's what upset us so much, that and the howling, though I suppose we *were* rather idiots to be frightened and run like that!" Mollie tried to laugh, remembering her age and her seniority in the Company. " But he took us by surprise, peering out of the raspberries like that."

" Of course, I quite understand, but all the same I'm sure there's no need to be frightened, my children." Kitty sprang up from her seat on the parapet, determined to take the matter in

hand at once. " Look here, let's go back to the place where you saw him, and tackle this savage of yours together."

" Yes, do let's," Mollie agreed after a moment's hesitation, and the others followed their two leaders.

They reached the vegetable garden and the raspberry canes, only to find that there was no sign of the startling apparition himself. But Byrde, pulling aside the tangle, pointed out triumphantly that the bushes behind were trampled down and crushed.

" You can see where he *was*, anyway," she said. " And he must have come in through that little door in the wall; there's a sort of path beaten down all the way to it."

The door proved to be open, and beyond it a damp, mossy path led through an overgrown shrubbery of rhododendrons, which rose on either side as high as trees, with dark hollows underneath their twisted trunks. It was rather a weird, dim place even on this sunny afternoon, with a dank chill hanging about it; and Kitty noticed that the three girls, as they walked, glanced round nervously, as though expecting more fierce faces to peer out at them.

But she was determined herself to get to the bottom of the affair and settle it once and for all,

before the infection spread and the whole camp was attacked by nerves almost before it had started. She spoke with brisk cheerfulness.

" I'll tell you what, girls, we'll go down to the Lodge and ask Mrs. Cooper about it. I'm sure she'll be able to tell us all there is to tell about this Indian of yours."

But Mrs. Cooper was not so helpful as Loot had hoped.

" I don't know, I'm sure, Miss; I've never see'd anybody like *that* about," she said, wiping soapy arms on her apron. " Not but what it might well be one o' the lads from the village playin' tricks. They're main vexed, you see, the boys, 'cause the gents that 'as the fishing won't let 'em go near the river, not if it was ever so. An' 'ard on the children 'tis, like my pore little Ernie, who mayn't go catching tiddlers like 'e always did, what with the barbary wire an' all they've put up, tearin' their trousies somethin' cruel."

" Well, of course, if the water is preserved, Mrs. Cooper, they've a right to make a fuss if anyone goes near to disturb the fish," said Loot. " Ernie must come and see if he can find some tiddlers in the swimming pool in the Park, sometime—we haven't any barbed wire there! So you think this person they saw may have been one of the village boys dressed up?"

"Like as not, Miss—just to annoy the gents. They lives in the boat'ouse, you know, down on the river, the gents do, an' does for themselves. Not often seen in the village, they isn't— gets almost everythink down from London. But I've nothink against 'em meself; very civil to me they was when they just come 'ere, and after all, what I say is, if people likes to keep theirselves *to* theirselves, why, 'tis their own business and no one else's! Not as I 'olds with the barbary wire. . . ."

"Thanks, Mrs. Cooper," Kitty interrupted the flow of talk which seemed likely to go on for ever, and the four departed.

For a time they walked up the drive in silence; then Loot spoke cheerfully:

"Well, that's almost certain to be the explanation of your Indian, and I think we'd better tell the others that these village boys are going about dressed up, otherwise they may get a nasty scare, as you did."

"I dare say it's all right to *tell* them so, but all the same it isn't true," Byrde said deliberately. "Because it wasn't a boy dressed up; it was a real Red Indian."

And since it was quite evident that the two others agreed with Byrde, poor Kitty felt rather like a lost person in a forest, who has come back after walking in a circle to the exact place from which she started. She spoke rather sharply in her perplexity over the situation.

" Well, I hope you won't tell the other girls that, and frighten them, Byrde. I'm sure you're making a mistake, and if the whole Company get scared and nervy—well, we shall simply have to break up the camp and go home, that's all. I can do it at a moment's notice, and I shall if there's any trouble over this silly Red Indian affair; I can't run the risk of any girls being upset."

Kitty's tones were resolute, and Mollie at once took alarm at such a suggestion.

" Oh! Loot, don't talk about such an awful thing after everything has turned out so splendidly," she said. " Of *course* we won't say anything to frighten the others, will we, you two?"

" Of course not!" Dina agreed eagerly. " And after all, I dare say it *wasn't* a real Indian; I don't see how it could be. It's much more likely to have been someone pretending."

Byrde did not look convinced; Byrde's small pale face had an extremely obstinate expression, and she spoke stiffly:

" You needn't be afraid, any of you; I'm

not going to make trouble. I shan't say anything about anybody to anyone."

And with this promise Kitty was obliged to be satisfied.

CHAPTER IV

Warning to Trespassers

At breakfast next morning everybody decided that nobody could have imagined that they were less than three miles as the crow flies from their ordinary everyday homes. Except for bird and beast noises, the night had been as absolutely silent as though they had been in the middle of the New Forest, and somehow the big red house did not seem to make them feel less far away. And it was another perfectly gorgeous morning.

There was no sign of any living thing except bees and butterflies and wasps in the walled garden when Mollie and Dina led a foraging party there, and it was the greatest fun to gather one's own fruit and vegetables—carrots and onions for the stew, a few rather small peas, turnip-tops and raspberries and loganberries for a " fool ". The Company had been told casually that the village boys might try to scare them by dressing up, but the information had not worried them in the least.

" If they do, we'll jolly well think of some way to scare them back," Pam remarked. " They've no right to come into *our* gardens, have they, Loot? Cheek, I call it!"

It had been settled that they would go nowhere particular that morning, but take out a tea picnic in the afternoon. And so after the camp jobs were done, after the formalities when the Colour Party ran up the Union Jack to the top of the flagstaff duly erected midway along the terrace, after kit inspection, after the wood and water and milk patrols had done their duties, all except the cooking patrol, busy with the preparations for dinner, went their several ways of exploration.

As usual, Gerry, Kathy and Chrissy found themselves together; one of the triplets never seemed quite happy or complete without the other two, and they wandered off in their usual fashion, linked together arm in arm.

" It's just like a desert island," Gerry repeated. " And there's no telling what we may discover if we explore in an old, old place like this—ruins, p'raps, or buried treasure."

" Or skeletons of people who've got caught in hollow trees or fallen into wells, or something," Kathy, whose taste in literature was rather gruesome, suggested cheerfully. " That's a thing we've often read about in old houses too, haven't we?"

"Well, if there are, we don't want to find them," Chrissy said emphatically. "Let's go into that copsy sort of place; it looks as though there'd be squirrels and all sorts of beasts there ; it's awfully like the woods in the ' Wind in the Willows ', where there were fierce little faces looking out everywhere. Wouldn't it be frightfully exciting if we found a badger?"

There did not seem to be any badgers out walking, but the wood was exciting all the same. One of the first things they saw was a squirrel, which skimmed up a tree trunk like a furry flash of lightning, and next they discovered a small brown owl sitting on a bough, as motionless as though it had been stuffed; even when they stood close beneath it, it did not attempt to fly away.

"Look, it's opening one eye!" Chrissy cried excitedly. "It winked at us—it distinctly winked! Would an *ordinary* owl do that?"

But at an attempt to climb up and stroke it, the extraordinary owl opened both yellow eyes and flopped away, leaving the triplets to continue their explorations further and further into the wood. It attracted them on and on as woods do, showing them one fascinating little path and

then another, which simply *had* to be investigated, until finally a particularly alluring pathlet
led them straight to a barbed wire entanglement
which barred their way completely.

Such barbed wire, too! Thick and strong and
spiky, and stretching away as far as they could
see in both directions, twisting round tree
trunks and wriggling through bushes like a
very unpleasant kind of snake.

" S'pose this is the part preserved for fishing,
where we're not to go," Gerry remarked. " Then
the river must be through there somewhere."

" Don't see it!" Chrissy was screwing up her
eyes and peering through the bushes. " Look
here, we'd better find out just where the barbed
wire *does* go, hadn't we? Then we shall know
exactly where we're *not* to go."

Gerry and Chrissy agreed with this reasoning,
and the three proceeded to follow the prickly
barrier through the wood.

" Oh, why do forbidden places always look so
specially lovely!" Kathy sighed after a while.
" There's the water through there, all cool and
gleamy, and we mayn't touch a single drop of
it."

" Well, they can't keep us from looking, anyway," Gerry said, and proceeded to scramble up
a tree from which she could get a better view.

That tree was very close to the barbed
wire; some of the boughs indeed stretched
right over into the forbidden territory. And
it was when Gerry was balancing on one of these
boughs and craning her neck to get a nearer
view of things that something happened.

" The wire goes right across the river a bit
lower down—big twists of it close down to the
water so that a boat couldn't possibly get
along," she informed her sisters. " It doesn't
look as though anyone could even swim past it,
and p'raps there's more under the water too."

" There is—so I don't advise any of you
young ladies to try to get through."

It was a very stern voice that spoke, and a
very stern-looking person to whom it belonged.
He was standing only a few yards away, his
brown breeches and gaiters and greenish coat
and hat almost invisible amongst the trees.
He was tall and dark with black eyebrows
almost meeting in a frown as he came a few
steps farther forward and spoke again.

" What are you doing here—trespassing?"

" We're *not*!" Gerry slid down and faced the
newcomer bravely. " We were only looking."

" It seemed so! Well, I'll trouble you not
even to *look*. This land is strictly preserved."

" We know. We were only finding out which

part was which, so that we shouldn't trespass by mistake," Kathy explained gravely, but the dark man only laughed in an unpleasant way.

" Why are you in the Favour Royal grounds at all?" he asked. " They're not open to the public."

" Because we're living at Favour Royal, a whole Company of us—Guides," Chrissy answered this time—the triplets usually took turns in that and other ways. " Lord Lorimer gave us permission to camp here, but we know all about the river being preserved."

" Yet the first thing you do is to come hanging round, and discussing whether you could swim through the barrier. I won't have it, I tell you."

" We weren't—we won't—we didn't! . . ." The triplets all began to speak together, then broke off and looked at each other helplessly, crimson faced.

" Well, if I catch you here again, I shall report it to the police," the tall man said grimly. " And I may as well tell you, too, that we keep a couple of very fierce dogs at the boat-house, to tackle trespassers. It wouldn't do any good to explain to *them* that you were only looking. You and your little friends had better bear that in mind—but we shan't bother you if you don't interfere with us."

Gerry, Kathy and Chrissy walked slowly away, and knew even without turning round their heads that the man was watching them go, watching them out of sight. And it was not until then that any of the three spoke.

" Well, we certainly shan't want to go near *him* again, disagreeable pig!" Chrissy said decidedly. " Hadn't he got a cruel face, just like a villain in a film?"

" He was very good-looking, *I* thought," Kathy remarked, and the other two stared at her. To begin with, the " I " was unusual, for the triplets always seemed to think the same thing.

" Well—if you *like* black hair and black eyes. . . ."

" I do, rather, and that teeny little black moustache," Kathy said calmly. " He's frightfully romantic-looking, not a bit like anyone here for ordinary fishing."

" Why do you suppose he's here, then?" Gerry and Chrissy demanded together, amazed at this independence of opinion expressed by their triplet.

" Of course I don't *know* . . . but I've got a sort of a kind of idea . . ." Kathy said slowly. " He's so aristocratic-looking—and Loot said she didn't know him by sight, so it would be quite safe his being here."

" Who?" Chrissy demanded.

" Why . . . Lord Lorimer. He's too poor to live here properly, so I b'lieve he's doing it in disguise, at the boat-house, because he just can't bear to leave the place. And of course that would be why he doesn't want people poking round, recognizing him. It's not just my own idea; I read somewhere about an earl dressing up as a gamekeeper," Kathy concluded modestly.

Both her sisters stared in more amazement than before, but with a certain amount of respect. After all, Kathy's idea *might* be possible, and it would be a tremendously thrilling sort of thing to believe.

" That look of his *might* have been just sadness, of course, not hatefulness," Chrissy reflected. " And he certainly has a face like somebody in a book, not just an everyday sort of person."

" P'raps we could find out from Loot what her cousin's like," suggested Gerry practically, and the others agreed that this was a good plan.

However, the answer to the question put by Chrissy with elaborate carelessness at dinnertime was not particularly helpful to their romance.

" Ralph? Oh! he was a very ordinary little

boy," Kitty answered. " Freckled, and brownish hair . . . nobody that you'd look at twice."

" Well, *that* isn't like the fishing man," Chrissy remarked when the triplets were alone, but Kathy only answered calmly:

" That's nothing. People change—and brown hair often goes dark, you know. Besides, he may have dyed it as a disguise. I'm certainer than ever that he'll turn out to be the Earl!"

CHAPTER V

Bluebeard's Chamber

"'Favour Royal owes its name to the romantic tradition that Queen Elizabeth presented the house and dem . . . dem . . . dem-es-ne'—however do you pronounce that word, Loot?"

"I don't, if I can help it!" Kitty laughed. "Go on, Dina, miss it out."

"'To a handsome young courtier, Robert Lorimer, through royal favour. It is a fine red-brick edifice built in the characteristic Elizabethan style, with later additions sufficiently in harmony with the original structure. The linen-fold panelling in the hall and the ornate ornamentations of the ceiling in the long gallery are particularly noticeable features . . .' um . . . um . . . um . . . and a lot more about ceilings and things. I think I'll skip a bit. . . ." Dina murmured, fluttering over the pages of the little paper-covered guide-book to Favour Royal which Loot had ordered from the station bookstall at Knutsbridge.

It was a wet day, this third of their camping,

and the Company had determined to spend it in exploring the house thoroughly.

Not that there was much to see, for practically all the rooms were emptied of furniture, with nothing left of what had once been there except discoloured patches on the walls where pictures had hung or bureaux and cabinets stood. Mice scuttled across the floor when doors were opened; in one room a bat was discovered hanging head downwards, like a small leathery umbrella, from the end of a curtain pole.

The greyness of the day peering at them through the dirty windows added to the dreariness of everything, and none of the Guides was particularly sorry when at last they reached the kitchen where a big wood fire was blazing, and a pleasant odour of prospective Irish stew hung on the warm air.

And it was here that Dina discovered a more interesting part of the guide-book than that concerned with ceilings and panelling.

" Oh! listen to this, all of you!" she cried. " It's quite thrilling! ' As is only natural in so old a house, many legends and traditions are associated with Favour Royal, although, curiously enough, there is no haunted room, no ghostly visitant who is supposed to visit the actual mansion itself.' "

" I call that mean!" Byrde remarked. " A house like this just *ought* to have a real live spook. I could have fancied the ghost of Lady Something-or-Other in one of those cunning little powder-closet rooms."

" Wait! You haven't let me finish; there *is* a ghost!" Dina said. " ' According to popular gossip, it is in the stone-paved stable yard that a spectre still walks in the shape of the famous " Long Man " of Favour Royal, especially in the vicinity of a disused well. Here it is said that an unhappy footman of unusually tall stature met with a tragic death in the early years of the Seventeenth Century, and here strange lights and a ghostly figure of immense height have been reported as seen by reputable witnesses even within the memory of local inhabitants.' "

" There! I was sure we should find there was a ghost if we waited long enough, only Dina was such a long time coming to it," Pam said triumphantly. " Do let's go and look at that well and the stone-paved stable yard. It isn't raining now."

" Pam, you know perfectly well that there are no such things as ghosts," Kitty protested, but Pam only answered sweetly:

" Of course I do, Loot darling, but one can be

frightfully interested in ghosts without really believing in them a bit, don't you think? So we simply must see the place where the ' Long Man ' is *supposed* to be, even if we know he isn't."

As the rest of the Company obviously agreed with Pam, Kitty yielded, and the whole party accordingly paddled out over the wet cobbles into the stable yard behind the main buildings of the house, which formed one side of the square stone-paved space.

To the right were the stables, ranges of stalls which had been empty of horses for so long that they had a very deserted air.

The third side of the yard, opposite the house, was taken up by a large brick archway with a turret and a clock to crown it, and with quarters for the coachman and his staff above and on each side of the entrance.

" And that was the harness-room and carriage-house." Kitty pointed to the buildings on the fourth side of the yard. " A big empty place that would have made a fine garage for cars, if poor Ralph had had the money to keep them. As it is, I suppose it's as empty as the stables now—and as dreary looking."

Having already investigated the bare stalls, with the names of horses on brass plates still

above them, " Regent ", " Kitty ", " Rufus ",
" Duke ", Pam and Mildred led the way across
to the other buildings. Grass grew between the
cobbles of the yard, and moss and golden lichen
covered the stone slabs round the well—" *The
Well* ", as Pam whispered to her companion,
with rusted chains hanging from a rotten beam
above it.

Instead of being open like the stable door,
however, that of the harness-room was barred
and padlocked. Not only that, but the windows
were heavily shuttered so that it was impossible
to see in.

" Funny!" Pam, doubled up, screwed her
head sideways to examine a crack beneath one
of these shutters. " Why should an empty
coach-house be locked up when everything else
is open?"

" It's a nuisance, too," Mollie said, with a
professional eye turned upon the building.
" Just think what a splendid place this would
have been to stow our tents and gear, if the
weather turns really permanently wet."

" Well, we shall just have to manage with the
whole of the rest of Favour Royal, and honestly
I don't think that we can complain," laughed
Loot. " Don't be greedy, Mollie!"

" Yes, but it's so *funny*!" Pam persisted. " It

just makes one long to see inside, to know why it's shut up like this."

"Doesn't it?" Dora tiptoed before a knot-hole in another shuttered window, whilst Pollie folded herself in two to investigate the door. "Anything mysterious like this is such a thrill."

"Well, you are a set of inquisitive little Fatimas!" Kitty surveyed her Company with amusement. "Whatever do you think can be hidden there? Do you suppose it's the bodies of the seven wives of my cousin, Bluebeard?"

"No, of course not!" Dora moved away from her window rather sheepishly, but Pam, still extremely busy with her own investigations, remarked calmly:

"Well—there *is* a queer sort of smell coming from inside, rather like something dead."

"Pam! Don't be so horrid!" Margaret ejaculated.

"But there *is*! Probably it's just mice or rats who've crawled in and died there," Pam per-sisted. "But I'm not making it up that there *is* a funny smell; come and sniff it yourself, Margaret."

"Thanks — I don't want to," Margaret answered disgustedly, whilst Mollie remarked reasonably that almost any place would smell fusty if it was shut up for some time.

"This isn't exactly fustiness," Pam pronounced. "It's more . . . more . . . it *might* be a dead cat. Anyway, I don't think it's very wholesome."

"Then stop sniffing it and come away, you horrid little pig!" Margaret displayed an eldersisterly exasperation with her persistent junior, and Pam reluctantly obeyed.

"I vote we go back to the kitchen, and the fire," Prue said, with a little shiver. "It's a bit chilly, and this is such a gloomy sort of place."

"Yes, it feels kind of haunted, doesn't it? By the well especially," said Pam, the irrepressible. "I do wonder if the long footman's body is still down there. It *might* be, you know—the skeleton, anyway."

"Pam, you really are a bit too bad!" Kitty's patience gave out at last. "Let's hope that dinner will soon be ready, and then you'll have something else to think about."

"Well, but there couldn't be anything more interesting than ghosts and mysteries, even if we don't believe in them," Pam said pensively, in an effort for that last word in an argument which her persistence so often secured for her.

But this time Kitty did not intend things to be left quite like that. She had noticed Prue's little shiver, caught nervous Mildred's glance towards the old well, and she spoke with determination.

" Look here, girls! I just want you all to understand thoroughly that I don't like and I won't have all this silly talk about ghosts and mysteries while we're at Favour Royal. And the first person I catch talking such nonsense again will be sent straight back home to Knutsbridge. That's all I've got to say, but I mean it."

There was silence for a moment before Margaret spoke, with a baleful eye upon her younger sister, who gazed back calmly.

" We all agree, I'm sure, Loot, and I think it's very ungrateful to make up silly mysteries about a place that's been lent to us so frightfully kindly."

" Oh, so do I!" said Pam earnestly, and Kitty found herself smiling almost against her will at this turning of the tables.

" Well—remember!" she said, and left it at that.

CHAPTER VI

Meet Maurice the Mascot

The morning after the wet day was gorgeous; clear and bright and cloudless, and almost too good to be true. At least that was Dora's opinion, and Dora's father, Mr. Harling, was a farmer, and had taught his daughter weatherlore. In fact, the Company considered Dora a living barometer, and also their especial authority on birds, beasts and botany, so that it was only an inferiority complex of the deepest dye which made her declare that outsize feet were her one distinguishing mark amongst the Guides.

" It's a ' fox '," Dora pronounced, looking up at the sky, as she and Letty Lawson went on six o'clock rounds, distributing two biscuits per Guide.

" A——?" Letty looked an interrogation mark, if that is possible.

" ' Fox!' A deceiving foxy day—a day that pretends it's going to be fine weather when there's more wet to come," Dora explained.

" But it'll be all right this morning, anyhow."

" It's heavenly," Letty said, depositing the last two biscuits on the flap of Pollie's sleeping-bag with an admonitory poke to the half-awake owner, and emerging from the tent to munch her own ration. " Let's race down the hill to the hedge and back."

The hill sloped down from the terrace and camp to a hedge which must have been white with May in spring, and was now patched with red where the haws were ripening, in thick bunches.

" It's supposed to mean a hard winter when there are so many berries for the birds," Dora remarked, as the two Guides paused for a moment by the hedge, panting after their run. " Goodness! How wet everything is; if I'd had shoes on they'd have been soaked through and through."

" Yes, it's a bit marshy down here." Letty lifted one foot with a squelching sound. " Of course the river's quite close, only there are such thick bushes between us and it. The preservers don't really need all that barbed wire the triplets told us about to keep people out, along here, anyway."

" You talk as if they were jam-makers—preservers!" laughed Dora, and then gave a sudden little squeak of excitement. " Oh, *look*, Letty—the lamb! The duck!"

It was thus that he, hereinafter known as Maurice the Mascot, presented himself to his prospective adopters, if that is the right term. He was not, strictly speaking, either a lamb or a duck, but he was small and innocent and appealing in his soft furriness, as he nibbled at a thick stalk of sow-thistle, his round head very much on one side, and peering up at the two girls.

Brown, about the size of a rat, with round, black eyes, he munched greedily and seemed quite unafraid of the strange females who watched him. Even when Dora made a sudden grab and picked him up, he only kicked and squeaked a little protestingly, without appearing really alarmed.

" What *is* he?" Letty asked. " Do you think he'll bite?"

" Of course he won't, the pet angel," Dora promised rashly. " He's a vole—that's what he is."

" A vole. . . . Oh! That's a water-rat, isn't it? Like ' Ratty ' in ' The Wind in the Willows'!"

" There are land voles and water voles and this is a land one. Look! His ducky little paws are all furry underneath, and a water rat's are bare. That's one of the differences."

" His tail's rather bare too," Letty said.

" Yes, poor pet—the fur's got rubbed off it, somehow, and it's sort of flattened. P'raps he's been in a trap. Letty, I'm going to take him back and tame him; he shall be the Company Mascot—I'm sure that's just why he turned up, to bring us luck, didn't you, pettest!"

The small beast cocked his head on one side and looked up intelligently. He really did not seem in the least afraid of Dora, but Letty was not surprised at that. Dora could tame anything, and made pets of the most unlikely creatures—toads, a field mouse, all kinds of birds. So this newest addition to her menagerie returned with the Guides to breakfast, and was introduced to the Company as Maurice the Mascot.

As he did not seem to care for either porridge, bread-and-milk or sausage, he was afterwards taken by his new mistress to the kitchen garden to choose something for himself. After a good deal of snuffling about, he made a hearty meal of lettuce and rhubarb stalks, so that the food question was solved and Maurice established as a member of the camp, with a Tate's sugar box as a kennel.

And—for the moment—that is all there is to be told about Maurice, except that as Gerry pointed out later in the day, his adoption did not seem to bring much luck in the first place, even to Dora herself.

For the same afternoon brought an unpleasant adventure.

The whole Company had gone exploring, since the " fox " day was still sunshiny and beautiful. They had walked for a couple of miles through the flat country beyond Favour Royal, where there were sometimes tiny streams between the fields instead of hedges, crossed by planks for bridges. And for part of the way a raised road ran across waste ground with very green patches here and there, studded with white waving cottongrass, which looked just as though Bo Peep's sheep had passed that way and left tufts of fairy wool on the grass stems.

Treacherous boggy country stretched as far as the high railway embankment which seemed to stride across it like some Roman wall, carrying the line safely on its broad back, with the marshes on one side and the wide stretch of water known as Maredale Mere on the other.

They went through the bricked-up cutting at the end of the embankment, and wandered part way round the Mere, a fascinating place where velvety brown bulrushes and yellow iris grew, and white and yellow water-lilies—terribly tempting as water plants always are.

" But we can't pick them to-day, girls," Kitty decided. " There isn't time, and you'd get so wet. We'll come again and hire a boat— they keep some on the farther side—and bring back a load of rushes and water-lilies."

" And I believe if we looked we should find flowering rush, lovely pinky blossoms," Dora said eagerly. " It's tremendously rare, but this is just the place."

" If it's here, we'll find it," Loot promised. " But the sooner we get back to camp now the better. Those clouds mean rain. We'll keep along by the river, it's quicker; we can reach the towpath beyond the far end of the embankment."

The first part of the towpath journey back was not particularly exciting, being flat and bare. It was not until they got quite near Favour Royal that trees and bushes began to appear on the banks, big willows with twisted branches, dipping in the stream, elders with bunches of blackening berries. The path became much narrower, much closer to the edge, and fringed with loose-strife and meadow-sweet.

Presently Kitty noticed that the triplets were

hanging back, lingering behind the others, glancing round them rather nervously.

" Come on, you three!" she called. " We shall be so late for tea if we don't hurry."

" We were thinking . . ." Gerry began hesitatingly, and Kathy chimed in:

" That we're getting *rather* near the preserved part of the river."

" And we don't want to trespass again," Chrissy finished gravely.

" Dear me! You're very conscientious all of a sudden!" Kitty said, laughing. " But you needn't be afraid, we won't trespass. We'll turn off before we come to the barbed wire."

" Yes, we'd better . . . some *time* before, don't you think?" Kathy said anxiously. " You see—there are those dogs. . . . They don't *want* people here."

" Oh, we shan't disturb them," Loot promised lightly. " Look! there's the barrier across the river, right at the far end of this reach; they've certainly made a very uninviting-looking entanglement. I wonder if it goes right down to the river bottom so that fish can't get out!"

" Yes, we're sure it does," Chrissy said seriously. " He *said* nobody swimming could pass."

" Well, I'm sure none of us want to try! Now we must begin to look out; there's a narrow path through this copse somewhere."

Before they discovered the path they were, in the opinion of the triplets, uncomfortably close to the preserved area, and they expected every moment to see the man appear or, still worse, the ferocious dogs. But there was no sight or sound except an occasional plop-plop of fishes on the surface, catching flies, and presently the fainter tinkling sound of big drops of rain falling into the water, one by one.

" It's beginning, and it's going to be a heavy shower." Kitty looked at the clouding sky anxiously. " Quick! Let's find that track; we shall be more sheltered in the copse than out here where it's open—the place must be quite close."

All the girls closed up together, crowding the narrow track, so that Dora and Gerry were on the extreme edge of the river bank. And then . . . nobody saw exactly how it happened or at what precise minute . . . but suddenly there were startled cries, stumblings, scufflings, and a queer, dull, squelching sound. . . .

Where part of the towpath had been, there was a big irregular gap; great masses of earth, matted together with roots, had fallen away, and lay heaped and tilted in the river. And in the muddy hole three or four of the girls were struggling for a foothold, others had just managed to scramble back on to the safer part of the path, whilst down in the river itself Gerry was floundering and splashing with Dora clinging to the bank.

In a moment Kitty was waist-deep in the water, hauling Gerry out, whilst half a dozen willing hands were extended to help Dora to climb up the bank. When at last all the party were in safety, half of them at least looked the veriest mudlarks it is possible to imagine, plastered with sticky clay from head to foot.

And Gerry, frightened by the shock and drenched through and through with muddy water, was sobbing hysterically:

" It's *them* — it's the fish-preservers — they made it as a trap. They c-cut away the path, s-so that we should f-fall in if we c-came n-near their horrible f-fish. . . ."

" Gerry, Gerry, don't be so absurd, child!" Kitty cried, shaking herself rather like a dog. " Is it likely that any people would do such a thing as that? You're upset and talking nonsense."

" It's n-not—it's n-n-not!" Gerry, thoroughly demoralized, went on sobbing wildly. "P-people

who'd set d-dogs would set traps. . . . They
did—they did!"

" What *really* happened, of course, is that the
river has undermined the bank and the path,"
Margaret said sensibly. " Then our weight
made it give way. Or pr'aps there's a stream
running down here."

" Don't see one." Dora, who had been also
scrutinizing the bank, shook her head. " No,
it must just have been the river lapping and
lapping underneath, though it's funny with such
a firm-looking bank."

" Cheer up, Gerry—you're not dead yet!"
cried Pam. " And I got my mouth full of mud
that tastes worse than water."

" No, none of us are dead, or even hurt,
which is rather a wonder, all things considered,"
said Kitty briskly. " But I've never seen a more
disreputable looking crew!"

" Just as though we'd been playing rugger on
a muddy ground!" Dora surveyed her mud-
encrusted legs cheerfully. " But here's something like a path, Loot."

" That's the one—quite close as I thought,"
Kitty said. " Now—the quicker the better . . .
double! I think hot baths, hot tea, and a camp-
fire in the kitchen with the biggest logs we can
find are indicated—those of us who are not

river- and tear-drenched will be rain-drenched before we're back!"

It was surprising how that cheering and warming prospect shortened the comfortless journey back to camp. Kitty certainly knew how to restore the muddied spirits of her Company, and soon Favour Royal seemed to be staring surprisedly with all its blank windows at the sound of the strains of " John Brown's Body " coming cheerfully homeward through the rain.

CHAPTER VII

Results of a Wetting

Though nobody was hurt, the wetting of the afternoon had certain results—quite a string of them, in fact. Long after " Lights Out ", when all the Company were supposed to be asleep, Margaret was roused by a muffled sniffing from the sleeping bag next to hers in the tent which she shared with the triplets.

Margaret's sense of responsibility as a Patrol Leader was awake as soon as herself.

" What's up, Gerry?" she asked softly.

Gerry, who during the course of a hilarious camp-fire had seemed entirely restored in spirits, sniffed again.

" It's—my tooth," she gulped. " Aching horribly! S'pose it was getting wet this afternoon."

" Poor kid!" Kind-hearted Margaret rubbed the sleepiness out of her eyes and sat up. " I wonder what we can do for it."

" D-don't b-bother," Gerry sobbed forlornly. " It—it m-might wake the others. B-but ooh! it does jump so!"

" Would Kathy and Chrissy have a sort of community toothache too, if we did? Good gracious! That *would* be a business!" Margaret laughed under her breath, then sat up and thought rapidly.

Iodine and other remedies were in the hospital tent, but she couldn't get at them without rousing Loot, and that didn't seem fair. Rapidly she ran over toothache cures in her mind, until she reached one which their old family nurse had always recommended. A salt-bag—yes, that could be managed; there was plenty of salt in the kitchen, and she could use the soft cover of her hot-water bottle as a bag. The oven under the big fireplace would still be warm enough to heat the salt.

" If you lie still and wait just a very little and don't wake the others, I'll fetch you a lovely hot salt-bag," she whispered to the softly sniffing Gerry. " It's frightfully comforting—you'll be asleep in two ticks and forget all about the wretched tooth."

" Oh, thank you, Mar!" whispered back Gerry gratefully; and the elder girl pulled on rubber Wellington boots and a long coat, tucked her hot-water bottle under her arm, and set off, electric torch in hand.

It was quite fine now, with a moon shining between clouds. Margaret found no difficulty in reaching the kitchen, and, as she had expected, there was still a glow of red embers in the big fireplace. Filling the bag with salt, she rapidly stitched up the top and then put it in the oven to heat, after which there was nothing to do but wait, and discover, now that she was idle, what an eerie place the huge kitchen was, with the queer shadows cast by the single candle which she had lighted, on the whitewashed walls, and the dark, dark corners where other shadows lurked.

Margaret looked at her wrist watch. Two o'clock nearly—what an uncanny time to be alone in the great old house! Wouldn't Pam imagine ghosts everywhere if she were here!

"I rather wish she was, though!" Margaret thought. "It would be quite fun if there was anyone to talk to."

She wandered across to one of the shuttered windows, and peered through a heart-shaped hole in it, which was just on a level with her eyes. It looked out upon the stone-paved stable yard; she could see the outline of the old well, and it was not exactly the view which

Margaret would have chosen at that moment.

For an instant she quite thought that she saw something—someone—moving near the well, but of course that was simply imagination. She longed to go back to the fire—longed still more to be once again in the tent creeping into her cosy sleeping bag, but a kind of fascination seemed to keep her at the window, glue her eyes to that hole in the shutter.

And then she saw something which was not imagination.

There, shutting in one side of the yard, was the coach-house, to all appearance shuttered and barred just as when they had tried to get in. But now under the door and round the shutters were streaks of light shining out into the darkness.

Margaret stood motionless, staring, little cold shivers running down her back. She seemed to hear Dina's voice again, reading from the Favour Royal guide-book about this very stable yard.

" Here strange lights have been seen . . . and a figure of immense height. . . ."

There were the strange lights; would the ghost of the Long Man appear soon?

" I—I don't think I can bear it if it does!" Margaret whispered to herself, clenching her hands, and then tried to pull herself together, telling herself almost fiercely that there weren't such things as ghosts, that the lights, most likely, had some quite ordinary explanation. Perhaps a tramp was sleeping there, thinking the house was empty . . . but then, how could he have got in? Or perhaps the place was on fire, but at that sudden thought all the practical side of Margaret rose to the surface, making her forget ghosts and all such creepy possibilities.

If it was a fire, she must do something and do it at once; there wasn't the faintest doubt of that.

In another moment Margaret stood outside the back door in the yard itself. The strips of yellow light still gleamed steadily under the door and shutters; it didn't *look* like a fire, and there was no smell or sound of crackling or burning. Margaret took a few hesitating steps forward, paused, and found her voice with a great effort.

" Is—is there anyone there?" she called, very weakly and shakily; then screwed up her eyes tightly as she stood waiting for an answer—dreading an answer.

But none came. There was not a sound, and when Margaret opened her eyes again, not a glimmer of light. All was as dark and silent as the rest of the stables, and as she stood there staring perplexedly, the girl wondered if she could have been mistaken, if there never had been those gleaming streaks, if they had been some kind of reflection of the moonlight all the time.

Suddenly in a kind of panic Margaret backed into the house again, shut and bolted the kitchen door, and busied herself with extracting the now almost overheated salt-bag from the oven.

She rolled it up in her coat, put out the candle, and hurried out through the side door by which she had entered, avoiding the stable yard altogether. Without letting herself stop to think even for a second, she made her way softly round the house, back to the terrace and the sleeping camp, back to her tent and the unsleeping Gerry.

For the tooth was still jumping agonizingly, although Gerry had heroically refrained from waking her triplets. She was so delighted to see Margaret with her remedy, that the elder girl forgot everything else in comforting the unfortunate sufferer, and tucking her up cosily with the warm salt-bag under her cheek. And it acted like a miracle; in less than ten minutes Gerry was sound asleep, and Margaret, back in her own bag, had time to think.

But the more she thought, the less could she make of her adventure, the less certain she felt as to whether she had seen anything at all, and the less inclined to tell anyone else about the occurrences of the night. After what Loot had said, after the way in which she herself had snubbed Pam, she could not really be the one to raise a question of ghosts; she felt ashamed even to let herself think of such a thing.

Yet . . . if the lights hadn't been ghostly or imaginary, what were they? If there had really been someone, or more than one person, in the coach-house, oughtn't she to do something about it?

Margaret's mind was by this time in such a muddle and so thoroughly tired out as well, like the whole of her body, that she could not think clearly. But all the same it was not until the darkness in the tent had turned to grey that she fell asleep, and she was awake again before the arrival of the early morning biscuits.

Nibbling those same water-wafers, whilst the triplets chattered like starlings and Gerry proclaimed that the salt-bag had completely cured her toothache, Margaret decided to say nothing as yet—to wait and see if anything else happened, anything more certain. A hurried visit to the stable yard told her that there was no sign of anything amiss; the doors and windows were shuttered and barred as before, the cobbles wet and gleaming, cleaned by a recent shower.

" Just fancy—or reflections," Margaret told herself, and tried to believe that her mind and her conscience were perfectly satisfied, and that she need never think about those mysterious lights again.

CHAPTER VIII

Pam Cooks

" ' A teacupful of grated Parmesan cheese,' "
Pam murmured. " Well, it's to be hoped
Canadian Cheddar will do as well; I'm sure
Mrs. Pepps at the shop would never have heard
of the other. ' Half a pound of macaroni '—
that wouldn't go far with all of us; it's probably
meant for about two people. How on earth am
I to know how much to use? I do wish these
books would tell you how to make everything
for *one* person; then it would be easy enough
to multiply by *us*."

Propping up the paper-covered cookery book
in front of her, Pam studied it frowningly. If
she hadn't volunteered it wouldn't be so bad,
but she had suggested herself that she should
make macaroni cheese for supper, had boasted
of knowing exactly how to do it; in fact, had
made the Company expect something very
extra special.

" And I do know how to make it directly I've
got the amounts right," Pam reassured herself.

" That's the only catch. Well, the best thing will be to lay out fourteen helpings of macaroni —good big ones. Everybody's so frightfully hungry in camp."

A few minutes later the kitchen table was spread with fourteen piles of uncooked macaroni, which Pam contemplated anxiously, adding here a stick and there a stick.

" It swells when it's boiled," she murmured. " So that each lot will look a good deal more after cooking—but I don't want to be mean. There! I think that's about right! Now for the cheese!"

The macaroni swept together made a large pile; it would need a good deal of cheese to flavour it properly, Pam decided, and macaroni cheese that was just milk pudding with a cheesy taste instead of a sweet one was so very unsatisfactory. Hers should be rich—luscious— Pam licked her lips at the very thought of the beautifully browned, cheese-sprinkled top, the soft creamy inside, that almost melted in one's mouth.

She began to grate cheese vigorously, and found it rather a fascinating occupation to watch the pile of shavings grow and grow. There were lots of little bits that wouldn't grate, and it seemed simplest to eat them, just to prevent waste. . . . And then, in the end, she had obviously grated too much even for a really rich dish.

" It isn't nice if you *overdo* the cheese," Pam reflected. " But I mustn't waste it; if I eat it now I shan't want so much at supper-time, and there'll be more for the others."

Refreshed and rather replete after a double handful of cheese shavings, Pam returned to the serious business of cooking. Salt—pepper—milk—— Slowly stew the macaroni. . . . And she must see to it that the oven was just the right heat, so as to brown it beautifully.

Pam heaved a long sigh of relief when the cooking in the dixie was really under way; she sat on the edge of the table, used the cookery book to fan her hot face, and wondered what she should do to pass the time until the macaroni was ready for the next process.

" I wonder what real cooks do," she thought. " They must have such a tremendous lot of time to spare between whiles. It's too early to get supper ready. If I start jamming the bread for sandwiches, it will only bring out thousands of wasps. I'll do a little exploring, I think; perhaps I might find some more *Punches*."

For Favour Royal had proved to be really and truly a little like the deserted wreck of the

Swiss Family Robinson. It might be an empty house, but there were all sorts of treasures hidden away in cupboards under stairs, in the depths of dresser-drawers, or the top of the huge linen press in the passage—a decayed croquet set, with comically narrow old-fashioned hoops, a bundle of innumerable old neckties, best of all, a huge pile of unbound *Punches*. Those had actually been discovered by Letty inside the big boiler in the wash-house, much mice-eaten.

So one never knew what one might find or where one might find it, and Pam set out on a further voyage of discovery, with all the feelings of an Elizabethan Merchant Adventurer visiting the Spanish Main.

There was that little door in the farther scullery which seemed to belong to an unexplored cupboard. The key had proved so rusty that it was impossible to turn it, but with patience and a little oil Pam had her reward. After a good deal of fidgeting, wrenching and lubrication, the stiff wards of the lock finally turned, creakingly, and the door was open upon the musty smelling dimness within.

It was more than a cupboard; it was almost like a little room, but without any window or furniture except for a dingy curtain hanging from a shelf across one corner. But behind that there might be all sorts of things . . . there *was* something bulging out the curtain. Just a pile of rubbish, but then rubbish was often terribly interesting, and good Guides could make something of anything—those *Punches* were to be sewn together into volumes, and put into brown-paper covers for the hospital, with the mouse-nibbled bits cut off. . . .

Hopefully Pam pursued her investigations, whilst the macaroni stewed cosily in the big dixie.

The rubbish turned out to be so absorbing that Pam almost spoiled her cooking. She was only just in time to save the macaroni before it stewed away to a messy paste, but still a miss was as good as a mile, and soon, with the cheese added and lumps of butter melting on the browning tops in each baking dish, the good work was going forward prosperously, and smelling deliciously already.

" Oh! how thirsty that cheese has made me!" Pam sighed. " Or pr'aps it's the dust in the cupboard. Well, there's plenty of milk."

She drank two big mugs full, and then devoted herself to jam-sandwich making. She did want to have everything ready for the rest of the Company when they came back from their walk—and there they were! She could hear the strains of " Old Stable Jacket " in the distance.

Well, macaroni cheese which smelt like a savoury dream, sandwiches with unstinted strawberry jam, *and* as an extra the surprise she had found in the cupboard. . . . The camp ought not to forget easily the day when they left Pam to cook for them!

They'd be here in a very few minutes now; it was almost time to dish up; steps and song sounded as though they had nearly reached the terrace, coming up over the turfy slope beyond.

Pam listened. The singing broke short off— then it began again after a minute or so, but there was something queer about it now, something that did not sound quite natural. And almost before Pam realized that anyone was coming, Mildred was in the kitchen, running noiselessly in her rubber-soled shoes over the stone floor.

" Pam!" Her face was white, her voice sounded shaky and frightened. " Didn't you know? . . . haven't you heard anything . . . anything happening?"

" Where do you mean . . . what?" Pam looked up perplexedly. " I didn't hear anything before you came."

" Out on the terrace—in the camp?"

" I've been in here, cooking," Pam answered.

" Come! Loot said everybody must—she told us to go on singing so that they—they——" Mildred's voice failed, but she was pulling Pam by the arm, and together they went out into the side yard, round the corner of the house to the terrace, straight into the little group of Guides who stood there, singing still, loudly, rather stridently, in a forced kind of way: " John Brown's donkey has a red morocco tail!" But even while they sang, all heads were turned in one direction, towards the camp and the tents, and Mildred's hand tightened on Pam's arm as she pointed with a shaking finger.

" Look!" she whispered unsteadily. " But d-don't say anything, pretend you d-don't see."

Pam looked. The flaps of the nearest tent were partly brailed up, enough to show the feet of someone standing just inside—booted feet, a man's feet, motionless, waiting. . . .

" S-sing too," Mildred gasped. " And look *there*—but go on singing."

Another tent—Pam's own—and here again the feet of a man just visible, part of the up-turned soles showing that he was lying down.

" And you can just see the tip of one toe sticking out from those bushes just by the store tent—there's another there," Mildred's excited whisper went on. " Besides—there's someone under the bed in Loot's tent; she saw him as she passed."

Pam stood motionless, her hands tightly clasped; she mustn't give in, mustn't show anything when the others were behaving so bravely, acting like well-drilled soldiers. And Loot was giving her orders, to be passed round in whispers; three were to go to one tent, four to another, four more to the bushes, whilst Loot and two others went to her own tent.

" And be ready to hold them when they come out—they'll probably try to make a dash." That was the principal order, and Pam found herself, with Mildred, going towards her own tent and the concealed man. A moment of tense silence, then Loot's voice, strong and firm, as she stood in the tent door:

" Come out at once! What are you doing there?"

There was no answer; nothing happened. Kitty spoke again.

" Whatever you men want, the game's up!"

Still not a sound. And suddenly Kitty sprang forward, seized the foot which showed under her low camp-bed, and gave a fierce tug.

Next instant she had fallen backwards, was sitting on the terrace, with a surprised look on her face and an empty boot in her hand.

"Oh!—it c-came off!" stammered Mildred; but Kitty was already on her feet, in the tent, looking under the bed. Next instant she was by the bushes, and had once more snatched up —a manless boot!

And Pam could contain her emotions no longer; she collapsed in a heap by her tent, shaking from head to foot with stifled laughter.

"Oh! oh!" she gasped. "Your faces—the solemnness!"

"Pam!" Kitty was staring at her, as well as the whole Company. "How did you? . . . where? . . . when? . . ."

"I found them—in the cupboard—in the scullery," Pam gurgled. "A whole pile—of old boots. That gave me—the idea. But I never, never thought it would take you all in so splendidly! Oh! . . . your faces! And the singing—b-b-burglars in camp! . . ."

Again she collapsed helplessly, but this time beneath the weight of a combined attack of sister Guides, shaking, scolding, exclaiming.

"Pam, you little wretch!"

"You *beast*!"

"How dare you!"

"Was *that* why you offered to stay and cook the supper?"

" Just to play a trick like this!"

" No; it wasn't—I didn't! I never thought of it till I found those old boots!" Pam protested, struggling to her feet. " And I've done you the loveliest macaroni cheese . . . to make up! Can't you *smell* it?"

They could. The smell had stolen out to the terrace on the evening air, and reminded the Company of the fact that they were too hungry even to think of any further vengeance on Pam, the deceiver.

And the macaroni cheese was good, so good, so rich and so plentiful, that it was a thoroughly overeaten party of Guides who toyed with the jam sandwiches later.

As for Pam, she could not even toy.

" I think it was the m-milk, I drank rather a lot on top of tasting rather a lot of raw cheese," so she accounted for her sudden greenish pallor. " I—I think I'll go and lie down, I'm feeling so frightfully—awfully sick. . . ."

The victim of culinary experiments departed precipitately, followed by Kitty and the helpful quartermasters. But Margaret, with the memory of the fraud still rankling, only remarked with cold vindictiveness, as she watched her sister's disappearance into the Red Cross tent:

" Serve you right, young Pam!"

CHAPTER IX

Nightmare

Macaroni cheese, in bulk and extremely cheesy, combined with jam sandwiches and hot chocolate as a beverage—another of Pam's specialities—is not a good supper to sleep upon. Most of the Company had come to that conclusion long before midnight, and almost all of them had vowed a vow that they would never look cheese in the face again, especially in combination with macaroni.

Kitty, too, was kept awake by the need to minister to the worst sufferers, even after Pam, very limp and empty and hugging a hot-water bottle, was sleeping off the effects of her extra indiscretion in the way of diet.

So it happened that it was a restless and wakeful camp at Favour Royal that night, a camp hardly likely to be surprised by any form of nightmare which might visit them. Even Maurice the Vole, who had gnawed his way already through several wooden boxes, scuffled and scratched restlessly inside the huge old zinc bath which Dora had found in one of the attics and converted into a home for the Mascot by covering the top with a piece of stout wire netting.

For this reason it cannot be said that many were wakened by the sound which broke the night silence some time after twelve o'clock, although it roused some who were at last half asleep.

"What's that?" Mildred lifted a startled face, and a drowsy mutter came from Prue in the next bag:

"Owl! . . ."

"More like a hyena!" Dora, wideawake, sat up. "Letty, you're nearest the door, look out and see if you can see anything. It might be a wolf or something escaped from a Show."

With this cheerful possibility in view and just as another hideous wailing howl burst out from somewhere quite close at hand, Letty peeped timidly round the tent flap, and at once drew back with a frightened cry.

"Oh! . . . What is it? There . . . over by the house . . . an *awful* thing! . . ." With a pillow-muffled howl, Letty buried her face in her sleeping bag, and Dora scrambled over her prostrate body to reconnoitre, and to be thoroughly startled in her turn by what she saw.

The whole camp was now awake. Heads were poked out of all the tent flaps, amidst a buzz and murmur of exclamations.

It was a dark night, moonless, starless; almost the only light came from something— something which stood by the corner of the house, dimly outlined against the dark brick.

Far taller than any man, it seemed to be a man's figure, dressed in something like a long dark cloak. For there was a face, pale, faintly luminous, giving all the light there was, as the head moved slowly from side to side, whilst again the terrible wail burst out.

" Oh! it's the ghost! It's the Long Man!"

It was Mildred who cried out, peeping over Dora's shoulder, but the words sent a shiver through almost everyone in the camp. For what else could it be, that figure almost double man-size, which was now moving slowly along the terrace nearer to the camp.

" The Long Man . . . the Long Man! . . ."

A frightened whisper ran round, and even Kitty found it hard to make her voice sound as reassuring as she could have wished. But she tried her hardest to laugh naturally as she spoke:

" Nonsense! . . . Nonsense, girls!" she cried.

" You *know* there's no such thing—you *know*! . . ."

Another hideous howl interrupted her, and it was a fresh voice which spoke as the sound died away, in a slow drawl which was somehow reassuring to everyone.

" Guess that noise doesn't cut any ice with *me*; I've heard it before. Just gives away that it's a man and no spook—a man trying to scare us. So. . . ."

On the last word Byrde had moved more quickly than the slowness of her voice could have promised, making a dart forward along the terrace, with arm outstretched as though to clutch at the long dark cloak of the apparition.

But she was some distance away; before she could reach it, the towering figure had disappeared round the corner of the house, walking with immense strides, and at the same time Kitty caught the American girl by the arm, pulling her back.

" Byrde! . . . Stop! You mustn't follow, especially if he's a real man; he might hurt you. Let him go now—tell us what you mean."

" Mean?" Byrde's usually pale face was flushed and excited as she stood there, very small and slim, in black-and-white striped pyjamas and the inevitable horn-rimmed spec-

tacles. " Why, I mean that I knew at once who
it was by that war-whoop; it's the Red Indian
we saw in the garden, the one you didn't believe
in, trying to frighten us again."

" Oh, you mean it's one of the village boys
that Mrs. Cooper spoke about, playing tricks!"
Kitty said, and her voice sounded relieved.

" Well, no, I don't; I don't believe it *is*
just boys," Byrde said slowly. " I'm pretty
sure it's men trying real hard to make us right
scared."

" But why should they, why should anyone
want to do that?" Kitty asked in bewilderment.
" We're here by permission; we're certainly
not doing any harm to anybody."

" Can't help it! I'll bet anything there's
someone wants to frighten us off Favour Royal,
wants us out of the way," Byrde repeated
obstinately, and received sudden support from
the tent door where the triplets stood in a
closely pressed together group of three.

" It's those preservers, they want to get
rid of us," Gerry declared shrilly. " You don't
know how fierce he looked—the one who said
they'd set dogs on us . . . and it *must* have
been them who set the trap and tried to drown
us in the river!"

" Oh no, Gerry, I'm sure it wasn't. I'm

certain that was just an accident," Kitty protested, but this time it was Margaret who interrupted, speaking in her quiet, practical way.

" I don't know about *that* part; at least, I think that was just accidental, but I'm pretty sure that funny things are going on, Loot, things that we don't know about. I wasn't going to say anything until I was sure, but perhaps I'd better now. . . ." Margaret stopped to draw breath, then went on with the story of the mysterious lights in the coach-house, whilst the rest of the Company clustered round closely to listen.

At the end Loot spoke thoughtfully:

" It might very well have been a tramp or tramps, you know, who somehow got in there to sleep; it's just the sort of thing they do. And I can't see, anyhow, that there's anything to connect the lights in the coach-house with the people who've hired the fishing."

There was silence for a moment; then Margaret said slowly:

" No, I suppose not, but——"

And somehow the whole Company had the air of echoing that " but ".

Kitty spoke in rather an exasperated voice, for she was inclined to think that the vivid imaginations of some of her Guides were rather running away with them, making mountains from molehills.

" Well, girls, what do you want me to do? Write to my cousin and say that our camp is being made uncomfortable, and we don't want to stay any longer?"

" Oh no, no!"

" Oh! Loot, you couldn't do such a thing as that!"

" Of *course* we want to stay!"

" We didn't mean anything of that sort!"

" We simply love being here!"

It was a perfect chorus of protest, all the Guides talking at once in the effort to reassure their leader.

" Then what do you want?" Kitty repeated. " Shall I report matters to the police, say we want to be protected against ghosts and Red Indians and mysterious lights. . . ."

The protesting chorus burst out more loudly than ever, followed by Byrde's slow voice, speaking alone:

" Nat-rally I can't answer for everyone, but I guess what we most of us want is to get to the bottom of the mystery, if there *is* a mystery, all by ourselves and without telling anyone else anything about it. My! girls, it's just a real

live detective drama, and we don't need anybody else butting in on us, do we? At least,
that's how I feel about it."

From the murmured sounds of approval
which followed it was plain that Byrde had
expressed the feelings of all her fellow Guides,
and Kitty felt decidedly relieved at this attitude.

" Well, then, that's settled!" she said briskly.
" We're not wanting to call in any help, and
we're going to be very practical and sensible.
And the best way of showing it at the moment
is by going to bed. We shall all be the limpest
of wet rags by to-morrow if we don't."

" Just one thing first," Byrde begged. " I do
want to go and see if that thing left any tracks
over by the wall there, while they're fresh."

" Footprints—oh yes!" Pam cried excitedly.
" It's been raining a bit, so they'd show."

" I don't reckon it'll be footprints," Byrde
said drily, producing a neat electric torch from
her pocket and walking quickly along the
terrace towards the place where the apparition
had appeared.

The others crowded behind, watching eagerly
as Byrde turned the circle of light from her
torch this way and that, finally holding it steadily
over a patch of damp pavement near the house
wall.

" It was about here . . ." she murmured. " Yes . . . I thought so. . . . It was. . . . Just what I should have expected to find, the only thing it could be, really."

" Don't be so horribly Sherlock-Holmesey!" Pam burst out impatiently. " What is it, where is it? I can't see any footmarks."

" Naturally not, but *that's* what there is!" Byrde threw the light full upon a round blotch on the wet surface, upon another much more clearly marked as a neat depression in a pad of moss.

" Looks as if someone had prodded with a big stick," Pam commented.

" It would look like that, my dear Watson," Byrde said gravely. " But it just means this, that I know how we can *all* turn ourselves into that kind of spook if we want to, and we will, too! We can do the scaring, I reckon, if it *is* boys playing tricks. Now, if there had been footmarks. . . ."

" Yes, that's what I hoped they'd be," chimed in Pam. " Footprints as clues to who it was."

" If there had been footmarks," Byrde repeated impressively, " I should have thought that it might be really a spook!"

CHAPTER X

Laying the Ghost

The weather was rather like one of those cakes made in layers, fine and wet days alternately, and the day following the night alarm happened to be a rainy layer. But for once there were no grumbles. Byrde announced at breakfast, which was eaten sitting on boxes and logs round the kitchen fire, that she would show anyone who liked just how to make a spook, and the suggestion was enthusiastically welcomed by all the Guides.

" There's plenty of what we need in the big shed over there," Byrde said thoughtfully. " Reckon we'll turn out just as good a model as that big boob last night, maybe better."

It was arranged accordingly that Kitty should go to their nearest local post office for letters, and to make some necessary purchases, whilst all the others worked under Byrde's instructions and also prepared the dinner.

For Kitty rightly considered that the good

hard work to which, as it seemed, Byrde intended to set them, would be an excellent remedy for any nerves which might remain affected by last night's happenings—not to mention last night's supper.

Even when she came back from her wet and muddy expedition, she decided not to disturb her Company. The sounds of laughter, hammering and sawing proceeded from the shed, and the stew simmering at one side of the fire needed no attention. Kitty accordingly indulged in a hot bath, and an hour or so of letter writing before the Cooking Patrol appeared to dish up dinner, full and brimming over with their morning's occupation and its results.

" But we don't want you to see anything until everything's ready, Loot," Pam said importantly. " Only I *do* think Byrde's clever; she seems to know such a lot about such a lot of things."

" Lucky, too; she's been to such a lot of places, and that's the way to learn things," Pollie added. " If *we'd* been to the south of France, we'd most likely have known what she did about the s——"

" S-sh!" Pam interrupted. " We want it to be a surprise; you're spoiling it all, Pollie."

Pollie subsided, and except for mysterious hints and glances at each other, all the Company kept their secret during the meal that followed, departing in a body afterwards, back to the shed.

But Kitty was too glad to see them happy and occupied to feel any sense of grievance over their desertion. She called after her vanishing Guides that she would see about tea, and then settled down to an afternoon of stocking darning very contentedly, varying her employment later in the afternoon by making some rock-cakes for tea.

It was when these were baking and the water for tea set on to boil, that Kitty went out on to the terrace to carry her neat balls of darned stockings back to her tent. The rain had stopped, but it was a grey lowering afternoon, already very dark for the time of day, with the pattering sound of raindrops falling from the overloaded leaves coming from trees and shrubs on all sides.

Just as Kitty emerged from her tent, round the corner of the house, where the apparition had been seen the night before, came a weird procession. One by one they emerged on to the terrace, six inhumanly tall figures at least eight feet in height, walking with long strides. They were covered with long flowing draperies which hid even where their faces should have been, except for huge round eyes which gleamed red or green or yellow.

Although prepared for something of the kind, it must be confessed that Kitty felt a little creepy as those uncanny shapes advanced silently towards her, and then, all together, set up a most unearthly wailing sound. She was almost relieved when the wail lapsed into giggles, and seven Guides in human shape came racing round the corner, all talking at once in chorus with the ghosts.

" Aren't we horrible?"

" Aren't they splendid?"

" Loot, darling, you looked quite scared when we appeared, you really did!"

" Don't you think we're quite as bad as the one last night?"

" I think you're appalling!" Kitty assured them solemnly. " I can't think how you've done it!"

" Well, you see." The leading ghost subsided upon the parapet, and in doing so revealed something of her make-up. " I saw at once from the marks on the terrace how that creature had made himself so tall. He was on stilts, and I do know something about *them*, because I stayed for nearly a year with Poppa and Momma in the Basque country in France, where all the peasants use them in the Landes—it's boggy marshy country, like this, only more so—and I learnt to——"

" And she's going to teach us *all* to stilt-walk," Pam's voice burst from the smallest of the ghosts, interrupting Byrde's slower narrative. " We only had time to make these six pairs, but we shall all have them by to-morrow and be a Stilt Company. And it's a gorgeous feeling, walking on them, Loot, darling—you'll have to have a pair too, and——"

Pam's enthusiasm collapsed with a slither and a crash, as her stilts slid from under her and deposited her ignominiously on the terrace in a tangle of ghostly draperies. But she was quite unhurt, and proceeded to pick herself up and display the secrets of her costume to Kitty.

" We used that pile of old curtains, and don't you think our eyes are beautifully horrible? They're just coloured paper—look, pasted on cardboard with big eyeholes cut in them! And then to make them glow we used electric torches fixed to our heads with elastic, only we hadn't really enough torches to go round."

" That man last night lit up his whole face, somehow, but we reckoned we were quite horrid enough," Byrde drawled.

" I should think so!" Kitty laughed. " In all

my experience of ghosts, I can safely say that I've never seen any so terrifying. And I think the stilts are a great idea quite apart from anything else; I used to have a pair as a child, and I loved them. But it's nearly tea-time; hadn't you better get out of those alarming costumes and be your natural selves again?"

Again there was a chorus, this time of protest.

" Oh no, Loot, we do want to walk round a bit first!" Margaret, the tallest ghost, explained. " Just down the drive as far as the Lodge and round the boundaries a bit. You see, we thought it would be such a good thing if anyone *did* see us, especially if the anyones happened to be *the* ones. It would show them that we can do ghosts as well—whoever they are."

" Yes, I see the idea," Kitty said. " Well, then, you had better start at once. Do we all join the procession?"

" Oh, *yes*!" Letty answered for the stiltless Guides. " We can't all be out of it."

So, led by the six spooks in single file, the procession set out and solemnly paraded the grounds of Favour Royal, skirting the grazing ground in the Park and the hedge along the riverside, striding down the avenue to the Lodge gates, and nearly sending some youthful members of Mrs. Cooper's family into hysterics.

Even Mrs. Cooper herself gave a cry of horror when she came to the door to see what was amiss, and had to be reassured by Loot.

"You see," Kitty explained to the lodge-keeper, "someone—probably as you said yourself, one of the village boys—has been trying to frighten my Guides by playing ghost. So this is just to show that they can do the same."

"Well, I never did! And 'orrifying they are, too!" Mrs. Cooper stared amazedly. "I 'ope they won't be walking round often, miss, I'm sure as 'ow they'd give me a turn, even if I *did* know as they was only play-actin', and as for my pore little Ernie and Gladdie—they'd be scared out of their wits."

"Oh no, Mrs. Cooper, I promise that they shan't frighten you again," Kitty said. "You needn't be afraid. Only *we* don't like people trying to frighten us. Now, come along, girls, we must get back to tea, or my scones will be all burnt."

With the spectres stilt-racing ahead in long strides, they returned to camp and tea in the kitchen, filled now with the fragrance of newly baked scones. Soon the stilts were piled, the curtain draperies removed, and the ghosts themselves once again; whilst Byrde, disengaging the elastic which secured the electric torch to her hair, remarked as she subsided upon a soap-box and carefully selected a buttery scone:

" Well, I guess that spook of last night is well and truly laid!"

CHAPTER XI

A Very Queer Thing

Kitty really blessed Byrde for her introduction of stilts into the camp during the days which followed, for they were mostly wet and, as all Guides know, likely to hang heavy on hand in consequence.

But the stilts could be used just as well in the big rooms and long galleries as out of doors, and after such intensive practice several of the Company became very expert indeed at the sport.

There had turned out to be plenty of suitable wood in the big shed to fit out all the Guides with stilts, and Margaret and Pam were good carpenters, whilst Byrde proved herself as neat-handed and inventive in this as she was in almost everything else. Kitty, too, soon regained all her old skill on stilts—after all, her small-girlhood days were not so very far away —and when they set out upon their first hike, each provided, for extra safety, with a long pole, the party had a most impressive appearance.

"And it's so sensible too!" Pam cried exultantly. "However fast it rains, we can't get our feet wet, we're *miles* above all the mud and slush. And everybody knows it's getting feet wet that is much the most dangerous of all in catching cold. So stilts must be frightfully healthy; everyone ought to be taught to walk on them as soon as they can stand."

After the expedition there was still greater enthusiasm for their new means of progression. The lanes had been mere streams, the fields bogs, the marshy ground inches under water and mud, and through it all the stilt-walkers had managed to stride dry-shod, and with very few casualties in the way of tumbles. They even managed to cross a stream at a place which would have ordinarily meant splashing over ankle-deep on half-submerged stepping-stones.

For there was water out everywhere on the low ground between Favour Royal and the railway embankment, more water than had ever been known before, as they were told by the woman at the cottage where they had tea.

"'Tis some as tell the lake do be leakin' through th' 'bankment," the old woman said. "But my man says there's no break in't, seemin'ly. It's this martal wet summer, that's what 'tis."

After tea the party had gone on to the embankment, but there certainly did not appear to be any breaks in it, only a few rabbit holes here and there and a general sodden wetness like that of the whole countryside. And so they splashed back to Favour Royal, rejoicing in their stilts.

That night, since for once it did not rain, they had a camp-fire on the terrace, and a war dance on stilts invented and led by Byrde, to the accompaniment of wild whoops. Afterwards Pam attempted a solo in the Russian style, and it was while she was endeavouring to kick out each leg in front of her alternately, after the fashion of those gaily booted dancers, that the Very Queer Thing happened—for capital letters are really needed to do justice to its queerness.

Pam kicked out, slipped, tried to recover herself, and came down in a mixture of stilts and waving legs, rather like a daddy-long-legs in a fit, as Margaret unfeelingly remarked.

" You're not hurt, are you, Pam?" Kitty asked, between anxiety and laughter. " You really mustn't, you know—you might break your legs quite easily. . . . Oh!—I beg your pardon. . . . I didn't see. . . . Did you want anything?"

For, suddenly and unexpectedly, a man had stepped into the circle of camp firelight, just opposite to where Kitty sat on an upturned log, with clustered triplets sprawling beside her.

Some of the girls and Kitty herself began to scramble and stumble to their feet, quite taken by surprise; but the man spoke in a pleasant voice, and raising one hand in an apologetic way:

" Oh, please—don't get up—don't disturb yourselves—I'd hate to do that. . . . I didn't come to upset a pleasant evening, and I can see that you are all enjoying yourselves tremendously. I take it that you are the leader here, Miss . . . Miss? . . ."

" Cree," Kitty answered, recovering her wits. " Is there anything we can do—did you want me for anything?"

" Why no, not exactly . . . as a matter of fact. . . ." The strange man laughed in a cheerful, friendly way. " I've really come by way of apology more than anything else. We— a friend and I—rent the fishing here, you know. . . . We're staying down in the boat-house."

Here was excitement indeed! Every eye in the camp-fire circle was fixed upon the newcomer in thrilled suspense. One of the preservers—one of the enemy come into the camp, and in such a friendly way. . . . He didn't look like an enemy either; he was much too laughing and friendly, sitting down—yes, actually sitting down! . . ."

" May I?" He drew up a section of a log and subsided upon it. " The fire looks so jolly. Yes, I really came to apologize; I'm afraid we've seemed very unsociable and—well, unwelcoming, but my friend is rather a fanatic where fishing is concerned—takes it much more seriously than I do!"

He looked round with a little laugh, and now that he was sitting in the full glow of firelight, all the Guides could see him quite plainly. He was youngish and smartish and fairish and palish, with very twinkling greenish eyes and a tiny moustache. He wore a belted trench coat and a felt hat dragged down over his ears, and he sat with his knees well apart and his hands deep in his pockets, those very bright eyes glancing round the circle.

" Well, we know of course that no one likes trespassers on ground—or water—that is preserved," Kitty began, but the stranger interrupted.

" One doesn't need to be unpleasant, though,

unless there *is* trespass, and I gather that my friend was rather—well—possibly a bit ogreish when he met some of these young ladies down near our domain. I'm really afraid he may have frightened them a bit."

" He *was* rather fierce—it was us he spoke to," Gerry said, in her serious way. " Of course, we weren't frightened. . . ."

" But we *did* think he might know that we wouldn't trespass, being Guides," Chrissy added.

" Well, you see, he hasn't come across Guides much, perhaps," the stranger said gravely. " He's different to me. . . ."

" Yes, he's *quite* different to you," Gerry agreed gravely. " Much more . . . more severe."

" I'm sure he didn't mean it—he's a good chap, really. He wanted me to make you understand that he was sorry he upset you. He'd have come himself, only—well—he's not keen on Society—shy, you know. Oh! and there's another thing! That wretched servant of mine— I'm afraid *he* was trying deliberately to frighten you; I only heard of it lately, and I was very sick about it."

" You mean the Red Indian who howled at us?" Byrde, hugging her knees, eyes very bright behind her horn-rimmed glasses, burst out.

The man glanced at her.

" You're a sharp young lady," he said. " Lou's a half-caste Indian, yes—came with me from Canada. A faithful fellow, but stupid. Directly he discovered there were strangers here, his one idea was to drive them away from his precious fishing, by primitive methods, eh? Well, now I've—or rather, we—made my confession, people, and I hope I may be forgiven."

" Of course!" Kitty said. " We're very glad to have it all cleared up, aren't we, girls?"

A murmur of assent ran round the fire, and the stranger laughed, looking round cheerfully.

" Good!" he said. " And now to show that we are all friends together, may I stay for a bit and join in the fun? I used to be a good hand at a chorus, and it'll remind me of my old camping days in the backwoods."

It would have been difficult to refuse such a pleasantly made request, and Dina threw on some more wood to make the fire blaze up, whilst Mollie hospitably handed round the home-made toffee. Soon they were all singing again, at first rather shyly, but soon forgetting that a stranger was present, except in hearing the unusual strength and volume of the choruses in which he joined heartily with a fine baritone voice.

What a noise they made, echoing back from the front of the stately house! Old favourites followed each other rapidly, and the culmination was a grand chorus of " Phairson had a Feud "—with their new friend providing a most realistic bagpipe obligato with lips and hands.

When there was a moment's pause in the concert, he broke in with:

" I wonder if you know this, it's a little song the voyageurs—the French half-breeds, you know—sing on the rivers in Canada."

And in a few minutes he had them all laughing at a ridiculous song which began:

> " Oh, Jean Baptiste, vy 'ave you greased
> Your li'l dog's nose with tar!"

and went on to explain that it was to prevent the little dog from catching the catarrh!

After this the stranger rose and stood in the firelight, beaming round the circle of Guides.

" Well, I must be off now," he said. " I'll go back the way I came, down the slope here to the river bank. I hope you'll let me join you again some time."

" We shall be delighted," Kitty said warmly, and next moment he had disappeared in the shadows beyond the firelight, leaving the Guides to their comment and discussion.

"Well, I'm awfully glad he came," Mollie said, stretching and yawning. "It's much nicer to feel we're friendly with the fishing people, isn't it?"

"*Much* nicer," Kitty agreed heartily. "Evidently all the bother was with this half-Indian servant, and they certainly won't let him play tricks on us again. He was really quite nice, wasn't he, this Mr. —— Why, how funny! We never asked his name and he forgot to tell us! We've never heard the names of either of them, if it comes to that. I must ask Mrs. Cooper some time. Well—bed, all of you! It's late!"

CHAPTER XII

Byrde Makes a Discovery

Of all the Guides, only Byrde had kept rather silent while the rest were discussing the pleasantness and politeness of the stranger from the boat-house. She sat staring into the fire, her pointed chin supported in her hands, and when Pam demanded whether she didn't think their visitor awfully nice, only answered " I suppose so!" in her coolest and most non-committal way, without adding anything more.

But when Byrde talked least she was thinking all the more, as her companions had discovered, and the result of her thoughts on this occasion was that she rose very early next morning, before the patrol had been round with their biscuits, before the sun was fully out, or the heavy white mists had cleared away from the low ground below the camp and the terrace.

As she was one of the cooks for the day, the others were not surprised to find Byrde in the kitchen a little later, making the fire in her usual neat and business-like way, a job which never seemed to leave her grimy or smutty as it did most people.

But when the wood was crackling away merrily, and the kettle set on to boil and the sausages pricked with a fork and ready to go into the frying-pan—their actual cooking being the job allotted to Letty on this occasion—Byrde touched Margaret's arm, and spoke in her slow way:

" I've got something rather queer to show you—it might have gone after breakfast," she said, and led the way without another word into the stable yard.

" It all looks just ordinary!" Margaret glanced round perplexedly.

" Well, it isn't!" Byrde said calmly, and went across to the big gateway, stood there, pointing at something on the ground.

" Look!" she said, and Margaret looked, screwed up her eyes, looked again and whistled.

" Marks of wheels—a biggish cart, I should think," she said. " But . . . when, I wonder!"

" After the rain yesterday afternoon," Byrde said. " They weren't there at dinner-time—Prue and I washed the yard down with buckets of water and it dried off. There weren't any marks of this kind."

" But——" Margaret wrinkled up her forehead again. " There wasn't any cart here in the evening, Byrde—we *must* have heard it."

" I wonder . . . with all that noise we were making with the singing . . . especially after the fishing man came," Byrde said slowly.

" Byrde, do you mean—do you think——?"

" Guess I haven't made up my mind yet *what* to think," Byrde drawled. " But there's something else to show you, that I found out just now."

She walked quickly across the yard to the door of the coach-house and gave it a push with her shoulder. It opened easily, and Margaret stared with a little gasp.

" It's unlocked—unbolted!" she cried.

" Yep!" Byrde said calmly. " And look!—see here!"

Again she pointed to the ground, and again Margaret saw the marks of wheels close by the coach-house door.

" Coming through the gate to the door—going from the door to the gate—and if there hadn't been just enough rain to muddy the cobbles a bit, we should never have known it, *or* if there had been rain in the night to wash the marks away," Byrde said.

" But surely if anyone came with a cart he

—they—would have let us know what they wanted," Margaret said.

" Guess that would depend on what they wanted! They might just as lief we didn't know they'd been here—they *might* send someone to help us sing and make such a noise that we wouldn't know, that we wouldn't hear," Byrde said dreamily.

" Byrde, do you really think that man last night—— Oh! I don't believe it! He *said*, why he came; you *are* a suspicious little wretch!"

" I've not said that I suspected anything— anybody—anyone yet," Byrde remarked coolly. " Don't you go putting bad ideas into my head. Well, anyway, there's nothing in the coach-house now, not a thing—except a smell."

Margaret pushed open the door and went in. It was a big place—big enough, as Kitty had said, to hold several cars — but quite empty.

Margaret sniffed and screwed up her face.

" There *is* a smell!" she said. " And it's rather, as Pam said, like something dead. P'raps we'd better leave the door open to air it out, unless there's anything still here."

" No, I think it's gone—the something dead; I think it's been taken away—in the cart—last night," Byrde said deliberately, pausing between each phrase.

" Oh, I do think you're rather trying to make a mystery about nothing—really I do!" Margaret broke out with exasperation, and Byrde raised her neat dark eyebrows.

" Do you? Well, p'raps I am," she said placidly. " I'm quite ready to be satisfied with an explanation, if you can give me one."

But Margaret couldn't, although she declared peevishly that she didn't think any explanation was necessary, that it was all probably quite simple and nothing whatever to fuss about, if they only knew the truth.

" But I'm *not* fussing!" Byrde protested gently.

" Oh! you're maddening! And you'd like other people to fuss, if you don't fuss yourself. Are you going to tell Loot all this?"

" N-no, I don't think so," Byrde reflected. " Prob'bly she'd say the same as you do. No, I reckon I'll wait till I know more—or less, and p'raps that won't be ever. I'll leave somebody else to find out that the coach-house is open. I thought I'd like *you* to see what I'd seen, that's all. Just in case anything else happens."

" Well, I don't think it amounts to much,"

Margaret said candidly. " And now we really must go back and help them to dish up breakfast."

" Ye-es." Byrde stood just inside the coachhouse looking about her without moving. " D'you notice how much cleaner one half of the floor is than the other, as though all *this* part had been covered by something till lately?"

She walked across to the cleaner side and stared down at the stone floor thoughtfully. Then she bent and pressed the tip of one finger upon it, stood up to examine the finger-tip intently.

" H'm," she said. " H'm—yes—p'raps!"

" Byrde, you're rapidly driving me insane," Margaret said. " I can understand the feelings of Watson now exactly; he must have wanted to kill Sherlock Holmes over and over again. Have you discovered something or have you not?"

" I don't know," Byrde answered. " And anyway, it's breakfast now."

Not another word would she say. And when after breakfast Kitty remarked: " Well, now that all the mysteries are cleared up, I do hope we shall have a comfortable, ordinary camp again," it was Byrde who answered in her placid drawl:

" Yes, Loot, I *do* hope so!"

CHAPTER XIII

Kathy Walks Alone

" And now that we're all friendly, it would be nice to find out whether the dark one really *is* Lord Lorimer," Kathy said pensively, darning her socks in the after-dinner rest-hour, as she and her triplets reclined in the privacy of their tent.

For Kathy stuck to things like a limpet, and she had never given up her idea about the identity of the dark " preserver ". Indeed, now she considered that events had increased the probability of her being right.

" The one who came to the camp-fire said that his friend didn't like society, but, of course, he *meant* that he didn't want Loot to see him; that's why he's been so—so seclusive all along. But they'll *have* to see each other some time if things are going to come right, and it would be splendid if we could do anything to help," Kathy said earnestly.

But the triplets did not always and invariably think the same, and neither Gerry nor Chrissy had any great belief in Kathy's idea, although they loyally tried to pretend that they agreed with her.

" Don't see what we could do," Chrissy said doubtfully.

" Don't suppose he *wants* any help," Gerry added.

" How do we know unless we ask him?" Kathy demanded. " That's the only way really to find out."

" Ask him?"

Gerry and Chrissy stared, but Kathy was thoroughly in earnest.

" Yes!" she persisted. " Very likely he's hoping that one of us will—take messages, you know, and that sort of thing. Probably it's why he sent his friend to make friends the other night, so as to—to get in touch. And that's why they haven't told us any names—because he doesn't want us to know what *his* name is."

It all sounded very convincing to Kathy, not so to the others.

" Well, *we* can't get in touch with him, and it's quite certain we don't mean to try," Chrissy yawned. " With the fierce dogs and barbed wire and everything. *That* doesn't look as though he yearned for our help!"

Then it was that Kathy surprised her sisters completely and, incidentally, used the first person singular for almost the first time in her life.

" *I* am going to try," she said calmly, finishing her darn and snapping off the wool.

" *You?*" Gerry and Chrissy gasped together.

" Yes," Kathy nodded. " To-day."

" How?"

" Just go down to the river and look about. There's no need for you to come if you don't want to."

This also was unprecedented, for the triplets always hunted in a leash. But Gerry rose to the occasion.

" Thanks. We don't mean to," she said with dignity.

After that not one of them found anything else to say, which was a third extraordinary thing. And when, after tea, Kathy disappeared during the preparations for a long walk, neither of the others made any comment, and no one else noticed it. Somehow, it was always taken for granted that where two of the three were, the other could not possibly be far away.

So Kathy from behind a bush watched the rest of the party disappear, laughing and talking, and then set off herself in the opposite direction, feeling just a little bit lonely because she was not used to doing things by herself.

She did not go in the direction of the place where the river bank had broken down under the Guides and tried to drown them. The boat-house was at the other end of that stretch of river which belonged to Favour Royal and was let to the fish preservers, and Kathy's idea was to get as near to the boat-house as she could, on the chance of meeting one of its inmates.

Here the river widened out a good deal into a kind of small shallow lake, and Kathy wandered along the edge until she reached the boundary, where brushwood and barbed wire made a tangled barrier across the path, and the wire could be seen carried over the river so that no boat could pass.

" But I shouldn't think it stopped the fish from coming in and out," Kathy thought. " What fun it would be if I had a fishing-rod and caught some *just* outside their own bit of river!"

As she had not so much as a bent pin and a bit of string, there was nothing to be done in that direction, and pretty soon Kathy was tired of dawdling on the river bank and began to wish that she had gone with the others. There was the boat-house, a whitish building, with a verandah sticking out over the river and the whole place mounted on legs. It did not look a very inviting dwelling, and there was no sign of life about it, not even smoke from the stove-pipe chimney.

" I suppose they're all out fishing round the corner somewhere," Kathy thought, for the river made such a sharp bend just beyond the boat-house that it looked almost as though it ended there.

Kathy turned and began to stroll slowly back along the bank, looking more closely now at the big reed beds which fringed it, in search of bulrushes. If she could get some of the huge brown velvety ones it would make such a good reason for her lonely expedition, without saying anything more about it.

But she could not find any bulrushes, or even yellow flags or pink flowering rush. What Kathy did discover out of the ordinary was something very different, something which she had not at first noticed at all, because it was so much hidden amongst the reeds.

Now that she *did* see it, it was the queerest thing, shaped rather like a huge bee-hive, and about four feet high. It seemed to be made of twigs and leaves and reeds and stalks of water weeds, all plastered together with mud, quite dry and firm, and with a rounded top.

" A sort of little house," Kathy thought. " I do wonder who made it and what it's for."

It was quite close to the bank, and Kathy found it easy enough to scramble through the rushes and look at it carefully. Yes, it *was* like an old-fashioned bee-skep, only there was nothing inside, as Kathy soon discovered by tilting it up and looking underneath—just dry plastered mud and a stuffy smell.

" Big enough to get inside—and I could, if I sort of propped it up on the rushes and wriggled under," Kathy reflected. " I'd feel rather like Moses-in-the-bulrushes, or hot crumpets under a cover, but it would be fun to try exactly *how* it felt."

To go as far as that, with Kathy, meant trying a thing in earnest, for she was almost as inquisitive as a kitten when it came to climbing into or under anything, or examining holes and corners. Hidey-places were a passion with her, and she could squeeze herself into the most unlikely holes and crannies.

That being so, it was " just Kathy " as Gerry and Chrissy would have said, to creep into the queer little rush-house and squat inside, in a funny greeny-browny sort of darkness, for most of the light oozed in under the edge where the erection was a little tilted to one side. In the hive itself there was not the tiniest crack or cranny to serve as a window-slit.

It was cramped and horribly smelly and stuffy, too much so, even for Kathy. Only a very few minutes were needed to satisfy her thoroughly about her feelings in the queer little place, and she was just preparing to wriggle out again when she heard something and sat still, listening, ears pricked up.

Could it be the rest of the Company coming back from their walk along the river bank? If so, Kathy decided, she would sit tight in her hiding-place, and surprise them afterwards by telling them exactly what they all said as they walked past—for Kathy's ears were particularly sharp and her memory particularly good.

Chuckling to herself, she lay as low as any Brer Rabbit and said " nuffin ", whilst the steps came nearer and nearer along the river bank.

But it did not take long for Kathy to decide that these were *not* the steps of the Guides; they were heavier, fewer, and when their owners spoke there could no longer be any doubt about the matter. For these were men's voices, and voices, too, which Kathy recognized almost at once.

"You must have been making a mistake, Harry," said the first voice—and *that* was the deep, stern voice of the romantic dark man, the man who, Kathy had decided, was Lord Lorimer, the man who had spoken so angrily to her and her triplets at their first meeting. The voice which answered was that of the stranger who had made himself so friendly at the camp-fire, but now it did not sound quite so pleasant.

"I could have sworn that I saw someone going along the path in this direction, *and* sworn that it was one of those confounded kids," he said, in a growling sort of way.

"I thought you were such friends with all of them now, since you paid your evening call!" the other man said with a laugh, and his companion answered in a tone which made Kathy give a little shiver.

"*They* thought so—oh yes, *they* thought so! I bluffed them completely. They hadn't the slightest notion that we wanted 'em to sit snug and mind their own business that evening—and all the time, for that matter. But that's the worst of girls and women, they *can't* mind their own business!"

"Then they have to be made to," the dark man with the deep voice said, in a grim sort

of way. " And if I catch one of those confounded girls spying about here again——!"

He broke off without finishing, but Kathy,
trying to make herself smaller than any human
girl ever *could* be made, shivered. For sometimes what people leave out sounds so much
worse than what they say.

CHAPTER XIV

"M" for Mystery

There was nothing to be done except sit tighter than ever. If the men once suspected she was there——and now it was Kathy who broke off, leaving things unsaid and unthought of too, as far as possible.

For, of course, they would believe that she had got into her hiding-place in order to spy upon them, and, of course, it looked uncommonly like it, one couldn't help seeing that.

"Oh! why was I such an idiot as to want to get in here!" poor Kathy thought; and all the time kept on listening with ears that seemed to be sharpened by fear. The men were evidently standing still now, quite close to her hiding-place, for their footsteps had stopped and their voices got no farther away as they went on talking.

"Lou had a pretty good catch last night— more than we've ever got since we started."

That was their visitor speaking, the one whom the other had called Harry.

" Yes, the river's full of 'em now—we'd make our fortunes if we could only have 'em in fast enough, before——"

" Before we have another sort of catch, eh?" How different his way of laughing was now! It had sounded so pleasant and friendly that night round the camp-fire.

" Well, of course, it can't go on indefinitely; things are bound to leak out——"

" They are already—leaking out, I mean. We can't stop 'em, worse luck!"

" Don't see how they can trace the leakage to us."

" Not just *as* leakage. But if they put two and two together and make investigations, things'll look ugly, although I don't see myself that there's any question of illegality."

" Oh, don't you? Well, you're more of a fool than I thought, Harry—deceiving yourself like that. You know as well as I do what we're up against by having anything to do with M——"

" Ssh! The less we use that name the better; you know we agreed not to," Harry said uneasily. " If one of the kids from the village, even, overheard and blabbed——"

" *Or* one of those precious Guide girls of

yours, eh?" The deep-voiced man laughed.
" Mind you, I don't say that Lorimer or anyone else wouldn't have a job to fix anything on
to us, but we don't want interference whilst the
fishing is good, and now that Lou has got his
hand in. He's a treasure—up to all the tricks,
and won't stand nonsense from anyone."

" You're right. The want of a store is a
sickening nuisance though, now . . . cleaning and
curing such a business . . ."

Ah! they were moving away now; there was
the sound of steps and their voices were getting
fainter, so that Kathy was not quite sure of
the last word. Then a pause, and the dark
man's voice sounded louder again, as though he
had turned.

" What about that place in the reeds—shall
we have a look as we're here?—just see if there's
anything there?"

" Oh, not a scrap of use till to-night; it's
only apt to disturb things to work by daylight,
Lou says . . . frightens 'em. We'll come along
with the nets after dark."

" Well—I don't know—seems to me as
though we might as well——"

The speaker was evidently still hesitating, and
Kathy drew herself closer and closer together,
as though that would be any protection. For

if they really did come to the reeds and began to search about, it was absolutely certain that they would find her in her hiding-place, and then—then——

Kathy had never really known what it meant to be cold with fright before. But after what seemed like long minutes of suspense, the men evidently decided that Harry was in the right. Their voices and steps grew fainter—fainter— died away into the distance, until all was silent again.

Yet even then Kathy did not dare to move for quite a long while. Perhaps they might come back, perhaps they might be watching, perhaps —perhaps—anyway, she was afraid to take the risk.

And when at last she crawled out, very cautiously, very slowly, she was so stiff and cramped that she could hardly move, could not have run away if the enemy had appeared again. How her legs and her back and her shoulders ached! It was not until she had rubbed and stretched herself for fully ten minutes that she was able to walk at all, and then only very slowly and painfully. But as soon as she could, she crept away amongst the trees; as long as she was on the path by the river she felt as though at least three pairs of eyes were watching her from the boat-house, as though at any moment she might hear angry voices—shouts . . .

" So this is what it feels like to be a spy!" thought Kathy, scurrying along through the undergrowth like a frightened rabbit. " Oh! I wish I hadn't—it's—it's so uncomfortable to *know* things, or half know them, because I'm not sure of anything really, except—except that he *isn't* Lord Lorimer. I'm quite certain of *that* now, anyway, and I feel as though I'd been a perfect little idiot even to think it could be possible. Who am I to tell? *What* am I to tell? Oh dear, I *do* feel miserable!"

Stumbling along, cold and aching and hungrier than she knew, poor Kathy began to cry, just from sheer uncomfortableness of body and mind.

And then—steps again, somewhere near, and she crouched down, holding her breath, only to give a little squeal of fear when someone came suddenly round the bush which sheltered her.

" Why, Kathy! What's the matter? It's only *us*!"

With a gasp of relief she realized that it was only Gerry and Chrissy, speaking in chorus.

" When we found you weren't back, we were a bit bothered—but we knew which way you'd gone, so we came. But what a *mess* you're in—

all mud and dust and bits of grass. *And* what a smell! Where have you been?"

Chrissy and Gerry were sniffing round their triplet like puppies, wrinkling up their noses expressively. But Kathy only repeated wearily, with a little choking sob:

" I h-hid—and it was dirty—and smelly—I couldn't help it!"

" You needn't tell us that—whew!" Chrissy puckered up her face. " Look here, come along quick and have a wash. And then after supper you'll explain to us all about it."

This programme was followed. A clean and sweetened, warmed and refreshed Kathy related her adventures in the cosiness of the kitchen to the assembled Company, and a kind of general discussion followed—a putting together of the bits of the jigsaw to see what pattern it made, as Pam expressed it.

Kathy's memory was good, so that she was able to repeat almost every word the men had said in her hearing.

Yet at the end of it all, the puzzle was not by any means finished; there was not even enough put together to tell what it was all about, what sort of pattern it was meant to make.

" It only comes to this," Loot said, trying to

sum up matters, " that the men at the boat-house are doing *something* they want to hide, but we don't know what—that it isn't really illegal and would be hard to fix on them as yet, and—and that they're very much afraid those confounded Guides will find out something more! Well, that's just what we confounded Guides must do—somehow!"

There was a murmur of applause from the Guides, and Margaret said:

" You mean—before we say anything outside —report anything?"

" Yes!" Kitty nodded emphatically. " The less said the better, till we're surer. If rumours got out, it would put the men on their guard, and, at present, we've really nothing definite to tell the police, have we? *Or* my cousin. They'd simply laugh at us if we couldn't say what we think it all means; up to now, even with what Kathy heard, it just seems to be a lot of vague clues that don't lead us anywhere. No, we must wait and see—although if nothing more happens before we leave, I should feel bound to tell Ralph that we suspect *something's* up. But in the meantime we'll keep a sharp look-out, although we mustn't let this queer business spoil our camp or worry us too much."

" Spoil it! Oh, Loot, it's the *making* of it!"

Pam cried enthusiastically. "It's so exciting, such a lovely change!"

"H'm—perhaps." Kitty, feeling her responsibilities, looked a little doubtful. "Well, anyhow, girls, understand this: you are *not* to go off sleuthing by yourselves, in the way Kathy did to-day. It isn't safe; these men seem to be nasty customers. So—all lone trails are forbidden—promise me that."

A community promise was given by the whole Company, and the council of war began to disperse with sundry yawns, although the keener spirits, like Pam, would have liked to continue the consultation until midnight.

And Kathy, weary as she was, still puzzled her brain over one point, the clue, perhaps, to the whole.

"If only we knew what that word was they wouldn't say—if only we could just find out what M stands for!" she said.

"My! honey, that's simple enough," Byrde drawled. "I can tell you *that* on my head!"

"What do you mean?" Kathy demanded. "How *can* you know?"

"Easy!" The American girl chuckled. "M for Mystery, of course!"

CHAPTER XV

Flooded In

It was all very well to talk of finding out things and solving mysteries, but what can one do when it just rains and rains and rains? And that is how the weather behaved for days after Kathy's adventure.

" I don't believe even bloodhounds would be able to do anything in the detecting way when it's pouring cats and dogs," Pam said gloomily. " Besides, I'm sure criminals wouldn't *do* crimes in this weather. It's so discouraging."

" The only person who really seems to like the rain is Maurice the Mascot," remarked Dora. " The way that creature grows! He's nearly twice as big as when we found him."

" He's bound to grow, eating as he does— it's the only thing he *does* do," Letty said discouragingly. " He's about the most uninteresting pet I ever came across; when he isn't eating he sleeps all day long, and then gets up and scratches all night."

" He isn't uninteresting if you really study him properly." Dora, as the original discoverer of Maurice, was always up in arms at once to defend him. " He can dig in the most marvellous way—at least he does a lot of it with his teeth; he could get through *anything*, I believe, except that old bath I keep him in."

" You don't *dig* with teeth," Pollie said scornfully. " That's nibbling or gnawing."

" Well, but he does it with his paws, too," argued Dora. " He got out under the wall of the tool-house like—like lightning. I just shut him up there for a few minutes."

" He's such an ugly little beast," Letty said. " Even *you* can't say he's pretty, Dora, with that skinny, scaly looking tail and simply *no* chin."

" His coat's getting lovely—awf'ly thick and soft," the loyal Dora declared. " And—and he has a very pleasant expression in his eyes."

" Well, *I* like cuddlesome pets, like kittens and puppies," Letty persisted. " And you can't say that Maurice is that. For one thing, he smells frightfully—much worse than white mice."

That accusation Dora could not deny, so she retired with dignity to feed the bone of con-

tention, who was scratching wildly in his zinc
bath to show that he was hungry.

It must be owned that time hung rather heavy
on the hands of the Guides. They had explored
the house from top to bottom, and stilt-walking
in the corridors had begun to pall; it was not
much fun after using them out of doors. Certainly a Guide is supposed to smile and sing
under all sorts of conditions, but when Prue
on this particular day began to carol cheerfully
" Pack up Your Troubles in Your Old Kit-bag ",
all the rest of the Company rose and rent her,
and accused her most unfairly of making things
worse than they were before.

" It's horribly bad manners to be bright when
other people aren't," Letty said severely. " It's
simply a mockery."

Whereat poor Prue, who had had the best
possible intentions, collapsed utterly and made
no more attempts to raise the spirits of the
party.

The cooking patrol were the best off; they
at least had something definite to do, and they
earned the thanks of their companions by preparing a particularly good dinner. But the
stew was of such surpassing richness and onion-
iness, and the treacle roll so seductive, that
almost everybody overate themselves; and this,

combined with want of exercise, deepened the gloom during the afternoon hours.

It was really an inspiration, even if she owed it to the very badness of the weather, which made Kitty decide that it was impossible to sleep that night in the tents. Camp must be moved into the warmth and dryness of the big kitchen, and all hands were set to work at once. Indigestion was forgotten in the exertion and excitement of running to and fro with bundles of bedding and mattresses and all the other gear from the tents, and it was a brilliant thought which made Dina suggest that bathing costumes were the only suitable wear for such an occasion.

In this garb, bare-legged, bare-armed and bare-headed, the Guides dashed to and fro between terrace and kitchen, using their ground sheets and waterproofs to cover their burdens instead of themselves. Cosy rows of beds were made up, some of them, as in upper berths, upon the tops of the long carving tables and huge flat dressers, others on boxes raised above the stone floor; and when all was finished there were hot baths for everybody before returning to normal clothing, with the wet bathing kit hung up to drip in the scullery.

" I felt after dinner as though I could never eat anything again in my life," Pam announced over the top of a huge slice of bread and gooseberry jam. "But now I've actually got quite an appetite for my tea."

"It's a very good thing that Favour Royal is on a little hill of its own," Kitty said. "For I do believe otherwise we should have been flooded out. I've never seen such rain—or heard it, either! Just listen!"

It seemed to be sweeping down in a solid sheet of water, which blotted out everything only a few yards from the windows. Swish—swish—it came like spurts from a hose against the sides of the house, and the trees bent over under the sheer weight of the downpour, helped now by a rising wind.

"What it must be like down on the flat marshes between here and the embankment, I can't imagine," Margaret said. "Don't you remember how bad it was round those cottages the day we went for the hike on stilts? And then there'd been no rain to call rain compared with this. I should think they'd simply be flooded out."

"It can't be awfully nice for those men in the boat-house on the river," Dina remarked. "A place on legs just sticking up out of the water, with the water coming higher and higher —ugh! Think of the dampness and the slugs and spiders and things—all creepy crawly!"

"Well, I don't pity them a bit, however creepy-crawly they are," Margaret said decisively. "They've *asked* for it."

"Yes, they needn't be down there at all, doing mysterious crimes that begin with an M," agreed Kathy. "You wouldn't any of you feel a bit sorry about them if you'd heard the way they talked about *you*. It would serve them right if they were *drowned*."

This was said with a vindictiveness so unlike Kathy that everybody laughed except her triplets, who thoroughly agreed that nothing could be too bad for such malefactors as Kathy had described to them.

"I'm sure they deserve it more than all the innocent kittens who die that way," Gerry said defiantly.

"Yes—or even *mice*," Chrissy, who was very tender-hearted, added. "Poor little darlings, *they* only steal cheese and things, and I'm sure they never mean to be wicked."

"Well, I don't think we'll bother about the boat-house men and their crimes until we know just what they've done," Kitty said sensibly. "In the meantime I think toffee-making is indicated for this evening—what do you say, girls? Let's try that new chocolate sort."

As it grew darker the wind rose more and more, and the rain fell with even greater heaviness. Somehow singing or dancing to the gramophone seemed impossible on such a night; they talked and ate toffee and drew close to the fire, and listened more to the storm than to each other, whatever they might pretend.

" I know now exactly what Noah and the others must have felt like in the Ark," Pam said. " Sitting stuck on the top of Mount Ararat, with the Flood all round, and wondering whether it was ever going to stop, poor dears."

" We'd better go to bed and sleep it out," Kitty said. " Very likely we shall wake to find a lovely day, with the storm all blown away. It surely can't go on like this much longer."

But it could and did—and Kitty soon found that she had been over-optimistic when she talked of sleep. Very few of them found it possible to do more than doze, starting awake every now and then at an extra loud gust of wind or battering of rain, or when a dull crash told that a tree had been blown down.

It was in the early hours of the morning, when a grim grey light was taking the place of blackness, that one of these storm sounds came so loud that it roused every one in the kitchen, and Kitty sat up and looked round at her flock. It was not a crash this time, more like a heavy thud, a dull, booming roar.

" I wouldn't have thought it was possible. It really does seem to be worse than ever," she said. " I fancy there must have been what they call a cloud-burst or something of that kind. The rain just now was like solid water falling."

" I do believe it's getting a little less now, though," said Margaret, after a pause. " Perhaps that was a kind of clearing up shower and it will stop soon."

Although that did not seem likely to happen, the rain was certainly a little less after another hour or so, and the wind had fallen considerably, so much so that Kitty, who had gone over to one of the windows to look out, stood listening with a rather puzzled expression.

" I don't know what it is—there seems to be another kind of noise . . . different," she said. " Can you hear it, Mollie? You've got such quick ears. It's not exactly rain or wind—at least, I don't believe so."

Mollie listened, frowning.

" I think—" she said slowly; " I think it's the river roaring—it must be."

" The river? But we can't hear a sound of it here as a rule." Kitty looked quite startled. " You mean—it must be in flood? And, if so—

girls, let's go upstairs and look. It's quite light enough to see now, and we can get a view from those skylight windows at the top of the house for miles and miles."

Everybody welcomed the suggestion, and there was a general scramble into coats and dressing-gowns and slippers, and a scurry to be the first to follow Kitty up the stairs in the chilly grey light of early morning, which made everything, even each other's faces, look queer and unearthly.

On the top landing they all crowded towards the skylight windows, which were on all four sides of a kind of " look-out " shaft or tower. And from everyone who could see came a simultaneous gasp. Pam had talked of being in the Ark on Mount Ararat, but did not dream how true her words were.

For Favour Royal on its mound had really and truly become an island, entirely surrounded by water. In every direction, north, south, east and west, the floods were out, sheets of grey-brown, dreary-looking water, covering field and marsh and ditch, with the tops of trees or high hedges sticking up, little islets in the water-waste, and a low grey sky which seemed still heavy with rain brooding over all. The course of the river showed as a double line of tree tops; otherwise it would have been almost impossible to say where it was.

It was like looking out on to a different world, so different that it was not easy at first to make out just what the changes were.

Byrde was the one to notice something really important, and she spoke in a queer, excited voice, with more American accent than usual.

" Say! I guess something has happened, something real bad. Look over there—to the embankment!"

" It's between those high tree tops one sees it—and on the farther side, isn't it?" Kitty said slowly. " But . . . I don't see it at all."

" No, because it's not there," Byrde said, still in the same dry voice. " It's gone—the embankment and the row of telegraph posts along it. Part of it, anyway."

CHAPTER XVI

The Stork Company

" That must have been the queer noise that woke us all up," Kitty said after a pause, during which everyone was trying to take in the news. " The embankment bursting—Maredale Mere breaking through and helping to flood the whole country."

" And it wasn't very long ago," Byrde said. " There won't have been a train along since it happened—yet. At this time in the morning there are very few on that line, very little traffic at all."

Nobody questioned Byrde's statement. She always had an uncanny knowledge about trains and times, and a wonderful memory where such things were concerned.

" But when the six-forty from Elwick junction *does* come along, they won't know the embankment's breached—communication must be cut by the telegraph poles being down."

" Oh, Byrde, do you mean there's the risk of an accident?" Kitty said anxiously.

" I certainly do, unless we can get word through somehow, warn them in some way."

" Then we *must*—we'll telephone to Elwick junction at once," Kitty said resolutely, and turned towards the stairs.

" H'm," was all Byrde remarked, but she said it again with a different intonation when, after ten minutes of fruitless " Hallo's " and " Are you there's?" growing each time more impatient, Kitty turned away from the instrument with a hopeless expression.

" I can't get any answer at all—not the faintest sound," she said. " It's just—dead."

" I thought it would be like that," Byrde remarked calmly. " The wires are down, of course—we can't communicate with anyone at all."

" Then what's to be done? No, you needn't answer, Byrde. I'm beginning to see myself, only I felt absolutely stupid at first. We must try to get over to the line—what's left of it— and give a warning."

" That's just about the only thing to do, to *try* to do," Byrde nodded quietly. " P'raps we'll be able to find a boat."

" If we can't, there are the stilts. We can get along with them, surely?" Pam cried excitedly. " That's what they're for, isn't it?

You said those people used them in water—
baskets, or whatever they're called."

"In marshes—in boggy ground—but a real
flood's a different matter." Byrde shook her
head gravely. "But we might try—don't you
think so, Loot? We're all pretty nippy on the
stilts now."

"Yes, we might try—see how far we can get."
Kitty was looking desperately worried. "But
you *must* obey me, girls, and you *must* be prepared to go back if I think it's dangerous and
tell you to. I'm responsible for the lot of you,
remember—and I suppose I *ought* to be making
plans to send you all straight home, somehow or
other."

But this was a threat which reduced the
whole Company to instant and abject obedience.
Anything rather than *that*—any amount of discipline sooner than break up camp just at this
most exciting moment. All promised fervently
that they would not question a word Loot said,
and all flew downstairs to scramble into wet-
weather clothes and to collect stilts and sticks.
Something too bad to be talked about carelessly
made one and all hurry, the feeling that lives
might depend upon their haste, that if they
weren't quick there might be a horrible accident, or even if they were . . .

And so it was in a remarkably short space of time that the whole party were trooping through the grounds, eating biscuits, bread-and-butter, apples, toffee—anything in the way of an impromptu breakfast which they had been able to collect as they swept through the kitchen.

The rain had stopped, though the clouds still hung very low. At first, paths and grass were not wetter than they would naturally be in stormy weather, but presently the ground dipped, and they began to reach what Pam, with a remembrance of newspaper language, called " the flooded area ".

It was past what was called the " Lower Lodge " where no one lived, some distance down the road which led out straight across the low, marshy country. They had been going at quite a quick jog-trot, and suddenly Pam and Pollie, who were leading, pulled up and called back that they had splashed into water—it was across the road and over their shoe-tops.

" Stilts!" Pam cried, and had already mounted upon hers before the rest of the party came up, and was testing the depth of the water, pronouncing that it was only about up to the stilt's ankle.

" We'll get along beautifully, stalking like storks," she cried. " Oh! do come on, everybody. It's quite easy walking on the road through the water."

So, for a time, it proved. The water was not more than a couple of feet in depth, and the stilt-walkers were raised well above it and progressed quite rapidly with the aid of their sticks.

They must have been quite a mile on their way before they saw or heard any sign of life, and then it came in the form of a shout from across the partly submerged hedge on their right.

" Hi! Hi! Help!" It was rather a feeble yell, and there on what was evidently a dip stood a thatched cottage, submerged above the level of the door. On the roof, perched on the eave of an upper window, rather precariously, was an old woman, wrapped in a shawl and waving a duster.

" Me oold man's just inside," she called. " Can't git out 'ere on roof on 'count of 'is stiff leg."

" Is he safe?" shouted Kitty.

" Ef water doan't coom mooch 'igher, but like's not it wull—cuvver roof likely."

" I don't think so at present." Kitty tried to sound reassuring. " Anyhow, we'll come as soon as we can and help you—we're going to try and find a boat."

" Theer's one—or should be—down on river, where that 'igh white postie be," the marooned old woman shouted. " Tied to bank, it wuz—on'y bank be gone. Doan't 'ee be long now, there's dearies!"

With renewed promises the Stork Company stalked on, but this was only the first of a series of encounters, if they could be called so. For now there were more and more small farms and cottages near the road, and almost all had their forlorn inhabitants perched upon the roofs, greeting the Guides with cries for help.

" But we can't go to them till we've got hold of a boat," Kitty decided. " Here, on the road, we're fairly safe on our stilts; there's a good firm surface under us, and the road itself is raised well up above the level of the rest. But if we once wandered off into those bogs and marshy fields—well, we could sink down just as easily on stilts as without them. Besides, the railway line and the embankment is our first job, and the quicker the better."

" And those people are pretty safe on their roofs, after all," argued Margaret. " Even if not particularly comfortable. All right! Coo-oo-ooming soon! Bringing boat!"

These last encouraging remarks were shouted at the top of her voice to another group of derelict cottagers, the last building, as it happened, before the stretch of sheer marsh—now an almost unruffled lake—between them and the railway embankment.

It was nearly broad daylight now, and the whole extent of the damage could be roughly seen. All the telegraph wires were down, the poles toppling and slanting this way and that, and subsiding into a perfect tangle where a big breach showed in the embankment itself, a gap where it had collapsed entirely and let the water of the lake come pouring through, leaving part of the railway lines suspended in the air.

Not only this, but a good part of the rest of the embankment, near the gap, seemed to be subsiding, slipping sideways.

"Most likely none of it is really safe." Byrde looked up, her eyes quick and observant behind her glasses. "It's simply frightful to think what would happen if a train ran on to it without knowing."

"Yes—until we could see it plainly, I couldn't help fancying all the time what we *might* find," Kitty said gravely. "And the danger really isn't over yet, until we've been able to tell the railway people."

"You're sure right there, Loot," Byrde agreed. "Some of us have just got to get on to the line and leg it as far as the first signal-box. Then the man there will be able to put everyone wise about the breakdown."

"It sounds an awfully dull way of doing it," Pam said regretfully, as they looked for a way up on to the embankment. "In a book it would be quite different. We should have reached the railway line just as an express train was dashing along at full speed to fall over the gap. And we should have sprung in front, only barely in time to make it pull up—or p'raps been killed in doing it."

"You'll be killed by falling down on your head if you talk all the time you're climbing up," Margaret said unkindly. "Here's a place where it ought to be pretty easy to get to the top—who's coming?"

"Three or four will be enough," Kitty said. "You seem to be on your way already, Margaret and Pam—and I'll come. You, Byrde?"

"No-oo," Byrde said slowly. "Guess there's plenty enough of you without me, and I rather think I'll stay and look at the embankment. I want to see how it all happened."

"Why, because of the floods—the extra water from the rain; it's easy enough to see," Kitty said.

"I'm not so sure. Anyway——"

" Well, it doesn't matter." Kitty sounded rather impatient. " You come, Dina—that'll be plenty, only we'd better start."

Finding rather perilous footholds in the wet muddy clay, the rescue party scrambled up to the top of the embankment, and set off along the line, Pam still lamenting.

" We ought to have something red to wave— a danger signal, you know. Or there was a story about a man who'd not got a red tie or scarf or anything, so he cut himself and let the blood drop into a bottle and then the light shone through and showed red——"

" Pam, you do have the most gruesome ideas —come on, girls, let's run!" Kitty laughed and led the way, jumping from sleeper to sleeper, whilst Pam's voice floated back to the group at the foot of the embankment.

" Well, but it's much better to *think* of all the things one could do in emergencies, so's to be always ready——"

CHAPTER XVII

The Ark, Favour Royal

" It's a very very queer thing "—only it was
" vurry " that Byrde said, relapsing into marked
American under the stress of emotion, as Mollie
put it—" why this embankment should have
gone all to bits just where it did."

" I should have thought it was simply what
Loot said—floods and rain," Letty remarked,
prodding at the wet clay with one of her stilts.

" Well, but I ask you! Wasn't it built to
stand that sort of thing, with the lake there and
all? No—there's something else, I believe,
something that made it unsafe *before* the floods
happened at all, though of course they helped
to bring it down."

Byrde moved slowly along the foot of the
embankment, with her head bent down almost
on a level with her knees, until she reached the
big gap, when she straightened herself up and
gazed at it thoughtfully.

" All these holes——" she murmured. " Look,

you can see here—regular tunnels, running right away underneath. It shows where the ground has all fallen away; you couldn't see how far they went otherwise. It's almost like a bit of honeycomb, isn't it? And it was bound to make it unsafe."

"Rabbit burrows," Dora pronounced, looking at the remains of the holes and tunnels with all the air of an expert.

"Ye-es! *Water*-rabbits," Byrde drawled, in her absent-minded way.

"Water-rabbits? What rot! There's no such thing, anyway in England." Dora laughed derisively. "Perhaps you have them in the States!"

"No, we don't; that's just what I meant, that I'd never heard of such a beast," Byrde explained. "All the same, only water-rabbits could have lived in those burrows, because when the lake was full, before it broke through and overflowed, a lot of the openings would have been under water—see? And the tunnels full of it."

"Yes," Dora confessed, rather nonplussed. "I suppose they would."

"So that rather does away with the idea of rabbits, *or* rats, *or* foxes."

"Perhaps it's some sort of fish—although I

never heard of such a thing," Dora said dubiously. " A fish that burrowed!"

" Perhaps," Byrde agreed slowly, and resumed her careful examination of the embankment, whilst the other girls scrambled up to the top out of the general wetness, and clustered together there like a flock of rather damp and dispirited birds amongst puddles and railway sleepers.

Presently the voices of the other party could be heard returning along the line, and their arrival with news raised the spirits of the rest considerably.

" We've done it—saved the train, although it was all rather tame." Pam as usual secured the first words. " All the same, we *did* hear it whistling in the distance, and if we hadn't been in time there *would* prob'bly have been a frightful railway accident, with a terrible number of casualties, and——"

" Oh, Pam, we'll hope it mightn't have been as bad as that," Kitty interrupted.

" Why? I *like* to think it would," Pam declared with morbid satisfaction. " It's no good having saved a train if nothing would have happened to it if we hadn't—now is it?"

" Well, at any rate it's quite likely there would have been a more or less bad accident

—the man in the signal-box said that," Kitty
allowed. " He was very grateful, girls; they
had not any idea that the embankment was
down, although he was beginning to think that
the communications had gone wrong, because
he had had no messages. Anyhow, he stopped
the train——"

" It was only a goods one, *not* an express—
another disappointing thing," Pam interjected.
" Goods trains are so dull; they don't come
roaring along and have to be stopped when
they're at full speed with brakes grinding and
steam hissing——"

" Pam, *do* be quiet for a minute and let me
finish telling the others about it. The train
was stopped, and we had to tell the guard just
what happened, and he's sending back at once
to the junction for a breakdown gang to investigate things and wire the news through. He
said the authorities would be very grateful
to us for the prompt manner in which we had
acted, and for bringing the information so
clearly and quickly; and he said, like the signal-
man, that we *might* have averted a serious
accident. And so I think, girls, that we may
really pat ourselves on the backs as a Company
—*and* set to work to see what we can do next,"
Kitty concluded.

" Breakfast," Pam murmured. " We're rather starving, Loot—we might fall off our stilts from exhaustion."

" Well, we certainly can't get any breakfast before we're back at Favour Royal," Kitty said. " And I do think that first we ought to try and find that boat the old woman told us about; it's the only way we can help the flooded-out people, by taking them off in a boat."

There was a general chorus of agreement, regardless of the pangs of hunger which most of the Guides were feeling. The party who had remained behind on the embankment were anxious to share with the train-rescuers in life-saving operations, and they all mounted their stilts once more and set off splashing vigorously along the submerged roadway, and keeping a look-out for the "white postie" which the old woman on the cottage roof had given as a land—or water—mark.

They made it out at last, sticking up near a clump of willows on what was evidently the course of the river, some distance away from where they stood.

And the waste of water of a quite unknown and unknowable depth between them and the post looked singularly uninviting in the grey morning light. Pam, venturing off the road for only a few yards, floundered into a deep, soft patch at once, and had to be hauled back to a securer footing by Margaret and Dina, and Kitty shook her head gravely.

" That won't do," she said. " Stilts aren't safe where you can't see where you're going."

And then Mildred, usually such a quiet member of the Company, surprised them all.

" I could swim over and see if the boat's there," she said, in her soft, rather timid-sounding voice. " And if it is, I'll tow it back."

" You, Mildred? Yes, of course you're one of our best swimmers, but you couldn't with your clothes on," Kitty said.

" I wouldn't try. But I've got my bathing costume on underneath," Mildred explained gravely. " You see, I thought it was just as well to be prepared. So if someone would just help me to get off my top things——"

This undressing business was managed without any particular difficulty, jumper and gym tunic being slipped off over Mildred's head, showing her very tall and thin in her dark blue bathing kit. Even her gum-boots were removed easily enough, and in a few minutes she was wading away towards the willows and the white post, feeling her way with a stick.

For some distance the water did not reach

above Mildred's knees; then it suddenly became waist-deep, and almost at once she was swimming, pushing the stick along in front of her.

" I do hope there are no weeds or roots— nothing that she'll get entangled in." Kitty watched the steady progress of the sleek fair head anxiously. " I wonder if I ought to have let her go alone!"

" I'm sure she'll be perfectly all right," Dina assured her, supported by a chorus from the other Guides. " None of us is a patch on Mildred where swimming is concerned—she's like an eel in the water."

But all the same, Kitty strained her eyes to see what happened when Mildred reached the willow clump and disappeared from sight for what seemed an interminably long time. At last she came into sight again, still swimming steadily, and towing behind her a large boat at the end of a rope.

" Oh, good for Mildred!" Kitty cried, and a shout of encouragement from her fellow Guides went across the muddy water to the swimmer, who came towards them with a slow, regular stroke, her pale face bearing Mildred's usual grave, intent expression.

At a little distance from the road and the group of Guides the boat grounded, and Mildred waded towards them, still holding the end of the painter.

" It's got oars and a boat-hook and everything," she said, with an air of serious triumph. " Three pairs of oars, and it will hold *quite* a lot of people, besides the rowers, too."

" Yes, it's a grand boat—well done, our Mildred!" Kitty said, and Mildred, who secretly and silently adored their lieutenant, flushed pale pink with delight.

It now remained to settle who should form the crew of their newly acquired lifeboat.

" I feel like the man with the fox and the goose, as though I *must* try to be in two places at once," Kitty said rather distractedly; but a general chorus immediately declared that she *must* be in the boat.

" You row so beautifully, Loot dear."

" You've simply *got* to be Captain."

" The others can easily manage with Margaret—and she's no good in a boat."

Half a dozen voices at once proclaimed, whilst Margaret herself staunchly agreed that she would manage beautifully.

It was arranged, therefore, after a little further discussion, that Kitty, with Dina, Mollie, Letty, and Byrde as coxswain, should go in the boat, whilst the rest of the Company in charge of Margaret returned to Favour Royal and set about preparing breakfast on a grand scale, and providing plenty of hot water and warm wraps as well as a good fire, with a view to possible refugees.

The lifeboat, meanwhile, would collect a load as soon as it could, and bring them to refuge at Favour Royal, which really did seem to be playing the part of an Ark for the surrounding countryside in its flooded state.

The stilt party plodded off along the road, whilst the lifeboat crew embarked in their vessel and set off rowing steadily towards the nearest group of cottages, on the first of which three small children and their parents were all ranged astride the roof, looking like queer birds, whilst the water had reached above the level of the attic window-sills.

It was not by any means an easy task to transfer the family from the roof to the boat, for two of the children were terrified and in tears, and the mother loaded with a great variety of bundles. But at last it was managed, and the damp group crouched forlornly in the stern of the boat, as it was pulled off in the direction of the next cottage.

Here there was only one human inhabitant, perched on the top of an outhouse, a middle-aged woman whose husband had gone to a town twenty miles away the day before, and had evidently been unable to come back.

But rescue here was complicated by the fact that the woman had three cats, which were clinging to different parts of the thatched roof of the cottage, and could not be persuaded to look upon the Guides as friends and rescuers. They spat, they swore, they scratched, they retreated to inaccessible points, they refused to listen to coaxings or threats.

When Mollie had almost fallen headlong into a partially submerged water-butt in an attempt to secure the mildest of the three, Kitty was driven to declare that they really could not take any more risks on the cats' accounts. But this only led to tears and wailings from their mistress, who vowed that she would never leave without her precious pets, and at last all three were secured and added to the crew of the boat, together with their owner.

" We haven't room for many more this trip," Kitty decided. " But we *must* try to take that poor old woman and her husband. After all, she deserves it; she told us where the boat was."

Accordingly, after promising various other desert-islanders marooned on their own house-roofs that they would come back before very long, they made their way to the cottage where the old woman still clung to the thatch above the window of the room within which her " oold man " was imprisoned.

The poor soul was waving her duster very feebly now, and seemed pathetically delighted at the reappearance of the Guides in the boat. She was so stiff and cramped that Dina and Letty were obliged to climb up on to the roof and help her down, and the business of getting out the old man was even more difficult, since the room was half filled with water, and he had climbed up on to a chest of drawers, which had to be dragged by slow degrees near the window before he could be hauled out and lowered into the boat.

Then began a long pull and a strong pull homewards with their loaded craft, although it was no great distance. When the water became too shallow to row farther, they moored the boat to a tree trunk and disembarked, crew and passengers and cargo, to wade for the little distance that remained before they reached dry land.

And a queer little procession it was that mounted the slope to Favour Royal, and limped and stumbled into the warmth of the great kitchen.

CHAPTER XVIII

In the Ark

With Prue and Pollie to relieve Letty and
Dina, and Dora, who was strong but clumsy,
as an extra one, the lifeboat made two more
rescue expeditions in quick succession, and the
kitchen became more like the Ark than ever
when half a dozen fowls, a canary, a fox terrier,
two ferrets, and a lame kitten were added to the
other animal inhabitants.

Breakfast was ready when the first party
arrived, and never had hot tea and toast with
anchovy paste and potted tongue to eke out a
limited sausage ration been more welcome. But
when the last contingent was safely landed at
Favour Royal the question of supplies became
very acute, and the two quartermasters came to
consult Kitty with very grave faces.

" We've got a good lot of tea still and plenty
of cocoa," Mollie said. " But we're running
out of sugar and there's no more milk, and as
for things to *eat*——!"

"There's practically nothing left except a tin of biscuits and some pickles," Dina supplemented solemnly. "Everybody was so fearfully starved that I suppose we weren't careful enough. We ought to have made some sort of rationing arrangement to begin with."

Kitty considered the problem seriously.

"We'd better row over and see if that little baker's shop at the cross-roads is still anyway above water," she said. "I suppose it's quite useless to think of telephoning anywhere?"

"Quite!" Mollie shook her head. "We tried, first thing, just to make sure. We can't get a sound out of it; the wires must be down completely. Oh! we're absolutely cut off, there's no doubt of that!"

"Not while we've got our gallant craft," Kitty said cheerfully. "Don't look so despondent, my dears—we'll weather the storm somehow and reach harbour—bless me! How nautical I'm getting! Well, that baker's shop is the first port to try for."

The shop in question was only about a quarter of a mile from the Lodge gates of Favour Royal, and the search party under Kitty soon discovered that the water had only just flooded its cellars and they were able to make bread as usual. All the same, the baker had not known what to do, as the cart could not go its rounds, and there seemed no way of reaching his customers.

The Guides came rather like fairy godmothers to his rescue, with the proposal that they would not only take all his present stock, but as much more as he could bake, as well as cakes and biscuits to feed their large family of refugees.

"And we have lots of potatoes and other vegetables." Dina was brightening up now. "Oh! we'll do, Loot! One can't *starve* on bread and potatoes and vegetables, can one? And plenty of tea—we want sugar, though."

It seemed that the baker could supply a fair amount of that necessity, and he also had several dozen of eggs, which they bore off in triumph, together with as much bread as they could carry. The baker himself promised to bring some more later.

Half-way back to the house Dina paused with an exclamation of dismay.

"I'd forgotten one thing that we've run out of completely," she said. "And that's butter."

"Well, I'm afraid we shall have to try to manage without either that or milk at present," Kitty said.

"But—dry bread!" Dina still looked disconsolate; her pride as a good caterer was

hurt. " And the kiddies finished up the last
of the jam just now at breakfast."

" Well—make some more!" Kitty laughed.
" There are any amount of plums in the garden
—and apples. So with some of the baker's
sugar—Dina, my child, I fear you are lacking in
initiative."

Dina said no more, but walked the remainder
of the way back to the house in thoughtful
silence. She remained thoughtful whilst arrangements were being made for launching the lifeboat again and declined to be one of the crew,
saying that she had other things to attend to.

The Raven, so called because it was large
and black and went from the Ark, set out
once more and picked up two more boat-
loads of passengers and their baggage. But the
news of the flood had spread and there were
other boats at work, so that after the second
journey Kitty decided that they had done
enough salvage for the day.

There remained plenty of other business in
disposing of their refugees. Mrs. Cooper at the
Lodge was willing to help, and brought spare
rugs and other things to make up beds in some
of the empty rooms, whilst her husband came
with a load of bracken which he had been drying
in a shed, to use instead of mattresses.

" I've taken it for granted that my cousin would want me to use the rooms," Kitty said. " It's the only thing to do, as I can't telephone to anyone. And it's just as well that my father is a banker in Knutsbridge—that seems to make the baker quite happy about trusting me and getting his money. Wherever has Dina gone to? I want to settle with her where to stow the foodstuff when it comes. Has anybody seen her?"

Somebody had, it appeared; somebody had noticed her going off to the kitchen garden with the triplets some time before, carrying baskets.

" Probably to get in some vegetables," Kitty said. " It's quite fine now, so she thought it a good opportunity, I expect. Well, I'll go and see her there before I forget about it."

Approaching the kitchen garden, Kitty sniffed with a puzzled expression. What *was* this warm, pleasant smell, and where could it come from? But next moment she knew, and paused behind a tangle of raspberry canes to watch and laugh to herself over the scene.

Dina and the triplets were there and they were extremely busy. They had made a big fire under a small pent-roof in a corner of the wall, where the ground was dry; a beautiful glowing

fire above which was slung the biggest dixie.
It was the dixie from which the delicious smell
came, as Dina, damp and crimson of face,
stirred it with a long stick and encouraged the
triplets, sitting on three upturned pails and
working away most strenuously peeling and
slicing apples.

"Hurry up!" Dina was saying. "This lot
is just done, and I want to get another started
while the fire is so good. We'll just pour it
off into the big enamel basins—— Oh!"

This was a startled exclamation as Kitty
appeared walking down the path, and Dina
almost dropped her stick into the boiling
cauldron in her surprise.

"You needn't tell me what you're doing—it
smells to the heavens!" Kitty said. "But Dina,
my dear, what a splendid idea!"

"Why, it was yours—you said yourself that
I ought to make some jam." Dina spoke half
reproachfully. "And I thought if I did, it
ought to be as quickly as possible—all that
dry bread, you know. Then it seemed simpler to
make it here, on the spot, without having to
carry in the fruit and mess up the kitchen—and
I do believe this is a really good batch of jam."

It was, Kitty pronounced solemnly as she
sampled a "taster" of the plum-and-apple

jam, and helped to pour it out into the big basins to cool.

"For it really doesn't seem worth while potting it, does it?" Dina said. "It'll be eaten up so quickly by all of us that it won't have time to go bad or anything. Besides, I'll tie greased paper over the basins that aren't in use. Now, I'm just going to get some more water and we'll start the next batch—have you got enough apples ready, triplets?"

"Dina, my child——" Kitty contemplated her quartermaster solemnly. "Never, never again will I say, or even think that you are lacking in initiative. Lacking! You're simply bubbling over with it!"

CHAPTER XIX

"The Dove"

That first exhausting day of rescue and salvage was over, and small wonder if all concerned, preservers and preserved, were thoroughly tired out. The Guides had been on foot or on stilts or rowing or otherwise exerting themselves since soon after four in the morning, and that on the top of a sleepless night owing to the storm. And as for the rescued cottagers, most of them had spent the better part of that same night perched upon their roofs, which could not be regarded as a restful occupation.

No wonder that whether on bracken or straw or bare boards, in sleeping bags or under rugs or ground-sheets, or even coats and waterproofs when other bedding failed, they all slept so soundly that not a soul in Favour Royal would have been waked that night by the worst storm in the world.

As it happened, it was quite calm and peaceful, and it was a very yawning and sleepy-eyed cooking patrol who roused themselves early next morning to prepare breakfast for their large family, with Dora attached as a supernumerary at her own request to attend to the wants of the animal population of the Ark.

There was not much cooking to be done beyond tea and porridge; breakfast consisted mainly of bread and jam, but nobody complained and there was the prospect of a hearty dinner, as a large piece of salt beef had been secured during one of their voyages the day before. This was to be boiled for dinner with plenty of vegetables, and Mollie had undertaken the task; whilst Prue and Letty, who adored children, were to be in charge of the " crèche ", the ten babies and small boys and girls who had been amongst those taken from the flooded cottages and were " parked " in one of the big empty rooms.

The elder refugees, together with some of the Guides, were setting forth on a voyage of exploration to see how things were going as far as the flood was concerned, using *The Raven* and the stilts of the Company. But Kitty considered that she and some half-dozen of the girls were enough for this expedition, and she gave her decision after deliberation.

" Triplets, I think you had better stay behind

this morning," she said. " We can't *all* go, and if Mollie and Prue and Letty are busy with their particular jobs, they can't attend to things in general—and one never knows what may turn up. So I'm going to leave you three in charge to deal with anything that happens in the way of emergencies, and to be at hand to help anyone who needs it. I can count on you, can't I?"

Looking very serious and important, the triplets gave their promise, and Kitty felt satisfied that her little speech had had its effect and soothed any wounded vanity at being left behind. She had spoken rather strongly just for that purpose; later she was to wish that she had not made *quite* such a touching appeal to such very romantic and conscientious individuals as Gerry, Kathy and Chrissy.

In the meantime the triplets felt extremely important and very much like knights left to defend a beleaguered castle, full of helpless women and children. They paced up and down the terrace as though it had been battlements, and gazed out over the greyish, muddy expanse of water which covered all the lower ground as though—to mix the metaphor—it had been uncharted seas and they a kind of threefold Columbus.

The flood reached up to the bottom of the grassy slope below the house, and only a very little of the hedge which bounded it was visible, with the tops of the trees beyond which fringed what had once been river and towpath. Everybody had been so busy on the farther side of the house on the preceding day that this aspect had been rather neglected, and it was quite exciting to try and make out all the changes which the flood had made, what one could still see or couldn't see, of the ordinary everyday landmarks.

Certainly standing there on the terrace it felt like being on the deck of the Ark, watching floating branches and pieces of wood and other oddments, such as an old basket and the tattered remains of an umbrella, which looked very absurd and out of place, bobbing up and down.

It was Chrissy's sharp eyes which discovered something more exciting than all this flotsam and jetsam.

" Look! Over there, by that clump of holly!" She pointed away towards part of the shrubbery which curved round on that side of the house. " There's something white—a big thing, partly hidden by the bushes—stuck in them."

" It looks like—— Yes! it is!" Kathy screwed up her eyes. " It's a boat."

" Washed up from the river most likely,"
Gerry added. " A small white boat."

" We ought to get it before it's washed away
somewhere else," Kathy announced decisively.
" Just think how useful it would be to have a
second boat, besides *The Raven*."

" Yes, of course—let's see about it at once,"
Gerry and Chrissy agreed in chorus.

Fortunately the place where the small white
boat was cast up was not in very deep water.
Bare-legged and tucking up their tunics as high
as possible, the triplets managed to reach it
without getting so very wet, and to pull it out
from the bushes in which it was entangled. It
was a most attractive little boat, they all decided,
painted a creamy-white, with two pairs of sculls
safely lashed inside, and so light that it would
be very easy to manage.

It seemed urgently necessary to prove that
at once, and all three scrambled in and rowed
away in style in their newly captured vessel,
Gerry and Kathy at the oars, Chrissy steering.

" Isn't it a *darling*!" Chrissy said. " Like a
feather. And it's so white and pretty. If the
big boat's *The Raven*, this ought to be called
The Dove, don't you think? It's *like* a dove."

As the other two thoroughly agreed, the boat
was accordingly christened *The Dove*, since,

fortunately, she had no other name painted anywhere about her.

After cruising about for some little time, the three decided that they must not leave their post for too long, and rowed to the bottom of the slope, pulling the little boat up upon the grass, well out of the water.

" Well, that's a really good piece of work," Gerry said with satisfaction. " Won't Loot be pleased to know that we've got another boat, and won't it be useful? We can go off rescuing by ourselves."

" Don't you think we might go for another row in it later?" suggested Chrissy. " Just to practise our rowing."

" Oh yes, and take Maurice," Kathy added. " He *is* having such a dull time, poor darling; he's not been out of his bath for ages and ages, and he's always scratching."

" Well, p'raps later," Gerry decided. " But not just yet, in case anything——"

And it was just then that something *did* happen, taking the words out of Gerry's mouth.

Kathy's quick eyes caught sight of it first, a little flutter of something over the tree-tops. It looked like the end of a pole, and on it— what *was* that?

" It's a sort of white flag," Chrissy said

eagerly. "With dark marks on it—letters, aren't they? Only they're too much folded up to see. Oh! look, it's blowing out!"

A breeze obligingly unfurled and partly spread out the white flag at that moment, giving glimpses of roughly shaped block letters, a bit of one, that of another being displayed, and then all together.

Almost simultaneously it dawned upon the triplets what that writing was.

" S—O—S!" broke from them in an ex- cited shout, and Gerry added, rather un- necessarily:

" Somebody wants help!"

" The boat!" Kathy gasped. " Quick! we must go at once! We can't wait to tell the others. Don't waste a single minute!"

It was wonderfully thrilling to race down the terrace steps and the green slope beyond, just as though they were a lifeboat crew summoned by a signal of distress from a wreck. Not until they were in the boat and rowing along did any of them really think about where they were going, and then it was Kathy at the tiller who suddenly dropped the ropes and exclaimed:

" It's the men at the boat-house—yes, that's who it is! They've put a sort of flagstaff on the roof—it's just where that part of the river bank ought to be, only the water has sort of mixed things up."

Both the other triplets ceased rowing and looked over their shoulders at their goal.

"Yes, Kathy's right! It *is* the boat-house men; there's a bit of the building through the trees—look!—the end of the roof!"

Gerry and Chrissy turned round again and all three stared at each other gravely.

"It seems a funny thing to go and rescue *them*," Gerry said gravely. "After the way they've behaved, and the crimes we know they're doing, and—and everything that's bad about them."

"Yes, and the way they spoke about *us*," Chrissy added. "What Kathy heard. It's cheek of them to expect us to help—they don't deserve it."

Kathy's cheeks had grown very red, and she clutched the tiller ropes tightly in both hands.

"They don't deserve it," she said with a little gasp; "but we must save them, all the same. We can't let them be drowned; if we did we'd be almost like *murderers*—'specially because we wished it. Yes, we did—the night before last. We said that they were much worse than kittens and things, and *ought* to be drowned. Well, that's what's happening, just as though it was in answer to our wish, and so—and so— we've simply *got* to go and save them—that's all!"

Kathy finished her long speech with an air of breathless defiance, but she met with no opposition from her triplets, as perhaps she had expected. Both of them nodded gravely.

" Yes, we must!" said Gerry. " There's no doubt about it."

" We must!" echoed Chrissy; and they set off rowing steadily in the direction of the S.O.S. signal.

CHAPTER XX

S.O.S.

It took longer than one would have expected. That was because they could not go as a crow flies, but more as a duck swims, and they had to row along until they reached a gap in the belt of trees between them and the place where the river usually was. For even though those trees were standing in water and fairly deep water too, it would not have been possible to push the boat along between them.

At last they found a fairly clear place, and after a little careful navigation amongst almost submerged bushes, reached the river itself, the swollen, altered river, with no towpaths or boundaries.

But before they reached the river they had had time to make another discovery.

" D'you know——" Kathy, less occupied than her sisters, remarked; " the bottom of this boat is very wet—it's sort of oozing up through the boards."

"Leaks," Gerry said briefly, glancing down. "But not much—yet, anyway. We'll have to start baling if it gets bad."

"What with?" Kathy inquired practically. "There doesn't seem to be anything of a baley sort——"

"Oh! well, p'raps we shan't need it, and you *must* attend to the steering," Gerry said impatiently. "Just round this next bend we'll come to the boat-house."

So Kathy concentrated on her task, and the other two on theirs. In a few moments they were within sight, not only of the boat-house, but of its three inhabitants, all perched upon the semi flat roof round an open skylight. The building looked very queer, for its "legs" and lower story were under the water, which seemed to reach just to the floor of the upper story.

Kathy, the only one of the Guides who could see what they were coming to, stared with all her eyes. How strange it was, those three sitting there who were Men of Mystery with a very big M. There was the big dark one, whom she hated badly, but still secretly thought a little bit romantic; there was the fairer, smaller one called Harry, who had made himself so pleasant at their camp-fire and who was really such a sneak. And lastly, and much queerer looking than the others—the man who must be Lou, short and broad, with a copper-yellow face, a flattened nose, beady black eyes, and a fringe of black hair over a low forehead. Byrde's Indian—and a horrid-looking creature, Kathy decided. But really at the moment they all looked too wet and draggled to be frightening.

They were quite close to the boat-house now; Kathy could see in through the window of the upper story that the water was just lapping about on the floor, but no more than that. It was a low room, with a skylight opening on to the roof.

" Hullo!—you saw our signal, then?"

It was the dark man who spoke first, with a smile which was probably meant to be pleasant.

" Yes," Kathy answered briefly. Remembering the uncomfortable moments she had spent hiding amongst the reeds, she really could not manage to be frightfully polite.

" Why!—it's our little trespassing friends!" This time the smile wasn't pleasant.

" Perhaps you'd rather we didn't trespass now—we can easily go back!" Chrissy said over her shoulder, and Harry laughed.

" One for you, old man! And I think it was jolly bad form to bring up that old matter.

I'm uncommonly grateful myself—but then, I've already made friends with these young ladies, haven't I?"

He appealed to Kathy, but she still remembered too much, and answered coldly and stiffly:

" Real friends are the same behind one's back."

" What a sphinx-like remark!" He laughed, but rather uneasily. " Well, we'll talk about that later. Meanwhile, as we're fearfully stiff and cramped——"

He shuffled along the roof as though preparing to drop into the boat, and the other men also began to move. Kathy, leaning forward, spoke hurriedly.

" There won't be room for all of them at once, will there, Gerry? They'd better let us row them ashore one by one, hadn't they, Chrissy?"

" No, there's certainly not room for everyone at once——"

Harry had swung himself down as he spoke, into the boat. " So *this* is the best thing to be done."

Before Kathy realized what he was talking about, he had seized her round the waist and swung her up into the arms of the dark man, who set her down beside him on the roof, too startled and breathless to collect wits or voice for a moment.

And before she had recovered either, Chrissy was being swung up beside her, and the Indian was down in the boat taking her place on the thwart.

Gerry, on her feet, was speaking indignantly.

"How dare you! What do you mean by it?"

"Come on—you'd rather be with your sisters, I imagine, than stay with us—up you go!"

And all three triplets were now on the roof, with the dark man swinging himself down and pushing the boat away from the side of the house.

"You thieves! Robbers! Oh!—we know about you!" Kathy in her fury was beyond prudence, and she fairly raged at the three men, her hands clenched. "We know that you've been doing something here—something bad— something you don't want found out!"

The dark man was scowling now.

"You do, do you?" he snarled. "Well, much good may it do you!"

Harry and Lou had already seized the oars and they were beginning to row away, when Chrissy gave an involuntary cry.

"You'd better be careful—that boat's leaking

—it won't take your weight!" she exclaimed.

It was true. The water, which had only oozed in slowly under the comparatively light weight of the triplets, was now pouring into the boat, and it was sagging over sideways in a perilous manner.

" Curse it! Where's something to bale with?" Harry exclaimed; and Gerry shouted back:

" There isn't anything!"

" You knew it, did you—confound you!" The dark man's face was very ugly as he snarled up at the girls. " You tried to trap us, eh?"

" You didn't give us time to tell you, even if we'd remembered at the moment," Kathy told them. " But—it serves you right!"

" I say—they'll be drowned——" Chrissy gasped, for the boat was now gunwale under and evidently sinking fast. Lou had slipped into the water and was swimming alongside, grunting out a few words in some foreign language.

" Back to the boat-house!" Harry cried; and they began to plunge in that direction.

Then Kathy acted, promptly and unexpectedly, her round face pale and resolute.

" Quick! Help!" she summoned the others. " Let's shut down the skylight—now! They shan't get up on the roof—they can stay in the room underneath. Help me, both of you!"

Bang! Down went the skylight and the triplets proceeded to sit upon it after they had rammed the bolts home. As Kathy had seen, it was the only way that the men could reach the roof again, although it had been easy enough to drop down into the boat. Now they had only just time to cling to the window-sills to scramble into the room beneath, before the boat sank entirely under its two occupants, with much gurgling and bubbling.

" So that's the end of *The Dove* !" Kathy said mournfully. " And she was such a dear little boat!"

" She behaved just as she ought—sinking them," Chrissy remarked. " She stopped those horrible men from getting away."

" Well, what do we want them here for?" Gerry objected. " We'd be better without them."

" P'raps we should." Chrissy looked uncertain. " Or p'raps it's best for them to be here."

" *They* don't think so!" Kathy grinned rather impishly, for the sounds from the room beneath certainly seemed to tell of dissatisfaction to say the least of it. Loud voices, stampings up and down, bangings on the under part of the sky-light.

"But they shan't come up," Kathy said decisively. "And now *we* must use the S.O.S. flag."

It was one thing to use it, and quite another to be answered. They unlashed the flagstaff, raised it, waved it in order to make it more conspicuous, but nothing happened.

"The worst of it is," Gerry said, "that none of the others are awfully likely to be on the terrace and see any signal. Or upstairs, either; even when they come in they'll stay in the kitchen."

"*We* saw," Kathy maintained bravely. "And if we wait long enough they'll miss us and look about."

"We've *got* to wait," Chrissy remarked rue-fully. "But it won't be nice when—if it gets dark."

Such a prospect was so uninviting that all three fell silent in face of it.

"Well," Kathy said at last, "it's no worse for us than it was for all those people on the cottage roofs—and the flood was still flooding then. Tell you what!—let's sing. It might cheer us up rather, and "—with another impish flash—" it'll remind that pig down below of our camp-fire that night, and how he pretended to be friends.''

So they sang. They sang loudly and tried to forget how hungry they were and how delicious that salt beef would be tasting. They sang, until Chrissy broke off with something almost like a sob.

" Oh, *look*!" she cried. " There she comes!— *The Raven*! I—I *couldn't* have sung much longer. But—who is that strange man in the boat?"

CHAPTER XXI

Byrde Visits the Post Office

During the time of the discovery, the voyage,
and the wreck of *The Dove*, *The Raven* had
been busy carrying passengers and goods.

Some of the refugees had found their homes
rather less flooded, and had determined to live
in the upper stories now that they were able
to reach the houses by wading, and there was
hope that the water would soon be lower still.
A few of the others, who would probably be
homeless for some time to come, had been
established by Kitty in the uninhabited Lodge,
which was high and dry and big enough to
accommodate several families.

" For I'm perfectly positive Ralph would
want me to do it," she said. " I shall get to
him on the telephone as soon as I can—to-day
perhaps—but in the meanwhile there's the
place standing empty, and we can store what
furniture and things we can save in it as well;

it's so close to the edge of the floods. It would be an awful business bringing everything up to the big house."

Even carrying to the Lodge was no light matter, as well as rowing the heavy boat backwards and forwards. But the job was finished at last, and a small party, including Kitty, Margaret and Byrde, set off along the high road on their stilts to visit the post office some half a mile away.

" If the wires are repaired I shall try and get on to Ralph," Kitty said. " And anyway, there may be letters. Possibly, too, communication may be open with Knutsbridge, and if so I should like to let your people know that you're all right. It's just possible that *some* of them may be anxious about their precious brats!"

The post office, standing with a few other cottages on a kind of raised terrace, was well above the water itself, although isolated by the floods from the rest of the village.

The postmistress greeted the Guides as though she had been the inhabitant of a desert island catching a glimpse of a sail upon the horizon, and insisted upon feeding them all with home-made dandelion wine and rock cakes in her warm back parlour.

Yes, the telephone wires seemed to be working again, she told them, and, dearie, dearie me!— there was a post in this morning, but it hadn't so much as been sorted yet—— She'd been that upside-downsy and put about with all these dreadful happenings.

Accordingly, Kitty established herself in the telephone box, first to communicate with the relations of the Guides in Knutsbridge, and then to try to get into touch with Lord Lorimer, tell him of the state of things at Favour Royal, and ask his advice.

Meanwhile, as this seemed likely to be a lengthy proceeding, Margaret and the others toasted their toes by the fire in the parlour, sucked bull's-eyes purchased from the post-mistress, who was also the local confectioner, tobacconist, stationer and newsagent, and enjoyed the rest after their arduous labours.

All except Byrde; she remained in the post office part of the establishment and went through the mail-bag with the postmistress, taking charge of all the Favour Royal letters for future distribution.

This job finished, and after Mrs. Jubb had retired to put on her husband's dinner to cook, Byrde remained behind the postal counter and gazed with interest at the various pigeon-holes and shelves and boxes, with their more or less dusty contents.

Mrs. Jubb didn't very often have occasion to send telegrams, she decided; the packets of forms were quite yellow and dog-eared with age. And it didn't look as though anybody had ever taken any interest in customs forms.

" Only six people with gun licences." Byrde read the list gravely. " And one of them the vicar; looks funny, somehow. I don't believe she registers many parcels; that sealing-wax must have been in use for years—— Wonder what all these little leaflets and folders are about—pretty dry, I expect. Foot and Mouth Disease, Studies Concerning the Handling of Milk, Investigations of Celery Diseases and their Control. I didn't even know that celery *had* diseases! Ensilage—now what on earth is that? Oh! I see, they're all published by the Ministry of Agriculture and Fisheries and the Department of Agriculture for Scotland— His Majesty's Stationery Office."

Byrde surveyed her grimy fingers with disgust; they were dusty things, these small leaflets and pamphlets, and didn't seem likely to repay further investigation.

" I always thought I could read 'most anything," she murmured. " But these sure have me beat for dryness. Hul-lo! What's this? A picture of—yes, it's him! Now, what on earth—— I wonder if I've struck big business just by accident?"

Byrde subsided on to the leather-topped stool behind the counter and remained absorbed for minute after minute in the small pamphlet of six pages with pictures, numbered cryptically, Form No. A. 767 L.P. (Second Edition).

She studied it and studied it with queer expressions passing over her face—perplexity, anger, something like triumph. Finally, when the click of the telephone-box door intimated that Kitty had at last finished, Byrde crumpled up the paper hurriedly and thrust it into her pocket.

" Oh! what a time that took!" Kitty pushed her hat straight. " I'm sick of saying ' Hello!' I got all the Knutsbridge people quite easily, but that cousin of mine! *Nobody* knows where he is; I simply can't run him to earth, so I had to give it up. I'll have to write and trust that the letter will be delivered somehow, sometime, somewhere! In charge of the shop, Byrde? Where are the others? Sick of waiting for me?"

Byrde explained, but said nothing about the paper in her pocket, as she gathered together the other booklets and put them back into their pigeon-hole. There was a good deal of thinking still to be done before she told anybody anything, for Byrde was distinctly cautious about jumping to conclusions. All the same, two and two seemed to be making four unexpectedly often, as she deliberated upon the facts which she had been studying so profoundly. It was like getting the one important clue in a crossword puzzle; all the other letters began to fit in as though by magic.

" Well!" Kitty looked round her flock as they assembled on the terrace outside the post office and prepared to resume their stilts. " I should think we might as well go back to dinner now. There doesn't seem anything else important to be done at present."

As all the others fervently agreed, they started for Favour Royal, and had almost reached the Lodge gates when a motor-car came splashing along the road through the water which reached half-way up its wheels.

It pulled up, and a young man looked out and called cheerfully, waving his hat:

" Hullo! Is that you, old thing?"

The Guides stared, scandalized at this method of addressing their lieutenant, and Kitty frowned and drew herself up.

" I'm afraid you're making a mistake——"

she began, and then suddenly broke off with:
" Why!—*Ralph*! You've got just the same face
as when you were a little boy, only higher
up!"

" Same old red hair and freckles—what?"
The young man grinned. " Well, I might
retaliate. I knew you at once, otherwise I
shouldn't have dared to address you as I did,
of course. Your attendant Guides made it
more of a certainty."

Kitty laughed.

" Well, girls, I suppose I needn't tell you
that this is my cousin, Lord Lorimer, our host
at Favour Royal," she said. " And not a bit
more grown up than when he was ten years old.
Ralph, I've spent half the morning trying
to run you down on the telephone, so it's a
tremendous comfort to see you here."

" I saw in the papers about the happenings
here, so I thought I'd better come and see
whether my property was completely washed
away—including my dear cousin and her Guide
Company." Lord Lorimer grinned. " And
I've already heard at the station about your
life-saving operations on the railway line and
elsewhere."

" Oh! that's nothing! But I've been using
Favour Royal as a sort of refugee camp for the

flooded-outs, and I did want to get your permission for that and a lot of other things."

" You've got it in advance!"

" Thanks! I knew you *would* say that. But
now you'd better come back with us to a boiled
beef dinner, before we settle anything more."

" Good! Nothing I'd like better—and I've
got to have more than just a general introduction to all my Guide guests." Lord Lorimer
grinned again so pleasantly as he spoke that
the whole of the Company present unanimously
fell in love with him, as Pam said afterwards, and
Byrde declared under her breath to Dora:

" He's not a bit like a Lord—I'd have sure
expected him to be quite different, more
pompous and stiff."

" English peers aren't," Dora said in a lofty
manner, as though her acquaintance with the
aristocracy was very large; for one mustn't let
down one's country before a foreigner. But
she added loyally: " Although I don't suppose
many are as nice as Lord Lorimer—being
Loot's cousin."

Meanwhile Kitty, walking ahead with the
same cousin, had been suddenly reminded of
the Mystery by a question of Lord Lorimer's.

" By the way, have you seen anything of
the chap I let the fishing to—Masterman?

There are three of them there, living in the boat-house, I believe—he and his friend and a servant."

" Yes, there are three of them—though I only know one by sight myself," Kitty said. " The fact is, Ralph, I've often wondered whether I oughtn't to write to you about those men, only I waited to know more—— It's a mystery, isn't it, girls?—quite an exciting one; the men at the boat-house seem to be up to something, and we haven't the slightest idea what it is except that they don't want to be found out."

" We have—at least, *I* have!" Byrde suddenly burst out.

" *You*, Byrde? Since when?" Kitty looked amazed.

" Since about half an hour ago I've known pretty well for sure what those men are up to," the American girl said slowly and deliberately. " But I want to tell them of it to their faces—just to make certain."

CHAPTER XXII

What "M" Meant

And from that determination nothing would make Byrde budge.

" I don't want to say anything till I'm dead sure," she maintained obstinately. " And I can't be dead sure till I see their faces when I show them something. So if you'd just let me go on oystering till then, I'd be real glad."

" Well, I'm quite sure we shall never make you say anything you don't want to!" Kitty laughed. " You *can* be as tight-mouthed as one of your own clams, Byrde."

" What are these fellows like?" Lord Lorimer asked. " I never saw either of them myself— we settled everything by letter."

" Well, the only one I've seen was extremely ordinary," Kitty said. " But I understand that the others are more of the correct villainous type, and certainly they *have* done some most peculiar things."

She proceeded to give details, helped by the

other girls who gathered round eagerly, remembering, reminding, and succeeding in leaving Lord Lorimer completely puzzled. And meanwhile Byrde, with the clue to the mystery in the small leaflet crumpled up in her pocket, stalked along wearing her most oysterlike expression.

It had been decided that before they did anything further the salt beef dinner should be disposed of, but when they reached Favour Royal it was only to find that the best laid schemes of mice—and Guides—had once more miscarried.

For Prue and Mollie met them with anxious faces and minds so disturbed that they did not even notice the presence of Lord Lorimer for some minutes after the meeting.

" Oh! Loot! The triplets have gone—disappeared!" Mollie cried, and Prue corroborated:

" We can't find them *anywhere*!"

" The triplets? But where can they have gone?" Kitty asked. " I told them particularly to stay at Favour Royal and they promised——"

" Well, they've *gone*!" Prue was very nearly in tears. " And I do believe it's those horrible men—I'm sure they've kidnapped them—it was the triplets who seemed to come across them most, you know, always—and p'raps they found out that Kathy overheard all that about what they were doing, and the M mystery."

" It does seem very queer altogether." Kitty was looking extremely worried. " The triplets aren't usually disobedient, and they faithfully promised not to go off exploring on their stilts."

" The only other thing is th-that th-they may be d-drowned," wailed poor Prue, bursting into tears at the very thought. " Anyway, they're not anywhere in the house."

All thought of dinner was set aside for the time being; but it was not very long before the S.O.S. flag was seen waving above the tree-tops down by the river, and from the top of the house it could actually be made out that the signals came from the boat-house roof.

" Then it *is* the triplets, and they *have* been kidnapped by those awful men!" Prue declared triumphantly. " Oh! Loot, we must go and rescue them at once!"

But this was not quite so easily done as said, since *The Raven* was the only means of reaching the river, and *The Raven* was at the other side of the Favour Royal estate, where they had left it when they adjourned to the post office. The only thing to be done was to start the rescue party from that point, and the next consideration was as to who should make up that party.

Kitty and Lord Lorimer went—or were to go without saying, and Byrde with her closely guarded secret was also a matter of course. Margaret, Pam, Letty and Dina were finally selected for the rest of the crew as strong rowers, and they set off at once.

The other Guides, somewhat disconsolate, were cheered by the suggestion that they should contrive, as quickly as possible, an answering signal to reassure the triplets—if it were the triplets. But the manufacture of a flag from a white tablecloth with the word " Coming!" in enormous letters took so long that it served no useful purpose in the end— except to provide the deserted members of the Company with occupation. But after all that was better than nothing.

Meanwhile the rescue party had reached *The Raven*, embarked, and set out in the direction of the river. It was not so difficult from this side to reach the channel as the triplets had found it during their voyage in *The Dove*, for the banks were more open, with fewer trees.

Byrde had disappeared for a few minutes before they started, and sat with something tightly buttoned inside her coat, and a more tense and mysterious expression than ever,

refusing to row—" until later "—as she observed
cryptically.

The flood water was covered with floating
debris, but when they reached the main course
of the river and rowed along it between the
submerged banks, it was to discover that the
curious wire entanglement across it, which the
men at the boat-house had erected to keep out
trespassers, was still partly in place.

Lord Lorimer frowned and shook his head
over it.

" Can't think what on earth the beggars put
it up for," he said. " Except to keep boats
from passing along. And I never blocked the
river myself in that way, or gave them authority
to do it when they took over the fishing rights.
That's illegal on their part, anyhow."

" You see—they just couldn't have people
start guessing what they were doing," Byrde
said. " That's what it was."

Round another bend—and there at last was
the boat-house, islanded in the water, and
there, too, on its roof, to Kitty's enormous
relief, the unmistakable figures of the triplets,
grouped on the skyline round the flagstaff, with
its S.O.S. signal waving bravely over their
heads.

The rest of the distance was covered very

quickly, but long before they actually came up to the boat-house Byrde had made another dramatic discovery.

" They're there!—those men!" she cried. " Inside the house—there, don't you see? One of the men's banging on the underside of the skylight."

" Yes!" Lord Lorimer chuckled as he glanced over his shoulder. " It looks to me, Kitty, as though your triplets had kidnapped the men, rather than the other way about!"

" They do look real mad, too," Byrde said, and added with satisfaction: " And they'll be madder still before *I*'ve done with them!"

As the boat came closer, the men inside the room stopped their efforts to force up the skylight, and Harry came out on to the little balcony with a pretence of great friendliness, such as he had shown on the camp-fire evening.

" Well, we're uncommonly glad to see you," he said. " It's been an uncomfortable business, being marooned here, and we shall be glad to be taken off, I can tell you. I suppose you've not got a flask on you, sir?" He spoke to Lord Lorimer. " You see, we're chilled through— been in the water."

" Because they stole our boat and it sank with them," Kathy chimed in unexpectedly from the roof, and Chrissy added excitedly.

"Yes, they stole it—and it would have served them right if they'd been drowned!"

Harry scowled and turned red.

"We were only going to fetch help," he blustered. "We'll explain all about that if you take us off."

"But we're not going to take you off for a little," Byrde spoke in her coolest and most deliberate tones. "Not until we've talked a bit."

"What d'you mean?" Harry glanced at her furiously.

"I certainly mean just that," Byrde said placidly. "We've got quite an earful to say because, you see, we've just been put wise to what you're doing."

Byrde's drawl, Byrde's accent, were much more pronounced than usual, but somehow she had so completely taken charge of the situation that no one else in the boat said anything at the moment. They just waited and listened as she went on slowly—and the triplets on the roof leant over to listen too, as though they had got an extra good place in the gallery of a theatre to see and hear everything.

"You see, we guessed quite a while ago that you weren't here just for ordinary fishing.

And we knew that you wouldn't have minded us camping at the house—if you hadn't had something to hide," said Byrde.

" No one wants a lot of children messing about near preserved water," the dark man snarled, with a furious glance.

" But we weren't near," Byrde said sweetly. " Only, of course, it was a nuisance our being at the house, just when you were using the coach-house as a store—and playing spooks didn't keep us away from it. But then you *did* manage to get all the stuff away that evening when Mr.—er—Harry came to the concert to distract our attention."

" What do you mean?" Harry snapped out.

" Well, I can't talk more plainly unless I put it all in words of one syllable," Byrde said patiently. " But the most important thing we've discovered is—what M stands for!"

" What!"

Both men, utterly taken by surprise, spoke together.

Byrde stood up in the boat, drew something from under her coat, and held it up with a dramatic gesture.

" There!" she cried. " M for Mascot and Maurice—and Musquash!"

CHAPTER XXIII

Finishing Touches

Maurice the Mascot kicked and squeaked lustily, and an answering squeal broke from Dora at sight of him. But the effect upon the men in the boat-house was extraordinary.

"Where did you get the beast?" Harry stammered.

"He strayed out of your musquash preserve," Byrde said. "But we didn't know he was a Musquash, Musk Rat, Fiber Zibethicus or Ondatra Qibethica until I found all about them in a Government book besides—and a lot of other things, too."

"But stop a bit—I don't quite understand what you're getting at," Lord Lorimer interrupted. "*What* have they been doing?"

"Breeding musk rats or musquashes—for their fur!" Byrde said triumphantly. "And nobody's allowed to—nobody's supposed to bring them into any country because they do such a frightful lot of damage."

" Oh!—rubbish!" The dark man spoke contemptuously. " What damage do you pretend has been done, you little idiot?"

" What damage?" None of her companions had ever imagined that Byrde could look so fierce; her eyes were positively blazing behind her spectacles. " Oh! nothing—except that you're responsible for the greater part of this flood damage—that you might have been the cause of a serious railway accident. Yes—you may sneer, but the railway embankment that gave way and let through the lake only did it because it was riddled through and through with the burrows of the musk rats, just like a honey-comb. I saw it, only I didn't know at first what it meant—and that's what they do; it's in the book."

Byrde paused a second to take breath, then ploughed on:

" They began by undermining the river banks—*that* nearly drowned several of us by breaking down, but of course, *you* wouldn't have cared. And then Kathy hid in one of their ' lodges '—she didn't know what it was, but there's a picture of it here, the round house the beasts build to keep food in. So she heard you say a lot about the numbers you were catching, and how it might get you into trouble

—only we still thought it was just fish. But, of course—that's why you've got that Indian to help you, because musquashes come from North America and he knew about trapping the beasts."

" But Byrde—dear!" Kitty took advantage of another pause for breath. " The railway embankment—is it *possible* that there could be enough of them to undermine it?"

" Possible! of course it is!" Byrde sounded quite indignant. " Why, do you know that a pair taken to some country or other had twenty million descendants in five years? That just shows—and I expect they brought a lot of pairs. It says—the book—that they breed with extreme rapidity, and more so in England than anywhere else. And they travel, too, both in water and on land—some have gone twenty miles in a week. They're the most terrible pests!"

" Darling Maurice!" Dora was almost crying. " To think that he should turn out to be a pest!"

" Well, I'm real glad you found him," Byrde said. " Because if I hadn't found his photograph in the book at the post office I'd never have known that it *was* musquashes."

" And then you wouldn't have been able

to give us this most interesting lecture on their habits and customs—we'd have missed a lot, wouldn't we?" The dark man spoke in an ugly sneering voice. " All the same, this doesn't cut much ice where *we*'re concerned, my dear young lady. We're not responsible to a pack of Girl Guides for what we do, or don't do—only to Lord Lorimer, from whom we rent the fishing rights and who has never found any fault with our doings."

" No—not until now," Lord Lorimer spoke grimly. " But only because he didn't happen to know what those things were."

" And may I ask who called upon *you* to interfere?" the dark man demanded furiously.

" Nobody—only, you see, I chance to be Lord Lorimer," the young man said gently; and at that, as Pam said afterwards, " those men just shrivelled up. Only they glared as though they'd like to kill us—and I expect they just *would*."

" There's no law against it," Harry muttered, but Lord Lorimer answered calmly:

" That remains to be seen—and anyway, I've got a case against you for introducing pests on my estate. And, if my eyes don't deceive me, here in the very nick of time comes a police patrol boat. They'll be able to help us to inquire

into the matter, and take you to dryer quarters
as well."

The small motor-launch, manned by three
constables and a sergeant, who were out in-
specting the floods, responded at once to Lord
Lorimer's signal, and agreed to take charge of
the three " preservers " pending inquiries. It
was quite plain, too, that the sergeant thought
the charge a serious one, and did not believe the
offenders would get off lightly from an investigation.

" Matter of a big fine, I shouldn't wonder,"
said the sergeant. " And so it ought to be,
with the damage that may have been done.
It'll be a big business exterminating the beasts,
too. Well, anyway, the young ladies have done
a good bit of work in discovering the mischief,
that's all I can say."

" Only he ought to have said ' lady ', because
it was Byrde who did it," Pam remarked, as
they all sat in the Favour Royal kitchen eating
the long-delayed salt beef, which was now more
in the nature of a stew.

" Oh no, Dora really began it when she
caught Maurice the Mascot," Byrde objected.
" And the triplets carried on, especially Kathy;
she really did the most difficult bit of sleuthing,
hiding in that musky, ratty lodge to listen to

the men. I only sort of put the finishing touches, and that was more by good luck than anything else."

"Well, anyhow, it has been an eventful camp, and one that we shan't forget in a hurry," Kitty said. "And we shouldn't have had a camp at all if it hadn't been for you and Favour Royal, Ralph, so we do thank you, don't we, girls?"

"It looks as though I shouldn't have had any Favour Royal left at all, if it hadn't been for you!" Lord Lorimer laughed. "So since you've saved the estate from being entirely undermined by musk rats, the thanks are due to you."

"And that's 'Love All '," said Byrde gravely. "A happy-ever-after ending."

Which was really the finish of the Favour Royal camp. But Dora still regrets Maurice, Mascot, Musquash and Mystery, who was duly dispatched to the Zoological Gardens. It seems to her very hard that her pet should be called a pest.

With the Speedwell Patrol
by
Marjorie Taylor

ABOUT THIS STORY

Mary Blair, Leader of the Speedwell Patrol, makes friends with Dawn Clive who lives next door and is an invalid, her back having been injured in an accident. Her father is supposed to have been killed in an aeroplane crash in the Himalayas. Dawn is persuaded to join the Speedwells and takes a new pleasure in life and manages to share some of their interests and the lively doings of the Blair family.

When she is ordered to Switzerland by her doctor, Mary goes with her. In Switzerland they meet a man who knows that Colonel Clive was not killed, but that, believing his little daughter to be dead, he chose to remain in the secret Tibetan valley where the plane had crashed. Mary's Uncle David, an explorer, grows interested, and eventually sets out by air, with a party including her, to try to find the missing man. Their efforts are successful, and after many difficulties he is brought back to civilization, to find his daughter Dawn well and strong, cured by an operation, and full of the fresh courage inspired in her by contact with the Guides.

Contents

With the Speedwell Patrol

CHAPTER I

The Wanderer Arrives

" I think that's everything." Mary Blair, Leader of the Speedwell Patrol, cast a critical glance around their Corner in the big school gym. " No pencils or anything left lying about? Well, good-bye till to-morrow, you folks, and don't forget about that Morse!"

" Now home to the joys of prep!" her Second sighed. " That algebra——!"

Mary laughed, as having saluted Captain good-bye the two picked up their books and set off together. " At least you've a house to yourself to do it in! What about poor me returning to three young brothers and two sisters, all of whom seem firmly determined that if I do any prep at all it shall be theirs!"

" Yet you know you wouldn't swop one of them for the world."

" No, I don't suppose I would! Though young Dick is a holy terror, now he's turned thirteen and thinks he is no end of a man! I wish I could get him to join Scouts. But luckily I'm becoming like Dad, who can write his sermons in the midst of any old din!"

Then the talk turned to their Patrol, and they discussed future plans till Mary's corner was reached. " Well, if we manage the half of this they ought to be the best Guides in Glasgow!" she grinned in farewell. " But somehow it never quite comes off! Cheerio till to-morrow then, and good luck with the maths!"

Quickening her pace, Mary swung down Arnold Drive: for she had noticed a familiar shabby sports car at the door of No. 12. Uncle David was in! Less chance than ever of doing homework—but it was worth it for one of his all too rare visits.

Young Hunter had seen her coming from the window, and the door was flung open in bois-terous welcome as she climbed the steps.

" Uncle David's here!" he bawled cheerfully. " C'mon, slowcoach, he was askin' for you!"

" Who's a slowcoach?" she asked, tousling his already wild brown hair. " Dick home from school?"

" Yeh, we're all back. You're always late on your old Guide day!"

" I'll just run up and tidy—won't be a jiffy!"

From the sitting-room she could hear the strains of "The Rippling Brook" being proudly crashed out on the piano. Ten-year-old Margaret was playing her party piece—which the others always said sounded more like a storm at sea.

Mary's room was up two flights of stairs, at the very top of the tall, rambling house. It was a tiny place, but all her own: which was something in a family of six. The sole privilege, as she sometimes said, of being the eldest.

Vigorously brushing her short fair hair before the window, she looked much more like her tomboy brother Dick than his dignified fifteen-year-old " big sister ". With all their frequent quarrels they bore a strong resemblance. Margaret came next: a self-contained young person, who at ten was rather inclined to patronize both of them. Eight-year-old Hunter was ardent admirer and slave of brother Dick, and a sturdy, sporting little fellow. So also was the toddler, five-year-old Hamish; while Maureen was only a baby of twelve months, and adored by all of them.

Suddenly the strains of a violin made Mary cease her brushing and crane out of the small window. There it was again! Who *was* it who played so beautifully? It surely must be the little invalid girl next door.

The sound seemed to be coming from the back garden, and it was such a perfect spring evening that it seemed quite likely she might be out there. But crane as she would Mary could not see over the dividing wall. A tall oak tree grew against their side of it, and its budding green foliage quite obscured the view.

" Curiosity, my child," she told herself severely. Still it *was* rather tantalizing.

The house next door had stood empty for

more than a year, so there had been quite a
flutter in the Blair household when an army of
painters and workmen had announced a new
tenant. It had been bought by a widow, a Mrs.
Donaldson, and she and her little daughter
lived there all alone but for the servants. Mary
had only seen the daughter—at least she
supposed her to be that—on the day that they
moved in. Aged about twelve, she was an
invalid: a thin, big-eyed slip of a thing who
had been carried up the steps in a flat spinal
chair. That was a month ago, but beyond this
occasional sound of violin playing she had
heard no more.

" *Mary!*" Dick's lusty bellow, inclined to
crack now on the top notes. " You gone to
sleep up there?"

" Sorry—coming!" Throwing down the
hairbrush she fled downstairs, taking the last
flight as a breathless slide upon the well-worn
banister.

" Whoa there!" Her father received her at
the bottom, as she slid neatly into his arms.
" Come on, lass, your Uncle David's got some

important bit of news to tell us, and he would insist on waiting till you arrived!"

The Reverend Arthur Blair had the smile of a schoolboy still, though his shoulders were bent and hair was going grey with the cares of his large family, and even larger family of parishioners. It was a contradictory face, with the broad, finely modelled forehead of a thinker and the eyes of a dreamer, belied by the square common sense of his chin and humorous nose.

Mary kissed him heartily. "Well, here I am, darling! How's the Wanderer?"

"Let him answer for himself!" boomed a deep voice, and as they entered the sitting-room Professor David Blair rose up from the hearthrug where he had been teasing Hamish, and stretched himself to his full magnificent height. A giant of a man, with short brown beard and fierce bushy eyebrows, he seemed to tower above them all.

"You've grown!" said Mary decidedly.

"Or it is probably I who have shrunk," his brother smiled. "Now, tell us your good news, David."

"No, we're all to guess!" Margaret cried importantly. "In turns, properly, beginning with the youngest."

"Gug-goo-laa-a-a!" supplied Maureen, who was lying by the window on her mother's lap —which Uncle David said was probably quite correct.

Hamish came next, and standing square upon his sturdy legs: "You're gonna be 'nengine driver!" he announced all in one breath.

"No—a soldier!" Hunter cut in.

"Both wrong!"

"My turn now, then!" Margaret bounced with importance on the piano-stool. "*I* know what it is, Uncle, you've finished your book on—on—whatever it is."

"The Ethnological and Racial Characteristics of Western Europe." The Professor tugged his beard ruefully. "No, my dear, I wish you were right—but I haven't!"

"You're going to buy a new racer!" Dick offered it more in the tone of an event he hoped for than one he really expected, for in the same breath he added: "Now Mary's shot!"

Mary wrinkled her short nose. " You're going away again, Oh Wanderer! Either to study North African pygmies or South Australian aborigines, or something worse! Being an ethnologist is the finest excuse I know for globe trotting."

" What exactly *is* an eth-thingame?" Margaret asked plaintively.

" It means, madam, one who studies the varieties of the human race. Its ancient cultures—and barbarisms." He turned with a twinkle towards his brother and his wife. " You two not risking a guess?"

The Rev. Arthur shook his head. " We are too wise! I only bet that it's something mad! From nursery days you were always a restless harum-scarum, while I was content to stay at home with a book—and now they've made you a professor for it."

" Well, Mary was the nearest of any of you!" he announced, drawing Hamish up on to his knee. " I *am* going away again—but I've been left a fortune to do it with!"

" *What?*"

" It's true!" His blue eyes twinkled delightedly. " Remember my old Chief Hewitson, Arthur? He's died out in Borneo, and I've just had a letter from the lawyers to say that he left me money ' to equip a scientific expedition for purposes of investigation and discovery of little-known races.' Isn't it stupendous?"

" And where are you off to?"

" I don't know." He became serious and tugged at his beard. " It's too big a matter to be rushed, and I may take months to decide. I've been getting some interesting information about an African pygmy tribe (right again, Mary!), but I'm not sure until I've heard more. I should like something *really* out of the way for the *Wanderer's* first trip."

" The *Wanderer*——?"

He beamed at them. " Oh, didn't I tell you? I'm going to buy a real ship and call her that! I can be busy choosing her and fitting her out while I decide where to go."

" You'll take others with you?"

" Just one or two. A doctor, an interpreter, a couple of experts: I've had 'em chosen in my mind's eye for years, in the hopes that I might ever get such a chance."

"Well, I'm jolly sure you deserve it!" Mary gave him an affectionate squeeze. "Your old Chief must have thought no end of your brains, to have left you this money. Wish I could come with you!"

"Pah, what use would a girl be?" Dick demanded. "Going to buy a *ship*—oh, you *are* a lucky dog!"

Mary linked her arm through her father's, as they two fell behind in the procession to the dining-room for tea.

"Poor Dad, you're thinking what you could have done for the parish with all that money— aren't you?"

He smiled down at her rather sadly. "I don't grudge it to him, my dear! But yes— when I think of some of the sufferings that sum might relieve——"

"I know. But, Dad, I've got a funny feeling about that money. I feel that it *is* going to do much good—in ways we do not dream of yet."

"Little prophetess!"

After tea Uncle David departed, boisterously
" seen off " by the entire family. Dick had his
head inside the bonnet of the car, and withdrew it reluctantly with the request, " You'll
let me know—if you *should* be wanting a cabin
boy?" Then the car shot forward, and in a
cloud of dust roared down the drive.

Mary slipped away from the others, and
dodged back into the empty sitting-room.
That algebra——! But even as she thought of
it, the piano, standing temptingly open, called
to her. It was so often occupied by the little
ones at their scales and practising, that it
seemed ages since she herself had touched it.
That little thing of Grieg's——

Half guiltily she slipped on to the stool, and
as her hands strayed over the worn and yellow
keys, grubby still from Margaret's fingers, she
forgot everything else. . . .

The door burst open and Dick's tousled
head shot round. " Oh, here you are——!"

Her hands dropped to her lap. " How
wonderful it must be," she whispered dreamily,
" to be able to do that."

" To play decently, you mean?"

" No, to compose. To create great tunes, beauty out of nothing— Oh, you don't understand!"

" I don't—but it's maths that are bothering me, that's why I came for you. Be a brick and solve this problem for me."

" Oh, Dick, I've got tons of my own——!"

" Well, you weren't doing them. Be a sport!"

" Then I'm jolly well going to show you how to do it yourself, lazybones!"

He listened to her explanations with a painstaking frown, and scratched his head when she had finished. " If ten men carried five loads of bricks a day—— Yeh, if I had the stuff I could *do* it all right, but I hate mucking about with bits of paper. Thanks a lot—an' now come out an' see a new way I've got of climbing up our tree!"

" My lad, I've got some work to do——!"

" Piffle, you were just making a row on the piano! Come on!" And ignoring all protests he dragged her from the room.

For town houses, Arnold Drive boasted large back gardens. Though the flowers that Mrs. Blair hopefully attempted to rear were blighted with smuts from their earliest youth, yet the grass grew healthily; and a broad green patch of it was a pleasant sight on a warm April evening like this. High walls separated the gardens from each other, and against one of these grew the tall oak tree which had been a friend of all the children. They had played houses under it, hung swings from it, and taken many a tumble from its knotted branches.

" What a perfect evening!" Mary exclaimed. " It's so still! Listen, you can hear the traffic in Great Western Road!"

" And the cuckoo!" retorted Dick rudely. " I didn't bring you out to write spring poems, but to see my new method. I can get up to the top in three steps—look!"

He hurled his stocky little form into the air, caught a high branch, and swung himself like a monkey feet first into the one above it. From there a couple more springs landed him neatly into the topmost fork.

"Easy!" Mary jeered.

"Oh, is it? Well, do it then!" Swinging lightly to the ground he challenged her indignantly.

"I'll do nothing so undignified——!"

"Yah, you're afraid! I dare you to!"

The ancient dare always found a hole in Mary's dignity, and with a swirl of short skirts she launched herself upon the tree. Gym was not taught at her school for nothing, and with surprising ease she repeated her brother's feat.

"Not bad for a girl," he admitted, looking up at her. "Your legs are longer than mine— Oh, there's Mother calling me." He turned reluctantly towards the house.

Mary smiled as she leant back against the trunk. Nice up here—why, you could get a good view of the next-door garden, the tree hung right over on their side.

A sound directly beneath her made Mary peer downwards cautiously. The next-door-girl *was* out. She lay almost flat upon a low deck-chair, a light rug over her, and her thin white hands fondled a violin.

Mary held her breath as she saw her raise it slowly upwards to her chin. She nestled in to it caressingly, then raised her bow and drew it softly across the strings. The melody she played was hardly more than a breath: an entrancing, hesitating, thread of sound, but it held the whole soul of this quiet spring evening in its notes. As it died away on a half plaintive note of questioning, Mary's enthusiasm overcame her cautiousness. " Bravo!" she cried. " Oh, bravo, that was splendid!"

The girl started, and raised wide black eyes to the excited figure looking down on her. A smile lit up her rather wistful face.

" Hullo—I didn't know that you were still up there!"

" I say, I hope we haven't been making an awful row—disturbing you?"

" I like listening to you. Could—couldn't you come over this side and talk to me a bit?"

" I'd love to!" Promptly obeying the invitation, Mary slid along a drooping bough and dropped lightly to the ground. " Good afternoon!" she grinned. " By the way, my name is Mary Blair!"

" Mine is Dawn Clive."

" Clive? I thought it was Donaldson——?"

She shook her head. " Oh no! Mrs. Donaldson is just my aunt." Her thin fingers picked nervously at the violin strings, and Mary noted anxiously that her lip was trembling. But a moment later she gained control again and smiled up at her visitor. " I see you're a Guide! What badges are these? Cook's — oh, and Musician's! You'll be the one I heard playing a few minutes ago. I wish I knew something about music."

" But—you play *beautifully*."

" It's all made up, though. I mean, I know my notes and that's about all. Aunt doesn't think it's good for me to trouble about really learning things, but she lets me play about with the violin inventing little tunes for myself."

" Then you're a genius!" said Mary promptly. " I've always envied people who can compose; I can only read what other people have written down for me."

" Written?   Oh, you mean those mystical black dots on paper," Dawn chuckled. " That's all double Dutch to me. Who was it played the ' Typhoon ' earlier this afternoon?"

" The ' Rippling Brook ', you mean," Mary laughed. " That's my little sister Margaret."

" Oh, the one that I call Prudence." Dawn flushed. " I hope you won't mind—but I've got names for all of you!"

" Poor kid!" Mary thought, " she's *lonely*." Aloud she said: " What's mine—do tell."

" Oh, I just called you ' the Guide '," she confessed frankly. " Your brother is Desmond, from *Daring Desmond*, a book I once had. Now let me see some more badges: Hiker, you're a very all-round person."

" You know all about Guides then?" Mary was puzzled.

" A little. There was a Company at my school, but I wasn't old enough to join them."

" Then you haven't always been——?" Mary broke off short and shook herself, for she saw Dawn's hand close tight around the violin, and her sensitively cut lips quivered again.

" No.   This was an accident."   She was
making an obvious effort to speak carelessly,
and her dark brows arched up in a puckish
smile.   " I had a funny experience in connexion
with that.   Not many people of my age can
say that they've been reported dead on the
front page of a newspaper!   But I have—in big
letters!"

CHAPTER II

The Concert

Mary looked at her in bewilderment. " Dead? But why on earth——?"

Dawn smiled. " Well, I nearly was! But you mean, why did they consider me important enough to mention the fact? You see, my father was Colonel Clifford Clive."

Mary had sunk down beside her on the grass, and a thoughtful pucker formed between her brows. Where on earth had she heard that name before? It was familiar, but there were so many names in newspapers and books it was impossible to keep track of them all. Dawn so obviously expected her to know him.

Suddenly her memory switched back, and a light came to her eyes.

" Clifford Clive the airman? Oh, *now* I remember! He smashed nearly every record there was, didn't he?"

27

Dawn nodded proudly. " Yes. Until—until he was lost."

In the sudden silence that seemed to have fallen over the sunny garden, Mary could hear Hunter's shrill young voice drifting across the wall. He seemed to be shouting down to someone from the window. " Hi, Dick, come up here! All my caterpillars have got *out* of the matchbox!" Poor Hunter, the insects he so ardently collected were always eluding him! . . . Notes heavily and methodically ascending and descending the scale, told that Margaret had begun her evening practising. . . . It was a queer feeling to be listening to one's family from outside like this—from " over the wall ". How lucky she was to have them all. The contrast between her lot and Dawn's brought a strangely painful tightness to her throat, as she laid one hand upon the other's arm.

" Don't tell me if it hurts you—please!"

" I think I'd like to tell you." Dawn's voice was steady now. " It was nearly two years ago. He was on a record round-the-world flight, and reached New Zealand ahead of

time. From there he was to have crossed
the Pacific to Russia—but he never arrived.
The weather had been bad, but whether it was
that or engine trouble we'll never know. Search-
parties kept on as long as there was any hope,
but no trace of Dad or his mechanic was ever
found."

" You haven't told me yet why *you* were
reported dead?" Mary spoke with a false
briskness, in an effort to break this awful
tension and make Dawn smile.

" I chose the moment when the newspapers
were full of the search for Daddy, to fall out
of a tree beside the school playground! I had
really climbed it to get away from people who
—who would sympathize. I don't remember
any more about it, but my spine was injured
and I was terribly ill for a long time. Of course
anything about me was ' news ' just then, and
one newspaper was a wee bit previous and
reported ' Death of Missing Airman's Daughter '! They had to correct it in their next
edition, for I *did* recover! But the doctors
say I'll never walk again. When I got well

enough to go out in a spinal chair, Aunt Katherine gave up her flat and bought this house because of the garden for me to lie out in."

" I see. Well, that was a real stroke of luck for both of us, for I'm sure you and I are going to be great pals!"

The pale face on the pillow flushed delightedly. " I'm glad you climbed that tree. If you knew how much I've *wanted* to speak to you. But it was only when I saw you in the tree that I had the courage. You see, I felt I simply *had* to make you come down quickly somehow, for I'm so nervous of seeing people climbing trees now."

" Poor Dawn! But a fall on that soft grass is a very different matter from a school play-ground. I'm afraid Dick and Hunter tumble out of it twenty times a day."

" Yes, I've seen them."

Mary reluctantly scrambled to her feet and brushed the clinging grass blades from her uniform.

" Prep is calling, alas! In fact, maths are

sitting very heavily upon my conscience. I'll
have to go now, Dawn, but I'll come again
to-morrow if I may."

" *Please* do! Aunt's out now, but I know
she'll be most terribly pleased."

" Thanks very much. I'll introduce the rest
of the family—in relays. You don't mind if I
go the way I came?"

With a little jump she caught the trailing
bough again and dragged herself up; then
waving good-bye from the top of the old tree,
dropped down on her own side of the wall
once more. . . .

Dick was spread upon the sitting-room
hearthrug, carving out a wooden boat for
Hamish. He greeted her with a grin.

" What on earth have you been doing?
Writing spring sonnets on the top of the oak
tree?"

" No, idiot! I've had an adventure!" Still
a trifle breathless she plumped down on a
chair. " I've been over the wall, talking to
that poor girl next door——"

" Poor? Why, the Donaldsons are rolling in

money! A house that size for two people, and tons of servants——"

" Maybe one day you'll learn that money isn't the only thing that matters——"

" Yeh, when I'm as old and wise as you!"

" You're a long way off it yet!" Mary was unruffled. " Money isn't doing Dawn much good now that she's injured her back and has to lie there flat all day. And her name is not Donaldson: it's Clive. She's Clifford Clive's daughter!"

Interested at last, Dick dropped his knife and gaped at her.

" The chap who broke the Atlantic record three times? Oh, he was *super*! Gosh, I—I wouldn't mind meeting that kid."

" You shall! She has long admired you from afar—and calls you Daring Desmond, by the way."

" Och, baloney!"

But she saw that Dick was pleased, his face had flushed beneath its freckles. His knowledge of the missing aviator proved far greater than her own, and he could reel off all his various records and achievements. Apparently at that date he had worshipped anything connected with the air, an enthusiasm which had now partially transferred itself to racing motors.

Mrs. Blair's voice drifted downstairs, calling Hamish up to bed, and there were yells of laughter as Dick hustled him to his feet and chased him up to her. Only then did Mary realize that her father was sitting in the window seat, buried behind his newspaper.

He put it down now with a rustle and smiled at her. " Come and tell me more about your adventure."

" Dad!" She ran across to him. " Did you hear what I was saying? She's such a sweet kid, only twelve, and I'm so terribly sorry for her having to lie there all day like that. She's too young to be sort of—resigned."

" Yes, Grandmamma!" he teased.

" Oh, you know what I mean! I think she's been horribly lonely too, but there are enough of *us* to change all that! I wish you could hear her play the violin. You know, Dad, I feel I was *meant* to go over that wall this afternoon, and that something big is going to come out of it."

He nodded slowly. " Aye, maybe you're right. There's a purpose behind most things we do, lassie. It will be good if you can make things cheerier for her, for her father was a very gallant man."

What a day of excitements, Mary reflected as she scrambled into bed; but she would certainly have to rise very early in the morning to make up for lost time on that maths. As she had prophesied to her Second—it had been very hard to give *that* any attention.

After school next afternoon, Mary went round to pay her first formal call upon Dawn Clive. She was lying out in the garden again, and this time her aunt was sitting with her. Her thin face flushed with pleasure as she introduced her new friend.

Mrs. Donaldson was a tall, grey-haired lady, dressed in widow's black, whom Mary had secretly thought rather formidable; but after a few minutes she changed her mind. She was quiet and reserved, being rather shy herself,

Mary sensed; but there was no doubting her welcome. When presently she went indoors, Mary carried her chair down to the house, and Mrs. Donaldson spoke to her earnestly.

" You've no idea how much good you have done Dawn already. She's more cheerful than I've seen her for a long time. Do come over just as often as you choose, for the poor child needs the companionship of young people, but with lying there so long she has rather grown beyond most girls of her own age."

Dawn had her violin tucked beneath her chin when Mary returned to her, and her dark eyes smiled as she lifted the bow. " This is a tune I made for you. Do you like it?"

Spellbound, Mary listened to a tune as light and gay, and full of laughter and the joy of life, as yesterday's had been sad. The swing of it had Mary on her feet.

" That made me want to *dance*! My dear, you're a magician, and next time I come I'm going to bring music-paper and try and write down some of your tunes—it's a sin they should be wasted."

Dawn laughed. "They're just rubbish. Now, you promised to tell me all about your clever uncle with the beard."

Nothing loath, Mary recounted some of the Professor's hair-raising adventures among little-known tribes, and was in the midst of describing his wonderful legacy and the new expedition he was fitting out, when a voice broke in on them.

"Hullo, you two!" From the top of the tree Dick's tousled head and freckled face grinned rather shyly down. "You promised to introduce me, Mary."

"So I did! Dawn, this is my little brother Dick——"

"Little yourself!" With a snort of scorn he dropped down beside them. Then regarding Dawn with the respectful admiration due to a hero's daughter, he announced: "I heard you playing, from our garden. That was a nice tune! Look here, why shouldn't we have a concert?"

"A concert?"

"Yes!" Dick had forgotten all shyness in

enthusiasm for his plan, and squatting cross-legged on the grass beside Dawn's chair he might have known her now for years. "Mary is always selling sticky toffee an' stuff for her old Patrol funds—this is a much more original idea. You could play the violin and Mary the piano—she's not bad really!—and I can tootle a bit on the mouth-organ, an' Margaret an' Hunter can have combs and paper. Hamish can give a rumble on his drum at intervals—an' even wee Maureen could blow her trumpet. You could write a symphony for us."

Dawn was shaking with laughter. "It sounds *too* gorgeous! Who will the audience be?"

"Oh, Mum an' Dad, and your aunt, and perhaps Uncle David would come, and I could rake in a few fellows from school. We'd charge 'em twopence each. We'd have it in our garden," he added after a hasty glance at the neat flower-beds surrounding No. 11's tidy plot. "It's used to a lot of people an' nothing can spoil *our* grass. 'Sides our piano stands right in the window, so if we had it open they'd hear beautifully."

To Mary's delight, Dawn seemed really attracted by the idea of the " concert ", and so she backed it up for all her worth. It was a real adventure to the little invalid, and her eyes sparkled with fun and excitement.

Next day Mary wheeled her through to their garden, an adventure in itself, and she met the rest of the family and held an impromptu rehearsal of the " orchestra ". Margaret had been given the post of conductor, having declined comb and paper as beneath her dignity. And now on every visit that she payed next door Mary played over her favourite solos on Mrs. Donaldson's fine grand piano, and Dawn improvised her own violin accompaniment to them. Her ear was amazing. Unable to read a note, she had only to hear a tune twice over to render it perfectly.

On Dick's urging she *did* compose one or two rousing march tunes which the whole " orchestra " learnt by heart: and also promised to play some of her own " ideas ", as she called them, as solos. Mary was making valiant efforts to transcribe some of these tunes. At first she found it very difficult, but gradually began to get the knack of jotting down the main notes of a melody and filling in the " frills " after a second hearing. At home she would play them over on the piano, and her father agreed that many were extremely lovely. But Dawn never ceased to be amused about her bothering.

The Saturday fixed for the concert dawned at last, and from early morning many anxious glances were cast up at the sky, from both sides of the garden wall.

Mary had her whole Patrol coming, having cheerfully assured them they could all pay twopence towards their own funds. While Dick, Margaret, and Hunter were producing between them quite a goodly bunch of their schoolfellows. Mrs. Donaldson and Mr. and Mrs. Blair had all accepted their invitations, but Professor Blair had sent a regretful scrawl to assure them that " his spirit would be with them, but the flesh was terribly busy ".

At two-thirty Mary called for Dawn and wheeled her round to their garden, where the whole family assisted to settle her comfortably in her own specially extended deck-chair where she could recline almost flat among cushions.

Margaret was taking her position as conductor very seriously. She had insisted on being dressed in her very best pale blue frock, and had persuaded Dick to white paint one of the bird-cage spars for her baton. Even Dick and Hunter had brushed their hair in honour of the occasion; and small Hamish was bursting with pride, stationed with his drum inside the garden gate collecting twopences. Mary was in uniform, as were the rest of her Patrol, who arrived early to dispose the audience among the miscellaneous collection of chairs Dick had spread out upon the grass, and to sell them the sweets they had been making during the week.

Dawn was introduced to the Speedwell Patrol, and beamed shyly upon them all. She was completely tongue-tied at the moment, but Mary knew that as soon as she raised her bow she would forget them all, and in a world of her own would reign complete mistress.

The audience was beginning to arrive. Mrs. Donaldson was conducted with honour to the front chair, with the Rev. Arthur and Mrs. Blair on either side of her. Baby Maureen sat upon her mother's knee, clutching her trumpet to show that she too " belonged " to the orchestra. Soon every seat was occupied, and quite a number of Hunter's small friends were scattered on their tummies in the grass.

Punctually at three o'clock the concert commenced. From her position at the piano inside the sitting - room window, Mary anxiously scanned the faces of the audience to see how each item was received. The first " orchestral " piece seemed to be really appreciated— and in the open air sounded surprisingly well. Dawn had given them just the right sort of lively tune; and the piano and violin carried it forward with a swing, while Dick and Hunter harmonized most skilfully on mouth-organ and paper and comb. Even Hamish, thanks to Margaret's energetic baton, produced his drum tattoos at just the right moments.

Items followed one another swiftly. Mary

played alone while Dawn rested; Mary and Dawn played together; and Dick and Hunter rendered an amazing " Ragtime Potpourri ". But it was Dawn's solo items which caused by far the most applause. Forgetting, as Mary had known she would, the very existence of her audience, she made her violin speak, in notes of purest, liquid beauty. Such gay little, sad little, mad little tunes she played—some of which Mary had never heard before. Creations of the moment, spontaneous outpourings of that vivid, dauntless little spirit, who lay there so quietly with big black eyes fixed upon the fleecy clouds that floated overhead. The audience seemed to recognize their rare, elusive quality: and gave to those short fragments a greater enthusiasm than even her most fault-less rendering of a well-known sonata, with the piano, had won.

After the interval, when cups of tea, pre-pared by the Guides, were handed round, the concert merrily cantered through its second half. A last orchestral item brought the pro-gramme to a close, and the players rollicked through it with complete abandon. A lusty (and quite unrehearsed!) trumpet blast from Maureen, during the final bars, was the success of the evening. Then the National Anthem, and it was ended.

Mary, with her Patrol, was kept busy seeing off their guests, and when she at length returned to Dawn she found her father in conversation with her.

" I'm just telling this lassie that she's a fine wee musician," he smiled. " She made your concert for you, Mary, and I'm sure she ought to be adopted an honorary Speedwell, or whatever you are!"

" You bet we're grateful to her!" Mary beamed. " My Second's just counting the cash with gloating eyes, over in the corner there! I've quite decided, Dad, that Dawn has got to *be* a Guide—Do you hear, madam? I've been telling you all about Posts."

" Yes—but I'm not going to be one."

" We'll not argue it now! You're tired, my dear, and I'm wheeling you right home to bed. It's been a wonderful concert!"

Two days later, when five of the Blair family were having tea with Dawn in her garden, the subject of Posts came up again. Dawn was so intensely keen and interested in all connected with Guiding, that Mary could not understand her continued refusal to join a Post Company.

" I know you'd love it, Dawn," she pleaded now. " You'd get a monthly Letter full of stories and competitions, and even be able to pass badges. It would keep you in touch with things—and most important of all, you would *be* a Guide."

" I know." With a restless little movement Dawn turned her head aside. " But—I can't." As always when the subject was introduced she seemed unhappy and restive.

Unwilling to worry her, Mary was about to change the subject, when Hunter's clear young voice cut in.

" That kind of Guides can't be much use, 'cos the only thing that's any use about Guides is hiking." He had never forgotten Mary's description of her last Patrol outing.

" Why shouldn't *we* hike?" Mary jerked

herself erect. " Dick, you're not the only one who has brain-waves! Dawn is as light as a feather in that flat basket-chair—You and I could easily push her out to the country, couldn't we?"

" In relays? Of course we could! Young Hunter and Margaret could be sent ahead by bus and meet us at the terminus——"

" And Hamish will look after Mother and Maureen—he'll be the only man at home." Mary skilfully anticipated that young gentleman's protests.

Dawn's eyes were shining. " And can we really light a fire—and cook sausages?"

" You bet we will!" Mention of food had fired Dick to enthusiasm. " This very Saturday, as ever was!"

" Ooh! This is *much* more thrilling than a concert!" But in her wildest dreams Dawn could not guess just *how* thrilling this hike, and its results, were going to be.

CHAPTER III

The Great Hike

The Saturday of the hike dawned dull and misty, but gradually increased to that fierce heat which Glasgow can know on some still summer days.

" Phew!" Mary gasped, as she paused in her labours of cutting sandwiches at the kitchen table. " Not just ideal weather for hiking, but we can't call off and disappoint Dawn now."

Dick nodded. " I'll do the first lap, if you like," he volunteered. " Might be a bit cooler on the way home. We needn't go far beyond Bearsden, and you can go out by bus with the kids and meet us at Bearsden cross."

" Oh, I'm afraid I'd better take her out myself!" Mary smiled as she pressed the top on the final sandwich. " She's still just a little bit shy of you, and right out to Bearsden alone might be rather overwhelming. She'll probably

46

get used to you during the day, and you can do the walk home."

" Well, let's split it. I'll meet you at Anniesland and take over from there."

They settled on that; and at half-past ten Mary went next door for Dawn, and having stowed away her packages in the bottom of her chair they set off on the Great Trek.

Dawn was looking radiant with joy and excitement: even the usual pallor of her cheeks was flushed to pink, and her big black eyes shone like two stars. Laughing, she raised a corner of the thin silk rug which covered her, and showed the familiar shape of her violin snuggled by her side.

" I had to bring him along!" she smiled. " Auntie thought I was quite daft, but I couldn't explain to her that I'd thought of a new tune in the middle of the night last night! I had the violin beside my bed, and I played it over *ever* so softly. I do want you to hear it, because it's your tune really—all caused by being so happy inside about to-day. And I think it's better than most of them."

" Then it must be jolly fine! We'll have a real concert when we arrive—I've never cooked sausages to music before!"

" Oh, but I'm going to cook a sausage too! Dick must find me an extra long stick, and I'll lean over the side!"

" You bet you will! No slacking allowed: it's all hands on deck when the Blair family go hiking! This will be young Margaret's first experience, and I bet she'll be disgusted by the lack of plates!"

They had turned into Great Western Road now, and the noise and bustle of the traffic silenced Dawn. She lay looking about her with quick, eager interest, taking in everything. The piquant beauty of her face, with its unusual contrast of white skin and dark colouring shown up against the pale green of the frock she wore, attracted many sympathetic smiles.

" I know this all so well," she murmured presently. " But it's years since I have been as far. I used to come this way to school, but it seems to have got much noisier since then."

" Um—Dad says it gets worse every day!

Look through there at the flowers in the Botanic Gardens, Dawn, aren't they a sight?"

" Oh!" She clasped her hands delightedly. " I do wish I knew the names of all of them! They're gorgeous!"

" We'll go and explore in there one day. I wonder if your chair would get through the door of the glass-houses? This is only the beginning of our outings, you know!"

" You don't know how wonderful it is to be at the beginning of something—not the end."

" My dear, don't talk as if you were ninety!"

" Oh, of course I'm still at the beginning of *time*," Dawn answered gravely. " But time itself can be—rather frightening when it stretches out, empty, in front of you. I thought I was at the end of *good* times, but you have taught me better."

The smile that she gave her then made Mary forget the heat of the sun, as she pushed with a will up the long, steady slope.

The rest of the road seemed to pass amazingly quickly after that, and when Dick came leaping off the tramcar at Anniesland (looking very business-like in shorts and a large haver-sack) Mary declared she was not tired.

" You can take a turn at the pushing if you like, but I'll walk on with you. Are the kids joining us at Bearsden?"

" Yep. Mum promised to see them into the bus, and we're to meet them at the cross. Hamish is quite consoled, and is strutting about in such a state of pride at ' taking care ' of Mum and Maureen that I think Hunter is beginning to wonder if it wouldn't have been more manly to stay at home."

Mary chuckled. Then as her brother took over the chair she waved a hand towards the huge expanse of distant bungalow roofs which marked the beginning of Knightswood, Glas-gow's largest housing scheme.

" Mustn't it have been beautiful when that was all a mighty forest?"

" But was it?"

" Of course it was, my son! What's the name of this canal bridge we're crossing now?"

" Temple——"

" Well, this district is called Temple because

there used to be a monastery of the Knights Templars here. So of course the big forest beside them became known as the Knights' Wood."

" How much will that be! Where do you get all your local history from?"

" Captain told us."

" Oh, those Guides again!" Dick groaned, and winked largely at Dawn. " Ask Mary where she learnt anything from how to boil an egg to sliding down the banisters and she'll say ' Guides ' quite automatically!"

Two pairs of hands made light work of the " Switchback's " hills, and they arrived in Bearsden in plenty of time to collect Margaret and Hunter. Then on for a short distance across the Stockiemuir, till a shady lane invited them and they hailed with joy the perfect field.

The youngsters set to work with a will, but as they had no idea what kind of twigs to get, Mary was soon forced to go to their assistance. It was news to Dick too that some woods would burn and others wouldn't, and he was becoming quite interested in naming the trees when Mary chuckled, " That's Guides again!"

But before the end of their meal he was treating Guiding with more respect. His ideas of cookery had not extended beyond a sausage on a stick; but the whole family regarded with admiration the dainty egg in orange skin which Mary made for Dawn, and were thrilled to be initiated into the mysteries of siskabobs. Even Margaret forgot to be dignified, and got deliciously " messy " with some very moist and grey-coloured dough.

After the meal Dawn demanded a story. " Please! I love the way you tell them, Mary. I'll play afterwards, but it's your turn first."

Mary chewed thoughtfully at a blade of grass. She had determined not to press Dawn about joining Guides, though the curious reluctance that she showed was still a mystery to her, but there could be no harm in getting her more interested in Guidey things. So she began the thrilling story of St. Patrick, the shepherd lad who was stolen by fierce Irish robbers; and when her hearers pleaded for more, followed it with St. George and St. Andrew.

Then on a page from Dick's notebook she

sketched the crosses for them, and showed how they build up into the Union Jack. A question from Hunter as to " how the flag stuck on the pole ", led to a demonstration of knotting, and Dawn's small fingers proved unusually deft and apt.

Dick grinned as he raised his tousled head from his first successful bowline. He was beginning to realize where all this led to.

" I'm prepared to admit," he announced judicially, " that there *may* be something in Scouting —Scouting, mind you; you girls just copied it!"

Mary let the insult pass, as she turned aside to hide the twinkle in her eye. This was a triumph: the first time Dick had admitted to any interest in Scouts.

" Well, Dawn must play to us now. Dick, put the dixie on again, and we'll have a cup of afternoon tea before we start for home. Now, my dear, we're dying for that new tune."

Dawn nestled her violin underneath her chin, and, as she raised her bow arm, smiled at them. " This is a song—*my* song—so you can call it Dawn Song if you like."

The first cool notes rose soft and clear on the still air, and as she listened Mary knew that this was the best that Dawn had yet produced.

It was a finished and a definite composition, in a way some of her other work was not. Many of her tunes were fragmentary things, without beginning or end; but this " Song " had perfect harmonic form, from the soft, slow notes of introduction, through the fascinating, laughing melody, to the whispered climax that was somehow just exactly " right ".

" Oh, Dawn, it's perfect! And it *is* a song— already I feel I want to hum it, for it's the kind of tune that gets inside your head and *makes* you sing. Play it again!"

She obeyed, while her little audience sat in rapt silence. Mary stole a glance at Dick, and noticed the dreamy expression in his eyes. He had a deep genuine love of music: which, however, he would have scorned to admit.

Thus it was that when the dixie boiled over he hastily grabbed at it with one hand, almost without looking. But that inattention was his own undoing; and his sudden yell of agony brought the violin to a screeching halt as Mary sprang over to him.

The carelessly held dixie had tipped and spilt its scalding contents on the grass—and over Dick's bare foot.

"Oh, poor boy—hang on, old man!" Inwardly Mary registered a prayer of thankfulness that her Guide first-aid outfit reposed in its usual pocket of her haversack. Hunter, obedient but terrified, fled to the stream for water for her, and very swiftly she had the picric lint applied and bandaged. Though white to the lips with pain, Dick gave her a plucky grin.

"Is—is he all right?" A very shaky little voice from the chair reminded Mary of poor Dawn, who still lay clutching her violin in an agony of apprehension.

"Fine!" she answered her briskly. "When he's had that cup of tea we're promising ourselves he'll be as right as rain. But he won't be able to use that foot for a little while."

"Then—then how shall we get home?"

" Oh, we'll manage!"

But all the time she was busy preparing the tea and making Dick's cup very sweet and strong, Mary's mind was busy on that same problem. How on earth *was* she to get them home? It was a good mile back to Bearsden: and anyway, could he manage in a bus by himself with one bare foot swathed in bandages? She would have to stay with Dawn (though, having walked the whole way out, the thought of pushing that long road back again made her realize just how tired she was); and then there were the young ones. Two small children, a spinal carriage, and a boy who couldn't stand were really a bit too much to tackle all at once, she reflected ruefully: but *something* had to be done about it.

So when they had damped out the ashes of their fire, Mary took command of things. " Dawn, would you mind if Dick sat on the end of your chair, just till we get into Bearsden? There's heaps of room for him to perch on the bottom there, with his legs hanging over."

" But you can't push me," he protested.

" Of course I can! Then you'll need to go on the bus with Hunter and Margaret; if we can get one that's not too crowded it should be all right for your foot."

Dick looked doubtful, but there was no other way, and so he hobbled on Mary's shoulder to the chair and perched himself upon it.

The strange little cavalcade set out along the bumpy lane, and Mary realized with dismay just what a difference Dick's weight made. The chair seemed more than twice as heavy, and the already weary muscles of her arms and legs ached protestingly with this new strain. Hunter tried to help, but the efforts of a very tired and sticky eight-year-old were not of much assistance.

How hot it was! By the time they reached the end of their lane Mary felt she had been a long way; she called the children to keep beside her as she turned her clumsy load into the main road.

" Look!" Margaret squealed. " Look, Mary, that's Uncle David's car!"

" Oh, it can't be——!"

But it was! Never had the familiar broad, squat nose of the shabby old two-seater appeared so beautiful, as the little party hailed it with arms and voice.

" Well, upon my word, what *have* you been up to this time?" The car had grunted to a halt as it drew level, and the Professor popped his bushy head over the side at them. A fair-haired young man, whom they did not know, was sitting beside him.

With a good deal of assistance Mary explained their dilemma, and asked if Dick could have a lift. " I think three can squash in quite easily, Uncle. He's not very big, and your car's nice and wide."

" Heaps of room—but you're going to be the third!" It was the strange young man who spoke, and his friendly smile as he jumped from the car made Mary like him immediately. " You're far too tired to tackle that walk, and I'm just longing for exercise. My name is Martin, by the way! Professor, won't you introduce me?"

The Professor chuckled in his beard as he presented his nephews and nieces and their friend: after which Mr. Martin took possession of Dawn's chair.

"You'll trust yourself to me, won't you?" he smiled. "Margaret and Hunter shall go along with us to the village, and then I'll see them into the bus."

"Rather!" Dawn declared. "I'm jolly glad that Mary should get a ride."

So they took no further notice of her protests, and Mary found herself between Dick and Uncle David in the car. A moment later they were snorting down the hill, and waving good-bye to Dawn and her new escort by the road.

Mary relaxed herself against the seat, deliciously aware that it was very good to be able to abandon all effort and do nothing.

The Professor's keen eyes beneath their bushy brows peered down at her. "You *are* tired, my lass! I'm glad John had the sense to make you come with me."

"It's far too good of him."

"Oh, he'll get on famously with Dawn!

She's a pretty kid that, and very like her father, from my memory of his photographs."

"When do you go off, Uncle?" Dick asked. "That legacy—haven't you spent it yet?"

"Not all of it! But I've got my ship now, son!"

"Ooh, have you?" Dick forgot his foot, as his eyes shone with eager excitement. "What's she like?"

"Not much, at present! But she's being turned inside out and fitted out down at the docks just now. She's to be called the *Wanderer*!"

"Your name!" Mary laughed.

"Aye! But at the moment neither of the Wanderers is very sure of where to wander *to*. That South American business came to nothing."

"The pygmy people?"

"Yes. The information was far from reliable, and I think myself they were only a branch of a tribe that's known quite well. Oh, I've got a good many other irons on the fire, but nothing definite yet. I'm determined not to waste this opportunity; I've got to know my game, and it's got to be *big* game, before I move. The expedition is chosen, though, to the last man, and I can get under way pretty quickly when necessary."

Dick heaved a sigh as they turned the corner into Arnold Drive. " I think I'll have to be an ethnologist after all, Uncle—it doesn't *sound* exciting, but it is!"

The Professor carried Dick indoors as though he had been a baby. Soon he was settled comfortably in bed, and Dr. Ross, who lived very conveniently a few doors away, was summoned to see the foot.

He pronounced the burn to be not so severe as they had feared, and greatly praised Mary's first-aid measures.

" That will heal up in no time!" he prophesied cheerfully. "Keep it up for a day or two, my boy, and we'll soon have you hopping round again!"

Greatly cheered by the news, Dick began to think with equanimity of a few days' holiday from school.

" I'll have to go in and see poor Dawn," Mary told her mother. After a wash and change she was feeling much cooler. " I think they ought to be here by now. I'll just slip in by the back garden and see if she's all right."

But as she entered the gate, the haunting melody of the Dawn Song came to Mary's ears. Dawn was still in her basket-chair, lying under the tree, and Mr. Martin sat beside her. He made a quick gesture of his hand for silence, and Mary stood motionless until the tune was finished. The expression on the young man's face intrigued her: he looked positively bursting with excitement, and by the end of the melody he was on his feet.

" By jimminy!" he shouted, " that's tremendous! My dear kid, do you realize what you've done?"

CHAPTER IV

The New Partnership

" What have I done?" Dawn spoke doubtfully, as if half afraid that she had misbehaved herself.

John Martin laughed excitedly, and scrubbed with an already familiar gesture at his boyishly fair hair.

" You've done what I've been quite unsuccessfully trying to do for a long time! You've composed the very tune the public are waiting for—the ideal antidote to jazz!"

" How do you mean?"

He grinned appealingly at Mary. " Can't you help me explain to her?"

" I've already told her how good it is, but she takes no notice of me!"

" No, I don't!" Dawn chuckled. " Mary's prejudiced!"

" Well, I am not. Now I'm speaking seriously, my child!" He had sat down again, and

63

emphasized his points with one long fore-finger. "That song is not a deathless master-piece, but it *is* a very beautiful and eminently *singable* song. Intelligent people everywhere are becoming tired of the cruder types of jazz, and there is a huge market waiting — in fact, gasping—for a clean, simple tune such as yours. It is not a difficult, intricate composition that is wanted, but a refrain that sings in one's memory as easily as jazz: because of its beauty, not its ' catchiness '."

"And you say you have tried to write one?" Mary was intensely interested. Leaning on Dawn's chair, her eyes shone with warm agreement of all he said.

He nodded ruefully. "I'm a musician—of sorts! I only say that in order to make this young lady place more faith in my words of wisdom!"

Dawn smiled as she slowly plucked her violin strings. "And you pretend that *I* have done what a real musician hasn't managed? When I can't read or write a note of music? Well, as Dick would say, I just can't swallow it! The Dawn Song is simply an idea that came into my head in the night, because I was feeling happy and excited."

" That's just its value—because it comes from real emotions."

From the distance they heard the sound of a violently hooting horn, and Mr. Martin leapt to his feet with a hasty glance at his watch. " Gracious me, I've been forgetting all about the poor Professor! I must fly, for he has an appointment in town to-night, and I'll be making him late." He shook hands firmly with Mary and then with Dawn. " Remember," he admonished her, " with suitable words that song's a winner! Thank you for playing to me."

" Thank *you* for bringing me home," she called after him, as his long legs vanished round the gate.

" What a nice man!" Mary exclaimed.

" Yes, isn't he? I say, how's Dick?"

" Splendid. We've had the doctor to see his foot, and he says it's not terribly bad. He'll soon be O.K. again."

" Oh, I'm so glad! Weren't we lucky to meet your uncle like that?"

" *And* that he had such an obliging friend with him! How did he know you played the violin?"

" Spotted the shape of it under the cover! He's one of the *noticing* kind, I think. Anyway, he made me promise to play to him as his ' wages '. So I came round the back way so as to do it here in the garden!"

" Have you not been in yet, then?"

" No, an' I don't expect Auntie knows I'm back, for she'll be sitting at the front of the house!"

" Come away in at once then, you monkey! She'll be thinking we've lost you down a rabbit hole or something awful, I'm sure!"

But Dawn only grinned, as she proudly displayed both arms. " I've gone quite *brown* —or perhaps it's only dirt!" she announced cheerfully. " Oh, Mary, wasn't it a thrilling hike?"

It was three days later before Mary managed to go in next door again. There had been an extra lot of home lessons to keep her busy in the evening, and she had also been kept more than usually occupied with helping her mother. Dick being laid up meant a good deal of extra fetching and carrying in the house, and baby Maureen had also been very fractious while cutting an extra troublesome tooth.

During that time she had heard the violin only once, but as the weather had become rather unsettled and windy she was not surprised that Dawn had not been lying in the garden.

On the Tuesday evening after their eventful hike, Mary hurried to get through her tasks, then arming herself with a couple of interesting books mounted the next-door steps.

Mrs. Donaldson had evidently seen her coming from the window, for the door was opened before she had touched the bell. Mary noticed immediately that her expression was both tired and worried.

" My dear, I'm afraid you can't see Dawn to-day. She has been in bed since yesterday with one of her attacks."

" Attacks? Oh dear, I *am* sorry! It wasn't anything to do with our outing, I hope—she didn't get too tired?"

" Oh no." Mrs. Donaldson cast a quick glance upwards to one of the higher windows, then motioned her to come inside. " Do come in for a minute, and I can explain to you."

As Mary followed her into the house she noticed how different (although exactly similar in size and shape) it was from No. 12. In place of that familiar shabbiness of worn carpets and somewhat battered furniture was a richness and luxury—and a sort of " unused " air about everything—very unlike the home in which six youngsters of all ages were growing up.

" Do tell me what is wrong with Dawn?" Anxiously she turned to Mrs. Donaldson as the sitting-room door closed behind them. " I didn't know that she was worse sometimes than others."

" She has gone far longer than usual without one of these attacks—thanks to your companionship." Mrs. Donaldson hesitated, then continued very quietly. " You must try to understand this: though the *result* is physical exhaustion, the cause is purely mental. A fit of violent grieving for her father begins it all. Poor child, she grieves for him constantly, I know, but sometimes during a sleepless night her emotions get the better of her: control *her*, as it were, instead of she controlling them. Then during this period of—shall we call it weakened mental resistance—the germs of self-pity creep in. Goodness knows she has full cause for it. To have lost both her father and the power to walk, within a few short days, would embitter many older minds than hers."

" But Dawn is not bitter!" Mary exclaimed.

" No, she is far from it. But just on these occasions when grief for her father has loosened things, so that self-pity can get a hold on her, she weeps uncontrollably for hours on end. As a result physical collapse sets in, for such emotional outbursts are terribly exhausting, and tell so much upon her slender strength that she becomes really ill. At present, I hope, she is sleeping peacefully. When it is over she usually sleeps like a log for hours, while nature restores the torn and weary battlefield."

"Poor Dawn," Mary whispered.   "Oh, poor Dawn!"

In the silence that fell upon the room she could hear the quiet ticking of the clock, then with a little sigh she rose to her feet.

"Will you tell Dawn I have been? And I shall come again to-morrow. But she does not need to see me if she does not feel like it."

"She will want to see you. I can't tell you how much your friendship has meant to her."

Those words somehow troubled Mary as she returned to her own house. She had done so little to deserve them yet. What did she really know of Dawn? She had touched only the fringes of her mind.

To the eager chorus of questions as to her prompt return, she merely replied that Dawn was tired and resting; then settled down to play draughts with the convalescent (and now thoroughly bored) Dick. After which she put Hamish and Hunter to bed: but during all the chasing and tickling, which was an inevitable

accompaniment of that process, her thoughts
kept jerking back to a lonely little figure overwhelmed by a passion of grief and yearning,
in the long, dark, empty hours of night. She
remembered what Dawn had said about being
sometimes *afraid* of the length of days, of time,
which stretched ahead of her. How terribly
" all wrong " to feel like that at twelve years
old.

" Oh, I do so want to help!" she whispered
as she knelt by her own bed that night. " Do
please let me help and be of some use to her."

When she called at No. 11 on her way home
from school next afternoon the maid had
evidently received instructions regarding her;
for she led her straight upstairs, and, tapping
on the door, ushered the visitor into Dawn's
bedroom.

It was a beautiful room, Mary realized with
the first quick glance. A carpet of leaf green
and walls of sunshine yellow showed up the
dainty light oak furniture, while the very
pretty curtains were palest green embroidered
with white flowers. The low wooden bed stood

against the further wall, and beneath its green silk coverlet lay Dawn; so thin and straight a little figure that she scarcely seemed to raise its smooth expanse. Like a frightened bird, Mary suddenly thought, pressed in the corner of its very gilded cage.

"Hullo, old thing! I've come to chatter to you for a while!"

"That's lovely. Thanks awfully for the books you left yesterday."

The voice sounded normal enough, but as she drew up a chair beside the bed Mary had to bite her lip to keep back an exclamation at the difference in Dawn's face. It showed how very slender her reserves of strength must really be, that these three days could have made such ravages upon them. Her cheeks were sunken in beneath their high, arched bones, and shadows like the pressure of an inky thumb lay under sombre eyes.

As their glances met a sudden flush crept up beneath Dawn's skin, and she turned her head away towards the wall. Very slowly she rolled it back again, and two black eyes, steady behind

a veil of mistiness, looked straight into Mary's
own. " Now you know," she said quietly.
" Now you *know* why I can't be a Guide."

" My dear—why not?"

" Because I'm a coward!" The words burst
out with almost frightening violence from that
motionless figure. " How can I promise to
keep your Laws, to smile and sing under all
difficulties, when I *know* that every little while
I must behave like this? If I were really strong
and brave I would have beaten this silly weakness—but I can't."

" And you never *can*—alone." Not a great
talker, Mary summoned all her powers to aid
her now as she bent over the bed. " Don't you
realize, Dawn, that it's just because you *are*
brave that these attacks happen? For days and
weeks on end you bottle your true feelings so
tightly down inside, that one day the cork is
bound to pop out and make a nasty mess. The
only cure for that is a safety valve—and oh,
my dear, do please use me as one!"

" A safety valve?"

" Yes. To let off steam gradually, and not

keep it held down until it gets to danger level. In other words, don't try too hard to suppress your quite natural grief and sadness, Dawn. Let me share things; and by good use of your safety valve there will be no need for ' explosions '!"

" You *are* a pal!" Dawn was smiling now, and some of that strained look had vanished from her face. " And I'll be proud to use you —safety valve!"

" It's settled then!" Mary grinned at her: rejoicing in that little triumph, but at the same time summoning all her forces to the attack again. " Now that you see how much easier things are when shared, don't you begin to realize what a comfort Post Guiding could be to you? To know that you are one of many hundreds striving for the same ideals and struggling against the same—or even worse— difficulties. It must help."

Dawn did not answer; and after a long moment's silence Mary spoke again, in a voice so quiet she still could hear the tick of Dawn's wrist watch, beating like a steady pulse upon the dressing-table.

" The Guide Promise says ' to do my *best* '. No Guide has ever kept her ten Laws perfectly. I know I've failed myself—horribly. But that Promise makes us rise and try again, for we know it is not only ourselves we let down when we fail. The Guide Spirit is really just the practical expression of Christianity, Dad says —Oh, I wish I could get him to explain to you, he could do it so much better than I can!"

" Oh no he couldn't!" Dawn's misty eyes joined with her lips in the sudden radiance of her smile, as she turned to face her friend. " He couldn't *show* it better than you do! Oh, Mary, you don't know how much I *want* to be a Guide, and you've made it so much clearer to me that I think I can be, soon. But I've got to get things straightened up inside me first; and when I'm ready—I'll tell you."

" Settled, partner!" she agreed.

A discreet knock at the door heralded the arrival of a maid with a daintily appointed tea-tray for two, which she laid out on a table by the bed.

" Mrs. Donaldson thought you would rather

have your tea up with Miss Dawn!" she smiled.

" How kind of your aunt!" Mary exclaimed. " The family will be thinking I'm lost, but never mind! Shall I pour out? Ooh, what a scrummy cake!"

" Isn't this fun? Just like another picnic!" Dawn chuckled.

But as she turned slightly to take the cup Mary offered her, a sharp spasm of pain twisted her face, while her lip was drawn tightly between her teeth.

" What is it?" Anxiously Mary sprang on to her feet. " Something's hurting you?"

" It's nothing. Sit down." The spasm had passed and Dawn was smiling again, though her breath still came unevenly. " It's only my back."

" But I didn't know your back hurt you."

" It never used to," she admitted frankly. " This is something new in the last week: a pain right at the bottom of my back where I never felt anything before."

" But you should tell your aunt and——"

" No." Dawn's refusal was the firmest and most definite word she had ever heard her utter, and her pointed chin stiffened determinedly. " That's one little thing at least I can be brave about. Give me a chance to feel for myself *some* self-respect, as a human being anyway, before I can think of being a Guide."

" But——" Mary was somewhat at a loss. During her healthy life she had never had to cope with physical suffering, beyond the usual knocks and bruises of the hockey field. " How can you keep quiet about pain? It must be awful."

Dawn smiled wisely. " It's one of the easy things! Pain *is* one of the things you can get your teeth into and hang on: and there's a sort of satisfaction when you have won the fight, without anyone having seen a battle was going on. Quite honestly, a good stiff pain to keep your thoughts busy can be a *help*, when there's danger of the other thing getting on top."

Mary knew that by " the other thing " she meant the tangle of grief and mental conflict which had conquered her two nights before.

She nodded understandingly, and then bit hard into her cake.

After the meal Dawn admitted with a chuckle that she had started composing words for the Dawn Song, and showed Mary the paper on which she had jotted her ideas. It was only a skeleton outline at present, with many blank lines and missing words, but the two settled down to finish it with great enthusiasm.

Mary had a natural gift for rhyming, many of her poems having appeared in the school magazine, and with her aid the "sticky" patches were soon overcome and the little verses completed.

It was by no means great poetry, but both rhythm and metre were correct; and the simple, straightforward lines about the beauty of day's dawning, and the fact that a new day and new hope always lay ahead of us, fitted perfectly into the tune.

That tune, Mary felt, was good enough to stand on its own legs without the aid of words; it was good enough for a publisher to buy it and have words written to it, if he did not care for theirs. For she had made up her mind, though not daring to tell Dawn, that the song *was* going to have its chance and be submitted for publication.

She made Dawn play it to her now, and raking music-paper and pen from among her case of lesson books, carefully took it down. Much practice was making her quick and expert at this task, and after three more hearings she was satisfied with her work.

It was late when she eventually took her leave, conscience stricken to realize how long she had stayed, but assured by Mrs. Donaldson, who had come up to join them, that the patient was vastly improved.

At home, school prep and a host of other duties awaited her, but she found time to steal off to the piano and play over her notes. The Dawn Song, sweet, joyous, and familiar, filled the room. Yes, she had got it perfectly.

Next morning Mary rose very early and copied out the song with painstaking neatness and perfection on her best paper. Then having obtained the address of a well-known publisher from some music on their own piano, she posted it on her way to school.

The deed was done! If it failed, no one need be any the wiser; but if successful——! She hugged herself to picture Dawn's astonishment and delight. . . .

A strange feeling of excitement still filled her as she raced up the steps of No. 11 on her way home from school, to pay a brief call on the invalid.

" I'm daft!" she told herself. " I know I won't hear anything for weeks or maybe months—— Still, I *do* feel something exciting's going to happen!"

Mrs. Donaldson met her in the hall and greeted her as " just the person I'm wanting!"

" My dear, I've got a big favour to ask of you!" she exclaimed.

" Anything I can do! How's Dawn?" Mary asked.

" Much better. The doctor was here to-day, and he says her nervous condition is back to normal. But he is not so pleased with her general health. The fact that this attack should have got her so low shows that her whole system is badly in need of toning up, and he recommends a complete change of air and scene. In fact, he wants me to take her to Switzerland."

" Oh, to Switzerland——!"

" Yes, and that's where the favour comes in! Dawn is terribly loath to go, because of leaving you, and if she is fretting all the good will be undone. So do you think you could possibly come with us, as my guest? I need not tell you what a help you would be to me and how much I would like to have you."

" *Oh!*" It was all that Mary could say just then. " Go to *Switzerland*? How perfectly, utterly, and completely thrilling!"

CHAPTER V

Switzerland

The Blair family were all wildly jealous of Mary's good fortune, and all had their own ways of expressing it.

" You lucky *dog*!" Dick growled. Words failed him. Hunter and Hamish were chiefly taken by her luck in escaping school, and the limitless possibilities for snowballing; while Margaret announced, " You'll need heaps of new dresses!" in a tone of admiration.

Mrs. Blair was at first doubtful of her daughter's accepting the invitation, as it would mean her missing nearly a month of school before the summer break-up, but her father championed her cause. " It's a chance she may not get again," he declared. " And I think the educational value of travelling abroad will be worth more to her than those missed lessons."

So it was settled; her father wrote a note of explanation to the Headmistress, while Mary joyfully told Mrs. Donaldson that she would be ready to set out with her on the date she had arranged—in about a week's time.

Dawn was radiant with excitement.

" I can't believe you're really coming!" she exclaimed on their first meeting. " I'm being thoroughly spoilt just now, by getting everything I want. You're sure you'd like to come?"

" *Like?*" Mary laughed at her. " Can't you see that this is just the greatest thrill I've ever had!"

" Then I'm able to do *you* a good turn at last, as well as doing myself one!" Dawn sighed contentedly.

" How is your back?" Mary inquired, with a sudden memory of her last visit. But Dawn brushed the subject impatiently aside.

" Don't talk about that. *I* haven't got time to notice it with so much else to think about!"

And what a lot there was to think about and do that week! Mary had to make expeditions into town with her mother, to obtain some necessary new clothes; and then there was the thrill of digging out the suitcases, untouched since the last family holiday on the Ayrshire coast, and beginning to stow her things away in them.

But these were not the only exciting events at No. 12 during those crowded days. Dick had returned to school: from which he returned on his second afternoon with a Recruit Form in his pocket, and the gruff announcement that he was joining Scouts. Though trying to be as casual as possible in her reception of this news, Mary felt that she had managed well. The interest aroused during their "hike" and by the first-aid she had been able to render to his foot, she had carefully fostered during his convalescence by the judicious lending of such things as *The Scout* and *Scouting for Boys*. Now her wordless battle had been won, and the determined scoffer had, of his own accord, changed his opinion.

Hunter lost no time after that in attaching himself to the school Cub Pack. He had secretly been longing to do this, but had loyally waited for his brother and leader's ban of disapproval to be lifted. Now that it was, he fairly let himself go in a spate of enthusiasm. Even Dick, when he realized he was not going to be teased or laughed at, relaxed his defences and began to talk of plans the " chaps in my Patrol " were making, and of camp in the summer time.

The house was breaking out in a rash of uniforms, Mr. Blair whimsically declared. " But it's an epidemic I'm very happy about!" he told Mary one evening with a little smile. " The B.P. germ is one worth catching, and I'm glad you carry it about with you!"

" I think even Margaret has been a trifle smitten!" Mary chuckled. " For she confided in me to-night that she felt ten was rather old to join Brownies, as she had ' never been very keen on childish things ', but she would be glad to help me with my Guides next year!"

" Yes, our Margaret is a very practical small person! But Guiding will teach her not to be so serious-minded about it, and will be the best thing in the world, I should imagine."

At last the great day of their departure arrived. They were to spend one night in London, and catch the boat-train to Dover the next day. Mary had puzzled not a little as to how such a journey would be possible for Dawn, but she now gained her first glimpse of luxury travelling, when no money has been spared to arrange for comfort and convenience.

Mrs. Donaldson had bought a special light carrying stretcher that was very comfortable for Dawn to lie upon; and on this she lay tucked up in rugs, her face pink and excited under her new hat, and was stowed away in the luxurious taxi whose back seat was wide enough for her to lie upon.

The whole Blair family lined the pavement to wave farewell, and Mary leaned far out of the window until they swung round the corner. Daddy flourishing his shabby hat, shoulders stooping rather wearily, but his dear, tired face smiling and happy as it always was. Mummy laughing and waving Maureen's podgy hand. Dick and Hunter flinging their caps into the air and shouting farewells and brotherly remarks at full power of lusty lungs. Five-year-old Hamish looking a trifle overwhelmed by it all and rather doubtful of whether he approved of big sisters being taken away; he stood sucking his thumb, and clung quite gratefully for once to the motherly hand Margaret offered him. Poor Margaret looking solemn too, neat and tidy in her school tunic and waving her handkerchief.

The last flutter had vanished, and Mary sank back on her seat. " Now we're off!" she told Dawn cheerfully. " We'll be so fat and sun-burnt when we get back I don't expect they'll know us!"

Dawn chuckled; but neither of them dreamt just what a shock the manner of their return *was* going to cause the inhabitants of Arnold Drive, and what amazing and incredible things were to happen during their absence.

Mrs. Donaldson was evidently an experienced traveller, and at the Central Station a little horde of porters seemed to spring up to attend to her. They had a reserved first-class compartment, and Dawn was laid comfortably along one of the seats. A stack of magazines was supplied for their amusement, and so the long journey down into England commenced.

It was late at night when they arrived in London, and drove straight to their hotel. Everywhere porters and commissionaires bobbed up to carry Dawn, and a luxurious lift rushed her to her bedroom. They must be very, very wealthy, Mary realized, but she was far from envying them. Mrs. Donaldson seemed a sad and lonely woman, not one half as happy as her own busy mother; while as for Dawn, money could do nothing to restore the two great things she had lost.

Mary shared Dawn's room that night, and when she found how much pleasure it gave her she resolved to keep with her during all the journey. For the first time for two long years Dawn was not lonely, and her dark eyes glowed with a new contentment in their depth. She was learning to use her safety valve, and the long, quiet talks they had together straightened some of her problems and brought her a new peace. While Mary grew very expert in knowing those little details which made just all the difference to her comfort; and in knowing too, though no word ever betrayed it, when the pain became especially bad.

They made the crossing very easily, and the journey across France, taken in easy stages because of Dawn, was an endless thrill to Mary's eager curiosity. Nevertheless she was not sorry when they reached their destination: a quiet little hotel at one of the less frequented beauty spots of the Swiss Alps. She felt that Dawn had had enough of travelling and was getting very tired.

The two girls had adjoining bedrooms here, leading out of each other and with their own bathroom attached. They were beautiful rooms, with a huge expanse of fine windows facing on to a view that took Mary's breath away.

" Isn't it *beautiful*?" she breathed, as she entered Dawn's room and found her lying entranced, with gaze fixed on those matchless snow-clad peaks. " Oh, I shall never know how to thank you and your aunt properly for this—it's a glimpse of fairyland!"

"We're going to be terribly happy here!" Dawn said with certainty. "And not only happy but—— Oh, I don't know!" She paused for a moment, then added quietly: "Well, I feel that I could write *real* music in this place."

"I know." Mary nodded understandingly. She sat curled up on the window-seat, with her chin cupped in her hands. "If I could do anything like that I'd feel I wanted to do it here. It's the *bigness* of everything somehow that makes you want to do big things."

"Yes. I've got it right down inside me somewhere—big music, I mean—much bigger than the Dawn Song. But I don't know if I'll ever be able to dig it up. You'll help me dig?"

"How can I help?"

"By just being you, and helping me to know myself, Safety Valve! Oh, can I have my violin now?"

"Of course you can! I was in the middle of unpacking, when this view encouraged me to idleness!"

Mary leapt briskly to the ground, and continued her interrupted task of stowing away

Dawn's belongings. Presently she came to the violin, safe within its leather case, and laid it in her arms.

She handled it joyfully, her long, thin fingers passing affectionately over the polished wood and drawing the bow across its strings. " My spade!" she murmured. " It does all the digging for me, if I just lie quiet and let whatever it finds come out."

" Well, I forbid any digging this evening!" Mary said firmly. " Your supper's coming up and then you're going to sleep. To-morrow we shall go a gorgeous walk together, for the porter told me your chair arrived here yesterday."

They went many walks together during the days that followed; Mary pushing Dawn's chair along the straight white road that stretched above the sleepy little village, and looked right across the valley to the majestic mountains at the other side. They had a special corner of their own for resting in and gazing at it all, before turning to walk back again.

They were sitting there one gorgeous afternoon while Mary read to Dawn a letter she had just received from Dick. A sprawly, hastily written epistle, it was full of information as to what the Beaver Patrol had been doing and were going to do, and they chuckled over it.

" He's as keen as mustard! It was our hike started that, Dawn!"

" Do you remember telling me then it was only the beginning of our adventures together? We little thought they'd lead as far as this!"

" And it's still the beginning."

" Do you feel that too?" Dawn turned to her eagerly. " I don't know what I'm waiting for, but I'm waiting for *something*! I feel just as if we were standing on the edge of—of a big discovery!"

" I know!" Mary admitted with a grin. " If I were writing a novel I would say: ' The fair maidens felt the hand of destiny had guided their footsteps to this place.' But being real life I merely think the strong air has gone a trifle to our heads!"

" Maybe! It'll be a wonderful place to dream and think about, but I wouldn't like not to see Glasgow again."

" Dirty, smoky old place!"

" But there's something about it——"

" The smell perhaps!"

Dawn chuckled. " Well, my elderly cynic, don't try to pretend *you* won't be glad to see it again!"

Mary smiled. " It's home, that's why. I've got seven good hefty roots there all waiting to drag me back, and I guess wherever your roots are is the real best place on earth."

She paused abruptly, realizing with a pang that poor Dawn had no " roots ". As her mother had died when she was born, her one and only possession had been the gallant airman father she had so adored. To change the subject, Mary hastily pointed across the valley to a low wooden building that nestled on the slopes almost opposite their hotel. " What is that place? Is it another hotel?"

" No, it's a small sanatorium. Our hall porter was airing his English on me this morning, and he told me all about it. The climate here is very good for advanced cases who can't stand a more exposed position. He seemed to think I ought to go there, but I assured him my lungs were not affected yet!"

"Poor things!" Mary whispered, looking across at that lonely building. . . .

The voice of the violin greeted her as she came up to bed that night. Dawn was propped up in bed, her eyes upon the window, playing a strange new tune. And what a strange, wild tune it was; a restless, seeking, incoherent thing, yet with a lost, questioning beauty of its own. It ended on a high, unfulfilled, almost wailing note, and the player dropped her arms and sighed.

"What's that?" Mary asked breathlessly.

"You can call it the Question Mark—an effort to express the feeling we were talking about this afternoon. The curtain shall now rise and the orchestra continue with the show! To talk sense: you're going ski-ing to-morrow afternoon."

"Am I?"

"Yes! You spend far too much time with me, and you're not getting enough practice. There's a big party of beginners—those jolly red-headed girls, and the fat Russel boy, and heaps more, going to try that hill opposite to-morrow, and you're jolly well going with them. Anyway, I'm going to compose some music and I don't want you!" she added loftily.

Dawn was very good at giving Mary her " marching orders " like this occasionally, and from the beginning she had insisted that she should practise ski-ing at least some part of every day. Mrs. Donaldson had given her a beautiful outfit, and she had hugely enjoyed floundering about with the other greenhorns on the easy slopes by the hotel. There were several young people staying there, and they had a hilarious time gaining their " snow legs " together, under the instruction of an expert skier.

But Mary was past the first stages now, and becoming daily more thrilled with the exciting sport. She was not yet very expert at turning, and still found the easiest method of stopping to sit down, but that did not deter her from setting forth in high spirits next day to seek new fields—or rather hills.

They were a merry party, laughing and shouting and snowballing each other, as they toiled up the long, powdery slopes and shot in a few mad seconds to the bottom.

Mary's cheeks were pink and glowing, and her eyes shone with excitement and laughter. The speed of the motion was intoxicating—almost like flying—and as she grew more proficient Mary became more reckless.

" Come on!" she cried. " There's a far steeper bit over here—a gorgeous straight slide right out of sight!"

" No thanks!" replied a very stout youth, who was stolidly plodding sideways up the hill. " You can go and break your neck by yourself. I prefer to stay where I know I've got something soft to land in!"

" Stick-in-the-muds!" called Mary cheerfully, and bending her knees in the approved fashion, she launched herself out over the edge.

Phew, what a pace! The keen air cut against her face and whistled in her ears, as she shot like a stone from a catapult down that hill. On and on, till she began to wonder rather anxiously just how to stop. If anything should come in front of her—— And something did! With a stab of horror, a little wooden shelter seemed to loom up out of the ground—and she was heading straight for it. Her efforts to swerve only seeming to increase her pace, Mary hastily and heavily sat down!

A husky chuckle greeted her, and looking up from this undignified position Mary saw that the shelter had an occupant.

Half lying in an adjustable chair, swathed round in rugs, sat a very thin young man. Painfully thin he was, with a too bright flush on each cheekbone, and close cropped sandy hair.

"Hurt yourself?" he inquired.

"Oh no! I say, I'm terribly sorry for disturbing you like this. Where am I?"

But she saw the answer to her own question as she scrambled to her feet. Over on her left stood the buildings of the sanatorium.

"You're in the sanatorium grounds."

"I'm awfully sorry."

" You needn't be! It's nice to have an un-expected visitor!" he smiled. " I get awful tired of the other patients, that's why I make them let me lie out here as much as possible, but it would be fine to talk to someone who has a new subject of conversation."

Something in his tones seemed to remind Mary of home; and almost on a venture she inquired: " Are you from Glasgow?"

His eyes widened. " Have I that tongue on me yet? Aye, I'm from Glasgow, or near it—Renfrew, to be exact. Are you from those parts yourself?"

" Rather! Born and bred!" She grinned at him.

" Fine! Oh, you and I must have a rare good crack—if you've time, miss," he added apolo-getically.

" Of course I will have!" There was some-thing strangely pathetic about this young Glasgow fellow, exiled so far from home, and obviously so very, very ill. He was terribly weak: she could see it was an effort to him to raise the magazine which lay on his lap. " Afraid

I can't stay just now," she added with a glance at her wrist watch, " as the people I am with will be expecting me to tea. But I'll come again to-morrow or the next day, if you're sure it won't tire you."

" That's mighty good of you, miss! It's a long while since I've heard anything but them Frenchies and other foreigners talking, and I'll never be good at that. You'll find me here, miss, any afternoon."

" Well, I promise I'll come back." She turned and waved to him as she moved away.

Poor fellow, he certainly looked an " advanced case ", and if it made him any happier to talk of Glasgow she must not grudge the time. " I wonder how he got here?" Mary thought. " It's so far from Renfrew! Why, that's the place where the big aerodrome is; I wonder if he's interested in flying? I must find out."

CHAPTER VI

An Incredible Story

Dawn was much interested in Mary's account of the Glasgow boy she had discovered in the sanatorium.

"Poor fellow, of course you must go and see him again! If he's been abroad for long it must be wonderful to hear his 'ain tongue'. What was his name?"

Mary chuckled. "Do you know, we never introduced ourselves! I just sat down in front of him with a bang and yelled 'Ow!' and he said 'Are you hurt?'—having most unsympathetically laughed first of all!"

"I'm not surprised at that!" Dawn grinned. "You must have looked a pretty priceless sight, I should imagine! Don't you agree, Aunt Katherine?"

"I'm only thankful that she didn't hurt herself!" Mrs. Donaldson exclaimed. "It's most interesting that you should have run into a fellow-townsman like that, Mary, and I must get you to take him a little basket of fruit from me next time you go."

"That's awfully kind of you, Mrs. Donaldson."

They were having tea together on the sunny terrace in front of the hotel, Dawn's light basket-chair drawn up beside the little table. She was looking heaps better since they came out here, Mary thought, glancing affectionately at the animated little face. Even her cheeks had filled out a trifle, and her face and arms were tanned brown by the sun; but there were still dark shadows beneath her eyes, brought there, Mary knew, by the strange new pain that was continually troubling her.

A diminutive page boy brought out letters to them on a tray. "But jus' arrive from England!" he beamed.

There were two for Mary, and she seized them eagerly; then could not suppress a sigh of disappointment when she saw the writings were those of her mother and a school friend.

Dawn's keen eyes were watching her, and

she chuckled softly. " Who *is* it you're expecting to hear from, Mary? I'll begin to grow suspicious soon, for every time the home mail comes you grab your letters and then peer around underneath everything to make sure you haven't missed one! Come now, confess!"

" Aha, that's my secret!" Mary laughed. For a moment she was tempted to tell her that the longed-for letter concerned *her*; that, in fact, she was daily hoping for word from the publishers to whom she had submitted her precious copy of the Dawn Song. It was for that reason that she had given her parents strict instructions to readdress any letter that might come for her—but no letter came. However, she suppressed the impulse to confide in Dawn. Much better to keep it as a complete surprise— *if* anything did happen!

Mary slept but lightly that night, for her dreams were uneasy and confused. About twelve o'clock she suddenly found herself broad awake and sitting up in bed: a wide strip of moonlight was flooding through the window and lay right at her feet.

Oh, how beautiful the mountains looked: they were unearthly and unreal by this white light! Spellbound she looked at them, until a soft, persistent sound caught at her ears. *Could* it be the violin? What was Dawn doing playing at this time of night?

Softly she crept out of bed and over to the dividing door. She pushed it ajar, and so bright was the moonlight in that room she could see it all quite plainly. Dawn's bed was bathed in radiance, and showed the strained and pinched expression of her small face, pressed close above the violin. She played with muted strings, a fluttering thread of sound, but so fast and passionately that her glinting bow was like a living flame.

" Dawn dear!" Mary ran across to the bed and knelt beside her. " What are you up to? Digging?"

" No—smothering this time." She dropped her violin and flung her arms round Mary's neck in a gesture as rare as it was surprising. " Oh, hold me very tight, please, just for one minute!"

Mary obeyed. She could feel the quivering of the thin little form within her arms, but presently she grew still and relaxed again.

" I've won!" Dawn whispered softly. " You helped a lot, but I *think* I was going to win whether you'd come or not."

" You mean——?"

" The pain began it." She was speaking quite calmly now. " It was very bad and I couldn't sleep; then when it stopped I had begun to think, and remember, too much. I would have given way—and been ill again—like I was before we came here; but I remembered things you'd said and managed to hang on. Now that I've once beaten it, I don't think it will ever happen again."

" Oh, my dear, I am so glad!" Mary slipped her arms round her again, and she cuddled close, smiling in the moonlight very sleepily.

" I feel so awfully happy! I'm a big step nearer now to being a Guide!"

Mary thought she slept, for she had lain in her arms a long time without moving, when suddenly her dark eyes opened and gazed straight across the valley to a single twinkling light which still burned in the sanatorium. "Poor man!" she said. "You will go and see him to-morrow, won't you? I can't bear to think of *anyone* being lonely now." Then sank into deep sleep. . . . But it was nearly an hour later before Mary gently freed herself, and tiptoed, stiff but happy, back to her own room. . . .

Dawn seemed particularly well and cheerful next day, and Mary left her on the terrace reading when she set off to pay her promised visit to the sanatorium. Mrs. Donaldson had given her a beautiful basket of grapes and other fruit to take with her, and carrying this she set off on her walk.

It was a beautiful day, with a sky of clearest blue above the snow-clad peaks, and Mary whistled merrily as she strode along. Her whole being was full and singing with joy; joy in Dawn's triumph of the night before, joy in her courage, and joy in the happier future which she felt sure lay ahead of them.

Her friend of yesterday was lying in the same

position in the shelter, and he greeted her eagerly. " My, this *is* good of you, miss!"

She gave him the fruit. " It's a little present from Mrs. Donaldson, the lady I'm staying with. She comes from Glasgow too! May I bag this chair? And now hadn't we better introduce ourselves—My name's Mary Blair!"

" And mine's Jim Brown—of Renfrew, as I said before!"

" That's where the aerodrome is; were you interested in flying?"

" Interested? Well, miss, that's my job! I'm a qualified air pilot and mechanic, but it's the mechanic's part of it that interested me most—though I've flown half round the world."

" I say, how thrilling!" Mary leant forward eagerly. " I bet you could tell some exciting stories!"

" Yes."

His face had gone stern and rather gloomy, and Mary felt that she had touched on the wrong subject. " Don't bother just now," she added hastily, " I'm only interested because the girl friend who is with me here is the daughter of a famous flier—that has made me rather air-minded!"

"You said the name was Donaldson?"

"Oh, Dawn is just her niece. *Her* name is Clive; daughter of Colonel Clifford Clive, the famous airman who was killed."

Jim Brown's face had drained of all blood to a ghastly pallor, and he moistened his dry lips twice before his croaking voice became audible.

"His daughter, you say? His daughter is *alive?*"

"Of course!" Sadly puzzled, Mary rose to her feet. "Are you ill? Can I do anything?"

He shook his head. "But he thought she was dead!" he repeated desperately. "He thought she was dead!"

"But I don't understand." Mary felt confused and puzzled. "Did you know Colonel Clive? But you can't mean that *he* thought Dawn was dead, because her accident came after he was lost. Oh, do you mean *you* thought she was dead?" A sudden light had come to her. "For I've just remembered her death *was* wrongly reported in one newspaper, but was corrected in the next edition!" And she repeated to him the story Dawn had told her that first day they met.

Brown listened to it in silence before he spoke again.

" Oh, I see how it happened. But it's cruel —cruel!"

" Did you know Colonel Clive?" Mary repeated her question.

The boy turned his wasted face full towards her. " Yes, miss. I was the mechanic who went with him on his last flight."

" *Oh!* When he was killed——?"

" The Colonel was not killed. Are you forgetting I'm meant to be dead too?"

Mary's face had turned very pale, and she gripped the sides of her chair till the rough wood cut into her palms. " What do you mean?" she whispered.

" Aye, I'll have to tell you the whole story now. I vowed to keep silence, but this alters things. I haven't long to live now, and maybe —maybe you've been kind of sent. A minute, miss, please, till I get my breath."

He was breathing in painful, panting gulps, and Mary could see that the excitement had been bad for him. She passed him some water that stood upon a side table, but her own hand shook so that it splashed over the glass. He drank, and then was seized with a gasping paroxysm of coughing which left him lying exhausted with closed eyes. But presently he opened them again and began speaking in a stronger, steadier voice.

"It was the storm that did it. We landed in an awful one, while crossing the Pacific, and were blown clean out of our course. The radio failed, and when it grew dark — black as pitch it was — we were pretty well at a loss to know *where* we were. Then the engine began to knock. That was the final nightmare. I doctored it all I knew, and the Colonel circled round as low as he dared: but it was impossible to see to make a landing. Flying blind we were—flying blind."

"And were you still over the sea?" Mary gasped out.

"Oh no. You see we'd covered a good bit

of our way, miss, before this storm came on, and after an hour or so of that blind flying, the Colonel he said to me, 'Brown,' he said, 'there's land beneath, but it can't be Russia.' That's where he was making for, you see, miss. 'It can't be Russia,' he says, 'but I think maybe it's China.' It was a really bad storm and some of his instruments were playing Old Harry and completely useless to us."

Jim Brown paused and Mary leaned forward anxiously. He passed a handkerchief across his moist forehead. "It haunts my dreams yet, miss, I can assure you! That darkness—then one awfu' flash as bright as day and we saw great mountains looming up in front of us. Under our very wings, as you might say. 'Rise!' I yells. 'Can't!' says the Colonel, very cool and steady like. 'Engine's gone, she hasn't another kick left in her. Hold on, lad!' Just as he finished speaking the engine stopped, and the silence that it left was—terrible. And then we crashed."

"On the mountains?"

"Yes. It was the Himalayas, miss. I'm not

much hand at geography, but you'll probably know that they're a great range that separates India and Tibet."

"Forbidden Tibet!"

"That's about all I know about it myself, miss! The Land of Mystery, they call it, and apparently it has always been very difficult indeed to penetrate their frontier. It was just on the Tibetan side of the range that we landed."

"But *how* did you land?" Mary cried desperately. "How is it you weren't killed, I mean?"

Jim Brown sat silent for a moment, then turned on her the full intensity of his sunken eyes. "This is going to sound utterly incredible, but you've got to believe me—you've *got* to believe me!"

"I *do* believe you. Please go on."

"By some miracle we crashed on a level plateau, some miles in extent, that is hidden in a sort of fold of those great mountains, high up on the Tibetan side. Not unnaturally it is unknown to white explorers, and its existence is unknown to the Tibetans too—except the strange race who inhabit it."

" Then there were people?"

" Yes. I'd better tell you straight away what it took us months to discover. They called themselves the Priests of Lukiang, and originally—that means several hundred years ago—it seems they were dissentient monks from a Lhasa monastery. They had escaped for refuge to the mountains, and the Colonel says they must have taken women with 'em from some of the villages that they passed. Anyway, they've been established there for hundreds of years, have built their own queer temple, and created their own priests to serve in it. A little lost civilization cut off from all the world. Those people saved our lives. They had never seen white men before, and treated us as gods. They pulled us from the blazing 'plane and nursed us back to life, for we were both unconscious for several days."

" But not injured?"

" The Colonel hurt his leg. After a while he was able to get around all right, but only limping and with the aid of a stick. But he was on his feet before I was, for I was critically ill for a long time, and when I did recover I was left with this lung trouble. Though these people were so good to us the Colonel was yearning to get away. He talked and longed continually for his little daughter. But the climb down to civilization was utterly impossible for a lame man, and seemed pretty well hopeless for a sound one. So things went on for about a year."

" A whole year?"

" Yes. I was only just beginning to get about again, and we had started making vague plans for me to climb back into India and summon help; but as I was utterly without idea of what direction to take, it is very unlikely I would ever have made it. Then the missionary arrived."

" A *missionary*?"

" Yes—I can tell you no one was more surprised than we were!" Brown gave the ghost of a chuckle. " The people of the Lukiang took it quite calmly that a black god should come to visit their two white ones! He was a young Indian missionary, an amazing fellow, very high caste and educated in England, who was working among some of the most outcast tribes of the Untouchables. He was on a holiday climbing expedition—queer idea of a holiday, *I* call it!—and, after weeks in the mountains, had lost the rest of his party and stumbled on our valley quite by accident. Oh, the joy and rejoicing there was when the Colonel had explained who we were! It was arranged that this young fellow should return to India as fast as possible, broadcast the glad news and have a Government 'plane sent to our rescue. If a 'plane knew just where to *look* for our valley, and flew low enough, they could locate it all right. The Colonel was fair crazy with excitement at the thought of getting back to England and his beloved daughter again. It was after supper that the Indian produced some ancient British newspapers from his kit. He said they were sent on to him from some other mission station, so they were *very* ancient before they got to his little backwoods outpost, but maybe we'd like to look at 'em. We said, you bet; and he gave one to me and one to the Colonel. The Colonel chuckled when he saw his had bits in it about his own disappearance—then he suddenly let out one awful cry. Oh, I'll never forget it! ' My daughter!' he cried. ' She's been killed—she is dead!' "

" Oh, it was *that* paper!"

" Aye, it was that paper, miss. He went into his hut and we did not see him again for hours; but when he came out he was calm and quiet— and absolutely determined. He was not going back. He cancelled all the plans that we had made, for he said that with Dawn gone he had nothing to return to and could not face civilization. She meant everything to him. So let him at least end his days in peace among these primitive people, who love him and to whom he is able to do some good. He made the Indian and myself promise most solemnly never to reveal that he was still alive; the world thought him dead—let him remain so. But he insisted I should go back with this fellow, as my health was in such urgent need of attention. I can't tell you what that journey was like," Brown shuddered. " It was beyond the worst horrors of nightmare. But by the time we arrived in India my trouble was too far gone for any cure. Since then I've passed from one hospital and sanatorium to another, and now am ending my days here."

" I am so sorry." Through all the dazed turmoil of Mary's mind came sincere pity for this poor lad. " Oh, I find it almost impossible to take in all you've told me!"

" You do think I've done right to tell? I've broken a promise, but he would never, never have stayed had he known his daughter was alive."

" Of course you've done right."

" Try and get to him—somehow, miss." A fury of coughing was shaking him. " I'm afraid you'll get no official help, for it's two years now since Colonel Clive disappeared, and they'd never believe such a queer story on just my word without no proof. You see, it would cost a mighty lot to fit up a search expedition—aeroplane is the only way to get at him."

" What *can* I do, then?"

But the cough was racking Brown too badly for speech. In terror Mary watched his thin body torn with it, and the handkerchief he raised to his lips was stained with blood.

At last he spoke in a gasping whisper, and pressed on her a scrap of paper from his pocket. " That's the compass reckoning of its position —the Valley of the Lukiang—when you get to the mountains. The Colonel did it himself with instruments he salvaged from our wreck. I've always kept it. Miss—I can't do more."

He was indeed utterly exhausted, and as Mary raised the glass of water to his lips she knew the thousand questions trembling on her tongue must wait unanswered.

CHAPTER VII

The Wanderer Decides

How Mary got through that evening she never quite knew. To answer Dawn's eager questions about her visit; to try and talk and be cheerful and bright and normal—when all the time this stupendous, terrible, new knowledge was burning in her brain—it was very hard. But she managed it somehow, and when the ordeal of supper was ended, pleaded a headache and escaped to her bedroom.

Alone at last, she tried most desperately to think. What could she do? What path was the right one for her to take?

Part of her longed to tell it all to Dawn: to hold her in her arms and say, " Your father is not dead! He is alive, and thinks that *you* are dead!" But Mary knew she could not dare do this. To raise false hopes, to give such news for nothing, would be too terrible for words.

She trusted utterly in all that Brown had told her: no one could have heard that poor boy's husky, gasping story and doubted his sincerity. But it was a year since he had left the Valley of the Lukiang; anything might have happened, the Colonel might even have died, since then.

When at last Mary climbed into bed, her tired brain was no nearer a solution of the problem. She knew only that she must go and see Brown again to-morrow: try and get answers to some of her hordes of anxious questions. Perhaps she ought to have got him to write it all out and sign a statement—though even then it would be only the word of a single man. Morning's pale light was beginning to slant into her room before she slept.

Next morning Mary took Dawn for a walk and spent all her time with her, for she explained that she must go back to the sanatorium that afternoon. Dawn was a trifle surprised at such a quick return, but agreed cheerfully: and immediately lunch was over Mary set off on the now familiar road.

But when she reached the shelter this time it was empty. Disappointed, Mary waited for a time, but as he did not come she summoned courage to approach the sanatorium itself.

A white-clad nurse came to the door, and in answer to Mary's shy inquiry she sadly shook her head. She spoke in French, but the main purport of her remarks was easy enough to understand. Jim Brown was dead. He had died early that morning of a sudden severe hæmorrhage.

Poor, poor fellow, Mary thought, as she walked sadly away. Into her tired mind there came the memory of what he had said about her being " sent " to him. Yes, there did seem a kind of definite plan about it all—that she had only just found him in time. Dad always said there was a pattern in everything, for those who had the eyes to see. The last time they had talked of that had been the evening Uncle David had come to tell them of his wonderful legacy—though it had been *she* who had told him she had a feeling that money was going to fulfil some good purpose in the world.

Uncle David! Mary stood stock-still in the middle of the narrow path, and a sudden light of hope burned in her eyes. The Wanderer! *Of course* that was the person she must consult in her great difficulty, and get him to use the money he had been left for the purpose of exploring *this* lost civilization.

Eagerly she strode on again, eager only to get back and start to write to him. Everything was fitting into shape perfectly, like the pieces of a puzzle. Surely there could be nothing more interesting and fascinating, from the ethnologist's point of view, than this remnant of a people who had been shut off from all outside influences for hundreds of years. So even if they did not find the Colonel, his time and money would not have been wasted. But they would find him—oh, they would.

Back at the hotel Mary dodged round by a side entrance to avoid being seen, and going straight to her room, commenced upon the letter. It was a long and difficult thing to write, for she explained in detail her finding of the young airman, and gave a full account of all that he had told her; at the same time emphasizing the need for privacy and the fact that no hint of it must be allowed to reach Dawn's ears.

Then Mary sketched out her own plan, and begged the Professor to consider it. "You are the only person I can think of who can help me, Uncle—and I do need help most desperately. Have you found any pygmies or people? Because if not, and you've still got that ship standing waiting— Oh, my dear old Wanderer, I do think you *ought* to do this thing. Even if Dawn's father is not there, those people of the Lukiang would be well worth your trouble, in a professional way. I mean, it would be a perfectly *right* way of using your old Chief's legacy, wouldn't it? And if you *should* find Colonel Clive—oh, think of it!"

The letter finished and stamped, she went out and posted it immediately, then joined the others at the tea-table. The news of Brown's death gave her legitimate excuse for being very quiet that evening.

Next day passed uneventfully, and the morning following a telegram arrived for Mary.

" Will join you in day or two. Announce
arrival and book me room. Will be very careful
about D.—Uncle."

Dawn was thrilled when Mary gave out that
her Uncle David was visiting Switzerland and
wanted a room at their hotel. She had been
much taken with him on their one meeting, the
occasion he had played knight-errant to the
hikers. Mrs. Donaldson was also much interested, as she knew Professor Blair by reputation
and was delighted at the thought of meeting him.

They arranged for the room, and then began
for Mary another period of waiting suspense.
But she made herself take part in everything as
usual: ski-ing, swimming in the lake, and
walking with Dawn, and the latter certainly
found nothing wanting in her cheery companionship.

They were at tea on the second day when
the Professor arrived. Mary could have cried
with joy at the sight of his dear, familiar form,
big and broad and burly, with his fierce brown
beard and absurd bristling eyebrows. He

looked so sane and safe and sure of things, the dear old Wanderer, that Mary flung her arms around his neck and buried her face in the good peaty smelling tweed of his jacket.

" Well, my lass, and how have you been behaving yourself? Hey, when you've finished ' dichting yer neb ' on my good jacket, maybe you'll introduce me properly!"

Laughing, Mary presented him to Mrs. Donaldson and to Dawn. His brown face crinkled into its very nicest smile as he bent over her hand; he *did* look very like Daddy sometimes, Mary thought.

" So we meet again, little lady! I was just thinking that Mary might have pushed you to the top of one of these mountains, and then you might want a lift home in my old bus— that's why I came out here!"

Dawn chuckled delightedly. " I hope you remembered to bring your car?"

" Bless my soul, I forgot all about that!" he exclaimed with mock chagrin.

Mrs. Donaldson inquired if he would be staying here long, but he shook his head.

"A day or two at most, probably. I'm a bird of passage at the moment, and very unsettled in my plans." Mary admired his easy composure.

It was some time before they had a chance to speak alone, and the Professor at once said that Mrs. Donaldson must be taken into their confidence.

"She'll be the best judge if there's any truth in the story or not. She must know her brother better than anyone else does, and can say if he was at all likely to have acted in this way."

Mary nodded. "We'll have to wait till Dawn's in bed, though. She'd be suspicious if the three of us shut ourselves up away from her."

So that evening, when Dawn was safely tucked in bed and Mary had assured her she would be coming up herself very shortly, the three assembled in Mrs. Donaldson's sitting-room. She looked mildly surprised when the Professor announced she was now to hear the real reason of his arrival in Switzerland.

"Better repeat the whole story to both of

us," he told Mary. "Excellent though your
letter was—I had to pay excess postage on it,
by the way!—I won't be sorry to hear the whole
thing over again. Mrs. Donaldson, this con-
cerns your brother, and I'm afraid I must ask
you to prepare for a considerable shock."

Firmly and steadily Mary repeated the whole
incredible affair. When she reached the fact
of Brown having been the Colonel's mechanic,
Mrs. Donaldson uttered a sudden breathless
murmur of astonishment; but from then on
she sat quite silent and motionless, with her
hands clasped in her lap.

"I'd better explain now where I come in,"
the Professor said, when Mary had finished.
And he stated the facts regarding his legacy.
"Mary knew I was swithering where to go,
and thinks I should use this money in the
Himalayan venture, quite as a business pro-
position even if I fail to find the Colonel. But
what I want to know from you is whether you
can conceive of your brother acting in this
way."

Mrs. Donaldson moved for the first time.

" Yes," she said very quietly. " Oh, I don't know if it is true or not—but it is most utterly the way that he *would* act. If he thought that Dawn was dead he would not want to face the world again." She paused a moment, and then continued haltingly: " My brother was in some ways a strange man. He adored his young wife almost too utterly, and when she died he—saved himself, I think—by transferring that affection, doubly intensified, to the baby. She was a trust that Muriel had left him, and as such filled his every waking thought. As Dawn grew older that affection ripened and deepened into comradeship as well as worship. He adored her to the exclusion of every other human relationship, and if he thought that she had died—well, the bottom and top of his whole world was gone."

" I think I understand," the Professor said.

" You have got to remember too what a moment this news came at," she continued. " Just when, after months of brooding, his spirits are raised to the skies by the hope of escape and return to her—he reads that she is dead. I am very sure that in that moment of reaction he must have felt there was nothing left for him to live for in the world at all."

Mary broke the silence that had fallen on the little room. " Jim Brown spoke the truth," she said firmly. " He was a dying man, who knew that he was dying. If you had seen him you could not have doubted him."

" I would gladly provide money for an expedition——" Mrs. Donaldson began. But the Professor broke in on her.

" I wouldn't lose the chance of this for the world, madam!"

" You'll do it, then?" Mary cried.

He smiled at her. " Didn't I tell you I was keeping this money for *big* game? To go down to fame as the discoverer of the people of the Lukiang! And if I *find* the Colonel——" He broke off, and turned to Mrs. Donaldson. " I think you had better leave this in my hands, for we will need official permission to fly into Tibetan territory, even though it is just over the edge of a mountain range: and my name is fairly well known in the right quarters, owing

to having done Government survey work in the
past. I don't think there will be any difficulty,
in this case at least, although of course it is
one of the stickiest frontiers in the world.
Anyway, I'll certainly do my best. I don't
think you need worry."

"I'll be deeply grateful if you will do this,
Professor."

"It's settled! Just a few days' delay while
I make the wires hum a bit, then when the
formalities are settled we'll go down and join
my ship."

"You've got it near here, Uncle?"

"Yes. I told 'em to wait for me at Monaco,
as they had to call in there for a member of the
party."

"Uncle David, I do believe you've quite
intended to do this all the time!" Mary declared.

He chuckled. "Have you ever known me to
refuse adventure, lass?"

"Can I go with you—*please*?"

"Well, in exchange for this," he was carefully stowing away the precious scrap of paper

with the pencilled compass directions, " I don't see I can very well refuse you. But mind, you're not to expect to go all the way, but be content to bide down in civilization."

It was very late when the discussion finally ended and Mary went up to bed. Cautiously she opened the door of Dawn's room and peeped in on her, heaving a sigh of relief to see that she was peacefully asleep. On tiptoe she crossed over to the bed and looked down on her peaceful sleeping face. " Oh, Dawn!" she whispered. " If only this is true, if only I can give your father back to you, I think I'll be the happiest person in the world!"

She had taken Dawn for their usual walk next morning, when she told her that she was going with her uncle. " He's really here on business," she explained. " And is arranging an expedition—somewhere near India. I'm going to sail with him, as far as India anyhow. It's such a wonderful chance: you won't mind, will you?"

" But why shouldn't I come too?" Dawn caught eagerly at her arm. " Oh, *please*, Mary!

If your uncle's got a boat of his own, wouldn't there be a *wee* corner for me?"

" Oh, my dear, I really don't know——!"

" Ask him, Mary, please, please, *please*! I couldn't bear to be left here without you. It would be worse than being lonely in Glasgow —much—after we've been so happy here together. Do you think I'm a frightful little pest?"

" Of course I don't! Dawn, I'd love to have you, and in a way I feel you ought to come. But I don't know just what Uncle will say about it!"

" If you asked him!" Dawn smiled and wrinkled a nose on which some tiny freckles were appearing. " He's very fond of you, you know!"

" He's very fond of *you*—that is my only hope!" Mary laughed.

If Dawn only knew the real purpose of this expedition, Mary thought as they turned for home again, there is no doubt she would have *insisted* on going with them. In a way it seemed a shame to prevent her, for if her father *was* found she ought to be as near as possible to him.

Mary used this argument when tackling the Professor after lunch. "Think if we did find the Colonel how wonderful it would be to be able to tell him his daughter was waiting for him down at the bottom—to be able to reunite them at once."

"Down at the bottom?" The Professor twinkled. "No, I'm afraid we'll not take her as far as that! But—if——"

"Oh, you *will* let her come, won't you? I'm sure she wouldn't be any bother, and I hate leaving her. You've no idea what a brave sort of person she really is, Uncle."

"I think I have—a little," he answered slowly. "Well, my dear, she can come, and of course her aunt also, on condition you all wait in Calcutta. That's where I'll head for, and not an inch farther are any of you coming!"

"Darling! We won't want to!" Mary jumped up and kissed him heartily upon the nose. "You really are a perfect lamb!"

"A lamb in lion's clothing, eh? Ah well,

lassie, it's a good thing the old *Wanderer* is a fairly commodious vessel, for I never reckoned on having passengers!"

"Passengers my eye!" Mary retorted. "I'll swing the yard-arm or whatever it is with the best of them! And Dawn can be ship's orchestra!" Then she fled upstairs to tell her the good news.

Dawn, though very joyful, was not as surprised as Mary had expected her to be. "I somehow *knew* I'd go!" she said happily. "Yes, one of those funny sort of 'fated' feelings we've been having lately! Oh, isn't it exciting?"

"Tremendously!" She turned to look out of the window, to hide a sudden glistening of tears that had sprung unbidden to her eyes.

"I've got a funny feeling," came Dawn's small voice from behind her, "that this voyage is going to be very important to me. Silly, isn't it?"

"Perhaps—it's not."

"Anyway, I've got you. And you don't know what a difference that has made to things, dear Safety Valve!"

" Has it really? But we're still at the beginning, Dawn—oh, let's always be at the *beginning* of fresh things!—And perhaps one day I shall really feel that I deserve your thanks. Not yet!"

Next day Mrs. Donaldson began her preparations for their departure, and they lived, as Dawn gaily expressed it, in constant expectation of " marching orders ". But it was more than a week before all the Professor's affairs were satisfactorily settled. At last, however, the final permit was received, and they started on their journey down to Italy.

" Oh, let us be in time!" Mary whispered, as she pressed her face against the railway carriage window. Dawn lay upon the seat opposite, her dreamy eyes fixed upon the flying countryside, and as Mary looked at her she breathed again: " Oh, please let us find him!"

CHAPTER VIII

A Thrilling Journey

Dawn was terribly tired by the time they boarded the *Wanderer* at Monaco. The long, trying journey, and the excitements of all the fresh places she had seen, combined to exhaust her, and though it was still early evening when they arrived she went straight to her cabin.

Mary accompanied her, and together they shared a picnic supper from a well-laden tray. It was a cosy little cabin with two bunks in it, which the two girls were to share; while Mrs. Donaldson had a smaller one to herself.

"Isn't it funny to be sleeping on a shelf!" Dawn chuckled. After the meal and a little rest, she had revived considerably, and was in the best of spirits. "You know I've never been on a real boat before, and I'm going to enjoy just every minute of it! What *is* that kind of wooden box stuck on the wall down there?"

" I'll show you!" Mary opened out the " box " and revealed a neat little wash-basin, made to stand out like a shelf when not folded up flat against the wall. " Isn't it cute? When you want to empty it you just tip it up and the water runs down this hole at the back, right down into the deep blue sea!"

" I always keep forgetting we are *on* the sea! Won't it be fun when we start moving?"

" Especially if we're both seasick!"

" Pig! Do tell me what you can see out of the window—porthole, I mean!"

Mary knelt on her own bunk and pressed her face against the small round opening. " I see water—very black! And a few boats, also very black, because it's too dark to see them properly. And on shore a lot of lights are twinkling, jolly pretty they look! That's all I see—oh, except a few stars have started to come out in the sky!"

" It sounds lovely!"

" Well, I suppose I'd better go to bed now." Mary flopped down on the bunk again and began pulling off her shoes. " We're nice and near each other, so if you snore all I've got to do is shy a boot at you!"

" I *don't* snore! But I believe I sometimes chatter horribly, so you had better keep some ammunition ready! I say, do let me play you a lullaby; I feel just in the mood for the Dawn Song to-night!"

Laughing, Mary gave her the violin, and presently the gay, sweet notes of the Dawn Song filled the air. In how many strange places had she heard that tune since first it sounded in a country lane beyond Bearsden.

Suddenly Mary's keen ears caught a footstep in the passage outside. Somebody had been passing, and had stopped at the sound of the violin. A half-smothered exclamation came to her, and then silence. When the tune ended she heard slow footsteps passing on again.

" You had an audience!" she chuckled, as Dawn laid down her bow. " What fun if we've got a musically-minded sailor on board, who whistles Beethoven in his bath!"

" Perhaps it was your uncle?"

" No fear! The darling hasn't a note of

music in him, and couldn't tell the difference between Chopin and Bach!"

"Maybe we'll solve the mystery in the morning," Dawn murmured sleepily, as she snuggled down into the clothes. "Goo' night, shipmate, pleasant dreams!"

Mary had been sleeping for some time when a strange sensation wakened her. She lay still for a moment wondering what it was: and then realized that the *Wanderer* was moving. So they were off! Off at last, on the first steps of this fantastic journey to an unknown land.

She whispered Dawn's name; but she was sleeping soundly, and only murmured "Daddy!" as she stirred a little in the embrace of some sweet dream.

A day of cloudless sunshine, twinkling upon the blue waters of the Mediterranean, greeted them when they went on deck next day. Mary wheeled Dawn's spinal carriage to a sheltered corner of the deck, and settled herself down beside her. Uncle David waved a cheery hand to them from farther along. He was deep in conversation with two members of his party; a learned-looking Mr. Hudson, who was an authority on languages and would act as interpreter to the party, and a tall, fair Swede whom the Professor described as " a brilliant scientific mind ".

" So it *is* the composer in person!" A voice behind them made Mary swing round, to see the cheery face of Mr. Martin, the Professor's friend who had pushed Dawn home after Dick's accident, standing just beside them. " I couldn't believe my ears when the first thing I heard when I got aboard last night was your Dawn Song! I thought it must have become world famous already, for the Prof never told me *you* were coming with us!"

" It was a last minute arrangement!" Dawn beamed. " I say, are you one of this party? Isn't that fun!"

The Professor came up and joined them. " Nice surprise for you!" he chuckled. " I didn't tell you this was the fellow we had to collect from Monaco! Well, John?" and he slapped him heartily on the shoulder. " You had turned in before I got back from my shore visit last night. How are things?"

"Fine! Yes, I was pretty tired, for I had rather a tough two days back there."

"So I heard. How is the patient?"

"Making good progress. He's going to pull round now all right."

Mary and Dawn had listened to this conversation with puzzled faces, and the latter now murmured, "Patient? But you're a musician, aren't you?"

"Who on earth told you that?" the Professor inquired. "He's a surgeon, my dear."

"*I* told them!" John Martin announced, as he flopped his long legs out in a deck-chair. "Anyway, I like to think I'm one, and I've *tried* pretty hard for several years! Though I dare say I'm guilty of making 'em think it was my profession instead of a most precious hobby—because I wanted this stubborn young lady to take me for an authority on the matter!"

Professor Blair slapped his thigh with a roar of laughter. "Well, if that isn't just like John Martin!" he chuckled. "To describe himself as a *musician*, when he's really one of the finest young surgeons in the country! Well, he's just been sent for by a rich old chap who developed appendicitis at Monte Carlo, and preferred to have John out from England than let anyone else touch him. That'll show you!"

" Nevertheless," said Dr. Martin with a friendly grin, " I'm still much more proud to call myself a musician than anything else: and I'd be prouder still if I could compose a tune like the Dawn Song!"

" Don't be silly!" Dawn laughed. " I never did believe you anyhow!"

The *Wanderer* stopped in Port Said for a couple of hours, and Dawn and Mary insisted on going ashore. Mrs. Donaldson, who had been abroad before, assured them that it was a dirty place and not worth looking at; but both girls were hugely thrilled by their first glimpse of the East, and Dr. Martin good-naturedly offered to accompany them.

Dawn was wide-eyed and radiant with excitement as Mary pushed her chair along the narrow streets. On every side, towering high above the flat-roofed houses, were white domes and minarets, standing out like etchings against the bright blue sky; and outside the queer shops stood wild-looking Arabs, all shouting at the pitch of their voices.

" What on earth *are* they saying?" Mary inquired.

" They're all telling you to come in and buy, and announcing how very superior their goods are to those of the thief and robber next door!" Dr. Martin grinned. " Well, there is one thing I think you ought to buy—a nice sun topi each. It's far too hot for those hats."

" It certainly *is* pretty sweltering," Mary agreed.

They followed the doctor's tall form into the dark interior of one of the shops, and there tried on a series of large white topis. " Hideous things!" Dawn called them, for, being lined with green inside they gave one's face a most bilious expression, she declared.

The dusky gentleman in charge spoke English, and was so polite and pressing a salesman that both girls indulged in a perfect orgy of

buying, and emerged laden with boxes of
Turkish Delight, ostrich-feather fans, and tinsel
scarves, which he declared to be " very good,
very rare ", but which the doctor said were
made in Manchester. Hot, sticky, and happy,
they at length returned to the boat.

All next day they were steaming slowly
through the Suez Canal, which fascinated Mary
more completely than anything she had yet
seen. The shining band of silver water beneath,
the strip of deep blue sky above, and sand-
wiched in between, a narrow bar of gold that
was the desert. It was like an ever-changing
picture book, that stretch of sand, and Mary
leant for hours upon the rail watching for its
next pages to unfold. When an Arab rode
past on his lean camel, the whole thing became
too completely and ridiculously like a coloured
Bible picture book of her first youth, now a
treasured possession of young Hamish's.

Dawn and Dr. Martin were very deep in
conversation to-day. Twice Mary had passed
them with their heads together talking earnestly,
and on one occasion she had heard Martin's

voice saying: " You can tell *me* the whole truth, Dawn, that is different."

He joined her at the rail that evening, and in silence they watched the glory of the sunset over the desert. As the mad riot of colours died away, his deep voice spoke quietly by her side. " I think I have never prayed more for anything than that we may find Colonel Clive."

" You know, then?" Mary asked.

" Yes, the Professor has told all his friends the real purpose of this voyage, under seal of secrecy. I was thrilled enough before, but it means doubly much to me now."

In the curved dome of darkness high above their heads the stars were kindling one by one, like brilliant jewels set out on black velvet; and as she gazed at them Mary murmured: " If wishes count for anything, we *must* succeed."

All during the days of scorching heat in the Red Sea Dawn remained placid and unusually cheerful, in spite of the fact that her pain was proving extra troublesome. Especially at night did it " get on top " of her, and she slept so little that Mary marvelled at her endurance.

Nearly every day she had one of her long talks with John Martin, and the rest of the time lay quietly strumming on her violin, or making friends with the crew, who all adored her.

They took in coal at Aden, a barren rocky spot that Mary found very depressing, then stoutly steamed on into the open waters of the Indian Ocean. Colombo, five days later, was the next port of call, and again Mary and Dawn made an excursion ashore. It was quite different from Aden's arid heat, being warm and green and moist; and once again the shops tempted and fascinated them. They spent all available money on carved ivory elephants, kimonos, and moonstones, to send back to the folks at home.

The Professor insisted they should all come as his guests to an hotel he knew of where they might sample real Eastern curry. Dr. Martin took Dawn's chair, so that Mary might have her first experience of rickshaw travelling. It was hugely exciting racing along in the little two-wheeled cart drawn by a grinning black boy, and the party were followed by small brown children who pelted them with big, sweet-smelling, waxy-looking flowers. The curry was exciting too, containing prawns and many other strange ingredients, and Dawn was vastly amused to find the correct way to eat it was with a fork *and* spoon.

Three days later they entered the mouth of the Hooghly River. It was late evening, and Mary went in search of Dawn to carry her off to bed. She found her as usual in conversation with Dr. Martin, and as Mary approached they suddenly shook hands and she heard the doctor's grave voice saying: "That's a bargain, signed and sealed, partner!"

"What's all the mystery about?" Mary inquired when they got into their cabin. "What's the bargain?"

"Aha, that's *my* secret!" Dawn grinned impishly. "You're not the only one who can have 'em, Miss Who Is Always Looking for Important Letters!"

"You'll probably know my secret soon!" Mary smiled.

"You'll know mine *very* soon." Dawn spoke

gravely now. " But I just can't tell you yet, Mary."

" My dear, I was only joking! Sure you're quite comfy? This is our last night in these wee bunks—till we go back."

As had happened once before, Mary was wakened in the night by a strange sensation: or this time it was *lack* of sensation. They were standing still. " We've arrived!" she whispered, and this time Dawn's voice answered her out of the dark. " Yes—we've arrived!" There was a note in it that Mary could not understand, a troubled note of almost—was it fear? But as she puzzled on it Mary fell asleep again.

Early next morning they disembarked at Kidderpore Dock, and had their first view of the great city of Calcutta. The Professor had taken rooms for Mrs. Donaldson and the two girls in a quiet hotel, and they drove out to it immediately.

Mary and Dawn shared a huge, airy room, whose impression of great spaciousness was increased by the whitewashed walls and very high ceiling. Their two beds stood like little islands in the midst of a perfect sea of matting: and the rest of the furniture, which consisted of two wardrobes, a dressing-table, and two chairs, all seemed vast distances apart from each other. The green mosquito-nets covering each bed were another new experience, and Dawn declared hers made her feel as though inside a meat-safe.

The Professor at once set about making his preparations for the trip, and after a good deal of discussion decided on the hiring of two aeroplanes. Some of the party had been keen to attempt the conquest of the mountains by climbing, as the Indian missionary's exploit had made it evident that this *could* be done; but Professor Blair felt that even should they find their way, months of valuable time must be lost by this method. He agreed with the Colonel's dead mechanic that air was by far the most hopeful means of penetrating to the hidden valley.

Mary saw little of her uncle save at meal times, for he was kept fully occupied in choosing his machines, engaging skilled and trustworthy pilots, and making a thousand other preparations. Both 'planes were to carry two passengers: Hudson, the Swede, Dr. Martin, and the Professor himself.

At last he joyfully told them that the arrangements were almost completed, and he thought they would be ready to start in about a couple of days. It was at the lunch table that the Professor made this announcement, and Mary noticed that Dr. Martin followed him after the meal with a quiet request that he might speak to him for one moment.

Tugging fiercely at his beard, as he always did when worried, her Uncle David joined Mary in the garden later and drew her aside from the others.

" Can't understand what's happened!" he declared. " But Martin says he's not going with us!"

" Not going?"

" No, and the only reason he gives is that he has more important business here. What on earth business can he have in Calcutta? But I can see he doesn't want to discuss the matter, and it's useless to try and change John from a decision. Not that it really matters if he goes or not, but I just can't understand it. He was one of the keenest members of the party, and has been doubly so since he knew the real purpose of it all—he takes such an interest in little Dawn."

" It certainly *is* queer," Mary murmured. But inwardly she felt that John Martin must have some very good reason for his refusal. If he said he had more important business here, well then, he had. She entirely agreed with the Professor that either cross-questioning or argument would be useless.

Mary told Dawn the strange news as they went to bed that night. There was nothing private about it now, and she had heard all the rest of the party discussing the matter in astonished tones.

" I don't suppose it really makes any difference to Uncle David," she added. " Except that there will be an empty seat in one of the 'planes. Oh, Dawn!" She paused with hairbrush upraised. " If it wasn't for leaving you, how I wish I could snaffle that empty place!"

"Well, why don't you persuade them to let you?" Dawn lay in bed, with a large magazine held before her face, and only her voice emerged from behind it.

"For one thing I don't think Uncle would——"

"Well, *try* him!"

"But, Dawn, what about you?" Mary spoke with surprise.

"I don't mind—honestly!" She had dropped the magazine now, and showed very bright eyes and a slight flush in either cheek. "I really don't mind a scrap! I—I've got a lot to do, and I'd honestly feel far happier if you went. I'd hate to think of your missing a chance like that just to stay with me."

"Well, I'll jolly well have an attempt at it!" What on earth had Dawn got to do, Mary wondered? Composing new music, probably. Oh, when *would* she hear from England about that song?

Next morning Mary began her siege of the

Professor, and after half an hour of wheedling won her point. " After all, you are the real head of this expedition!" he admitted with a smile. " So I suppose you may as well see it to the end. I've engaged a third small supply 'plane to follow us half-way, and wait to be called up if necessary. We'll need it if we find him."

If we find him! Mary hugged the words close up against her heart. Now that it had happened she could scarcely believe that it was true—that she herself would soon set eyes upon the Valley of the Lukiang, and know the answer to its hidden mysteries.

CHAPTER IX

Dawn's Secret

The last day in Calcutta! That was the first thought that came into Mary's head as she opened sleepy eyes next morning to blink at the cheerful black face of their little servant woman grinning at her through the filmy mist of the mosquito curtain.

" Missy Sahib awake? Want chota-hazri?" It was the inevitable morning greeting of this quaint little black person, clad in a spotless white sari, with demure soft eyes, and teeth stained red by chewing betel-nut.

Through the raised blinds the brilliant sunshine of another perfect day blazed in on them, and Mary leapt up and stretched herself energetically.

" Well, what are we going to do to-day?" she demanded.

" Everything!" Dawn answered promptly.

She seemed so wideawake that Mary wondered with a pang how long it was since she last slept. "We've hardly been outside the garden yet, and as it's your last day I'm determined to see the whole of Calcutta!"

"To fortify you for to-morrow!"

"I'll need it."

"Yes, the pain of losing me will be something 'orrible!" Mary agreed lightly. "By the way, I'll have to creep out of the room to try not to disturb you to-morrow morning, for I believe we're starting about the crack of dawn!"

"There is no danger of your disturbing me, Mary."

Something in her tone made Mary pause and look at her anxiously. "How do you mean? There is nothing wrong——?"

"No, of course not! Mary—I'm going to tell you that secret of mine after breakfast, somewhere out in the garden where we're alone. But it's only if you make two promises!"

"Two promises?"

"First that we'll go out our sightseeing expedition immediately afterwards, and that

you won't let it make a scrap of difference to
our jolly day!"

" Of course not, if you want to!"

" And second, that you'll take what I tell
you like a Guide!"

" What *do* you mean?"

" Why—smile and sing!"

" Dawn, what *is* all this about?" Mary
demanded.

But she merely shook her head with a gay
" Buck up, my child, or we'll be late for breakfast!"

On the breakfast table Mary found some
home mail, and seized it up eagerly. One
glance revealed that the long awaited letter
from the publishers was not there, but there
was one from her father, and a very bulky
envelope in Dick's sprawly writing.

She opened her father's instantly, and
propped it up before her as she ate. What
would Dad say? This was the first time she
had been able to hear from him since writing
to tell him of the strange quest that Uncle
David had undertaken. For she had told her

father everything: those two always shared things, and in all her life Mary had had no secret from him. He wrote just as he would speak, so sanely, quietly, and with such a sure confidence in the ultimate goodness of everything, that she seemed to see his dear, familiar face behind the closely written pages.

" My heart and my blessing go with you, dearest," he ended. " If it be God's Will that you should find Colonel Clive, your prophetic words about the good your uncle's money was to do will have been more than justified. And if you fail—I still ask blessing on the spirit and the courage which lie behind this Great Adventure."

As Mary carefully folded the pages and looked up she noticed with a shock how tired and haggard Mrs. Donaldson was looking. Her face was very sad and strained, and there were lines as if from a sleepless night, beneath her eyes. This waiting must surely be getting on her nerves. Thank goodness it was to-morrow that they went.

As she opened her second letter Mary

chuckled to discover that it contained notes from the whole family. There was even a ' drawing " from wee Maureen, who was exceedingly fond of wielding a lavish pencil over large sheets of paper.

" Look at this from Hamish!" she laughed, throwing a page across to Dawn. " I'm sure it's still sticky and smells slightly of his favourite acid balls! Don't you love the end of it? ' Hope you is well, dere Mary, an bring me home an ellyfunt or some little present. Hunter has los my white mice.' He evidently thinks an elephant would be a more convenient size not to get lost in the back garden!"

" From the number of crossings-out I should say Hunter has been helping with the spelling!" Dawn grinned. " What has *he* got to say for himself, by the way?"

" Oh, much more reasonable; he merely inquires if I can't bring back ' some sort of Indian beast '! Probably thinks they roam about the streets of Calcutta in hordes!"

" And Dick?"

" His is bursting with Scout news—there

never *was* such an intelligent Patrol as the Beavers, you'll be glad to hear! But listen to how he ends up! ' Now that you are having all those wonderful adventures, which is not fair for a mere girl, don't you think you *could* persuade Uncle to take me on as a cabin boy or something? I know I'd make a good one, and I ought to be seeing the world a bit at my time of life!' "

" You can see his grey hairs sweeping to the ground, can't you? And I love his modesty!"

" Dick always was a modest violet!" Mary laughed. " Let's turn to Margaret's for a refreshing change!" As she read the final neatly written sheet Mary's lips twitched and she gurgled delightedly. " This *is* a change! She thanks me for the little gloves I sent her from Switzerland, but solemnly warns me not to be extravagant! Then tells me to take as many photos as I can, but be sure and keep the camera straight, as she thinks I'm rather inclined to spoil 'em by tilting it! Oh, isn't that *exactly* like Margaret! They are a priceless bunch—all different!"

" And how lucky you are to have them all."

Mary nodded emphatically. " And don't I know I am! But they're yours too, Dawn— every one of those letters sends *you* love— You're an adopted member of the wild Blair clan!"

" You bet I am!" Dawn smiled, as she handed back Hamish's grubby letter. " Give my greetings to the clansmen next time you write!"

When the meal was over, Mary wheeled Dawn's chair out into the garden, and they found a sheltered little arbour where no one was likely to disturb them. Mary's mind was still full of her letters from home, and she smiled happily as she curled herself up on a cane seat. " Fire ahead, old thing!" she smiled. " What's the big, dark secret you were plotting aboard the old *Wanderer*?"

But Dawn did not answer for a moment or two. She lay very still, with her big black eyes fastened on the faint heat haze shimmering in the blue distance, then slowly turned her head till her eyes met and held her friend's.

" The reason Dr. Martin is staying behind is to operate on me."

" *Operate* on you? But, Dawn, my dear——!" Mary's laughter had all gone now, and she leant forward tensely. " But why—how——?"

" It's this pain. I confessed to him about it, you see. At least I didn't really need to *tell* him, for he seemed to *know*; but when I'd admitted what he'd guessed was true, he made me tell him everything."

" And—and what does it mean?"

" He examined me thoroughly, and he says it means the important nerve centre in my spine has been only paralysed by the shock of that fall—not killed. I may—oh, Mary, I *may* walk again! But it is urgent that the operation should be done at once; he did not want another day's delay, but I persuaded him to wait until —to-morrow."

" Oh, Dawn, Dawn my dearest!" Something hard and bitter was constricting Mary's throat as she took Dawn's thin brown hand and held it tight between her own. " Why, *why* didn't you tell me before?"

" Because I'm a coward!" she murmured with her whimsical little upward twisting smile.

" A coward?"

" Yes, that's why I couldn't tell any of you. Even now you must please not say a word to your uncle or any of them—not until your 'planes are right up in the sky! You see, I'm really—horribly funking this. And I just *couldn't* have been brave if everyone was fussing and being sorry. Do you understand?"

" Of course I do. Thank you for telling me."

" I felt you just must know, for our last day together. I knew you'd keep your promise and ' smile and sing '."

" And your aunt?"

" Dr. Martin told her last night. He had to get her permission, as I have no parents."

Mary dropped her head upon her hands. Now she knew the reason for Mrs. Donaldson's haggard expression. No parents! How utterly ironical that this should have occurred on the eve of their departure on the final stage of the search for her missing father. But John Martin knew all that, and therefore he must feel the need for the operation to be very urgent, as he did not wait for the result of their expedition.

Dawn's cool little voice cut across the tangle of her thoughts. " I wish you wouldn't mind so much, Mary. It's going to be all right. Do you remember how I first met Dr. Martin?"

" Very well indeed."

" It was the Dawn Song that made us friends, that day when he made me play it to him as his ' wages ' in our back garden. Don't you think that may be sort of symbolical? That his friendship and help may mean the beginning of a *real* dawn—the dawn of new hope and happiness in my own life?"

" Oh yes, I *do*!" Mary had raised her head, and though her eyes were hot with tears, looked squarely into the brave yet pleading little face at her elbow. " It *is* the beginning of new happiness, more than you have ever dreamed. I'm *sure* it is." In her mind there was a picture of the two 'planes that would sail off into the blue at dawn next day, and somewhere, *somehow* bring Dawn's father back to her. Then she burst out aloud: " But oh, I cannot go and leave you to-morrow! You must let me stay!"

Dawn shook her head emphatically. " I want you to go; I was so glad that it worked out that way. I'll have Aunt Katherine with me, you know, but I—I won't be pleasant company for a day or two. I've had operations before, so I haven't any delusions! It's not the sort of illness where you want someone to sit and hold your hand—only to be left in peace. But I expect he'll keep me under morphia for a while. I'd so much rather you were away from all the unpleasant part of it; it'll make me happy to think of you flying through the sky. And see what a lot you'll have to tell me when you get back again!"

" Yes!" Mary whispered fervently, " Oh yes, I *must* bring you back—news."

" And now!" Dawn declared cheerfully, " we must get off on our sightseeing expedition, and we're not going to talk another word about this business until I go into the Home to-night!"

"To-night?"

"Yes—that's why I said you couldn't disturb me to-morrow morning! There is an English Nursing Home here that Dr. Martin knows, and I'm to be installed there this evening. He will operate early in the morning —soon after you have left."

Mary sprang hastily to her feet, she could not trust her control any longer. "Come on then! Shall we collect your aunt? I'm afraid Uncle and the rest of the party are off on business as usual."

On the stairs up to Mrs. Donaldson's room she met John Martin, and his strong brown face was quiet and serious as he laid a detaining hand upon her arm. "If it is Mrs. Donaldson you're going to, she is lying down. She knows you two are going out together, but told me to ask you to excuse her."

"This business is worrying her terribly, isn't it?"

"Dawn has been telling you?" The doctor folded his arms upon the banister and sighed. "Yes, she feels it keenly that this should happen just when her brother may be found. But it is impossible to wait. If Dawn is to have any chance in life, this risk must be taken—*now*. It is her only hope, and it ought to have been done when she felt the first signs of that pain."

" And just how much chance is there?" Mary's eyes looked squarely into his.

He answered her with the simple honesty she so much appreciated in him. " It's about fifty-fifty. If it's completely successful she will walk again, and if it fails—I don't think she'll be any worse."

" I see."

" And now if you're off sightseeing may I come with you? I know this place well, and we might even explore the native quarter; that would amuse Dawn."

" Rather, do come!"

They had a marvellous day, with John Martin as most entertaining " tourist's guide ". All three were determinedly and firmly cheerful, but Dawn in particular seemed so truly and genuinely merry that Mary found herself

joining naturally in her laughter. Her complete
trust and affection in Martin was good to see,
and it was evident that they understood each
other perfectly.

First of all they sampled the European
quarter; walking down the main street, called
Chowringhee, where were situated all the
Clubs and many excellent shops. This street
faces the Maidan, a huge park which contained
among other things a race-course and cricket
and football grounds.

" Lucky dogs!" Mary commented.   " We
need a place like that in Glasgow!"

An endless stream of motors and carriages
drove across the Red Road in this park; among
them occasional shabby tikka-gharries and
smart little dogcarts (locally known as tum-
tums); in fact, all Calcutta seemed to be taking
the air.

" Looks very English and civilized, doesn't
it?" Martin observed, " till one of those goes
past!"   And he nodded his head towards a
strange equipage, like a box on wheels, which
was crammed with dark-skinned men and boys,

most gorgeously clad in rich purple, scarlet, and gold.

"It is such a nice *clean*-looking place!" Mary exclaimed, gazing admiringly up a broad street of pillared houses, each standing back from the road in its own palm-shaded compound.

"She's always comparing it with Glasgow!" Dawn chuckled. "But what *I* want to see is the native part!"

"Your wishes shall be obeyed, madam!" Dr. Martin bowed.

It was certainly an exciting contrast, to turn from all this clean spaciousness and by merely walking a few yards down a side street suddenly find oneself in a nest of narrow, unpaved, dirty streets, lined with open booths where half-naked men squatted upon the ground, selling lumps of sticky sweetmeats, and piles of other peculiar eatables that looked rather like unbaked scones. And everywhere little naked babies sprawled and tumbled in the dust, indiscriminately mixed up with goats and puppies.

"Now I know," Dawn murmured faintly,

" just exactly what is meant by the perfume of the East!"

Thrilling though it all was, they were not sorry to return to their own side again, and eat a hearty meal in a big shop famed for its peculiarly delicious chocolate cake.

For the last walk of the evening Mrs. Donaldson joined them, and Dr. Martin suggested they should go along the Strand: the name of a carriage-way down by the river where the great ships lay at anchor. In silence they strolled along, eyes fixed on the spars and masts as they became silhouetted against a glory of red and yellow, while the sun sank to his rest.

The two girls had drawn a little ahead of the others, and Dawn spoke very quietly.

" I want you to know that I am not afraid. I'm only afraid of *being* afraid—can you understand?"

" Perfectly."

" When I have come through this, Mary—whichever way it ends—I think I shall be ready then to be a Guide. And perhaps, perhaps I shall be a *real* one!"

" You are that now, in spirit," Mary answered gruffly. " Oh, Dawn, if I could only help you through!"

The last flame of red died from the sky, and darkness fell almost at once, with that abruptness peculiar to the Eastern world. Dr. Martin came up now and took Dawn's chair, and they turned their steps towards the Nursing Home.

Mrs. Donaldson went in with her niece and the young doctor, but Mary waited outside. She felt that they had said their real farewells. Dawn waved a hand as she disappeared within the big glass doors, and called to her, " Best of good luck to-morrow!"

Best of good luck indeed, Mary's heart echoed. Oh, if Dawn had only known just what it was that she was wishing for!

Mary waited till Mrs. Donaldson came out, and they walked home together. For once that calm and self-reliant lady was in need of comfort and reassurance which she could give, and Mary told her again and again that she felt certain she had acted wisely. " The hope of finding Colonel Clive is altogether too vague and slight to have risked Dawn's whole chances of future happiness by waiting for it. Dr. Martin is a fine man, and she is quite safe in his hands."

Yet in spite of her own brave words Mary slept little that night. Dawn's empty bed was a continual mute reminder by her side, and the topsy-turvy chaos of her own thoughts made it impossible to rest or even lie still.

Very early next morning she got up and dressed herself in her warmest clothes, then swallowed a hasty breakfast brought up by a sleepy-eyed servant. A car had been ordered to drive her out to where the 'planes awaited them, and very soon she found herself struggling into a heavy leather coat and goggles, and settling into the low bucket seat of the open plane which was being used.

In spite of herself some of the thrill was returning to things. It was for Dawn that they were setting off on this high adventure; to seek for and bring back her lost father. Even if the operation failed, and she could bring *him* to her, nothing else would matter very much.

The Professor had finished his final instructions, and the pilot of the third little 'plane nodded and walked back to his machine. Hudson and the Swede were seated in the second 'plane, and now her uncle climbed in beside Mary. With a zoom of powerful engines the great bird glided over the ground, and rose surely and steadily into the air, its companion closely following behind.

" We're off!" Professor Blair called cheerfully. " Now for beyond the borders of Forbidden Tibet!"

CHAPTER X

Death in the Lukiang

They had established a base among the foothills of the Himalayas, and from there the pilots were to take it in turn to make reconnaissance flights across the range. From the supply 'plane some tents had been produced, and Mary found her Guide knowledge useful when it came to pitching her own small shelter.

An excellent supper was cooked upon oil stoves, then as the evening chill increased they gathered close round a bright camp-fire.

"I wish Martin were here," the Professor murmured. "This is the kind of adventure he adores."

"I can tell you now why he didn't come, Uncle." Mary hunched her knees up to her chin, and her eyes were fixed upon the flames. "He operated on Dawn this morning."

"On *Dawn*? My dear, don't look like that!"

172

His strong arm slipped around her shoulders, and Mary found to her surprise that she was shaking uncontrollably.

" It's cold up here," she excused herself. " Oh, Uncle, if only I knew how things had gone!"

" She's in the best possible hands, child; John Martin is a splendid man. Was it something urgent?"

She nodded. " Yes. He thinks he may make her walk again, but it had to be done at once. Dawn didn't want anyone to know, for she couldn't keep a stiff upper lip if people were sympathizing and talking about it."

" Aye, I can understand. She's a brave lassie. Like father like daughter, eh?"

" If we could only find him for her——"

" We shall, I have it in my bones to-night. We shall."

Then a hot drink and off to bed. Just like camp, Mary thought, as she paused in the doorway of her little tent. Except that here the snow-capped majesty of a colossal mountain range brooded behind them, and to the left lay the dark spreading patch of shadow which was their three aeroplanes.

She did not expect to sleep, but to her own surprise slept deep and dreamlessly. Last night's wakefulness, the new experience of flying, and the long hours in this strong air, combined together to produce an exhaustion so complete that for a time all thoughts and questionings were banished from her mind.

At dawn next morning the flights began again, and by the time Mary emerged from her tent she found that the men had both been up two or three times. One of the 'planes was just landing as she arrived, but the pilot shook his head as he clambered stiffly out of it. " No luck at all, sir. But Bates is still up there, and he may have struck on something."

" Well, come and have breakfast, all of you!" The Professor raised a heated face from his beloved cooking stoves. " Hullo, Mary, has the scent of bacon dragged the sleeping beauty from her bower? Come and help me serve!"

They were in the middle of the meal when the second 'plane returned. It made a perfect landing, then the pilot came towards them at a shambling run.

" I've found it, sir!   At least I think so! Flying low I saw what looked just like a deep black fissure in the mountain, just over the Tibetan side.   That'll be the valley, I should think, sir."

" Good work, Bates." The Professor spoke quietly, and showed little sign of the excitement Mary knew that he was feeling. " Have some bacon, man, then we'll get on the job."

Nobody took very long over finishing that meal, and ten minutes later the party was stowing themselves away in the two aeroplanes. Mary and her uncle went with the man Bates, and their 'plane rose first into the air, followed by the Swedish scientist and Hudson.

They flew low, once the crest had been crossed, and Mary peered down excitedly when their pilot pointed. " There!" he shouted. " No one could possibly notice unless they were looking for it. I'm going to shut off the engine and drop now—it is the only way."

The rocky walls of the valley reared up on

either side of them, and after its narrow entrance they abruptly widened out into a broad ravine. The pilot caught his engine into spluttering life once more, and almost before they had time to realize it the ground rose up to meet them and they landed gracefully upon a broad level green stretch.

" Here we are, then!" Professor Blair pressed her hand excitedly as he pulled off his goggles and gazed round. " That'll be the village back there and—my word, they're coming out to welcome us!"

Out of every pointed, beehive-looking hut a stream of dark-skinned men and women was pouring. They were clad in strange garments of rough, unbleached and homespun cotton; and many of the men seemed to wear a straight " one-piece " sort of robe down to their ankles, dyed a vivid crimson shade, from which their bare black heads and arms protruded in startling contrast. They had fine features, these people of the Lukiang, clean cut and shapely, with Mongolian cheekbones, and only a hint of the almond eyes of their Chinese neighbours.

" Uncle, I don't believe they *are* welcoming us!" Mary's voice was suddenly sharp. " They seem to me to be pretty angry about something."

" Aye, I believe you're right!" The party had clambered to the ground now, and the Professor's great fist closed convulsively as he put one arm around his niece. " Hi, Hudson! Come here, you two!" he called. " For goodness' sake try and speak to them—find out what lingo they use."

Mr. Hudson shouted out some words, but the natives crowded closer and closer till they formed a solid ring round the two aeroplanes, but at a respectful distance of a yard or two away from them. They were obviously more than half afraid of the white men and their machines: but equally obvious was their anger. A continuous wild muttering rose and fell like the surging of an angry sea, and occasional threatening cries and even brandished fists were raised from the background.

Mary gazed around the sullen faces in bewilderment. She had pulled off her tight helmet, and the slanting rays of sun touched her tousled fair hair with gold. Somehow a hostile reception was the last thing she had expected. Brown's description of how good the people of the Lukiang had been to them, and how they had treated himself and Colonel Clive as gods, had led her to expect the same welcome. And where *was* the Colonel? Crane her head in every direction as she would, Mary could see no sign of a white face among that mass of swarthy skins.

Suddenly she realized that the crowd was staring at her with especial curiosity. Several of the red-robed men had gathered in a group and were pointing at her and whispering together. Mary flushed uncomfortably and lowered her eyes. If only Mr. Hudson could make them understand.

He seemed to be having a little more success now, and was talking to the tallest and most imposing looking of the red-robed men. A chain of beads, made of some sort of large white seeds, around his neck, and a strange red monogram painted upon his high forehead, marked him off as a person of importance. The conversation necessitated a good deal of forcible gesturing and pointing on both sides, but it was obvious that they were beginning to understand each other.

At length Mr. Hudson turned to the others. "They speak a weird sort of variant of one of the Chinese dialects," he explained. "They have evidently developed a lot of their own words and phrases during the last few hundred years of isolation, which makes it exceedingly difficult to understand. This fellow is the Chief High Priest, it seems, and about the only thing that I *can* clearly gather from him is that we are to regard ourselves as prisoners."

"But why?" Professor Blair protested. "Where is the Colonel? Tell them, Hudson, that we have come to see the White Chief. Find out where on earth he's hiding."

Mr. Hudson spoke to them again, but after a few moments an angry roar arose from the people. He turned back to his own party and nervously mopped his heated face. " I've made them savvy that all right, but it doesn't seem to have improved the situation! The idea of our having come to see the White Chief seems to have put the final seal on their disapproval. I thought Miss Mary said he was popular with them?"

"But he was!" Mary protested in astonishment. "Brown told me that they treated him like a god."

The attitude of the natives was getting rapidly more threatening, and the Professor's jaw set grim beneath its short brown beard. "Tell 'em we're here on peace!" he shouted to Hudson. "My goodness, Mary, I ought never to have let you come."

Before Mr. Hudson could speak again the people of the Lukiang, led by their red-robed priests, had closed in on their unwelcome visitors and begun to half push and half lead them towards the village. The two young airmen were eager to resist, but the Professor called out to them to go peacefully. "We are hopelessly outnumbered. They have not used any violence to us yet, and I forbid any of you to raise a hand to them until they do. We are obviously on the right track, as they understood when we spoke of the White Chief—but where *is* he?"

The natives led them into the centre of their little village, and thrust them into one of the largest of the odd-shaped huts. Mary felt thankful that their anger was still so clearly mixed with fear, as otherwise she felt they might have been far more roughly used.

The hut in which they were put was a bare, circular place, with a trodden mud floor and a small opening high up in the wall for admitting light and air. A portion of the space was shut off by a rough curtain, and they indicated by gestures that this would do for Mary to retire in. It contained a sort of couch formed of a pile of skins, and when Mary sat on this a young native girl suddenly bowed herself to the ground before her. She touched the floor with her forehead several times, then uttered some words in a pleading almost imploring tone. It was clear that they were not nearly so angry with her as with the men, but Mary could not understand what favour it was that they were asking of her.

As soon as they were left alone she joined the others in the main part of the hut. They were talking together anxiously, but the Professor broke off to smile at her cheerfully.

" Glad to see they're treating you with some respect, old lady! Well, they've got a guard all round this place, so the only thing we can do is to sit and wait for what will happen next!"

As he spoke the flap was raised and some bowls of food were thrust through to them. There was a great mound of rice, a dish of berries, and a hollow gourd of water.

" So they're not going to starve us!" the Professor beamed. " Come on, you folks, fall to—for we're going to need all we can get."

When they had eaten, the tall Swede suggested he should lift Mary to the high window opening. " She is the lightest," he explained. " And on my back might see something that is happening."

Mary mounted on his shoulders and peered

out. At what she saw first she could not suppress a chuckle. " They're binding our aeroplanes down with something—but so *very* gingerly! Now and then they leap back a few yards as if afraid they're going to bite!"

" That wouldn't stop us," one of the airmen growled. " If I could get my engine going——!"

" Yes, but *why* are they doing it?" The Professor's tone was puzzled. " Why are they so determined to keep us here?"

" Oh, they're coming!" Mary cried excitedly. " A sort of procession of those men in red, the priests, with the High Priest leading them. He's got a sort of canopy thing being held over his head—oh, it's all very important looking!"

" For goodness' sake let's be ready for them!" the Professor exclaimed. " Hudson, find out why they're treating us like this, and where the Colonel is—these are the two things we must know."

A flood of light shot into the dim interior of the hut, as two brawny young men pulled aside the barrier and revealed the procession of priests. The High Priest gravely squatted down in the doorway, two attendants holding the clumsy canopy above him, and with a dignified gesture he conveyed his readiness to parley.

A long conversation followed between him and Mr. Hudson, while the others waited as patiently as they could manage. Mary watched the changing play of expression on their interpreter's face. He seemed to be making some headway at last.

" I'm getting to it now," he told them suddenly. " And the news is bad, I'm afraid. Their White Chief is very ill; delirious as far as I can make out, for they say ' his spirit is talking with many voices '. They are certainly devoted to him, for they seem terribly upset about it. The reason they were so angry with us is because they think our coming heralds his death. Remember, we are the only white men they have seen except Clive, and they think we have come in our Great Birds to carry him away into the sky. That's the idea of shutting us up and trying to tie the 'planes and all that. It's rather pathetic."

" Do assure them that they are wrong, that we are friends of their White Chief," the Professor urged. " And for pity's sake get us permission to see him, even under escort. We must get to him *somehow*. My goodness, I hope he's not too bad."

The interpreter got down to it again, but by the resolute expressions and vigorous head-shakings of the priests, Mary could see he was not having much success with his request. With a sudden inspiration she pulled off her flying goggles, which she still wore thrust up on her forehead, and with a friendly smile held them out to the High Priest.

Her gift made a deep impression upon the whole assembly. A murmur of excitement ran through their ranks, while their leader bowed low as he accepted it and solemnly squinted through each eyepiece; then turned and gabbled something to his followers.

" They're terribly pleased!" Mr. Hudson whispered quickly. " The old chap says it must be an omen that you should give him your ' second eyes '. I can't quite make out what they regard you as, but you're evidently very important." He plunged into his persuasions again, and this time was more favourably received.

"We can see him," he reported at length, "provided Mary leads the way. It's the best I can manage."

Mary felt her whole body go stiff and prickly with excitement. Now at last she was to see Dawn's father, whom they had come these many thousand miles to find.

The procession of the priests was forming again, with the white men in the middle of it and Mary at their head. Steadily they marched across the silent village, watched by eager eyes from every doorway, till they came to a hut which stood a little isolated and apart from the others. It was bigger than any of them, and had a much larger window cut out from the wall.

At the entrance the priests fell back and made a pathway for them. The Professor motioned to his companions. "The rest of you wait here. If the man's ill, Mary and I will be enough to go in to him. Lead the way, lassie."

Mary's mind was centred upon Dawn as she stooped her head to that low doorway. What was happening to her now in far-away Calcutta? Was she thinking of her at this moment? Or too ill to think of anything?

They heard Clive's voice, even before their eyes had sought him out in that dim light. He moaned and babbled incoherent words in the fever of delirium, and now and then his voice rose sharply to a shriller note. " Dawn!" he cried. " Where are you, little one?" Then dropped to moans again.

Mary ran across the room and dropped on her knees by the tossing figure on the primitive couch, forgetting all else in a rush of pity for this thin, pain-racked figure, with the brown face drawn and wasted by fever. She laid one hand on his hot forehead and whispered gentle, soothing words. He was so like Dawn—so like her, and so very, very ill.

A young boy crouched at the head of the bed, gently fanning him with a bundle of dried grass. His eyes expressed dumb misery, and turned on Mary with anxious appeal.

The Professor bent low over the bed. " Clive!"
he said slowly and distinctly. " Clive, we are
friends, white people, who have come to take
you back to your daughter."

But the spirit of Clifford Clive was far beyond reach of his voice. He only looked at
them with unseeing eyes and moaned again.

" He can't recognize us," the Professor
sighed. " I know nothing of doctoring, worse
luck, but it's obvious he is pretty bad."

" Oh, don't say we've come too late?" Mary
cried unsteadily.

A sound behind made them both look round.
The High Priest had entered, and with folded
arms stood frowning down on them. With a
sweeping gesture he motioned Mr. Hudson
forward, and spoke a few slow, hissing words.

The interpreter's face turned very pale as
he translated them. " He says that if Clive
dies, all of us will be slain also."

CHAPTER XI

The 'Plane Returns

" What *can* we do about it?" Back in their own hut the little party faced each other, white faced and anxious. " Apart from our own skins, the man is obviously very ill and we must do something."

" None of you have any medical knowledge, I suppose?" The Professor spoke appealingly, and glanced with a faint hope from face to face.

Mr. Hudson, the young Swedish scientist, and the two airmen all shook their heads hopelessly, while Mary made a little gesture of helplessness. " I've got my Guide Sick Nurse Badge, and I can *see* he's suffering from a fever of some sort—but we haven't even a thermometer!"

" We'll have to get John Martin here." Professor Blair spoke with the sudden brisk certainty of a man who has made up his mind. "If things have gone all right he should be able to leave Dawn by now, shouldn't he, Mary?"

"Well, soon, I suppose. But how on earth could you get him here?"

"Aye, that's the problem."

"We can't," Mr. Hudson declared flatly. "We're close prisoners and this place is surrounded again."

"I'm not suggesting we should escape, but 'can't' is a word that has never figured in my vocabulary." Mary noticed that her uncle's kindly eyes shone with a steely gleam that she had never seen before. "We shall have to leave openly, but these people love the Colonel so much that it ought to be possible to make them understand it is for his good. Somehow, Hudson, you have got to explain it to them that we are sending for a great medicine man who will make their White Chief well."

"If only one 'plane went and the rest of us stayed behind as hostages it *might* be possible——" Hudson spoke doubtfully.

" It has got to be. Not only may it mean his life but all of ours."

Mary shivered slightly. It was all so unreal and so strangely nightmarish. Her uncle's firm hand pressed against her shoulder. " And when that 'plane goes you'll go on it! Though they've treated you very decently, I've never ceased to call myself a fool for having brought you. You can take Martin's place with poor old Dawn."

Mr. Hudson had been talking to one of the guards outside the doorway, endeavouring to get him to take a message to the High Priest, and at length the fellow moved off to obey. " Now for it!" he grinned ruefully. " Mary, for goodness' sake sit by me and beam. That seems to have a good effect on 'em!"

The High Priest came surprisingly quickly, and they saw that he had emerged from Colonel Clive's hut. Underneath its mask of solemn gravity his face looked tired and strained. It was clear that he had a very real affection for the sick man.

Mr. Hudson, in a firm yet persuasive voice,

began to talk; and this time the Professor intervened with an odd word or so. "This lingo is not so very different from Chinese!" he smiled to Mary. "I'm beginning to get the hang of it already!"

But in spite of their united efforts this matter of allowing a 'plane to leave was not going to prove an easy one. Despairingly Mary saw the slow hand of her watch creep twice around the full white circle of its dial, while weary and stiff she still sat on: still tried to smile now and then upon the dusky potentate in the red gown.

Just when she felt that this rumbling of unintelligible voices must go on for ever, a decision was reached. Her uncle moved over to her, mopping his streaming face upon his handkerchief.

"Phew, I don't think I've ever worked so hard in my life! Well, we've won—but it's only a qualified victory. One man can go in one 'plane to fetch Dr. Martin, and the rest of us must stay here as hostages for his return. But the one thing they will *not* under any circumstances allow is for you to leave with him. You're far too precious to them!"

"Why am I? I don't in the least want to go, Uncle, but *why* do they regard me as different from the rest of you?"

"Well, I've discovered that too. It seems that in their old legends the Spirit of Life is a golden-haired maiden—as much of an imaginary and legendary being to them as it would be for us to think of a green-haired maiden. For you must remember that they have never seen anything but the straight black locks of their own race. So when you came along, and the sun conveniently shone upon your hair, you can imagine it caused some excitement! Your presence is the only good omen about us, for they are still afraid that our real purpose is to take Clive's spirit away in our Great Birds, so they feel that only by hanging on to you is there any hope for him."

Mr. Hudson came over to them. "Bates says he'll leave at once, Professor."

The young pilot nodded his head, and glanced from his watch to the lengthening shadows.

" It'll mean night flying most of the way, but if I can get clear of this and over the mountain before the light goes I'll be O.K. It's easy going after that. No time to be lost, though."

Mr. Hudson was already communicating their decision to the priests, a little group of whom now stood outside the door, and a moment later the whole party was being escorted out again to the aeroplanes.

The whole village gathered round to watch as Bates climbed into the cockpit, and a murmur of astonishment went up as the pull of the powerful engine snapped the fibre ropes with which the 'plane was bound. He turned and waved to them as it taxied along the ground. " Cheer up, folks, I'll have the doctor here in no time!"

Up and up he rose, to disappear between the towering walls of the valley. No wonder they had been unscalable by a lame man with a bad leg, Mary thought. The sheer rocky walls, covered with scanty vegetation, seemed to slope inwards towards each other, and at the top were jutting, overhanging ledges. It must have been a superhuman feat for Jim Brown to have accomplished.

" You're dead tired, my dear." Back in their hut her uncle pushed her gently towards the curtain. " Lie down and sleep—there's nothing more that any of us can do to-night."

But though the sleep of exhaustion descended on her immediately, her dreams were lurid and uneasy. Dawn was in them all; Dawn and her father constantly interchanging, and both tossing in pain and misery.

Next morning they were well fed, and told that Mary was at liberty to walk about the village. The men, however, it was made quite clear, must stay in their hut.

" You go, lass," the Professor advised. " Try to get in to Clive if they'll let you, for you may be able to do some little things to make him more comfortable. Come back and cheer the captives now and then!"

The bright sunshine outside made Mary blink after the gloom of the hut, and as she walked across towards Clive's hut she was very conscious of scores of curious eyes fastened on her. But no one attempted to stop her, and when she reached the doorway the screen was drawn aside by a lad who stood outside.

Colonel Clive seemed much the same as yesterday, but the atmosphere of the hut struck her as hot and stifling. Two young boys knelt sad-eyed by the bed, and to them she made the motions of drinking till they understood and brought her water. With her handkerchief wrung out in fresh cold water, she bathed his face and hands and laid the cool wet cloth across his temples, then rearranged the tumbled couch and settled him more comfortably.

The boys seemed eager to do anything she wished, so greatly daring she flung wide the heavily screened entrance of the hut, and by gestures made it clear she wished it to remain so. They bowed their heads obediently. Light and air came streaming into the twilit gloom of the hut, and Clifford Clive ceased moaning and sighed gently as a cool breeze touched his burning cheeks.

The girl whom Mary had seen yesterday

entered now, with a bowl of fresh goat's milk. She bowed low as she offered it to her, and bowed again, with grateful eagerness, as Mary accepted it with a smile.

Gently raising the sick man's head, she put the bowl to his lips, and to her great delight he swallowed a few sips of it before turning aside.

There seemed nothing more now that she could do for him, so leaving the little boys vigorously wielding their impromptu fans, she wandered out into the air again.

If they returned immediately, Dr. Martin should be here to-night. Anxiously Mary looked up at the blue sky, as if half expecting to catch sight of him already. Oh, if only she knew how Dawn was getting on! Wearily she passed a hand across her aching eyes. What æons of time it seemed since she had said good-bye to her outside the Nursing Home.

Resolutely Mary thrust these thoughts to the background of her mind, and set herself to exploring this strange village of the people of the Lukiang; she owed it to her uncle to be able at least to *tell* him something of all this that he had come so far to see.

The village consisted of about two score of the pointed beehive huts: strange, primitive erections built of a hard clayey mud, plastered outside with fibrous grass and branches. In these small dwellings whole families lived and slept and fed themselves, and the little naked babies played and rolled about the ground outside. In this respect it reminded Mary of the native quarter of Calcutta, except that here the children and their surroundings were clean.

Both in the people and their houses Mary found a surprising degree of cleanliness; which, though she did not know it then, was largely due to Colonel Clive's influence. During the years he had spent with these simple folk he had taught them many things, and had done much to improve their health and conditions of life.

In some of the huts she found the women working at primitive hand-looms and spinning-wheels, weaving the coarse cloth of which their garments were made. She also watched with interest the dyeing of one of the red robes that the priests wore. It was done by the juice of a small berry that grew near. The children collected great quantities of it and they were boiled in water, then the cloth thrust into the crimson brew thus obtained.

But it was the strange rock temple that fascinated Mary most of all. She had wandered out of the actual streets of huts, looking with interest at the cultivated fields which stretched on either side of the village, when she first noticed it. The original settlers here, long, long ago, had taken advantage of a natural cave in one rocky wall of their valley, and gradually through successive generations had further excavated and enlarged it. The place was now a lofty and remarkable cavern, richly decorated with frescoes and carvings in the living rock. At the further end a squatting, Buddha-like image, roughly but forcefully hewn, completed a temple of primitive art which she felt sure would have caused her uncle endless excitement and delight.

In between these explorations Mary made

frequent returns to the other captive members of her party, but her accounts of all she had seen hardly served to rouse Professor Blair's despondent spirits.

" If I could only see it!" he groaned. " It sounds *too* perfect and unspoilt, the sort of place I've been looking for all my life, and now I'm shut up and can't get to it!"

" Wait till Dr. Martin comes and makes the Colonel better, they'll trust you then, Uncle! Do you think he will be here to-night?"

" Aye, I should say so, lassie."

Restlessly she wandered out again and back to Clive, to renew the wet head-cloth and help him drink.

But darkness began to fall, and still there was no sign of the returning 'plane. Mary's anxieties increased with every hour, and she stayed gazing helplessly up at the sky till her uncle called her in.

" They won't come now. Impossible to make a landing here after dark."

" But what can have happened?" she asked miserably.

" Och, nothing, lass. Something's kept him and he's just not been able to leave at once."

" But the only thing that can have kept him is Dawn. I'm so terrified it means that she is worse."

They all tried to reassure her, but Mary slept very little that night, and was out soon after daybreak next morning. Slowly the long hours of the second day of waiting crept past, with no sign of the return. Mary had ceased to find any interest in her surroundings, as between her thoughts of Dawn and her father her mind and nerves were on one continual rack of doubt and worry.

The evening shadows were beginning to lengthen again when a faint buzzing sound brought half the village out to gaze skywards, and Mary in the midst of them. It was the 'plane! With eager eyes she watched while it came swooping down, then skidded to a gentle halt beside its bound companion.

Breathlessly Mary rushed forward to meet them. A weary-looking Bates climbed stiffly from the cockpit; and on his heels came John

Martin, smiling at her cheerfully, but with heavy lines beneath his eyes and a face both tired and haggard looking.

" Oh, you've come at last——!"

" Engine trouble," the pilot explained briefly. " Had to come down at our base camp, and it was yesterday evening before I could get away. I flew to Calcutta overnight. Dr. Martin hadn't been in bed, but after I'd had a couple of hours' sleep he came with me right away."

" Oh, how is Dawn?" Mary could contain herself no longer.

" Heaps better!" Dr. Martin smiled at her. " I won't say it hasn't been an anxious business, and the first two or three days were the critical ones, but she's going to be all right."

" And it's successful?"

" Completely so, I think. I have every hope that she will walk again!"

" I'm so glad that I could cry!" In an over-whelming rush of relief and happiness Mary flung her arms round Dr. Martin's waist and hugged him heartily. " I'll just never be able to thank you properly, for I *do* love Dawn."

" So do I, my dear! And I want to tell you she's been *marvellously* plucky. Now take me to her father."

She led him to the door of the hut and watched him bend his long back to its low entrance, then fled to tell the others the news.

Martin joined them half an hour later. " What do you think of him?" the Professor inquired, after greetings had been exchanged.

" Oh, it's not nearly so alarming as it looks. One of those nasty ' foreign fevers ' as my old chief used to call 'em! He'd certainly have got worse without proper attention, but I've filled him up with quinine and done everything possible, and he's sleeping peacefully. There's no real danger now. I hope he'll be well enough to tell him about Dawn to-morrow."

" That will help?"

" Give him something to live *for*—at present he's making no effort."

Very deliberately John Martin stretched himself out on the rough mud floor and pillowed his head upon his instrument case. " Now I'm going to *sleep*!" he announced. " And anybody who rouses me for the next ten hours will be cold-bloodedly slaughtered!"

Next day the Professor and his party were allowed to leave their hut and wander as freely as Mary did. The attitude of the natives had undergone a complete change with Martin's arrival, for they realized that these men *were* doing their best for their beloved White Chief, and saw that the white medicine man's magic had already made a big improvement in him. Smiling faces and eager friendliness now met them everywhere; and the Professor, his anxiety about Clive relieved, was in a state of blissful happiness exploring and working with his two companions. The natives had christened him the Hairy Chief, and seemed to find his antics most amusing.

That afternoon Martin broke the news to the now conscious Colonel that his daughter was alive. He was with him for a long time, and when he came out Mary saw that his eyes were suspiciously bright and moist.

" Poor fellow! He simply wouldn't believe it was true at first, but when I'd told him every detail his joy was almost uncontrollable. He'll get well now all right, for his one thought and desire is to get strong and to go back to her. He must rest a while, but this evening you can go in and see him."

When she first entered his hut Mary felt that almost a miracle must have happened to improve him so. Bright-eyed and eager, though still very thin and weak, he struggled to sit up as she bent over him.

" Your uncle tells me I owe all this to you!" he smiled. " I owe you more than I can ever repay, or ever deserved."

" Nonsense!"

" It was cowardly to run away from life and stay on here, but I did not *want* life without Dawn." He pressed her hand. " Thank you for all you have done for my poor lass. Dr. Martin has told me a little of what you have meant to her."

Several more days passed peacefully in the Valley of the Lukiang, while Colonel Clive rapidly fought back to strength again. Every morning their third small aeroplane circled over the valley, waiting for the signal which would tell it to land and would mean the Colonel was ready to journey back to civilization.

"Won't be long now!" the Professor said one morning cheerfully, as he watched it flying away. "I'm coming back again though with a fresh expedition. There's months of work waiting here."

"Are you so sure it won't be long now?" Mr. Hudson spoke very gravely. "Have you ever considered how we're going to get Clive away from here? How we're going to make the natives let him go? You know what they were like at the beginning when they thought we'd come to steal him—why should they take it any better this time?"

CHAPTER XII

Glasgow Once More!

It was left to Colonel Clifford Clive himself to settle the method of his own departure.

"As soon as I can stand I'll call a meeting of the whole crowd of them in the temple," he explained. "It'll have to be done by reasoning and explaining, there is no other way. You found that when it came to being allowed to send for Dr. Martin."

"Yes." Mary was sitting cross-legged by his bed, while her uncle sprawled lazily against the wall. There were no chairs among the Lukiang. "They'll be terribly upset at losing you. Now I'm beginning to talk to the folks a bit, I can see how much they love you."

"I've been their father confessor, schoolmaster, and health visitor combined for two years! But really, Mary, it's that affection that I'm counting on; I've got to make them

14   207   (H 21)

understand that you have called me back to older loyalties, and to a life that I had thought was dead and gone."

"You can tell them I'm returning—if that's any consolation to 'em!" the Professor rumbled.

"We have got to bring them more than that." The Colonel was sitting upright, his lean brown hands clasped round his knees. "Now that this valley has been discovered by civilization, we have got to bring to them Christianity and a teacher of its Gospel. The original founders of this little colony were Lhasa monks who fled their monastery because they sought a purer faith. They have been long in finding it, but surely the reward of all their seeking is coming to them now."

"That's a thrilling thought!" Mary whispered.

"They are good people," he said simply. "I have done my utmost to prepare the ground; it is fallow now, but it needs a greater hand than mine to sow the seed."

So on the first day that he was well enough to walk on his own legs, Colonel Clive interviewed the High Priest and arranged for him to summon a meeting of all the village in the temple that afternoon.

It was an extraordinarily picturesque sight, and one which Mary was never to forget. They formed into a long procession, every man, woman, and child in the hidden village, and led by their red-robed priests, with Clive limping in the midst of them, marched out to the rock temple. The Professor and his party brought up the rear, and a thin, high chanting drifted back to their ears as the priests intoned some ancient invocation which floated like a wraith on the clear air.

When they entered the cavern the orderly crowd spread themselves out in silent rows, all kneeling on the ground. Clive was the only one left standing, and his tall form dominated them all, as leaning heavily upon his stick he looked with sad eyes at those simple folk with whom he had made his home.

When he began to speak, the Professor rapidly translated the gist of what he said in Mary's ear. He spoke in the language of metaphors, which they best understood, and his voice was vibrant with deep feeling.

He told them that the White Spirit of Life (and Mary felt eyes turning upon her yellow hair!) had come to tell him that his daughter whom he had thought dead was still alive, and was needing him. " And I must go to her, my people," he said quietly. " For her name is Dawn; and is it not fitting that the people of the Lukiang, which means Servants of the Dawn or Morning, should serve this little White Dawn Maiden? I ask you to serve her by sacrifice— the sacrifice of letting me go from you. But you will not be left alone, for the Hairy Chief is returning to you, and will bring with him many good gifts and rare treasures in his Great Birds. But the rarest treasure which white men will bring to you can only be won by those who tread the Road of Sacrifice. By the answer that you give me now, O People, you will prove your love for me. Let it not be shown a little thing."

Mary found herself holding her breath in the silence which followed on his words. Bowing themselves rhythmically to and fro, the priests were consulting their gods, and a ceaseless wailing sound arose from them. Real tears ran down many of their faces.

At length the High Priest rose to his feet, flung one arm on high, and uttered a few sonorous words.

" He says," the Professor translated, " ' The White Chief must go. Our blessing goes with him.' "

" I'd never have thought it possible!" Mr. Hudson gasped. " He has great personal magnetism."

" It is because they love him," Mary said simply.

Next morning they signalled to the circling aeroplane to land, and amid a scene of great bustle and activity the whole party packed themselves aboard the three 'planes. Colonel Clive went with Mary in Bates' machine, and the Professor and Dr. Martin occupied the third one. The people of the Lukiang pressed close around their White Chief in farewell, and many of the women were weeping. He stood

up and called a greeting to them. " Good-
bye, and thank you for all your goodness to
me. The Hairy Chief will return and bring
you many good things: yes, even the one Great
Gift which I have promised, for your hearts
are ready for it now."

Then they were off. In a few moments the
hidden valley and even the mountains themselves had been left behind, and they turned
their faces towards Calcutta.

" My mind can still hardly credit that I'm
going to Dawn!" the Colonel exclaimed. " Tell
me again about how you discovered poor Jim
Brown."

Mary repeated her story of that accidental
encounter in the sanatorium grounds; and he
nodded his head.

" Poor fellow, he was never strong. But a
fine mechanic and a plucky lad. What a lot
I do owe to you, little friend."

" Not one quarter what you owe to Dr.
Martin. It is he who is making Dawn walk
again."

" It is terrible to think of all she has gone

through in these last years. To me it is almost impossible to picture that restless, nimble sprite—not walking."

Mary did not answer. For her it was equally difficult to picture Dawn standing erect—but oh, how she *longed* to see her doing it.

It was late evening when they returned to their hotel, and the famous airman was re-united to his sister. Mrs. Donaldson wept tears of happiness as she clasped his thin travel-stained form, but knowing where his thoughts must be she spoke immediately of Dawn.

" You'll see her to-morrow, Clifford! We'll have to break the news to her first, as I haven't dared say anything yet." She turned to Dr. Martin. " She's getting on so splendidly! Sitting up in bed and as bright as a button— oh, to think it's two years since I've seen her *sit!*"

Dr. Martin was chosen to break the wonder-ful news to his little patient, and he went to the Nursing Home first thing next morning. Colonel Clive, Mrs. Donaldson, and Mary followed him, and sat waiting in an outer room. Presently he returned and beckoned to the Colonel, and Mary and Mrs. Donaldson were left alone.

They sat in silence for a while, and Mary's mind was very far away in the realms of thought. She was picturing that meeting between father and daughter who had each thought of the other as dead, and who had both been through so many and such terrible experiences since last they met. Suddenly Mrs. Donaldson gave a little exclamation.

" My dear, I'm carrying a letter of yours about with me in my bag! It came while you were away, and I put it in here not to forget it." She pulled a long envelope from her bag and smiled at its generous smothering of postmarks. " It seems to have been following us half round the world! Your people re-addressed it to Switzerland, and it just missed us there and seems to have been trying to catch up ever since!"

Mary took the letter and slit it open without much interest, then glanced carelessly at the printed sheet of paper it contained. Suddenly she stiffened and uttered a low whistle of excitement. " Crikey Christopher, it's come at last!"

The letter was from the music publishers, accepting the Dawn Song for publication at very generous rates, and hoping to be allowed to see further specimens of the author's work.

She told Mrs. Donaldson at once, and she was utterly amazed and delighted that her little niece's work should have been found worthy of print. They were still discussing it excitedly when Dr. Martin returned to them.

" You can go in and see her now, Mary. She really shouldn't have any more visitors, but naturally after all this time won't rest content until she sees you! But I don't think she had better see anyone more until later in the day," he added to Mrs. Donaldson, who nodded understandingly.

Mary followed John Martin's tall form down a clean white-painted corridor, her nostrils contracting at the unfamiliar smell of disinfectants and chloroform, and entered for the first time the bright and bare little room where Dawn had gone through her last ordeal.

How strange it was to see her sitting up in bed! Bolt upright, her cheeks flushed with excitement, her eyes like stars, a radiant Dawn swung round to welcome her. Colonel Clive sat close by her bed, his arm around his daughter's shoulders as if he could never bear to let her go again; and their two faces so near together, one tanned, one pale, presented a united picture of utter and inarticulate joy that brought a lump into Mary's throat.

" Mary!" Dawn threw out her hands towards her in an eager little gesture. " Oh, come and pinch me and make me sure I'm real!"

" We're both black and blue from pinching each other already!" Colonel Clive laughed. " But perhaps you could do it even harder!"

As she perched on the bed Dawn caught her hand and held it for a long moment of silence. " The three of us together," she whispered. " How often have I dreamt of this, as one dreams and longs for a thing that can never, never be. Mary, I'm not going to begin to try to thank you, for it will take my whole life-time to even start doing that."

"Nonsense, Dawn! It has just been luck—chance—what you will—that has put all this into my hands. It has been the biggest adventure, and the biggest privilege, of my life. Dr. Martin is the only person you have got to *thank* for anything."

"But even meeting him I owe to you—that day we hiked to Bearsden together, and poor old Dick burnt his foot. *Everything* traces back to you in the end, my dearest—Safety Valve!"

"If you'll stop talking piffle I've another surprise for you!" She laughed and thrust the letter into Dawn's hands. "Read that—and then I'll do some more pinching!"

The Colonel and his daughter read the letter together, and an explosive gasp burst from Dawn as she finished it.

"My Dawn Song to be *published?*" she gasped. "But how did they *get* it?"

"I sent it to them, of course! This is the solution of the mystery letter I was always waiting for—so now we have no more secrets!

And now perhaps you'll have to admit that *I* was right!"

" But what's all this about?" the Colonel demanded. " Has this infant been developing into a *composer* in my absence?"

" No, of course I haven't!" Dawn exclaimed. " I only think of tunes—and it's *this* child that's been writing them down!"

" Perhaps you'll engage me for your secretary one day, if you're not at the stage of dictating your songs straight into a dictaphone!" Mary chuckled. " Or can one dictate music?"

Dr. Martin came in then, to tell the visitors it was time to leave, and of course had to be shown the amazing letter.

" At last I am justified!" he declared. " Not for nothing did I call myself a musician—at least Mary believed me, if you didn't!"

" Mary again—the infallible one!" Dawn teased. But Mary saw she only laughed to keep the tears which filled her eyes from welling over.

Colonel Clive spent the whole of his days at the Nursing Home after that, and Mary joined them for a great deal of the time. The father and daughter had so much to talk about and to tell each other that their tongues wagged ceaselessly, but they always seemed to want Mary to be with them. It was a case where three *was* company, and Mary soon began to feel for Colonel Clive an affection only second to that for her own father.

Then came the great day when Dawn first left her bed and tried to walk. Slow progress at first between two nurses, but gradually she grew stronger and more sure of herself, till she was sitting up with her clothes on all day and making little excursions round about the room alone.

Oh, what a wonder and a joy it was! A joy so great that neither Mary nor Dawn managed to speak of it very much, but strove to hide the uncomfortable depth of their feelings under laughter and jokes.

Only one evening when they sat alone together did Dawn whisper softly: "We're still at the *beginning*, Mary, the beginning of a real life together. Dad says that of course I shall go to your school when we are home. And—and will you have me in your Guides?"

"You were made an honorary Speedwell long ago! Do you remember the concert you gave for them in our garden, in the dim past?"

"Long, long ago! Can you believe it is really only a few months? What an odd, unhappy little person I was then, and how patient you were with me!"

"You taught me far more than I ever taught you, Dawn."

Dawn smiled. "Well, you've got to do all the teaching now, Mary! Teach me how to be an ordinary schoolgirl, for I'm afraid I've forgotten quite a lot in these last years! Oh, but you don't know what it is to be looking *forward* to life again, not dreading the length of days any more. To have Daddy back, and my legs back—oh, Mary!"

Now the day for their return was settled, and when it came Dawn *walked* aboard the scrubbed decks of the dear old *Wanderer*; walked aboard the ship from which she had been carried on her stretcher chair when they berthed at

Calcutta. And she was leaning on the arms of Mary and her father: the father whom she had never expected then to see again.

The voyage back to Scotland was a very happy and merry one; and Mary and Dawn revisited, walking arm in arm, those places which Dawn had last explored lying flat upon her back.

She was a tall slip of a thing, well above Mary's shoulder though only twelve years old, for her years of lying had " stretched " her most amazingly. Tall and slim and graceful, Mary thought as she watched her with quiet pride. The colour daily growing in her cheeks and the shadows gone for ever from those big black eyes that sparkled now with joy and merriment.

Then they were sailing up the dear, familiar River Clyde, while Mary raced from side to side identifying well-known landmarks. But the actual reception when they reached the docks amazed and bewildered them. Somehow neither Mary nor Dawn had realized that the news of the dramatic discovery of the missing Colonel Clive had been flung by wireless to the far ends of the earth, and that all Glasgow waited eagerly to welcome back a hero whom they had thought dead.

A seething crowd of people fought around them as the gangway was lowered; pressmen clamoured for " just a few more details, please "; and cameras clicked unceasingly. Dawn had to face a regular battery of them, clinging to her father's arm, and emerged from the ordeal with an " Ouff!" of thankfulness.

" It's a distressing business having such a popular parent!" she grinned. " Will they always follow us about?"

" Oh, not for long! A respectable middle-aged gentleman with a limp will soon cease to be of any interest to them!"

" So you're never going to fly any more?"

" Never any more." He squeezed her arm. " My dear, do you think I'd ever leave you again? I've had enough of roving and am more than content to settle down with you and Aunt Katherine."

Then Mary saw the family, trying to make

their way towards them, at the same time as she caught Dick's lusty bellow from another direction. There he was, burrowing towards them, resplendent in Scout uniform and with five other boys upon his heels.

"Hullo!" he panted, "I've brought my Patrol to meet Colonel Clive! We had top marks in the Troop competition, and that's the prize we chose. Whew, is that sunburn or dirt you're covered in?" A typical brotherly greeting that made Mary know she really was home at last.

Now her father's arms were around her, and Mother, Maureen, and Hamish were all being hugged and kissed; while Hunter demanded to know what it *felt* like to go up in an aeroplane, and Margaret proudly displayed the scarf that she had sent her from Port Said. . . . What a marvellous, triumphal homecoming, with Dawn walking for the first time up the steps of her own home. . . .

A few months later Professor Blair set off again, with a new expedition, to examine the ancient culture of the people of the Lukiang;

but Colonel Clive showed no inclination to go with him. He had settled down happily and contentedly at No. 11, with his sister and Dawn.

Dawn was at school now; at school, and a Guide. A member of Mary's Speedwells at long last. She still continued composing music too, in " odd moments ", but the Dawn Song remained her own and Mary's favourite, and she played it very often when they met together.

" I love it," she murmured one evening, as the last soft notes died away and she laid aside her violin. " I love it for what it has meant to us since the day when I first played it. It has been a real ' Dawn Song ', hasn't it, Mary? The beginning of new life and new hope—a whole new world."

Mary nodded. " ' Every day a new dawn '," she quoted softly from the song. " We're *still* at the beginning, partner!"

" Of course!" Dawn smiled. " Guides are always at the beginning of adventures!"

The Island Camp
by
Margaret Middleton

ABOUT THIS STORY

Mysterious incidents begin almost at once to vary the routine of the Guide Camp and strange footmarks are found in the morning dew.

The big house nearby—a friendly house in other years —has new tenants who have no interest in Guides, regarding them rather as trespassers. Soon some of the girls realize that the camp is being spied upon, and start some counter-espionage which quickly involves them in unexpected excitements and more serious matters than they had bargained for. The climax is almost too thrilling for those closely concerned, but all ends well. Ordinary camp life and humour and mishaps form the background of this tale of mystery, and the Guides and Guiders are a lively and likeable lot.

Contents

To My Mother

" When love is an unerring light
And joy its own security."

THE ISLAND CAMP

CHAPTER I

The Lone Camp

Philippa Fleming sat astride her kitbag and tugged impatiently at the lace of her shoe, which had run into a knot. Behind her, under the rather scanty cover of a hedge, a figure submerged in a tangle of navy-blue garments was changing from its best uniform into a camp overall; and a score of yards away a third girl knelt, cutting the turf from a fireplace with a big sheath knife. A faint smell of wood smoke lingered in the air, and from beyond the hedge came the sound of voices and laughter, and the wooden knocking of mallet on tent peg.

Around Philippa, the grass was strewn with odds and ends of luggage, hurriedly dumped and as hurriedly opened, and the long shadows thrown by the evening sun had the effect of making each dump look twice its natural size. Philippa frowned as, after triumphing over the knot, she straightened herself to peel off her stocking.

"How are the others getting on, Joe?" she called to the girl at the fireplace. "Can you see?"

Joe Hamilton sat back on her heels, one earthy hand propping a thick roll of turf. The ground was on a slope, and in spite of the hedge a part of the neighbouring field was visible from where she knelt.

"One tent is up," she said, craning her neck, "and two are spread out on the farther side. I can't see this side because of the hedge, but Jean and Billy are using mallets. Their fire is built. I can hear the sticks crackling, and there is a very thin puff of smoke going straight up into the air."

Philippa gave another glance at the littered field, and frowned again as she pulled off her second stocking and plunged an exploratory hand into the kitbag in search of her plimsoles. With the company pitching camp was an orderly affair. Seconds went to help Q.M., while the rest of the patrol put up the tent, filled their palliasses, made their beds, unpacked, fetched a little wood, or water; and then, miraculously, supper was ready, the washing-up water was on, and camp was pitched and tidy.

Philippa rose, and hurrying barefoot up the field snatched a loaf of bread, a packet of butter, and some loosely wrapped slices of ham out of the reach of Joe's heels.

" You are dropping worms all over the place," she said, as that young woman waved a protesting sheath knife. " You roll those turfs about without a thought of where they are going."

Joe looked at her as haughtily as a hot and not too clean face would allow, then, without deigning to reply, turned her head.

" Hie!" she shouted over her shoulder. " Hester! Come and help me to do the work. Philippa has begun tidying."

The girl by the hedge gathered up her discarded uniform and dropped it on a pile of tightly rolled bedding.

" Not a bad idea in its way, tidying," she observed, as she approached. " But have you noticed that Philippa always tidies small things, things that are no trouble, such as potted meat jars, or billies somebody else has cleaned. Anything large or heavy, turfs, for instance, she seems to overlook. Now I, on the other hand——"

Hester stooped, and with a flourish picked up a fat sod and stumbled with it towards a ditch near-by. Unfortunately, she had reckoned without the very real weight of her burden. Joe's warning cry came too late. The turf unrolled, as turfs will in careless hands, and fell on her feet in crumbling jagged pieces, and the next moment Hester had fled across the field with Joe in irate pursuit.

Philippa watched them for a moment, Hester long and slender, leaping over the dumps of kit like a young gazelle, Joe square and sturdy, panting behind like an indignant bull, then, with a little shrug of her shoulders, continued to tidy. She spread a ground-sheet on the grass beneath an oak tree, dragged a box of stores towards it, and lifted a bread board on to the box to make a supper table. On a second ground-sheet she gathered up a collection of hats, haversacks, shoes, stockings, ties, a piece of soap, a number of tent pegs, and a canvas water bucket, and hid the whole pile from view under Hester's mackintosh. She carried two more of Joe's sods to the edge of the ditch and laid them down with gingerly care in the shade of an elder bush; and with four pegs and a small plank she found under the hedge, she made a stand upon which she arranged the billy cans and other kitchen dishes in a neat row.

" There," she said, stepping back and admiring her handiwork as Joe, puffing and panting, returned to squat once more beside the fireplace, " that is better, isn't it? How hot you look; almost hot enough to cook on. The Tartars do, you know—use themselves for cooking on, I mean. They put their joint of yak or llama or whatever it is on their saddles and then they sit on it and go for a long ride, and when they come back it is as tender as a grilled steak—at least so I have been told. Such a convenient idea. No bother with fires and frying pans, though for fussy people there might be drawbacks."

Joe, busy at her turfing, gave the grass an exasperated stab with her knife. She had wasted ten good minutes chasing Hester and now, with the evening drawing on, and with no fire to cook over, no tent to shelter them, no beds to sleep in, without wood, or water, or any of the other necessities of camp life, she felt in no mood to follow Philippa into a discussion upon Tartars and their habits.

" Do get hold of Hester and start on the tent," she implored. " We shall be so desperately late."

Philippa glanced at her wrist watch, gave a little exclamation, and set to work in a businesslike fashion on the knots of the tent sack. Between them, she and Hester pulled the tent from its bag, tipped out the pegs and counted them, and spread the canvas, umbrella-wise, in a circle on the ground, lacing the door, and stretching out the guylines to their utmost till they looked like the tentacles of a round white octopus. A silence fell. All three girls became absorbed in their jobs, working with a zeal that suggested slight qualms of conscience, while their shadows, growing steadily longer, slanted across the white fabric of the tent like the pointing fingers of a stern schoolmistress.

It was Philippa who broke the silence, stopping suddenly with upraised mallet in the very act of driving in a peg.

" Late!" she exclaimed, echoing the word Joe had spoken a full quarter of an hour before. " Late! But what for?"

" Supper, of course," Joe said, surprised no less by the tone of her voice than by the obviousness of her question.

" Supper!" Philippa, with a wave of her mallet, put suppers in their place. " Supper! They "—she pointed towards the hedge—" may have to hurry. They have supper at eight o'clock precisely and no dawdling. But we can have it when we like—now, or at midnight, or to-morrow morning. This is *our* camp."

Deliberately she dropped her mallet, sat down on the half-pegged-out tent, and stretching for her kitbag began a really satisfactory and exhaustive search for her plimsoles. The others watched her, blankly at first, then with a slowly dawning interest on their faces.

" I never thought of it like that," Hester said. " It *is* our camp. I believe this notion of Captain's is going to be better fun than we expected. Why "— Hester, following Philippa's example, threw her mallet on to the grass and lay down at full length on the tent, with her hands clasped behind her head— " it isn't just not being late for things. We can do any mortal thing we want to, and nothing we don't."

" What about the others?" asked Joe. " Your

patrols may be meek little ba-lambs, but if mine look over the hedge and see us all behindhand they will have something to say about it, and they won't say it tactfully, not a bit."

" And is it our fault if we are behindhand?" retorted Hester. " Didn't we help to unload the lorry and unpack the kitchen stuff while they went straight off to do their tents? Besides, who cares for the others. Mere children! ' They say. What say they? Let them say.' "

Joe, after a moment's thought, murmured " Umph!" and continued to build her fireplace. She could not help wondering how much Hester really would " Let them say ", if it came to the point. Moreover, knowing her captain, she felt that there might be more in this apparent freedom than met the eye.

The feeling was increased when, a little while later, Pamela Aldwyn herself strolled through the gate in the hedge to see how they were getting on. Hester and Philippa got up rather hastily to meet her. They had once or twice heard their captain express her opinion of laziness, and they were not sure whether they could explain the subtle difference between being lazy, as opposed to simply doing what one liked. Mrs. Aldwyn made no comment, however, but sat down beside Philippa, as if an unpitched tent were the most natural seat in the world.

" I have come round for a breather," she told them,

putting Philippa's half-empty kitbag behind her and leaning against it. " Things are going very well over there, but there is a good deal of gentle prodding to do, and it is pleasant to get away from the bustle. That is a good piece of turfing, Joe. No fear of scorching the edges on a square that size. Did you do it all?"

" She did," Hester said, before Joe had time to speak. " She has done it quite nicely, though she was a little clumsy with the first sod, let it fall to pieces, dropped it, you know."

" I see. And you caught it as it fell." Mrs. Aldwyn's eyes twinkled as she looked at the dusty brown streaks on Hester's overall. " It is a comfort to know that you two are here, helping poor Joe through her difficulties. And how are you enjoying yourselves?"

The three girls exchanged cautious glances.

" Very much," Philippa answered after a slight pause. " It is rather jolly not having to hurry over things."

" We are having supper at twelve o'clock," Joe mentioned, setting the last brick into her fireplace.

" Oh! Good!"

There was another moment's pause. This placid aquiescence left the girls a little breathless.

" It isn't that we want supper at twelve, exactly," Philippa explained. " It is just the feeling that— that——"

" I wondered how much longer you were going to be, getting that feeling," said Mrs. Aldwyn. " I am glad that you have at last begun to think the idea less foolish than you had supposed."

" Captain! We——"

" Oh, you were very polite, and after all, you couldn't help your thoughts. But there is no doubt that you are sometimes a little hidebound, and that you cling to the good old ways without so much as considering new ones. It is your age. Eve must have been a round twenty before she ate that apple."

Mrs. Aldwyn shook her head and sighed, then smiled at the three injured faces which confronted her.

" If nothing ever clung to anything," Joe said coldly, " the earth would fall slap out of the solar system, and that would be that."

" We don't mind new ideas in reasonable numbers," Hester said, " but we do like to know where we are. Look here, Captain! Do you really and honestly mean that we can do precisely as we like—eat when we like, sleep when we like, get up when we like, work when we like? Do just as we please, all day long?"

" You can "—Mrs. Aldwyn hesitated, choosing her words—" you can be as independent as you choose. After this evening nobody will come into your field unless you invite them. You must keep the bathing rules, of course, and report if you are ill or smash

15   (H 21)

yourselves up, but otherwise this is your camp, and you may run it as seems best to you. Is that clear enough?"

" Ye-es," said Hester. " I suppose so."

" No," said Joe. " I want to know why?"

Mrs. Aldwyn looked at her interrogatively.

" Why have you packed us off like this, to do as we like."

Again their captain hesitated, as if choosing her words.

" You are beautifully brought up Guides," she said at last. " I brought you up myself, so I ought to know. You manage your patrols most admirably. You are full of initiative and resourcefulness and self-reliance, and all the other qualities Guiding is supposed to develop. If you are given anything to do, it is always done. You make camp run like clockwork, and there isn't an idle moment in your day except those legally and officially dedicated to idleness. You are, in fact, model members of the community."

Mrs. Aldwyn looked from one to the other of her listeners, and the look was returned by three pairs of eyes, dark with suspicion.

" And so," she pursued, smiling a little, " I thought it might be a good plan to give you some leisure in which to meet yourselves as individuals. I should hate you to grow into the kind of people Robert Louis Stevenson describes, who are so taken up with ' busyness ' that the whole breathing world is a blank to them, and who, if they are taken away from their usual occupations, are left without one thought to rub against another. In a big camp there is bound to be a certain amount of organization and discipline, both of which are exceedingly good for you. But there is always a danger that you may use that self-same organization and discipline as a pair of mental crutches, to save your minds the trouble of walking on their own legs. And once you give way to crutches, before you know where you are you will be in the bath chair of routine. To have one's camp running on oiled wheels is one thing, but to have one's Guides running on tramlines is another—dear, dear! I have got involved in my metaphors!"

" You have," said Joe.

All three girls regarded her dismally.

" Just to think," muttered Hester, " of the years you have spent talking to us about being tidy and methodical and thorough."

" And how often you have told us," added Philippa, " that sloppiness was the root of all evil."

" So it is." Mrs. Aldwyn averted a pair of twinkling eyes from the field about her. " But things are not always what they seem, and a sudden attack of sloppiness may be due to reaction, or perhaps to a declaration of independence. The best of people get taken that way sometimes."

There was a silence. The shadows had by now
stretched so far that their grey edges melted into the
grass, and their soft flickering resembled the dancing
of ghostly elves rather than the fingers of an accusing
school-mam. An owl, waking early for his night's
work, hooted in the trees of the wood that lay westward of the camp; tiny lights winked out on the hill
beyond the creek, and two long reflections rippled
from the riding lights of a yacht anchored off a tumbledown jetty. The creek was at ebb tide, and the sands
and mud between stretches of sedge grass shone, an
opalescent mirror for a sky that would soon fade into
twilight. On the distant mainland a lighted train went
by with a faint clatter, vanishing one moment behind
invisible trees and houses, rushing out the next like
a fiery serpent. From many miles up the Channel a
deep continuous reverberation told of a liner weighing
anchor to sail half across the world.

Mrs. Aldwyn stood up.

" I must be going," she said reluctantly, turning
her back upon the sea, and on the grey hills with their
twinkling lights. " Ask me back again, sometimes.
It is so peaceful here."

The three girls went with her to the gate, where
she bade them good night. Then, as she was leaving
them, she paused.

" By the by," she said, " I had almost forgotten to
warn you—your mystery house——"

The girls looked at her, their faces lighting with a quick interest and curiosity.

"It has been let. Mrs. Weland told me so this afternoon; so don't go rapping at its knocker as you used to do last year."

CHAPTER II

A Door with a Brass Knocker

Dawn was sung in by a thrush perched high on a bough of the oak tree. Its voice summoned the other birds as a single note summons an orchestra, till from every tree and from every bush and hedge the heavens declared the glory of God and the firmament showed His handiwork. Eastward down the Channel the sky had a golden rim, but the sea itself was grey as steel, and beyond it the coast of England lay dark. The fields close at hand were without colour, and the trees stood cold against the light.

Philippa turned restlessly on her bed of straw. Unlike birds, humans are rarely at their happiest in the chill hours before sunrise. Sins of yesterday or yester-year meet and foregather; memories rise unbidden and unwelcomed; and conscience throws off his reasonable workaday guise and, leagued with Giant Despair, lies like a leaden weight upon his victim's chest.

Outwardly Philippa was an ordinary girl, pleasant to look at, with clear eyes and fair shining hair. Inwardly, being a sound sleeper and unused to the influences of five a.m., she was a monster. Or was she even a monster? Were her very sins not commonplace? Some people could sin magnificently, could crown their misdeeds with a halo of romance. Philippa, looking at herself in the bleak light of morning, found herself drab and insignificant. She was no monster, she was just a worm. The fact was humiliating to contemplate. She sighed profoundly.

By and by, the leaden weight upon her chest appeared to move. It was no less heavy, but it was farther down and perhaps easier to cope with therefore. Slowly the truth bore in upon her and she sat up in bed. Their midnight feast, that declaration of independence, had resolved itself into hasty mouthfuls of bread and ham and cold water swallowed in the intervals of work, unsatisfying at the time and now less than a memory.

" Breakfast!" thought Philippa with passionate intensity. " Porridge, bacon and eggs, and tea! Bread and marmalade!"

She looked at the others. Joe was hunched up under her blankets, but Hester wriggled, opened an eye, and shut it again. Like Philippa, neither of them had slept well. Time after time she had heard them turning and rustling on their palliasses, seeking to fit their weary bodies to the bumps and hollows of the ground. And to judge from the look in Hester's one visible eye, she, too, found the dawn a melancholy hour in which to waken.

Philippa slipped first one, then the other reluctant foot out of her warm bed; only now, when she was about to leave it, did her mattress feel suddenly comfortable. She rolled the legs of her pyjamas well above the knees, put on her coat, and left the tent, standing a moment in the doorway to watch the spreading band of gold in the sky. The fields were no longer colourless, but sparkled under a crystal canopy of gossamer, and from every blade of grass hung a cobweb jewelled with dew, delicate as fairy diamonds. The sea rippled silver; the trees were deep polished emeralds. The whole world was a treasure-house of glittering transient gems.

Philippa trod barefoot on the cold grass and shivered ecstatically. She wished the birds would sing again, but their praise was over, and they were busy with family affairs, though they chirruped in a preoccupied way now and then. She crossed to the kitchen, and her eye was caught by two long tracks, leading from the box which held their stores to the hedge, where the dew had been brushed away and the grass beneath showed dark against the shining field. Something inquisitive and purposeful had been to call, something also which was surely very small, for a larger animal would have left footprints rather than the trail of its whole body. Looking back, she saw with interest that her own footprints were surprisingly clear, and she planned, a little optimistically, to get up every fine morning and make a thorough study of tracking signs in dew.

At present, however, she must, like the birds, attend to more pressing household matters. She found the loaf, the marmalade, and two tomatoes left over from last night's supper, and returned after a little while to the tent with an appetizing platter of sandwiches. Joe was sitting half dressed on the edge of her bed, pulling on a pair of gum-boots. Hester lay as she had lain when Philippa left her, except that her eye was more definitely open. As it met Philippa's it shut again hastily. On no account, it said, was its owner to be considered awake.

Philippa set the plate down at the foot of the tent pole.

" There," she said. " Sit up at once. That's what you want!"

" What?" Hester repudiated her eye, and sat instantly bolt upright. " Philippa, you lamb! You angel! How did you guess?" She helped herself to sandwiches with either hand, and gazed at them lovingly before taking a bite out of each to establish her ownership.

" I have had such a sinking feeling," she went on. " It got mixed up with my dreams. I thought that I was a porcelain figure on a marble mantelpiece, and that I would break if I didn't put myself down very gently. Even when I woke up I felt fragile, and wondered if I was going to die young."

" Unlikely," said Joe.

" I was such a pretty little figure," Hester pursued dreamily. " A Chinese lady-Mandarin, with a long flowery coat all edged with gold brocade, and a deep blue petticoat and purple trousers—but I remember my head was loose. It nodded. In fact, I believe it came right off. Now, I wonder what made me think that!" She thumped her pillow inquiringly.

The others chuckled, and Philippa observed:

" A very natural thing for you to think. Did you find that it made much difference—not having a head, I mean?"

" No. It was stuck on again with gl—Philippa! I hate you—at least "—Hester took another sandwich— " I shall hate you in a minute or two, when I have had enough."

Philippa laughed again.

" I do love teasing Hester," she exclaimed. " It always takes her about thirty seconds to get there, and then she goes off plop. Never mind, Hetty, my love. You are not a pretty little figure now, far from it; and your head is as solid as a rock. There are always consolations."

" It is nothing of the sort."

" Then may I hope that it will nod if I ask you to do something?"

Hester's face fell.

"I might have known you would say that. What do you want?"

"Wood."

"Wood! Now!"

"We didn't fetch a stick last night. It's a goodish walk, and the fire will take a lot of coaxing in that new cold fireplace. Besides, you said——"

"I know I did: please don't remind me," sighed Hester, shivering as she turned her clothes out from under her pillow.

The sun was well above the horizon when they crossed the next-door field, and the world was no longer a treasure-house, though it still felt unusually fresh and clean and expectant. As they passed the tent doors the three girls were hailed by sundry coughs and grunts, and they waved back a friendly if slightly patronizing good-morning. The others, poor things, must keep the silence rule for another hour. Only now and again while they were in camp would they be allowed as a treat to get up at dawn. The joys of liberty brought an added sweetness to the sweet morning air.

"Not," Hester said, "that one really wants to get up at dawn very often. The first morning or two when one is wakeful, perhaps; but afterwards, when one has got used to sleeping on bumps, it is hard to feel as enthusiastic when the moment comes as one did the night before at camp fire—in fact "—concluded Hester candidly—" getting up at dawn is just another of those things we enjoy because we are supposed to and not because we do. When I am grown up I am going to have duties, and I am going to have pleasures, but I am not going to try to delude myself by mixing the labels."

" Your duties should be pleasures," said Joe primly.

" I don't care what they should be, it's what they are that matters. If I do enjoy my duties I'll call them pleasure. But if I don't, I shall call them dratted nuisances—though, I suppose, I shall have to do them just the same."

" I shall be sorry if you decide not to enjoy getting up early," said Philippa, and she told them about her schemes for tracking. " It was my own tracks in the dew that made me think of it," she added. " Look at the footprints we have left now. They are quite different from the ones I made. You could tell at once that I was barefoot. I thought it would be such fun if we made a set of casts to take back to our patrols; especially if we do it without telling anybody, because then it won't matter much if they go wrong."

" If you are proposing to make plaster casts in dew," Joe remarked, " it certainly will be wiser not to tell anybody."

" Not dew, stupid. Mud."

" Umph!" said Joe, for at that moment they reached

the stile into the wood, and even Philippa was forced to laugh.

" I don't mean at this very spot," she conceded. " Just here you get all the carts and the stray cows and horses, and the tractor going down to the beach for shingle. There is bound to be rather a mix up. It won't be so bad farther in."

She climbed the stile and walked on, her eyes fixed on the ground, though it gave her little encouragement. The path was deeply rutted and in many places trampled to mire; on either side was a thick belt of undergrowth, chiefly briars and brambles, and where, under the taller pine trees, there was a clear space, it was carpeted with a springy fibrous brown soil as dry as the path was muddy, on which, as Hester said impatiently, an elephant could hardly have left any lasting impression.

" I always have had my doubts of sleuth-hounds who could solve everything from the snapping of one twig," she added, " and besides, what animal with a grain of sense would risk its only fur on those briars?"

" Hester! Where was you riz', honey? Don't you know ' born 'n' bred in a briar patch, Brer Fox, born 'n' br——' Why, look at that!"

Philippa touched Hester's shoulder and pointed at the clearing ahead of them, where a score of rabbits were peacefully at breakfast.

The three girls crept forward on tiptoe, but even

on tiptoe twenty-four solid stone of girl could not hope to tread noiselessly over crackling pine twigs. The breakfast party broke up in a streak of white scuts, and vanished helter-skelter into the bushes on every side. Somewhat chagrined, the three naturalists spread out their ground-sheet and began to collect wood.

" Found any tracks yet?" Joe inquired, as Philippa, after a spurt of great energy, stood lost in thought gazing out between the trees to the sea.

" I have had another idea. Why shouldn't we build a hide and take photographs from it?"

" A what?" asked Hester.

" A hide—a hut of stakes and boughs, with a hole to watch through. You choose a place where you think animals are likely to come, and you put up your hut and leave it for a little while till they get used to it, and then you sit inside and watch. There have to be two or three of you, because you all go in, and then one comes out again, and as birds and animals don't do arithmetic they think the hut is empty."

" It sounds simple," Hester said. " Almost as simple as making casts in mud. Is that why you have only picked up those three long branches, instead of collecting wood?"

Philippa looked at her gleanings with a dissatisfied eye.

" These are not really tall enough or stout enough,"

she returned. " The wood is going to be a difficulty. Those fallen saplings are much too heavy, and the ordinary dead stuff is brittle and too small, and, of course, we can't cut any green."

" How much do you want?"

" About fifteen uprights and any amount of smaller brushwood for weaving in and out."

" Wouldn't it be better," Joe suggested, " to make a hessian hide? You could sling it from a tree, like a little tent, and if you found one place dull, you could move it to another."

" It would scare the birds, like a scarecrow."

" Not if you camouflaged it. Paint it all over in uneven patches of colour, mostly green. We could go into town this afternoon and buy paint or dyes of some sort."

" It would be quicker," Philippa agreed. " And another idea: we might fetch up a dozen or so bucketfuls of sand from the shore, and make a special wet sand patch. If we put down food, we would get our tracks, as well as photographs."

" Unbleached calico would be more fun to paint on than hessian," Hester put in, " and it is almost as cheap. We might even make our own dyes; I do love a really good mess." She gave a sudden little skip and tossed another armful of wood on to the groundsheet with an abandon that scattered the whole pile. " I am enjoying myself!" she cried. " It is such fun saying we will do this and that, without a by-your-leave to anybody—only "—her face fell—" I do feel rather a pig too. It seems a shame to enjoy yourself just because the others are not there."

" It does in a way," Philippa agreed. " But the others do expect you to be so perfect. Everything has to happen as it ought, and you have to know all about it beforehand. You can't really enjoy experiments if you have to try them out with people like Kitty Kennedy and Daphne Todd at your elbow, sniffing and saying ' call yourself a leader '. Not that Daphne is a bad child at heart, but she is at the difficult age."

" You should give her more to do," said Joe. " If she shared your experiments she would share your failures, and then she couldn't say anything. Don't you think we have enough? It is time we were getting back, and I should like to have breakfast ready five minutes ahead of the others."

They lifted the ground-sheet and bore it stretcher-wise through the bushes and up the path, debating as they went where to put their hide. The neighbourhood was a perfect one for their purpose. Over the brow of the hill beyond the steading, and on either side of the by-road down to the farm and the highway, there were woods, spreading for nearly a mile to the westward, and bounded on the east by the creek which ran far inland. Long ago the woods had been part of an oak forest, but many of the oaks had been felled, and in their place grew silver birches and pines and larch trees; and, as in the little wood by the camp, the undergrowth was thick with bushes. There were few footpaths, and picnic parties, thanks to the steep and stony road, were rare. In addition to the farm, there was only one other house, and that, a long rambling building, stood beyond the steading on the top of the hill looking out over a wide view of the sea and the surrounding countryside.

The three girls, taking a roundabout but easier way out of the woods with their load, passed one of the doors of this house on their way home. It was an unusual door, jet-black in a high white wall and fully ten yards from the house itself, with which it was connected by a covered stone passage. Hester eyed the knocker sadly.

" I do hate passing it without a single rap," she said. " I feel just as if I had refused to shake hands with an old friend. I wonder if the people who have taken it are nice," she added, in a voice which sounded dubious.

" They are from London," said Joe. " I met Billy last night coming back with the milk, and she said Mrs. Weland had been talking about them. A Mr. and Mrs. somebody. Mrs. is all eyebrows and high heels, and she gets her stores from London, even butter and eggs and vegetables and proper country things like that. The servants are foreigners, a man and a woman; and they all keep themselves to themselves, and sound none too popular."

" They haven't bothered to clean the brass," observed Hester. " That lion's head would look lovely if it were bright and shining against the black paint. It is funny how much you can tell about people from little things. I do wish they had been nice. They might have asked us to tea, and we could have seen the inside properly instead of peeking through the shutters. If only we had asked, I am sure Mr. Weland would have taken us over the house last year, only then it wouldn't have been a mystery. We did have fun, stalking round the garden and inventing stories, do you remember? There was that extraordinary fat grandfather clock half-way up the staircase that we said led into a priest's hole; you could just see it through the keyhole of the front door. And down below was the oak kist for the Bride of Lammermoor; and that arm-chair with the lion head arms. There were a lot of lions about the place, one way and another —oh well——"

She sighed as she turned towards the camp. The three girls gathered up the corners of the ground-sheet, and lifted their load of wood once more. Hester cast a last lingering backward glance at the knocker and sighed again.

" Here endeth our mystery house," she said. " We must go and cook the breakfast."

CHAPTER III

A Meeting by the Sea

They breakfasted not five, but thirty-five minutes earlier than the next-door camp, for although, as Philippa had prophesied, the fire needed some coaxing, they found that it took far less time to cook for three people than it takes to cook for twenty-three. They had finished their meal and stacked their plates ready for washing up before the warning whistle went for the other members of their company, and they rolled up the brailing of their tent to the singing of a distant grace.

They made no comment to one another, but they felt satisfied. This was the way leaders should camp when left to themselves. If they could do what they liked, then what they liked, they decided this morning, was going to be nothing less than perfection. Philippa, observing a small crease in her section of the brailing, unfastened it and rolled it up again till it was as tight and smooth as a well-boiled roly-poly pudding; and Joe, watching her, uttered an approving grunt.

They scoured the tent, straightened the pole by an

35

eighth of an inch, scrutinized each peg and guyline, and finally stood back to survey their handiwork with eyes which, critical though they were, could find no further fault. Leaving their beds out to air, they turned their attention to the kitchen, where, under Philippa's directions as arch tidier, they laboured steadily for an hour and a half, and when at last they climbed the intervening gate to join in prayers and colours with the others, they had good reason to be content with their first morning's work.

" Store tent, grease pit, incinerator and hanging larder," said Philippa, ticking each off on her fingers as she crossed the field. " We must finish the wood-shelter and make a pantry, and a proper dixie rack instead of the slipshod thing I put up last night, and then we shall be ready for anyone or anything."

" Let us come straight up from swimming and carry on," Joe said. " I do like to get things done so that I can play with an easy mind—and don't forget we must ask Captain if we can go into town this afternoon."

" Why need we ask?" demanded Hester. " Aren't we to do as we like?"

" Yes, but—well, it is manners. Besides, we should. She ought to have some idea of where we are. Suppose a telegram arrived to say that your whole family had been run over by a bus!"

" Two buses," corrected Hester. " There are six

of us, you know; one would hardly manage the lot. You ask her then, but don't say what for."

Mrs. Aldwyn, questioned on the way down to the sea, gave her consent without demur.

" Only," she added, " if it is stores you are buying, you can get them here. I would rather you came to us for all your food. Miss Ashe will order anything you want if you give her time."

" It is not food, thank you," Joe told her. " We are just going shopping."

Mrs. Aldwyn sighed, and wondered why it was that while other people's Guides planned wonderful tracks and hikes, her own always made straight for the nearest Woolworth's. She sighed again still more heavily as she answered her own question. Most companies reflect the character of their captain, and she could herself never resist a Woolworth's.

The first bathe was a short one, and by half-past eleven the three girls were back and engrossed in the wood-shelter, which was an intricate affair with a sloping roof, walls and a floor, invented by Philippa in the watches of the night.

" There," said Hester at last, snipping the string off the final lashing, " we have been hard at work since six o'clock or earlier, and now I propose a lightning strike. What do you say to a short rest hour, with canteen?"

" Well, usually," Philippa answered her very gravely,

" I say that I am so pleased it was able to come, and that I am delighted to see how its canteen is growing. And I don't mention its shortness in case its feelings should be hurt. Short fat people like to be talked to just like other people, don't they, Joe?"

" Ass!" said Joe. " Who is going to cook the dinner?"

" We all are, but we don't need to begin yet. Breakfast only took twenty minutes, porridge and all, this morning." Hester spread three ground-sheets in the shade of the oak tree, and crawled on her hands and knees into the miniature stores tent for the canteen box. " We must have some rest," she added in a voice which sounded muffled, either because of the tent, or from some other cause; " we shall be out all the afternoon."

They lay down, and the hot midday sun threw over them a dappled blanket of sunlight and shadow. It seemed a long time since they had wakened at dawn; their limbs ached with unaccustomed work, and they were sleepy and stiff after the stinging cold brine of their first swim. From the farm, far away over the hill, came the hum of a reaper, drowsy as the drone of a giant bee. Over the hedge sounded a murmuring of busy voices, interrupted now and again by clearer words called from one group to another. For a little while the cries mingled with their dreams, but presently the world faded out of all hearing, and they were sound asleep.

Joe was the first to stir, and in turning she flung an arm across Philippa, waking her. They lay for some moments in the languor that follows upon sleeping out of doors on a hot summer day, then Joe, blinking up into the green branches overhead and thinking of nothing at all, became aware of a quiet that was, somehow, disturbing. She could still hear the reaper; and a lark, springing up from the grass, sang itself out of sight in the blue sky; but neither of these sounds made up for the lack of something more familiar. She sat up sharply and stared over the hedge, then looked with incredulous eyes at her wrist watch.

" Philippa Fleming!" she cried, but softly, so that her voice should not carry too far in the still air. " Do you know that it is after three o'clock?"

Philippa, who had just curled round with her head on her arm for another snooze, rolled over and opened her eyes.

" What?" she said sleepily, then in her turn sat up. " What?" she repeated, this time very much awake.

Joe put a finger to her lips and pointed, first over the hedge, and then at Hester. She put a hand over Hester's mouth, while Philippa gently pinched her ear. Hester shook herself, and turned her back on them.

" G'way!" she muttered.

" It is three," Philippa whispered to her. " Three o'clock."

"Why shouldn't it be?" Hester, dragged from oblivion, yawned gigantically. "Perfectly good time."

"We have had no dinner," Philippa reminded her.

"You are always eating. Never met such people."

"Sh! They will hear you over there," cautioned Joe. "They have not finished their silent rest hour."

All three girls glanced towards the hedge, then at one another, and finally at their kitchen, with its spotless but empty fireplace; its sheltered pile of wood, chopped, stacked and sized in apple-pie order; and its array of shining tin dixies and clean white enamelware. They thought of the expedition planned for the afternoon, and of the length of time it would take to cook, eat, wash up, and restore everything to its present state of perfection. They thought also of the inquisitive faces which, attracted by smoke, and by the crackling of sticks and clanking of dixies, might peep over the hedge directly the rest hour drew to its close. At length Joe, with a long stretch and a yawn, stood up.

"Are you hungry?" she asked.

Hester and Philippa shook their heads. They were, as a matter of fact, slightly sick. They had eaten well rather than wisely of canteen, and moreover, the sun, creeping southwards while they slept, had for the past half-hour been shining full upon them.

"Then suppose we give ourselves a nice quiet lunch of bread and cheese, and take our kippers down to the beach for a supper hike, instead of going to town."

The others agreed indifferently. They felt no enthusiasm for kippers, and very little for bread and cheese, although a hollow emptiness inside made them eat readily enough when Joe set the loaf beside them.

" This is my third bread and buttery meal to-day," Hester observed rather pensively. " My fourth, in fact, if you count the slices left over for breakfast that we had for elevenses. I wonder if it is really nourishing! I am feeling fragile again, just as I did this morning."

" Head loose?" inquired Joe.

" My heart is not at all strong," Hester replied with a note of dignified reproof in her voice. " You will have to be very careful of me. You know that if anything were to happen to me here you would never forgive yourselves."

She finished her fifth slice of bread and cheese and handed her plate and knife to Joe to be washed up, while she herself leaned comfortably back between the roots of the tree to watch the others set about their preparations for a beach supper.

As their languor wore off and their energy was restored by their lunch, bread and buttery though it was, their change of plans grew more ambitious. Instead of going down to the sea, where they would probably find themselves surrounded by the younger Guides from next door, they decided to make for the mouth of the estuary; and later to carry out a voyage of exploration, following the twistings and windings of the creek through the woods to its source. At Joe's suggestion, Philippa and Hester improvised a hay-box in the small pit which they had dug, but had not yet used, for rubbish; while Joe herself lighted the fire, boiled a billyful of cocoa, and baked a hastily mixed panful of oatcakes, using for a girdle the lid of a biscuit tin which she afterwards hid under the wood-pile to be washed up at some future time. No matter when they returned, there was to be no question to-night of a cold supper eaten in hurried snatches.

The lane which led to the creek was steep and deeply rutted and, though the sun was high, almost completely shaded by the hedges on either side. For nearly a mile it lay between fields which last year had been grazing land, but which were now under corn. Farther down it crossed the outer fringe of the woods, and finally it emerged on to the wide flat margin of the creek, where it lost itself in a maze of green turfed footpaths that twisted hither and thither between the pools and inlets.

The way was pleasant between the tall green hedges, with their sweet tangle of honeysuckle and feathery travellers' joy. The girls sauntered along, stopping every now and then to pick up a likely piece of fuel, or to discuss which flowers could be used for dyes.

"You get green from cow parsley," Hester said, "which is a good thing, because you want plenty of green." She looked down the lane, where the cow parsley grew white and fine as a web of lace against the dark hedge. "Pear leaves give a lovely green, too, a sort of soft jade. Elderberries make a bluey purple, but they will hardly be ripe yet—there is woad, of course. I should love to try woad. I know just how it is done." Hester paused by a gate in the hedge and, leaning her elbows on the top bar and propping her chin on her hands, gazed abstractedly across the cornfields to the wood. "You pound the leaves into a pulp, and stand it in heaps for fifteen days. Then you roll it up into balls like butter, and dry it for a week, and then you crumble it into powder and mix it with water and turn it over every day for a fortnight. And then you leave it in a heap till you are ready to use it. It turns you green at first, but you go blue when you dry."

"It sounds a little slow," Philippa said, exchanging smiles with Joe. "Besides, isn't it carrying things rather far? I don't mind camouflaging my tent, or even my clothes; but I don't want to camouflage me. It might not come off."

"Have you seen any woad growing about here?" Joe inquired.

"I have never seen it at all. It is very rare, and I don't really know what it looks like, except that it is tall, and the flowers are bright yellow. Talking of yellows, St. John's wort——"

Joe climbed down from the gate.

" It's time we were going on," she said with some firmness. " There are only five hours of daylight left, and it will take you all that to cook one kipper in your present state, let alone go exploring afterwards."

They reached the shore at no great distance from the craft they had observed the previous night, which lay anchored off the tumbledown jetty, sheltered by a wide curve of the coast from the open sea. With some curiosity the three girls walked along the top of a dyke to look at her. She was not, as they had supposed from her colour in the distance, a yacht, but a big sea-going barge, painted white, high and broad in the bows, low amidships, and high again in the stern, where there was a roomy cabin with a small railed-in deck above. Her mast was no longer erect, but had been lowered and lay flat almost the full length of her deck. On her bows and stern her name and her port of origin appeared in big gold letters.

" Dutch," said Hester, as they went by, " or Flemish, perhaps. I wonder if she belongs to the people up at the Manor."

" Not to eyebrows and high heels, surely," exclaimed Philippa, observing the sturdy lines, and the dazzling whiteness of paint and deck. " Not that high heels aren't very well in their proper place, but one can't imagine them in the lane we have just come down, or looking after a fine workmanlike barge like that."

" They were in the lane, though," said Joe. " Didn't you see the prints of them? Dozens, some overlapping each other, tiny shaped heel marks, and pointed toes. She must come up and down pretty often."

" So that probably the barge is hers. Well, well! Different people have different tastes. If I trotted up and down that lane I shouldn't wear tiny high heels or such-like, and if I did, I would keep to the grass at the sides. Why walk in the mud?"

Joe shrugged her shoulders. She had found a little sandy hollow screened by gorse bushes, and she was more interested in getting her supper than in the vagaries of unknown ladies with eyebrows. While Hester and Philippa were unpacking their haversacks and making an orderly dump of their belongings, she laid a trapper's fire. With the thickest of the wood found on the way down, she built a shallow semi-circle, partially closing in the ends with two smooth flat stones tilted a little inwards. In front, but not too close, she heaped up a small pile of stones, and in the middle of the space thus enclosed she erected a criss-cross tower of smaller sticks, which she filled with shavings of birchbark, a handful of dried sweet chestnut leaves with their tassels, and some bracken and scraps of gorse. Finally, she drew from her pocket one small object which she inserted with great care in the very middle of the structure.

"Ready?" she asked, glancing at the supply of delicacies which had been spread out on a sheet of grease-proof paper.

"You have forgotten the potatoes. What was that?"

Joe took the three potatoes which had been scrubbed but not peeled, and scooping a small hole within the circle of her fireplace, laid them in it and covered them with a thin layer of pebbles.

"I don't believe they will bake," she said. "Heat never seems to strike down fiercely enough to cook things through. Still, we can try. We can finish them off in the ashes afterwards—what was what?"

"That thing you put into the fire?"

Joe fumbled in her pocket a second time and took out two small corks wrapped in a scrap of newspaper.

"It is a dodge I heard of from a New Zealander," she said, holding them out for Hester to see. "You soak them in paraffin and let them dry. They are supposed to light any fire that ever was laid anywhere. I tried one this morning, and it did go at the first match, though, of course, that wasn't much of a test."

"I call it cheating," said Hester, with a great air of disapproval. "When I light a hike fire, I light a hike fire. I don't use a labour-saving device replete with every modern convenience."

Joe's eyes twinkled. Hester very rarely did light fires of any kind, leaving that task as often as possible to other people.

" If I had invented the idea myself," she said, " I probably wouldn't approve of it either, but hearing of it from a Colonial makes it seem quite backwoody and squatterish. Cheating or not cheating, they are handy little things to carry around."

She put a match to her tinder and watched with satisfaction as the flame crept upwards and burst into a reassuring blaze. She fed it stick by stick till the hearthplace was filled with hot charred ashes and the logs at the back glowed red, throwing their heat forward. Then, on the smooth, tilted stones at either side, she laid half a dozen scones, the dough of which had been mixed before leaving camp. At the back of the fire she balanced a billy of water, and lastly, with one cautious eye on the billy can, which was a trifle shaky, she stretched out a hand towards Philippa.

" Kippers?" she inquired.

" Just coming."

Philippa had meantime been whittling three nails from a green, knotty oak twig. She laid the kippers on a small flat piece of board and pegged them to it, driving her oak nails through their tails; then she whisked over them with a dab of butter, sprinkled them with a touch of pepper, a modicum of salt, and the merest suggestion of sugar, and handed the board to Joe, who propped it against the little pile of stones heaped in front of the fire.

A pleasant sound arose as first the butter, then the golden-brown skin of the kippers began to hiss and fry. The girls sniffed hungrily, crouching round the fire and turning their scones this way and that. After ten or twelve minutes Joe unpegged the kippers, reversed them, and toasted the other side. Presently Hester threw a small handful of tea leaves, Australian fashion, into the boiling billy can, and Philippa, gingerly and with one or two smothered exclamations, removed the scones one by one from their baking stones and laid them, smoking hot and as light as feathers, on a plate by the fireside.

" What about the potatoes?" Hester asked.

Joe handed her the sizzling kippers to unpeg, and scraped aside the ashes with a piece of shell. She shook her head.

" Haven't begun to cook on the under side," she said. " I was afraid they wouldn't, and, in any case, they need at least half an hour. I'll put them round the fire on the scone stones, and we'll have them afterwards with butter—there!"

With a deep contented sigh she took her plate of kipper and scone on her lap, and leaned back against the side of the sand pit. There was a prolonged silence, broken only by the crackle of sticks and the fall of cinders in the fireplace. A faint breeze from the sea stirred among the gorse bushes, and the sand was pleasantly warm and smooth to the touch.

" This," said Hester at length, " is my idea of perfect camping." She tipped the skeleton of her kipper into the fire and wiped her plate with a handful of grass plucked from the border of the hollow. " As good a meal as you could wish for, and nothing to wash up afterwards, except one little wooden board and a tin billy that needs only to be rinsed. Even the dish-cloths can be burnt." She tore up a second handful of grass, gave her plate a final polish, and began on her second course. Her scone as she broke it open sent out a faint but delicious steamy aroma; she filled it with butter and a spoonful of brown sugar, shut it together again, and took an appetizing bite. " Let us do this every day," she concluded, when she could speak with politeness.

Joe inspected a potato and pushed it farther into the ashes.

" It would be fun," she said, " but we ought to have a proper dinner with vegetables and puddings at least every other day. The things one can cook without washing up are rather limited."

" There'th thothatheth," Hester began, " sausages," she corrected herself, swallowing another large bite. " wrapped in banana skins; and chops on forked sticks; and bacon and eggs and tomatoes; and we could do fresh herrings in wet newspaper, as they do small trout in the Highlands. And if you must have cabbage, boil it in a paper bag. You boil water that way, so why not cab——"

Hester broke off, and the others, following the direction of her gaze, saw two people climb from the barge into a small rowing boat and row themselves ashore.

" Mrs. Eyebrow-Heels of the Manor House," Hester exclaimed, " and that must be the foreign manservant with her. I hope she will pass close to us. Wouldn't it be fun if she turned out nice after all and took us aboard? I want to see the house, and I should just adore to see the barge."

The three watched interestedly from behind their screen of gorse bushes as the boat was beached.

" I think we had better cough or make a clatter of some sort," Joe said quietly, as the couple drew near. " It is so horrid to take people unawares. And don't goggle if you want to make a good impression, Hester."

" I am not goggling." Hester's protesting tones dropped suddenly. " I don't know that I do want to make a good impression," she muttered. " I think I would rather not be noticed at all."

Joe and Philippa, after another searching look, agreed with her. As one man they turned to their fire and became engrossed in the baking of their potatoes. Their desire to see the tenants of Manor and barge had vanished unexpectedly. They felt that what they had supposed to be friendly interest, now somehow stood revealed as vulgar curiosity, and reasonably or unreasonably they blamed the subject of that curiosity for the change.

But, whether they desired it or not, they quickly saw that they were not going to be passed by. The clatter of their plates had been heard, and the couple were walking straight towards them. They rose politely as the lady approached, hoping that their feelings were not too plainly written upon their faces. She might, after all, be quite pleasant, though a close sight of her held out small hopes of such a possibility. Her first words banished it entirely.

" What—" she demanded, and no matter what her listeners' faces might do, hers made no pretence of concealing her feelings, " what are you doing down here?"

The girls hesitated, disconcerted. Their plates lay scattered on the ground and half their supper was at that very moment baking on the fire; but they knew that the type of grown-up who asked obvious questions was apt to call obvious answers impertinent. To their own disgust, they felt guilty, though they had no reason in the world for doing so.

" I asked you "—the lady was tapping impatiently with her small high-heeled shoe—" what you were doing down here. Don't you know that this ground is private?"

"Private!" There was blank dismay in the three voices that echoed her.

"Yes. Private. It belongs to the Manor, and I won't have a riff-raff of trippers littering the place up with their picnics, and trampling all over the woods."

"But we aren't trippers," Joe explained. "We are Guides from the camp up at the top of the hill. We come down here quite often for meals on the beach, or at least we did last year, and nobody said anything."

"What you did last year doesn't interest me in the least. Weland had no business to let the fields at all, but since you are here, I can at least insist on you keeping to them. Please go back to your camp at once, and don't let me find you wandering about again."

"But—but—" Philippa stammered, seeing all her plans for stalking and tracking dwindle and fade into thin air, "surely you don't mean that we mustn't go into the woods either?"

"I most certainly mean it. The woods "— just for an instant their visitor seemed at a loss, but she went on quickly—" the woods are preserved for game, and if any of you are found trespassing, we shall prosecute. It is barely a week till the Twelfth."

"The Twelfth," Joe echoed, and broke off, looking surprised and puzzled.

"Please stop arguing and do as you are told."

There was a moment's pause, then in dead silence

Joe took the billy can, filled it at a pool, and emptied it over the dying fire. Conscious all the time of hostile eyes, the three girls buried the wet ashes under sand, gathered up their belongings, and packed their haversacks. They were hot with indignation, but uppermost in each mind was the restraining thought of their uniform. They would at least give this person no further cause to complain about Guides.

When, after apologizing and bidding her a conciliatory " good night ", they turned to climb the hill, no eyes, however hostile, could have found a trace of their activities, and the only sign which might have betrayed their feelings was the speed at which they marched up the lane. Not till they were at the top, and far out of sight or earshot, did any of them speak. Then Hester, vaulting the gate into their field, wiped the sand and mud from her shoes against the grass.

" That," she said, " is that. I am going straight across to Captain."

" No," said Joe quickly, putting out a detaining hand.

" Why not?"

" Because—well, not to-night. We shall give her a much more reasonable account in the morning when our tempers have had time to cool. Besides——"

" Well?"

" Oh, nothing. But I would rather wait till to-morrow, if you don't mind. Don't let's talk about it now."

Hester gave her shoes a final and vigorous polish. When Joe argued a point it was usually for a good reason.

" Very well," she conceded, " though I am bursting to talk about it. I shall spend the night thinking of all the nasty things I can say, and to-morrow I shall say them."

Joe found the kipper board and began to scrub it. She had ideas of her own about what was to be said to-morrow.

CHAPTER IV
Misadventure Next Door

To-morrow, however, brought with it other and more familiar troubles. A north-easterly wind swept the Channel, and rain fell like a slanting leaden curtain into a dark restless sea, blotting out the distant coast-lines, and wrapping the camp into a little grey isolated world of its own. Water streamed down the tent and ran in tiny dripping rivulets from ropes that stretched taut in spite of the wind. Pools of water gathered in the folds of the old ground-sheet which covered the hay-pit; sodden leaves clung to the roof of the wood stack; clammy unrecognizable fragments found their way into the larder and the store tent; and the ground round the fireplace and in the tent doorway became a slough of treacherous mud for unwary feet.

" I suppose this is why rude gutter urchins call us ' Girl Slides '," Hester said ruefully, entering the tent with unexpected force on her return from prayers.

The others followed her, crawling more cautiously

on their hands and knees under the laced-up door. Shivering a little, they discarded their wet shoes and mackintoshes, and scanned the roof of their home with anxious eyes. The rain drummed upon it steadily and persistently with a note which held out no hope of respite for many hours to come.

" If it had been going to leak it would have begun by now," Joe said. " We shall be all right unless we bump it." She edged round to the farther side of the pole with the careful stooping movements of the tent dweller, and wrapping her overcoat round her shoulders, made herself as comfortable as she could on a kitbag flanked by rolled-up bedding. " I wish," she concluded gloomily, " that we had not worked so hard yesterday. We have made all the gadgets we need, and I hate cluttering up the place with mere frills."

She gave a towel-rail a hopeful shake as she spoke, but it was in no need of repairs and stood as firmly as a towel-rail could reasonably be expected to stand.

Hester and Philippa sighed agreement. They had left the next-door camp in a state of mild bustle and confusion. A tent had leaked in the night, and its occupants were being transferred, bag and baggage, elsewhere. Their offers of help had been politely declined, and the three leaders had come away feeling that it was a little dull that matters should be left so much in the hands of their juniors.

They settled themselves down rather disconsolately to a long morning of books and letter-writing, interrupted only by occasional sallies from under the wet brailing to look at a world sodden as drearily as ever with drenching rain. At length Joe, more restless than the other two, stood up.

" I am going for a walk," she said, pulling on her mackintosh and buttoning the collar up round her ears. " It is my turn to cook, so I shall get wet anyhow; as well be hung for a walk as a sausage."

She scrambled under the door, and the depressing squelch of her shoes could be heard dying away up the field.

" I hope she will remember to keep away from the woods and the beach," Hester said. " She has some sort of an idea in her head, and has not just gone out for an ordinary walk or she wouldn't have hurried off without so much as suggesting that we should come too. I believe she means to call at the Manor and have it out with Mrs. Roberts."

" Not in a bathing cap!"

" Hm. Perhaps not. But she has something on her mind—I wish I had something on mine. I haven't even a mind to have anything on!" Hester yawned, stretched herself, and returned to the letter she was writing to an elderly aunt.

Whether her surmise was right or wrong, Joe was away for a very long time; so long, indeed, that her two friends had ceased to feel anxious about the dinner she was supposed to cook for them, and had become anxious about herself, before they heard the welcome flap of her mackintosh in the kitchen. She came crawling in presently, dripping like a sponge from every fold, but with a look of triumph on her face that no rain could wash away.

" I have something to tell you," she said, pausing on her hands and knees half in and half out of the tent. " I'll just get the fire going first. Throw me the matches."

" Where have you been?" Hester demanded, complying.

" Farm—yes? What is it?" Joe wriggled backwards as a voice called to her from the hedge. She vanished, and was absent for several minutes. When she came back her face had lost all its triumph and was white and very sober.

" There's been an accident," she said. " Captain wants us."

" An accident!"

For a second Hester and Philippa stared at her, while their hands, quicker than their brains, stretched out automatically in search of gum-boots.

" Who?"

" What has happened?"

" Miss Ashe. She stumbled when she was lifting the stew from the fire, and it went over her arm, right up beyond the elbow. It is pretty bad. Do hurry up."

Hester grabbed at her mackintosh.

" I have been wishing all the morning that something would happen to make them want us," she exclaimed in a voice filled with remorse, " but I never meant anything like this."

They found a disconsolate Company standing in scattered groups about the fireplace in the farther camp. Everything the Guides could do to help had been done, but the idea of going back to their tents seemed heartless and they waited, feeling that indifference to rain and wind and long wet grass would at least express their sympathy. It seemed even more heartless to carry out Philippa's suggestion and have dinner, but realizing that the most helpful thing they could do would be to do as they were told—they did it; and served, and ate, and washed up as if their quartermaster's life depended upon the thoroughness of each task.

Joe joined them half-way through the meal, after helping the patient and her several attendants into Mrs. Aldwyn's car. She brought with her a number of messages which had a reassuring ring, most of them being descriptions of what would happen should anyone allow bones or tea-leaves to get into the pigpail during the absence of authority. The drooping spirits of the Company began to revive, although they continued to show the depths of their feelings by being very polite and attentive to one another, and almost unnaturally obedient to their Patrol Leaders.

But good though the Guides might be, to the three leaders the afternoon and evening seemed endless; and it was a very weary trio that plodded back at last through the wet and the darkness to the little camp. They had urged Mrs. Aldwyn to let them stay with her for the night, but the rain, which had never slackened for a moment, was coming down more heavily than ever. To strike and re-pitch their own tent was out of the question, and sleeping quarters in the big camp were already cramped for lack of the tent which had had to be abandoned that morning.

" The worst that can happen," their captain pointed out, " is another leaky tent, and that would make your room far more valuable than your company. Miss Ashe "—she glanced at a much-bandaged quarter-master, who grinned sardonically—" declares that she never felt better in her life. And the Guides are being so supernaturally perfect that they will all have halos as well as badges to polish to-morrow. Off you go, you three, and have a good night's rest. You have more than earned it, bless you."

More grateful for their release than they cared to admit, even to one another, the three girls took their departure. They had run quiet games in the Guides' tents. They had run active games in the barn. They had seen that the invalid's bed was ready with hot bottles for her return, and that their captain's dinner was kept hot. They had supervised the cooking and serving of tea and supper. They had dealt with a casual young twelve-year-old who, at seven o'clock, confessed to four very wet blankets acquired, she could not imagine how, during the afternoon. They had held a most successful sing-song. And finally, after a rigorous inspection of clothes and bedding, they had seen the Company tucked up for the night, and had taken hot lemonade round to each tent.

" I never knew before," said Hester as they trudged back to their own field, " that Guiders actually worked."

" They don't," said Joe. " They only go round seeing to things as we have been doing this afternoon— did you remember to slacken the guylines of the store-tent when you did up the doors?"

" They were slackened before supper."

" That won't be enough. They shrink all the time in weather like this. We had better go back."

The night was so dark that they lost themselves on the short journey home and had to feel their way along by the hedge. Inside their tent, after groping blindly for torches, they made their beds, unable to stand upright, but creeping to and fro on their hands and knees for fear of hitting the wet canvas; and bumping one another continually in the confined space.

" If there weren't so much water about already,"

Hester exclaimed, rubbing her head after a particularly painful collision with the tent pole, " I should burst into tears."

" Come, come," said Philippa, who, being tidier than the other two, had found her belongings more quickly and was already snugly curled up in bed. " Remember that the habit of looking on the bright side of things is worth a thousand a year."

" I wish someone would look on the bright side of my pyjamas," muttered Hester. " Goodness knows where they've got to. I believe I have made my bed with my sleeping bag upside down—where did I lay that torch?" She fumbled about the floor of the tent and her fingers closed over something smooth and shiny. She snatched it up only to find that it was the inkbottle, which she had left uncorked when hurrying off before dinner. The others giggled unfeelingly.

" ' Smile awhile, and while you smile another smiles, and soon there's miles and miles of smiles,' " chanted Philippa.

Hester glowered at her.

" The laughter of fools is like the crackling of thorns under a pot," she retorted. " And if you don't stop, Philippa Fleming, I'll give the tent a good hard slap just above your pillow."

Joe and Philippa sat up, and their giggling stopped abruptly. When Hester was roused there was no saying to what lengths her wrath might carry her.

" Talking of pots," Philippa said hastily, to change the dangerous trend of the conversation, " it is Joe's turn to cook the breakfast to-morrow as she missed dinner to-day—and Joe, what was it you were going to tell us this morning when you were so late of coming back? Was it anything to do with that Roberts person?"

" Yes—half a minute——" Joe slipped out of bed to help Hester with her blankets. When at last all three girls were settled, and torches had been switched out, she went on. " Did you notice how Mrs. Roberts hesitated when you asked her about going into the woods?"

" I think I did, but yesterday evening seems so long ago that I have almost forgotten what happened."

" Well, she did. And when she talked about disturbing the game, I was pretty sure she was just inventing an excuse. You see, it is grouse shooting that begins next week, and there can't be any grouse round here because there is no heather, and heather is the chief thing a grouse eats. If these woods are preserved at all, it must be for pheasants, and pheasant shooting doesn't begin till October; the coverts are not usually shot till about the middle of November."

" Even so, she might think we would do a lot of damage."

" She might. But it sounded to me as if she simply didn't know what she was talking about. Besides, these woods weren't preserved last year; and the Manor House has not been let to the Roberts people very long, and you don't stock coverts all in five minutes."

" I suppose not. Go on."

" I went down to the farm and talked to Mrs. Weland about it, and she fetched Mr. Weland. He has been acting as Colonel Eskdale's agent for the estate, and the whole letting of the Manor has gone through his hands. He says that the woods are not preserved and haven't been for years. And he says that the Roberts have rented the Manor House only, and have not one jot nor tittle of right to anything else, and that in any case the whole stretch of land down by the shore and all along the coast is a public right-of-way."

There was a short pause, then Hester said inelegantly:

" Well, I am blowed!"

" There must be a mistake somewhere," exclaimed Philippa. " Are you positive Mr. Weland hasn't misunderstood you, Joe? Perhaps he thought you were asking about the copse where we always go wooding, and our own little stretch of beach."

" No. I told him exactly where we were—down at the foot of the lane where the barge is anchored—and exactly what Mrs. Roberts said to us; and he was so angry that he went to his safe and took out the letters

Mr. Roberts had written to him, and the agreement. The Manor has been taken, furnished, on a monthly lease for three months, with an option of extending the period."

" Does the agreement say in so many words ' no woods '?"

" Not exactly; but it talks about the Manor House being part of the property known as the Eskdale estate, and it mentions that the lessee is entitled to the produce from the gardens of the said house. I can't remember the precise words, but they were quite clear, even to me. And as Mr. Weland has rented the farm lands for over twenty years, and has been agent for the rest of the estate for at least ten, he must surely know what goes with the Manor and what doesn't."

" Then it must be the Roberts who have muddled things up, because Mrs. Roberts did say quite distinctly that the whole place was private, and that she would have us up for trespassing if we went there again."

" According to Mr. Weland there is no question of a muddle. It is just ' all of a piece with the rest of their goings on '. He ground his teeth, he was so angry, partly because of Mrs. Roberts meddling with his affairs, and partly because of us? They are dears, the Welands. They always talk of us as ' their own ' Guides."

" But," said Philippa, propping herself up on her elbows, " why on earth should they? Why should the Roberts, I mean, want to turn us out? We weren't doing any harm, lighting one small fire in a safe, sandy hollow. We weren't even making any noise, except a polite noise to let them know we were there—I wish we hadn't."

" It sounds to me a rummy, fishy show," said Hester, even less elegantly than before. " What about telling Captain?"

" I wondered about that this afternoon," Joe said, " but I thought she looked as if she had had enough to worry her for one day. If we really had trespassed, even by mistake, of course we should have had to own up at once. But as things are, there doesn't seem to be any urgent need to let her know just now that our new neighbours are bent on being disagreeable."

" But shouldn't we warn the rest of the Company? That Roberts woman might make some of the babes perfectly miserable if she talked to them as she talked to us."

" I don't think she will. Mr. Weland is writing—in fact he has written, he did it while I was there—to explain that we have permission to go where we like."

" In that case," said Hester after a moment's thought, " we can carry on with our hide. I am longing to try those dyes. If Captain doesn't want us for the whole of to-morrow, let's begin collecting the herbs. They ought to be nice and juicy and full of colour after all this rain."

Philippa lay back on her pillow, though she continued to shake her head in a puzzled way.

" Why?" she murmured. " Why? Well, well! I suppose they just don't like the look of us. We had better hang little bells round our necks and cry ' woe, woe ', to let them know when we are coming, as lepers do."

" We needn't bother for a day or two, at any rate," said Joe.

" Why not?"

" I believe they are away."

" How do you know?"

Joe turned over on her side and curled herself up.

" The barge has gone," she said. " I watched her sail this evening."

CHAPTER V

The Dyeing of the Hide

When she woke up to another wet morning Hester called for three hearty grumbles. She gave them herself, heading them with a firstly, secondly, and a thirdly, and each grumble was so clear and to the point that her companions could find nothing to add except applause.

Philippa, getting solemnly out of bed, made a little speech in which she expressed her deep gratitude to her eloquent and esteemed colleague, and proposed a vote of thanks. The motion was seconded by Joe and carried unanimously, after which the meeting adjourned very cheerfully to wash. It became even more cheerful when it saw upon leaving the tent that the clouds, though wet and stormy, were broken, revealing glimpses of blue sky as they went scudding before the wind.

Leaving Joe to her cooking, Hester and Philippa walked across the neighbouring field to inquire for the invalid, and to lend such hands as might be needed. Everybody was at work, and the preparations for breakfast were in full swing. It was plain that the Company meant to adapt itself to circumstances and, since it could no longer wholly rely upon its two Guiders, rely instead upon itself. By eleven o'clock the leaders found themselves once more free to follow their own devices, and after some discussion set out on their long-delayed shopping expedition.

"I read about dyes in the badge book yesterday morning," Hester told the other two. "The wool has to be prepared by boiling it in alum; it is called mordant——"

"But unbleached calico isn't wool," Philippa interrupted. "It is only cotton."

"The badge book doesn't say anything about calico; in fact it doesn't say very much about anything, except lichen dyes. We shall have to trust to luck and invent what we can't guess. The mordanting business is supposed to take four or five days, but we haven't time for all that. But we can at least get the stuff and be soaking it while we collect the flowers—besides, don't you think shopping in a nice, dry bus has its attractions?"

Joe and Philippa smiled. It did not take them long to guess that there were other nice, dry attractions besides the bus. They could not hope to reach the town in less than an hour; shopping would occupy the better part of another hour, and at one o'clock they had no doubt that Hester would, with an engaging air of innocence, discover an opportune restaurant. Although the glimpses of blue sky had become more frequent, rain was still falling, and it was Hester's turn to cook the dinner. Everything happened as they had foreseen, except that the air of innocence was accompanied by a wink, and they returned to camp at two o'clock, warm, dry, well-fed, and at peace with the world."

"What did I tell you?" exclaimed Hester, taking to herself entire credit for the first patch of watery sunshine. "Now we can go to work right away, without any tiresome cooking and washing up. What an enormous amount of time and talk and energy one does waste in camp on eating, or getting ready to eat, or clearing away after one has eaten."

"You wouldn't be much use as the wife of a pioneer," Joe said. "What would you do if you had to grow your food as well as cooking it; and spin your own wool, and weave your own cloth, and look after ten children, and fight a few Indians in between times."

"I shouldn't waste my time answering silly questions," returned Hester. "You put that alum on to boil, while Philippa and I cut out the calico and sew it."

They designed the hide by slinging the length of wide calico over a rope stretched from a tall pole to a short one, and cutting off the corners that trailed on the ground. The severed pieces and a spare half yard of the stuff made a curtain for the tall end, leaving the little one open so that they could creep in and out. There was no denying that the shelter when made was rather an odd shape. It looked as if it had sat down for a rest, and the two windows which Philippa cut in the upper end gave it a knowing and rakish expression. But, whatever its appearance, it held the three girls without bulging unduly if they sat still. They stitched it together, and by tea-time had it ready for the dixie of alum mordant which Joe had prepared.

The next stage was the collection of leaves, roots and flowers. But here, after an hour's hard search, even Hester's enthusiasm began to flag. For green dyes there were pear leaves and cow parsley in plenty; but other colours proved more elusive.

"If we found all the agrimony and St. John's wort in the field," Philippa said, "it wouldn't dye a pocket handkerchief. Can't you suggest anything else, Hester?"

"There's nettles," Hester replied. "Lots of them, and I am game to pick them, if you are."

"What colour do they dye?"

"Yellow. Dirty yellow."

Philippa laughed. "That sounds appropriate. We shall ' pine in thought, and in a green and yellow melancholy sit like Patience on a monument smiling at grief '. I don't know about the smiling, but we shall certainly need the patience."

"Hideous," muttered Hester, whose mind's eye

had pictured all the colours of the rainbow. " I wish we could find some birch bark, but we can't go peeling it off living trees, and I have seen no fallen ones, have you?"

" There is a young ash sapling down, if that is any use to you. It is over by the cliff."

" Ash." Hester's face brightened. " Ash should give us quite a good blue. What is its bark like?"

" Worse than its bite," responded Philippa gravely.

Hester looked at her with a stolidly wooden expression.

" Oh, I see! You are being funny! By the cliff, did you say? Then if Joe will lend me her turfing knife I'll go there now."

" Joe won't, and you won't," said Joe emphatically. " You will come right over here and help to pick nettles, as you said you would."

The nettles, though painful at first, soon lost their sting; and by the time an adequate supply had been gathered and laid beside the heap of cow parsley, the girls were handling them as easily as they handled a basin of onion skins rescued from the next-door camp, from which Hester engaged to distil a rich orange colour. It was supper-time before they finished collecting their raw materials, and further work had to be postponed till the morning; but they spent a useful hour after they were in bed inventing the recipes they proposed to follow. Their ideas were of the haziest;

but ignorance, they agreed, was probably bliss. And it was more amusing to experiment for themselves than to follow instructions out of a book.

The first step was to pound the nettles to a pulp; but when they tried, they soon found that this was easier said than done. Their tent mallet and tin basin made a poor substitute for pestle and mortar. Nothing daunted, they borrowed the mincing machine from the big camp, and in due course the green mash was put into the washing-up dixie, covered with water, and brought to the boil. Then they twisted a large stone into a corner of the calico, tied it tightly with string, and dropped it into the cabbagy liquid. The corner slowly took on a greenish-yellow hue, ugly, but undoubtedly darker than the original stuff; and presently they untied the stone and revealed a round dingy, yellow patch edged with little white streaks where the stuff had been twisted and tied.

" Too pale," Hester said, eyeing it critically. " We must give the next piece longer. I wonder if we could get on the ash and the cow parsley and dye three colours at a time; otherwise it will take days to finish the whole thing. The ash bark had better be soaked whole, Phil; poor Q.M.'s temperature would burst the thermometer if she found we had been putting trees through her treasured mincer. How was she this morning?"

" Up," Joe answered, " but rather the worse for

wear. Billy told me that it takes an hour and a half to dress her arm, counting the time needed for sterilizing things and getting ready, and Captain does it twice a day. It must keep her pretty busy."

" I wish she would let us help more; but she says the Guides are being such lambs there is no need. Let's have a party for them to-morrow, ask them to tea, and run sports and games afterwards. It would take them off her hands without giving them that you-can't-get-along-without-us feeling—I say! That pear-leaf green is going to be good!"

They lunched off bread and cheese, holding a slice in one hand while they poked and prodded, and stoked the fire, and held the overflowing yards of calico out of harm's way, with the other. The sun, repenting his two days' desertion, streamed down upon them. They grew hotter and hotter, and the wet dyed calico, getting heavier and more unmanageable, fell into the ashes and dragged on the ground by the fire-place, so that new and unintended stains were added to it. The supply of cow parsley ran out, and Philippa had to find more, and to stand like a hurdy-gurdy man turning the handle of the mincer till her arms ached. But in spite of all trials the girls persevered, and by tea-time a remarkable shelter, strangely patched with colours that had run into one another, and dotted here and there with white spots, was hung proudly over its poles to dry.

" It may look odd," said Hester, gazing at it affectionately, " but for camouflage it couldn't be bettered, unless it dries too pale. In the woods you will hardly be able to see it; it won't show at all at any distance."

The others uttered non-committal grunts. Whatever it might do at a distance in the woods, close at hand in the field the effect was far from beautiful. Hester was right, nevertheless. In the evening they bore it away, and after scouring the woods, put it up among some bushes, where it overlooked a clearing in the plantation at the foot of the lane by the creek. In the half light the dingy greens and yellows faded into their background and the misshapen patches held no unbroken lines to catch the eye. They spent another hour putting final touches to their handiwork, darkening the white spots with the aid of a humble mud pie, and came away at last with the feeling that their work had been well done; which is, perhaps, of all the feelings vouchsafed to mankind, the happiest.

" It seems a lot of trouble for the sake of watching a rabbit do its daily dozen before breakfast," Hester remarked, as they returned to camp, " but we have had a lot of fun out of it. What about putting down your sandpatch for tracks, Philippa? I should like to play with plaster casts. Patience on monuments never was my strong point. I would far rather do something."

" That is a good thing," Joe put in drily, " because it is your turn to do the supper. We'll leave the sandpatch to-night. For one thing, time is getting on, and for another, we shall know better after to-morrow morning where to spread it."

They went early to bed and, being tired, early to sleep. Philippa, as on her first night in camp, slept lightly, turning and tossing on her palliasse; and it was still dark when she woke just before four. She sat up with a sense of expectation that reminded her of Christmas mornings when she was little. She smiled as she recalled the bulging stockings that used to hang in the darkness at the foot of her bed, with shadowy crackers sticking out of the top. The memory cast a glamour over her present waking, and she felt sure that something nice was going to happen. She leaned towards Joe and Hester and gave each a little shake. Joe was roused at once, but Hester snuggled deeper into her pillow. Philippa shook her again.

" G'away!" she muttered.

" It is time to get up."

" 'Tisn't."

" It is, really."

" Dark."

" But don't you remember? We are going out to the hide. We must get there before dawn if we want to watch properly." Philippa emphasized her argument with a third and harder shake.

" Shup!" said Hester clearly, and rolling over, turned her back on them and settled down to sleep.

"Better leave her," counselled Joe. "She isn't really keen on the watching part. She probably wouldn't sit still, and that hide is close quarters at the best of times."

The air was cold when they crept out into the open field, and they pulled their coats about them, shivering. There was already a tinge of grey breaking through the darkness, but the woods were as black as midnight and at first, to untrained ears, as silent as the tomb. The girls moved gingerly, feeling their way before them, but for all their caution they sounded to themselves like two earthquakes crashing through the bushes. They found the hide, crawled in on hands and knees, spread a ground-sheet over the floor, and sat down to wait, wishing that their enthusiasm had not brought them there quite so early. There was nothing to do except listen, and they were too inexperienced to do more than guess at the meaning of the rustlings and cracklings which echoed around them. They were sleepy; not only their eyes, but every limb and muscle felt heavy, and they quickly found that straining to hear without being able to see made them sleepier. Philippa found herself wondering whether there might not be some justification for the sharp line which Hester drew between the pleasures one enjoyed, and the pleasures which other people said one ought to enjoy. The ground was cold and hard and uninviting, but she slipped down lower and lower upon it until, half crouching, half lying, she fell into a doze.

She was roused by the choir of birds, and for the second time that morning shook Joe into consciousness. The two girls scrambled to their knees, stretching their cramped bodies as best they might in the narrow space. Peering through their windows they saw the trees, grey in the half light, but with the first gleams of sunshine flickering through the branches. The vigil had begun.

For a time, though there were rustlings and whisperings in plenty, they saw little, and felt themselves to be almost as blind as they had been in the dark; but with the increasing daylight their eyes grew quicker to catch the movements of the world wakening around them. They saw a tree-creeper appear at the base of an oak sapling and climb up the trunk. It mounted in a leisurely spiral, disappearing round one side, appearing again at the other and darting its beak with swift continuous movements into the crevices of the wood. It reached the branches, flew down, climbed again, walked out along a branch and flew off to a fresh tree. A Jenny Wren flirted in and out among the bushes just beside the shelter, its comings and goings as neat and as surprising as if a conjurer were producing it out of a hat. A squirrel sat up for a breakfast of pine cone, holding the cone by one end and tidily stripping off the scales to reach the seeds beneath; but a jay screamed, and he dropped the cone before it was half finished and fled, scuttering up a tree and leaping from branch to branch with tail outstretched, till he vanished in the woods.

The girls peered out to find what had frightened him and could see nothing, but a couple of rabbits lolloping across the clearing turned suddenly and doubled back on their tracks.

" There may be a fox somewhere," Philippa whispered. " I heard one barking in the night."

" More likely us," Joe answered her, " only—sh!"

The jay screamed again, and they saw a pair of wood pigeons rise and go flapping towards the cornfields. Almost at the same moment they heard a woman's voice speaking softly and quite near at hand.

" We can't risk another journey. The light is too good."

" If we don't unload now "—the answering voice was a man's—" there will be another twenty-four hours' delay, and every day the tides keep us later."

A second masculine voice struck in.

" She is right, all the same, Roberts. The delay is a confounded nuisance, but we can't carry on in broad daylight. We shall have to get going earlier next time, Guides or no Guides. I won't come up to the Manor; I don't want those servants of yours to see me, and, in any case, it is quicker to cut straight through here to the car."

The last words were loud and clear, and before the

girls could stir the speaker appeared and came striding through the coppice within a few yards of their shelter. They held their breath. For all their innocence of trespass or intention, they had no wish to face Mrs. Roberts at this moment. The man walked on and passed into the woods. The sound of feet died away up the lane. Jenny Wren, perching on a twig almost at their elbow, ceased her warning " tick-tick " and burst into a triumphant " diddle-diddle-diddle-diddle-dree-ee ".

Philippa relaxed with a long sigh, but Joe kept a hand on her shoulder, warning her not to speak. Presently, from somewhere far away among the trees they heard a car being started up. It buzzed its way through the wood in first gear, changed up, and faded out of earshot.

" What is the time?" whispered Joe.

" After six."

" Give them a clear half-hour. They may not go straight back."

The two girls sat down and waited. They no longer had either eyes or ears for nature lore. At last Joe judged it safe to leave. They slipped out through the coppice, and instead of going up the lane, crossed it and squeezed through a gap in the hedge on the farther side, where they crept cautiously up the ditch. As they approached the camp they saw a thin wisp of smoke rising in the still air.

" That can't be Hester!" Philippa exclaimed, almost as startled as she had been in the woods.

It was Hester, nevertheless, and she waved to them and then, to their surprise, put her finger to her lips.

" What!" cried Joe. " Have things been happening to her too!"

They hurried towards the camp, but Hester, coming to meet them, drew them aside as they approached the tent.

" I want to show you something," she said, and leading them in a wide circle towards the tent door, she pointed to the grass.

Four lines of footprints showed dark in the shining dew. One was Joe's. One was Philippa's. One was Hester's. And one, leading down from the gate to the tent and back again, had been made by a pair of little pointed shoes with high French heels.

CHAPTER VI

The Tracks in the Wood

" I was so afraid the sun would have dried them up before you came back," said Hester, prodding a slice of bacon about the frying pan with a fork.

The other two squatted by the fireside, sniffing the fragrance appreciatively.

" But when did you discover them?" asked Philippa. " What made you get up so soon?"

" I guessed you would have had enough of observation in two hours or so, if you didn't fall asleep first, and I was pretty sure you would come back ravenous. It was a little after six when I first came out, and they showed even more plainly then."

" Just after six. That was while Mrs. Roberts was frightening us out of our wits in the hide. She can't have come here while we were awake or we should have heard her; so if the footprints were there at six, they must have been made while we were asleep, sometime in the middle of the night. That seems quite obvious."

" She probably came to see that we were asleep," Joe put in. " That second man said something about

' Guides or no Guides ', as if we were people he would have to guard against."

" It does look now as if they had some reason for wanting us out of the way," Hester said. " But it is a pity for their own sakes that they are so clumsy about it. If they had left us alone, we should never have given them a second thought. As it is——" She left her sentence unfinished, but her chin took on an obstinate tilt.

" As it is," Philippa echoed, " we itch to know what they are doing, and mean to find out if we can, only —I suppose it is all right."

" Suppose what is all right? I shouldn't take the rightness of our Manor friends for granted, if that is what you mean."

" I don't. I only mean, is it our business? Are we poking our noses?"

" No," said Hester. " It probably isn't our business. But people who walk into our camp in the middle of the night are making themselves our business, and they are going to get all the trouble they ask for. They are thrusting themselves upon us. ' Nemo me impune lacessit '," she finished, grandly. " Scotland's motto, and I am Scottish to the backbone."

" Umph!" said Joe. " There is another good Scotch saying, ' Ca' canny '. We may not like them coming into our camp, but it was no crime. They didn't do us any harm."

" And on the other hand if their mysterious business is all aboveboard we shan't do them any harm," retorted Hester.

" And how exactly do you propose to find out if it is aboveboard or not?"

" We know they are carrying on with it to-night," Philippa struck in, " so why shouldn't we take the chance and watch them?"

" Because Mrs. Roberts will come to look at us before they begin," said Joe. " She has not a beautiful and trusting character, one gathers."

There was a short and thoughtful silence, then Hester said:

" We must do something. I feel as if she had challenged us."

" And thrown down two shoes instead of a gauntlet," added Philippa, smiling a little. " As a beginning, why shouldn't we go down to the woods and find out where that car stood? It must have left tracks, and we might pick up some information, though goodness knows what."

She looked inquiringly at Joe, who nodded.

" I think we might venture that far. But however challenged we feel, we must not put ourselves in the wrong. When you get into scrapes, it is never the slightest use explaining to grown-ups that they began it. They just refuse to listen."

" There isn't going to be a scrape," declared Hester.

" Not even Mrs. Roberts can make a scrape out of going into a wood where a car has been. And, in any case, we don't propose to be seen by Mrs. Roberts. Our investigations "—Hester's voice became a little pompous—" will be strictly private."

This assertion notwithstanding, they felt far from strictly private when, after colours and prayers, they set out on their search. Even Hester admitted that she felt like a sandwichman, placarded behind and before in letters two feet high " Sleuth! Beware!" They sauntered self-consciously down the steep by-road between their camp and the main road, doing their best to look as if they were out for a pleasant morning's walk.

The road surface, though in places it had been mended with cartloads of pebbles from the beach, was for the most part thick with dust, and showed innumerable car tracks made by the tradesmen's vans which visited the camp and the Manor House. But although the girls scrutinized every gap where a car could have turned off the road into the woods, not a track could they find till they had reached the little bridge over the creek, where, being close to the main road and the zone of picnics, they found far too many. Hot and dusty after their walk, they sat down on the parapet of the bridge to think.

" This is really the best place to start from," Joe remarked, not at all discouraged. " We know that wherever else it went, the car must first have crossed this bridge in order to reach the woods at all. All we have to do now is to pick up the trail and follow it."

" But which trail are we to pick up? The place is a perfect car park."

Hester turned her eyes from the shining water of the creek, which mirrored trees and clouds and blue sky, to look disgustedly at orange peel, broken bottles, and dirty paper bags.

" If I wanted to drive a car into the woods at four o'clock in the morning for reasons that were wropt in mystery," said Joe, " I shouldn't go straight up a road that took me past a farm, not if I could help it."

" But could you? Is there any other path that would be passable for a car?"

" We'll make a cast round the car park and find out. The only thing to be said for picnickers with orange peel minds, is that they don't go far from the beaten track as a rule. If we come across any signs of enterprise, we'll follow them."

After exploring several misleading paths which ended in the bushes, the three found what they sought beyond the tract of grass by the waterside. Here, on a bumpy and moss-grown stretch of ground, Philippa saw tyre marks which wound away between the trees. By degrees the trees became more scattered and the track more defined until a distinct, if rough and narrow, path emerged by the border of the creek.

In spite of the difficulties which must have confronted the driver, there was no doubt that a car had travelled that way quite recently, for in addition to tread marks, every here and there lay small freshly broken twigs and branches, their leaves green, and their pith showing white where they had been snapped off.

The trail ended at last in a sheltered hollow under an oak tree. Tracks crossed and recrossed one another where the car had been backed and turned; and four clear, rather deeply imprinted tyre treads, with black drops of oil between them, marked the spot on which it had stood. A few yards away three paths met. One, the path along which the car had come; one leading towards the creek and the lane; and one disappearing among the bushes in the direction of the farm road.

The three girls glanced about them a little nervously. The undergrowth was thick, and they had discovered for themselves how easy it was to watch, or to be watched, unseen or unseeing. Instinctively they lowered their voices.

" What next?" asked Philippa.

All three looked again from the bushes to the paths, and back from paths to tyre prints. Joe studied the ground carefully and noted with satisfaction that their own soft canvas shoes left only blurred and vague traces on the springy moss. She walked over to the four deep tyre prints.

" It must have been a large car," she said. " It

drove up as far as this, and was left standing here, you can see by the sinking of the wheel tracks; then it backed to the crossroads there, without going forward at all from where it stood, so that those oil marks give us its length from the bonnet to the back axle. And the tyres look to me bigger than usual, though perhaps that is because they have sunk in so."

" They are not all alike," Hester observed, stooping to look at them more closely. " These three have long curly squiggles, while that rear one has square ones."

" It has had a bad puncture too. You can see a flaw in the treads every couple of yards where the outer cover has been vulcanized—I say "—Joe straightened herself—" suppose you try your hand at a cast, Philippa! I don't know what use it would be just now, exactly, but you never can tell. It might help to identify the car at some vital moment. It will be good practice in casting, if nothing else; the marks are so clear and deep."

" You did say something a few hours ago about being careful not to get into scrapes," hinted Philippa.

" Did I?" Joe grinned. " What a shocking memory I have, to be sure. If you and I fetch the plaster of paris, we can take the path to the hide and reach camp through the fields. We might pick up other tracks as we go. Hester can follow the third path to the farm, and see if she can borrow a copy of the *Autocar* to compare with the tyres—or if she would rather not go alone, you go with her, and I'll fetch the plaster."

"Not go alone!" Hester looked startled. "My dear Joe! What do you think is going to happen? After your calm and detached attitude this morning, too!"

Joe shrugged her shoulders.

"Come on, then," she said to Philippa. "It will take about three-quarters of an hour to get to camp, collect the things, and come back again; so you had better stop for a chat with Mrs. Weland, Hester. You don't want to be loitering about here longer than necessary."

Whether from their lack of skill in finding clues, or whether there were none to find, no further knowledge was gleaned on the way to and from camp. The three met again at the appointed time, and feeling that if they were caught now their actions would require a good deal of explanation, set anxiously to work. The plaster of paris was mixed into a smooth cream and poured first into the track of the patched tyre, and then into one of the others, and stout sticks were placed as barriers to prevent it spreading too widely. It took four mugfuls of mixture in each track to make a cast large and deep enough to satisfy Philippa, and while the girls were waiting for the plaster to harden, they studied Hester's motoring paper.

To identify the tyres from the advertisements

proved more difficult than they had expected. The punctured one they found quickly enough, but the remaining three resembled none of those shown, and when Hester did at last hit upon a possible likeness, it was an illustration of a foreign make of car, and the tyres themselves were neither named nor mentioned.

"Not that that matters," she said. "It may even be more helpful in a way. If three of the tyres on our car are French, we can be fairly sure that the car itself is French too, and if we are watching for it, we should be able to see a whole French car much quicker than we could notice three unusual tyres on an English one. It may even have a foreign number plate."

"Not with one English tyre," Joe returned. "The fourth tyre looks more like a French car with a British owner, or at least with an owner that lives in this country—how much have we found out? Let's check it. A large French car, six cylinder probably. Saloon —almost all big cars are saloons, it is a safe guess. English number plate. Odd tyres. Colour—I wonder if we could get a hint of its colour. It must have bumped a little, turning in that narrow space. We should be able to find a tiny fleck of paint on the thorn bushes, if we tried."

Joe walked towards the path up which the car had been driven, gazing intently at every bush and tree trunk.

" It has rubbed against——" she began, and broke off.

The others, absorbed in their own search, paid no heed to her silence till Hester, glancing round and seeing her standing stock-still with her eyes fixed on the ground, called out:

" What is the matter?"

" Come here a minute." There was a curious note in Joe's voice that brought her two companions hurrying towards her. Without a word she pointed to the ground, and they saw, outlined in stones, and stretching across the path from side to side, a large, plainly marked arrow. They stared, then Hester said with simple eloquence:

" Lumme!"

" It wasn't there when we came first," Joe said.

" It was not."

" Do you suppose the children have been here," Philippa suggested. " It is a regular tracking sign."

" Whoever made it," Joe rejoined, " must have watched us for quite a while. As sleuth hounds we seem to have something still to learn."

" Whoever made it," Hester said more optimistically, " doesn't seem to be at all unfriendly. Also he, or she, probably wants us to follow it up."

All three turned to look in the direction in which the arrow pointed. Simultaneously their eyes fell upon a pile of three small stones at no great distance away, and simultaneously they moved towards them. The stones directed them to a thick holly bush. Three more sent them to the stump of a beech tree on the bark of which was scrawled a square with a number inside and another pointing arrow. With rising excitement they paced out the distance, and after a short search found a heavy stone with a smaller one balanced above it, between two gnarled and twisted roots. A corner of paper showed white against the ground.

"Wait a minute!" Joe caught Hester's arm quickly as she stooped to take it out.

They stood quite still, listening intently, but the only sounds they heard were those of the woodlands; the rustling of leaves, birds singing, a dog barking down by the farm, and the faint distant thrum of the reaper. Presently Joe gave a nod.

"I think it is all right this time," she said, and Hester, tipping the stone up with her knuckles so as to leave no fingerprints, withdrew the paper. She unfolded it, with the others peering eagerly over her shoulder, and after a quick scrutiny handed it to Joe, her face falling.

"It is only a hoax," she exclaimed in a flat voice. "Just a lot of zigzags like a child's scribbling. It must have been the others after all."

Joe took it, frowning.

"The tracking signs looked like Guides, right enough," she admitted, "but I don't believe any of our people could have seen us without our hearing them. We did keep our ears open, and it is far harder to walk over this crackling underwood than the books on stalking seem to think." She studied the paper again, and her face brightened. " It looks like scribbling, but it is divided very definitely into words, you can tell by the lengths. It may be a cipher."

" If it is a cipher, then it is Captain's doing," declared Hester, her gloom persisting. " It will turn out to be morse, you see!"

Joe hesitated a moment longer, then tucked the paper away in her pocket.

" We can't wait to decipher it here," she said. " We have been hanging around too long as it is. Don't forget to erase the signs as we go back. Whether they are Captain's or not, we don't want any more people to know that we have been here."

They returned to the tyre tracks to find that the plaster had set thick and solid. Joe loosened it with her turfing knife, easing it out inch by inch so as to disturb the mould as little as possible. Should the motorist chance to return in daylight, there must be no trace of their work to catch his attention. Wrapping the two casts in Philippa's jersey, and packing them into a haversack, the three girls set out a little disconsolately for home. They had achieved at least as much as, if not more than, they had set out to do, but the excitement they had felt over the tracking signs, and their subsequent disappointment, had left them rather crestfallen. They took the path to the farm and came out on to the by-road half-way up the hill. They trudged up it wearily, the sun blistering the backs of their necks, and the dust rising in clouds from under their feet and making them sneeze.

" You know," Joe said suddenly, after they had climbed half a mile in silence, " I don't see how it could have been Captain. We started out directly after prayers and inspection, and that is when she does Miss Ashe's arm."

" Of course it was Captain," growled Hester. " Morse and a cipher, it is as plain as your face!"

" We can settle it by asking her," said Philippa, " but we had better decipher the message first. Come and sit in the kitchen, Joe, and tackle it while I get the dinner."

They reached the steading without having met a soul, climbed the gate into their field, and deposited their various burdens in the tent. Then Joe, with pencil and paper, squatted on the stores box in the shade of the oak tree.

" It is morse, sure enough," she said after a minute or two, " and quite easy to read, just a big V for a dash, and a small one for a dot, with a little hyphen joining the letters together. But "—she paused as she transcribed the letters, then added slowly, writing as she spoke — " I — don't — think — the — message — is — Captain's."

The others joined her and read, fascinated, as the words came one by one from the point of her pencil: " Secret and urgent. If you can do it without being seen, trail this car."

CHAPTER VII

The Cipher is Hard to Follow

" I don't believe it is Captain's," Joe repeated, digging the point of her pencil into the final dot, and twisting it this way and that. " How could she know there was a car there at all?"

" Tracks," said Hester.

" Hm, yes. She might have seen them. But would she send us off after a perfectly strange motor-car, just for a joke? It doesn't sound like her somehow. Besides, how did she come to be in the woods at eleven o'clock?"

" It may have been one of the Guides," Philippa said, " but it doesn't sound like them either, not with that zigzag morse."

Joe stood up, stretched herself, and passed a tidying hand over her hair.

" I shall be back in a jiffy," she said. " If you will get on with the chops, we can discuss over dinner what we are going to do. Don't forget there is all this afternoon's tea and games to get ready. We haven't much time for dallying. Any messages for Miss Ashe, Phil? It would be better if I had an excuse for calling."

" Love, of course, and a little more dripping, and I hope her arm is better—oh, and another swab if you can wring it out of her. I had forgotten that wretched party."

Philippa returned to her fire, where she let the chops burn while she watched Joe's retreating figure. Hester picked up the message and deciphered it afresh for herself, as if she hoped to find some vital word which Joe had overlooked!

" It must be Captain," she maintained for the twentieth time. " But if it isn't——"

" If it isn't, we shall do our best to trail a French six-cylinder saloon with three French tyres and one English one—we forgot to look for the colour, after seeing that arrow," said Philippa. " I wonder if we should go back."

" ' Secret and urgent,' " muttered Hester. " What exactly does that mean, I wonder."

" It probably means secret and urgent," Philippa answered rather drily.

" Yes, but secret from whom? Do you suppose Joe will tell Captain about it now?"

" Not if she intends to come back in a jiffy."

Hester carried the paper to the fire and warmed it carefully, without any visible effect.

" There is nothing else on it," she said. " Not another dot."

" Just as well, if you ask me," Philippa remarked.

" There is quite as much on it already as we can manage. You had better put it away. Hide it somewhere. If it turns out to be a joke, we can burn it. But if it doesn't, it had better be kept safe. If we do get into that scrape Joe mentioned, we may want it one of these days."

They waved eagerly when they saw Joe approach the stile. She shook her head, and continued to shake it with great emphasis as she climbed over.

" Not Captain?" cried Hester. " Not the others? Are you positive?"

" Perfectly positive." Joe crossed the grass and laid the dripping, but no swab, on the stores box. " They were just up from the beach, in their bathing wraps, when I went over. They have been down there since half-past eleven, and before that they were playing a return rounders match, Honesties against Daffs, while Captain was with Miss Ashe. She is in bed again—Miss Ashe, I mean. Nothing bad, but she ran a temperature last night after being up yesterday, and Captain is worried."

" You are certain it couldn't have been any of them? Not Bubbles, or Pat Franklin, or Pidgie? Pidgie is clever enough to have thought of the zigzags, I'm sure, and they are all three ready for any really good mischief that comes their way."

" Not just now. They are working like blacks, and haven't looked the road mischief is on since the accident. And in any case, not one of them was away from the camp at eleven o'clock."

" Then "—Philippa lifted the frying-pan from the fire and set it on a brick while she doled out the chops —" we must make up our minds what we are going to do, and how we are going to do it."

They sat down to dinner, rather surprised to find themselves hungry. They had been so preoccupied, that they had forgotten the length of time which had elapsed since breakfast.

" The first thing to decide," Joe said slowly, " is not ' what ', but ' if '."

" If?" Hester opened her eyes in surprise. " There isn't any ' if ', surely. Those tracking signs must have been made by a Guide, or someone who has been a Guide."

" Why not a Scout?" suggested Philippa mildly. " There are Scouts, you know."

" So much the better," rejoined Hester with a grin. She was a pretty girl. " I should enjoy helping a really nice Scout. But Scout or Guide, the real point is that we are to trail the Roberts crew, and that means that our Guide or Scout—let's call him the Gout—is on our side, or we are on his, whichever way you like to put it. And besides, isn't it our duty to help our Brister Gouts."

" Our what? Oh, I see. But can we take our Brister Gouts for granted? How do we know that the whole thing isn't a trap laid by our nice Mrs. Roberts herself?"

"My dear Joe," said Hester. "If Mrs. Roberts knows one thing about Guide tracking signs, I'll eat my boots—or her high-heeled shoes! No. It isn't ' if ' that worries me. It is ' how '."

There was a silence, while everybody ate ordinary dinner reflectively.

"We have two bicycles," Hester went on presently. "Q.M.'s and Miss Weland's. I know we can borrow Miss Weland's, because her mother told me that the last thing she did before we came, was to clean it and oil it and pump up the tyres, so that it would be there if we wanted it."

"We won't find it very easy to follow a six-cylinder car on bicycles," Joe said. "But they would be better than feet, which are our only alternative, as far as I can see. We could keep them at the barn, and slip down the hill and hide in the bushes beyond the bridge, and pick up the car as it goes past. The difficulty will be to avoid being seen. Navy-blue shows up at the best of times, but uniform, when the Roberts are already on their guard against Guides, is going to be a pretty stiff handicap."

"We can't borrow Miss Weland's clothes, as well as her bicycle," Philippa said doubtfully.

"We could. I believe we could borrow their skins, if we asked for them, but we won't. We must just do the best we can as we are." Joe dropped her melon rind into the fire, and rose to fetch the washing-up water. " If you will go down and ask for the bicycle, Philippa, Hester and I will get on with the things for the sports. The others said they would be here at three."

The afternoon was a strenuous one. Leaders and Company, meeting in the unfamiliar rôle of host and guest, found themselves unexpectedly shy; and their surprise at this unforeseen state of mind made them still shyer. At tea there were awkward silences interrupted by regrettable gigglings and whisperings; and more than one mug was upset, to the great embarrassment of its owner and the diversion of ill-behaved onlookers.

In spite of this slight initial constraint, the party showed no desire to go home, but, with the exception of a cook or two, remained enjoying its games, somewhat uproariously if the truth be told, till three whistles blown in chorus called it back to a very late supper.

" I hope they will settle down a little before bedtime," Joe said rather anxiously. " I suppose it is the reaction after four days of goodness. They seem to have been happy, anyway."

" So they jolly well ought," retorted Hester, " with three people taking all that trouble to amuse them. I am worn to a shadow."

Joe opened her mouth and then shut it again. She wondered whether, as Guides, she and Hester and Philippa had not sometimes been inclined to take the providing of amusement for granted. But, as was her habit, she kept that moral reflection to herself.

" We can't clear up all this mess to-night," Hester continued, standing in the middle of the kitchen and looking about her at the jammy remains of trays, plates, knives, and general litter. " It is getting on for nine, and we must have something to eat. I had almost no tea, there was so much to do, and we had to hurry over dinner too. Do you know "—Hester paused impressively—" we have actually been up and doing things almost without a pause since four o'clock this morning. No wonder we are tired!" She sat down on a tree root and gave a tremendous yawn at the thought.

Joe raked the ashes of the fire together vigorously, blew them into a flame, and put a billy of water on for cocoa.

" What about the Manor House?" she asked, glancing from Hester, who was propped wearily against the oak tree, to Philippa, who was scraping and stacking dirty dishes and dropping every second plate through sheer exhaustion. " Do you still want to keep watch to-night and find out what is being carried up from the barge?"

There was a prolonged and dismayed pause, then Philippa said faintly:

" We ought to. We may not get another chance."

" We shall have to be up before dawn, because of trailing the car," muttered Hester, " so a few hours earlier won't make much difference one way or the other. Only——"

She gave another yawn. It was hard to feel thrilled over an adventure when every bone in one's body was aching.

" If we are to watch," Joe said, " our best plan will be to wait until Mrs. Roberts has come and gone, and then go down across the fields to that gap in the hedge near our hide clearing. We can see a good deal from there, and if anything should go wrong, we have a chance of slipping back to camp which we wouldn't have if we were the other side of the lane. We shall have to come back before it is light, so as to get down to the bushes beyond the creek with our bicycles. If you could cut some bread and dripping, Hester, we could have supper in bed. We shall need all the rest we can get—and it is good dripping. It is in the basin I brought across this morning."

A very subdued little procession straggled across to the tent, bearing mugs and sandwiches. Joe and Hester scarcely spoke, but Philippa, who was apt to babble when she was tired, kept up a running chatter, half aloud, half to herself.

" ' Weary with toil I haste me to my bed,' " she murmured, unrolling her palliasse and smoothing out the blankets. " ' The dear repose for limbs with travel tired.' I wonder if Shakespeare ever camped! He seems to know all about it. ' But now begins a journey in my head To work my mind when body's work's expired.' Ugh, how true!". She crawled between the clothes and lay down, sighing. " I shall be creeping away from the lane and scooting down the hill on a bicycle all night, I know I shall. It will keep my drooping eyelids open wide looking on darkness——"

Joe leaned across her, picked up a slice of bread and dripping and pressed it into her mouth.

" Bite," she commanded. " A large bit that you can't talk through. You needn't bother about journeys working your mind, they can't work what isn't there; and as for drooping eyelids, it would be a blessing if they did keep open wide so that we could be sure of not missing Mrs. Roberts. But they won't. The only thing you ever open wide is your mouth—here! Take another bite."

" ' When I most wink,' " murmured Philippa, " ' then do mine eyes best see.' Don't you worry about Mrs. Roberts. I'll wake you when she comes—although "—her voice, muffled in blanket and dripping, grew indistinct—" whether I shall be able to wake Hester is quite another story."

For all her Shakespearean boasting she did neither,

and it was six o'clock and broad daylight when she
stirred, blinked, and started up, conscience-stricken.
The top of Hester's dark head was visible on its pillow,
but Joe's bed was empty and cold, cold even far down
between the blankets. She had evidently been gone
a long time.

Philippa peered out from under the tent brailing
at a silent deserted field, and a kitchen sordid with
yesterday's dirty plates. Then she huddled down
again into her bed and did her best to turn a deaf ear
to the call of duty. But she had two ears, and no
sooner did she turn one, than duty called into the
other. Sleep was banished. Conscience made her
palliasse a bed of thistles. And all ten Guide laws
walked unbidden into her head to remind her of disagreeable people who said: " I thought Guides were
supposed to——"

" Oh *blow!*" said Philippa.

She got up, dressed, went to the kitchen, and began
to wash the dishes. But if she expected to feel that
virtue which is its own reward, she was disappointed.
Conscience and Duty, standing one at either elbow,
told her that this tardy busyness was only a mask for
her anxiety about Joe. It was all very well to be washing dishes, but why had she not wakened as she had
promised? Philippa dried a plate and flung it angrily
on the ground. She found Conscience and Duty a
most unlovable couple.

The plate struck a pile of other plates, knocking them over, and their clatter brought Hester scurrying out of the tent to know what was wrong. Conscience at once told Philippa that this was what she had meant it to do, and that she was a pig. She flung the next plate down harder.

" Where is Joe?" cried Hester.

" How should I know," Philippa snapped. " Trailing that car, I suppose, as you ought to be doing."

" I like that! What about yourself?" Hester retreated indignantly to dress.

Fortunately for Conscience, who, being without tact, never knew when to stop arguing, and still more fortunately for the peace of the camp, Joe came back before Hester was ready, and her first words as she reached the kitchen were:

" I say, you have done a lot! We look quite respectable again—and Hester has got my bed out to air. You are a pair of bricks—what did you say?"

Philippa smiled happily.

" I was talking to Duty, telling her that ' her I now would serve more strictly '—no, no. I am quite all right. It was only an idea."

" We have both been rather worried about you," Hester explained, joining them. " That is why I tidied your bed. I thought it would be so sad to have to do it afterwards, if you turned out to be a corp. How did you get on. What happened?"

" Practically nothing. The bicycle idea is no good. We shall have to think of something else if we get another chance."

" When did you go?"

" Why didn't you wake us?"

" Did you see anything in the lane?"

" No. I didn't wake myself till after it was light, and you both looked so dead to the world that I hadn't the heart to disturb you. Besides, I thought one person would have a better chance of reaching the creek than two or three. It would have been different if it had been dark. I only just got down by the skin of my teeth. The car came along about three minutes after I had hidden."

" What was it like?"

Joe's face fell, and she answered with disgust:

" A seven-year-old Morris, just like Daddy's, only blue."

The disgust was reflected on the faces of her audience.

" Well, we are a clever lot," muttered Hester. " With our six-cylinder French saloon. Are you sure it was the right one?"

" It must have been. Two cars wouldn't be coming out of the woods at five in the morning. And it was a saloon. That was the only point we had right."

" But that was just a guess, while all the rest we

thought we had deduced. How far did you follow it?"

"Not at all, really. It was all right as far as the turning into the main road, because the last part of the lane twists and bends so that it had to go slowly and I could keep quite close without being seen. But on the main road I had to keep out of sight because of the reflecting mirror, and once it had got ahead I never saw it again. I went as far as that big fork beyond Woodmouth; I hoped I might be able to pick up its tyre tracks. But that is hopeless on a main road. There wasn't a thing to show which way it had gone, though I hunted for ages. We shall have to find some better plan if we try again—and we must disguise ourselves. Uniform is impossible."

"But shall we have the chance of trying again?" muttered Hester. "You didn't hear them talking, as you did yesterday?"

Joe shook her head. There was a short silence while they all sat plunged in thought. Disguise, when one was in camp with only Guide clothes in one's kitbag, was no easy matter. Presently Philippa rose, and still frowning meditatively began to break up sticks for the fire. They crackled sharply, almost as if an autumn frost had touched the still August morning. Joe's quick ears caught a sound which seemed to echo the snapping of the wood, a slow, steady chunk-chunk

that came faintly up from the sea. She stood for a
moment, shading her eyes with her hand.

"The barge is under way," she said, "and if it
goes out, it will probably come back again as it did
before. We may have our second chance, and this
time we must be ready for it."

CHAPTER VIII

Summons to the Manor

As soon as breakfast was over the three girls held a review of their belongings. They spread out clothes, and even bed-clothes, hoping that the display might reveal possibilities which they had overlooked; but all it revealed instead was the poverty of their resources. Philippa's offer of a very large red-and-blue striped blanket to be cut into jumper suits met with dubious headshakes. And there was no dubiety at all when Hester suggested that their cotton palliasses should be made into sleeveless frocks and dyed with home-brewed dyes.

" Dyes!" echoed Joe and Philippa with almost surprising unanimity, as they recalled the greens and yellows of the hide. " Dyes! Again! No jolly fear!"

" What we want," Joe added, " is a disguise. Not a fancy dress that will make the whole island turn round and stare."

" A frock like the hide," said Philippa, " wouldn't be a fancy dress. It would be a catastrophe." She shuddered, and picking up her Guide tie tried for the twentieth time to imagine it as a chic scarf twined round her neck. "The sleeveless frock idea is quite good, though," she added, holding the tie out at arm's length, considering it, and throwing it impatiently aside. "We could probably buy quite cheap stuff and make ourselves dresses. It only takes about two and a half yards and they are very easy to make. I have made three this summer—I have more than enough money. How much have you, Joe?"

"Five shillings."

"I am broke," said Hester, "but I am expecting a postal order from home any minute."

"There is a figured cotton in White's window at a reasonable price; rather pretty too. And it is thick, like casement cloth. We must have something that isn't transparent so that we don't need petticoats; we can't run to a whole trousseau. Two and a half yards for Hester and me, two and a quarter for Joe, that will leave us about—about—well, just about enough for extras and our bus fares. We don't need stockings, heaps of people don't wear them, or hats either, but we must have white sewing cotton—I hope your postal order does come soon, Hester."

It came opportunely that very morning, so that they were able to shop without the fear of spending more than they could afford. Moreover, the figured cotton was pretty enough to make the prospect of wearing the frocks a pleasure. Each girl chose a different colour and they found coloured belts to match at Woolworth's. Hester, who had two thick dark plaits, committed the additional extravagance of a cherry-coloured ribbon to match belt and dress; and all three girls returned from their morning's expedition in a more feminine frame of mind than they had felt since leaving home.

" Not that I am tired of camp," Hester remarked, as they left the bus and turned into their own lane, " or that I don't appreciate our luck in having a full-blown mystery at our very brailing, so to speak; but when I have been living in a tent for a week or so, I suddenly long to lie in a hot bath, and then get out and put on my fluffiest frock, and very best stockings, and powder my nose and—and—sit on a cushion and sew a fine seam, if you know what I mean." She unfolded the paper parcel of cherry-coloured ribbon, and pulling a plait over her shoulder, held the ribbon against her dark hair to observe the effect. " Most of all do I want to powder my nose," she concluded a little plaintively, pausing on the hill to mop a scarlet face.

" A wash would do it more good," said Joe, with greater truthfulness than tact. " You had better stop at the steading and put your head under the water tap. And though we can't offer you a cushion, you can sew a fine seam to your heart's content. There are three whole frocks to make, and no sewing-machine to run them up on."

Hester mopped her face again. She had forgotten that this particular item in her desires could be granted so easily and so soon.

" I do appreciate our mystery," she reiterated with a sigh, " but I begin to feel that there is a terrible lot of hard work attached to enjoying oneself."

The sight of the tap in the steading, dripping with cool splashing drops into the water butt, tempted all three girls into taking Joe's suggestion seriously. They quickly pulled off their ties, opened their collars, and rolled up their sleeves; and one by one they balanced themselves over the trough, their hands planted against the wall, their feet astride, while the cold delicious water poured over their faces till all three were splash-ing like watering-cans. Hester, with Philippa holding back her plaits, was in the middle of a second shower-bath when a deep, gruff voice called to them from across the yard.

" Hein!" it said.

Hester started, and one plait, jerked from Philippa's grasp, fell under the tap.

" Hein!" said the voice again.

It came from the passage doorway of the mystery house, where a burly, blue-bloused man was standing, the man whom they had seen with Mrs. Roberts down by the barge. The three girls stared at him. He had

18   (H 21)

a round close-cropped head, and a three days' growth of beard. His face was far from amiable. His blouse gaped open at the neck, his trousers were patched, and his feet were bare in leather, wooden-soled shoes. He beckoned them with a jerk of his head.

" Hein?" he said a third time, interrogatively. " Arrivez." He held the door open in unmistakable invitation.

" Do you want us?" asked Joe, startled.

He beckoned again, though obviously he had not understood.

" Arrivez," he repeated. " Ici."

The girls exchanged dismayed looks. They were very damp, rumpled and untidy. From Hester's wet plait a rivulet of water trickled down her uniform. Joe's hair was plastered in wet rat-tails over her face. Philippa had rolled down her stockings for coolness, and a long streak of dixie black smudged her bare leg. All three had flapping sleeves, bedraggled collars, and the uncomfortable feeling which comes from being interrupted by an unsympathetic grown-up in the middle of a noisy fit of the giggles. Although the grown-up in question was only a foreign manservant, the shade of Mrs. Roberts lurked acidly at his elbow.

For a painful moment they stood hesitating, then Hester took a step forward.

" Come on," she muttered, squeezing her plait between her two hands to wring the water out. " Let's

go in, we may discover something—he's all right "—
as Joe gave a warning " sh "—" you can see he
doesn't speak English. He doesn't seem to speak much
French either, for that matter, or perhaps he thinks
it would be wasted on us."

She stepped over the threshold, and the other two
followed her, feeling uncommonly like Christians
walking into the lion's den. They found themselves
in a long flagged passage, with dark, colour-washed
walls, and small, thick, honeycomb-glassed windows,
through which came very little light. The outer door
closed behind them with an unpleasant finality, and
to eyes fresh from the glare of sunshine the gloom
became almost blinding. Another door opening at
the opposite end of the passage brought them into a
kitchen, a bleak, comfortless place whose size suggested a whole troop of cooks, kitchen-maids, and
scullery-maids. It was occupied by one slatternly
woman, big-boned and heavily built, who eyed them
with a sullen curiosity and made some remark, in a
language which was neither French nor German but
faintly reminiscent of both, to the man. He grunted
a reply, a grunt being apparently the only mode of
speech in which he indulged, and clumped in front of
the three girls out of the kitchen, across a second passage and into the main hall, his wooden-soled shoes
clattering on the stone floor as if a regiment of cavalry
were riding through the house. He pushed aside a

curtain hung before an archway, herded the girls under it with another jerk of his head, uttered a final and slightly longer grunt, and left them.

They found themselves in a long lofty room. Facing them, all along the length of one wall, were windows, leading out to a veranda of grey stone covered with wistaria, and arched like the cloisters of a cathedral. Between the arches they saw the garden, with sunny green lawns stretching to the woods and the edge of the cliff, and beyond the trees, glimpses of the sea. For a second they forgot where they were, as they gazed at the beauty of old grey stone, green clustering leaves, sunlight and grass. They were recalled by the voice of Mrs. Roberts. She lay back in an arm-chair, her little flimsily-shod feet stretched out and crossed on a high footstool; her hair waved in a faultless line from brow to nape; her dress, of the palest green linen, was without crease or wrinkle; her hands, plump, white, and manicured, rested indolently on the arms of the chair. Only in her face, where nature had somehow failed, art failed too, and for all her care she was not agreeable to look at.

The distaste which the girls felt appeared to be fully reciprocated, for her gaze travelled deliberately over each in turn, from head to foot, and her expression did not fail to emphasize the contrast between the three, hot, untidy, and ill at ease, and herself, cool, nonchalant, and immaculate. The very manner in

which she refrained from spoken comment was morti-
fying, since it gave the girls no chance of excusing
themselves.

" I sent for you," she said at last, letting her eyes,
with faintly lifted brows, rest upon Philippa's dixie-
smudged legs, " to show you this letter."

It was the letter from Mr. Weland, written at Joe's
behest on the morning of Miss Ashe's accident. They
read it stolidly and handed it back without a word,
partly because they could think of nothing to say, and
partly because they had just learnt that silence was an
effective weapon. Mrs. Roberts tapped an impatient
toe. She did not seem to relish this use of her own
tactics, but she contrived to make them feel that while
her silence had been caustic, theirs was merely ill-
mannered.

" Well?" she asked, after waiting in vain for them
to say something.

Joe took a breath, but before she could speak Hester
had edged her aside and was answering with a bright
smile.

" Thank you. Thank you so much."

" Thank——" The toe stopped tapping. " There is
nothing to thank me——"

" Oh, but there is! It really is kind of you to let
us know that Mr. Weland has explained everything,
and that you are satisfied."

Philippa swallowed a giggle and disgorged it again

as a cough, while Mrs. Roberts's face lost its disdainful expression and grew several shades pinker.

" Satisfied!" she repeated sharply. " Mr. Weland has——"

" We knew it was just a misunderstanding." If silence was one good weapon, Hester was now evidently bent on showing that speech could be another. " We knew that you didn't really mean to keep us out of the woods and off the beach altogether. You see, we are very keen on nature study, and we have planned to——"

Mrs. Roberts broke in angrily.

" I don't care what you have planned," she began, then checked herself, and with a visible effort controlled her rising temper. When she went on, her voice was quiet but grim, and like Hester, she had discarded silence. For five minutes she talked with a vigour that brooked no interruption, and it was a dazed and subdued trio that at last found itself dismissed to stumble through the archway into the dark entrance hall. The man stood there waiting for them, and if before he had looked surly, now he was positively malevolent. They shivered as they entered the cold flagged passages, and when they reached the steading and came out once more into the hot sunshine and the familiar everyday surroundings of camp, Hester's teeth were chattering, and Philippa was white and cold under her freckles. They gathered up their ties and bits and pieces from the ledge by the water trough, and walked slowly down to the field.

Joe set to work straightway on fire and dinner, while Hester and Philippa changed from uniform into camp overalls, and chopped wood and laid the ground-sheets and table. Not till they were half-way through the meal did one of them, looking cautiously about her first, refer to the morning's interview.

"What were all the things she said?" muttered Hester. "Wire to Colonel Eskdale and have the camp sent home; write to Headquarters complaining of our rudeness and disobedience; get Mr. Weland turned out—I don't believe she can. Tenants can't be turned out at a moment's notice."

"He might loose his job as estate agent," said Philippa gloomily.

"And she is writing to the Island C.A.—why on earth did you give that away, Joe? She had never heard of Camp Advisers till you talked about them."

Joe speared another sausage out of the pan and regarded it, poised on the end of her fork, with a thoughtful scrutiny.

"The Island C.A.," she remarked, "knows all about the camp sites on the island, and just what you can and what you can't do on them. If Mrs. Roberts writes to her—but somehow, I don't think she will. Did it strike you as at all odd "—Joe, having inspected her sausage, put it down on her plate and cut off a large bite—" odd," she repeated, swallowing, " that Mrs. Roberts never once suggested reporting us to Captain?"

The expressions on the faces of the other two changed from gloom to interest.

" No," exclaimed Hester. " No more she did."

" You would think," Joe continued, " that if she really wanted to complain about our behaviour, the first person she would complain to would be the person in charge of us."

The others nodded; they saw this when it was pointed out to them.

" In fact, Captain is so obviously the proper person, that it almost looks as if Mrs. Roberts were avoiding her on purpose."

" It does. But why?"

" There might be inconvenient questions. It might not seem very difficult, perhaps, to frighten off three girls by threatening to complain about them to their Headquarters, but a grown-up, a grown-up like Captain, who has travelled half the world over, is quite another pair of shoes."

" How shoes do keep cropping up in this affair," said Philippa, laughing. " If we were in a thriller they would make quite a good title: ' The Mystery of the Louis Quinze Heels '—was it Louis Quinze or Louis Quatorze who had to wear such high heels because he was so little?"

" Louis Billion for all we care," retorted Hester.

" Don't be so tiresome—then you think we ought to go
ahead, Joe, and pay no attention to friend Roberts."

Joe hesitated, her face rather sober.

" What did worry me," she answered, after a moment, " was the very last thing she said. I don't think
you heard; you were half out of the room. But she
smiled a perfectly detestable smile, and she said that
we had better be careful, because Osterhaardt had had
orders to deal with us if we were troublesome."

" Oster—is that the man?"

" Yes."

" It doesn't sound a French name."

" I believe he must be Belgian. The language the
woman in the kitchen spoke may have been Flemish.
It wasn't French, not the lowest patois French."

" Osterhaardt," echoed Hester, frowning. " Not an
amiable gentleman. I don't much like the idea of
being dealt with by him."

There was a silence. Recalling the malevolent looks
which had followed them across the steading, Joe and
Philippa were entirely in accord with this opinion.
Presently Hester spoke again.

" I have just remembered another difficulty," she
said. " We have nothing but a pair of small nail
scissors to cut those frocks with, and curved ones, too."

" Are we going to need the frocks?" asked Joe in
a quiet voice, looking at her.

" Need them? What did we go and buy them for if

we don't need them? You said yourself that it was
hopeless to follow that car without a disguise."

" And Osterhaardt?"

Hester smiled, rather ruefully.

" Mrs. Roberts gave you an excellent piece of
advice, didn't she? She told you to be careful, so
careful we shall just have to be. You don't want to
back out, do you?"

Joe shook her head.

" I just wanted to be sure that you realized what
we were up against. In a way, in spite of that ' secret
and urgent ', we have been taking things fairly light-
heartedly, as a kind of joke. But there isn't going to
be much joke about it if we are caught now. A sense
of humour is not likely to be Mrs. Roberts's strong
point at the best of times, and to-day she struck me as
being very distinctly in earnest."

" Oh, distinctly," agreed Hester, whose first un-
easiness had, nevertheless, begun to fade. " But after
all, there are three of us, and we are in England in a
Guide camp. One can't imagine anything really
drastic happening with twenty stout Girl Guides next
door. They just don't make the right background for
melodrama. The idea of getting Mr. Weland into
trouble, or of having the Company reported to Headquarters, worries me much more than vague threats
of ' being dealt with '. But I am sure Joe is right,
and that it was pure bluff to frighten us away—I

think we ought to cut the patterns out in newspaper and pin them up before tackling the frocks themselves. We can't afford to make mistakes."

Hester got up as she spoke, and stretched herself before turning to fetch the parcel of materials. But her stretch ended abruptly, and she stood looking towards the creek with a slightly dismayed face.

" I hope we shall need the frocks," she exclaimed in a disgusted tone. " That barge is back again already."

CHAPTER IX

Hester Solves a Problem

" Why doesn't the stupid thing make up its own mind," grumbled Philippa. " Out one minute, in the next. How can anyone know what to expect?"

All three glowered at the distant jetty. This was the second time that their deductions had been at fault, and the thought was discouraging.

" Since anyone can't, apparently," Joe said at last, with a shrug of her shoulders, " anyone had better just carry on. We can at least be prepared. If you two would like to go over to the big camp and borrow some newspapers, I'll do the washing up. Better plait your hair, if it is dry, Hester. One question leads to another, and we aren't sure yet whether we are supposed to answer questions."

It was a point upon which their unknown ally was to advise them with almost uncanny promptness. When Hester and Philippa returned with bundles of newspapers they found Joe sitting on a log by the wood pile, while the unwashed dishes lay strewn about the kitchen.

" Look at this," she exclaimed, and handed them a scrap of paper.

On it, in the same zigzag code as before, was a message, with Joe's translation scribbled beneath it: " Brer Fox, he lay low 'n' sed nuffin'."

The girls exchanged glances, and then, as Hester returned the paper, grins. They felt suddenly relieved. After all their fears of the morning, there was something reassuring in the familiar words.

" Where did you find it?" Philippa asked.

" In the woodstack. It was under the tin biscuit lid that I used for baking oatcakes on, the day after we came. I hid the lid beneath the wood to save washing it and forgot all about it, but when I was at the stack just now, a corner was poking out, as if somebody had uncovered it on purpose. I wonder you didn't notice it before dinner."

" I did," said Hester, " and I kicked it in again. I thought if it had been unwashed all this time, it could wait a bit longer."

" Then it is a good thing you didn't kick any harder," said Joe severely. " It just shows how careful we must be. Goodness knows what we may miss if we let ourselves get slipshod."

" We wouldn't have missed much in this message," Hester retorted, argumentative because she felt herself to be in the wrong. " Doesn't tell us anything."

" I am glad we found it though!" Philippa interposed hastily. Remembering her own mood in the morning, she guessed that Hester's prickly conscience was about to make her disagreeable. " It does set our minds at ease for the next little while. We shall probably get another message when there is anything definite to do—and I believe that the Brister Gout will turn out to be a Guider."

" Why?" Hester's tone said that she was quite ready to be distracted from prickliness, but dignity demanded that the others should soothe her a little.

" Brer Fox is not the person one would expect a Scout to quote, somehow. And still more, I don't believe that a Scout would notice a lid under the woodpile. A nest, or a tracking sign, or a rare wild flower, yes; but not a lid that wanted washing. Whereas a Guider—well, look at Captain."

Joe and Hester looked, metaphorically speaking, at Captain, and grinned. Under Mrs. Aldwyn's eyes their sins seldom failed to find them out.

" I am sorry about that," said Hester. " I am afraid you are right, but it is a little dull. A nice Scout would have appealed to me more. I wonder who she is?"

Discussing this problem, they tidied the kitchen and retreated to their tent. They had agreed that the open field was no place in which to make disguises, and although the sun shone, and the oak trees cast cool green shadows across the grass, they turned their backs on temptation and, letting down the brailing and partially closing the door, resigned themselves to an afternoon of confinement.

Their work had to be carried on under difficulties. There was very little space in which to spread their newspapers for cutting out, and less in which to move about. They crept round their patterns on hands and knees, growing every moment hotter and stickier, but conscious all the time of an undercurrent of excitement which made the very difficulties welcome. They cut and pinned and tacked and stitched, Philippa and Hester chattering as usual about their own particular affair of the moment, and neither paying any heed to the other's conversation. By tea-time the basted dresses were ready to be tried on, and when, having sewed until it was too dark to see needle or thread, the three broke off work for the day, the harder part of their task was done.

" You may not look like Paris, precisely," said Hester, taking up a pleat on Joe's shoulder, thrusting a couple of pins through it, and standing back with her head on one side in a professional way, " but you are a charming picture of English girlhood, sweet, fresh, and modest, and—well, it's your own fault, you shouldn't have jerked."

Joe sniffed, and tried in vain to see a scratch at the back of her own neck.

"Take it off, and be careful how you pull," she commanded. "I shall have to unpick that shoulder, and that will make the third time. Why don't you talk less and think more—look out!"

"Looking out is just what I'm doing," retorted Hester, who, in drawing the dress over Joe's head, had retreated backwards through the tent door. "The barge!"

"Bother the barge. Get this thing off me, I can't breathe." Joe emerged from the scratchy folds and smoothed down her hair and her temper, both of which had been ruffled. "What about the barge? I am sick of the very word."

She followed Hester out of the tent and stood for a moment to peer into the gathering dusk. The boat itself was no longer visible, but its red-and-green lights were gliding down the creek to the sea, and again the faint chunk-chunk of its engine could be heard.

"It really does look as if it were off this time," said Philippa, as the lights were lost in the darkness of the open sea. "I am glad we have got on so well with the frocks."

"I should be gladder if we had hit on some ideas for following that car," Joe rejoined. "The frocks are only a part of our stock in trade. They are not going to do the whole job for us."

The other two frowned. After sewing almost without

a pause for seven hours they were in no mood to relish this reminder, true though it might be.

"What I want," Philippa announced, "is to find out what it is they do going up and down from the barge to the Manor in the middle of the night. As soon as these frocks are finished I am going to have a short rest cure, so that when the barge comes back I shall be all bright and brisk instead of sleeping through everything like an elderly pug."

"A rest cure!" Hester yawned. "We need it. Who would have thought that a little sewing could exhaust one so? It is odd, but I have never been so tired in any camp as I am in this one, and yet we always worked very hard with the Company, or thought we did. Harder than we do here."

"In the Company," Philippa observed, "we just did as we were told without bothering; but here we have to think for ourselves. Thinking is tiring when you are not used to it."

Hester eyed her friend suspiciously, but it was too dark to see whether her face was as innocent as her voice.

They cooked a sketchy supper by lantern light, and went rather silently to bed, where their dreams were haunted all night long by seams and patterns and needles and pins. By the following afternoon the dresses were finished and folded away, but no solution had been found to Joe's problem of how to follow the car; a problem which, directly they had nothing else to do, forced itself none too cheerfully upon them. They racked their brains over it, separately and together, and for twenty-four hours neither thought nor spoke of anything else. On the second day of the barge's absence they tried to avoid the subject, but it remained uppermost in their minds, and they found themselves drifting back to it from the most unexpected angles of conversation.

" It's no use," Hester declared at supper, when a debate on the Company's chances of winning the Divisional Cup had led by perfectly natural stages from last year's competition in hike fires to hikes in general, to a particular expedition to Friday Street, to the bus which had taken them there and which they had pushed up the hill, to the car which had ultimately rescued the bus and which had been, as Joe now recalled, a Morris saloon exactly like——
" It is no use," Hester repeated. " And anyhow I never did believe those detective stories in which everyone ignores the corpse waiting on the doorstep while they discuss a well-chosen meal. Not talking only makes things worse. My mind is running in circles and needs to be poked out of them."

" The bother is we are all in the same circles," said Philippa, " but waiting for inspiration doesn't seem to be much use. All I have done is to go over the things we can't do. We can't, on bicycles, keep up

with a car that is doing thirty to forty miles an hour;
and we can't interfere with its inside to reduce its
speed because we don't know how; and we can't
borrow Captain's two-seater because Hester and I
can't drive, and Joe won't."

" It is no use beginning that again," Joe said shortly.
" I tell you, I have only driven three times in my life,
and in any case a Humber is no more like a Morris
than you are like a chimpanzee—less, in fact. A
lot less."

Philippa snorted, and marked her disapproval by a
heavy silence.

" Well, then," Hester took up the tale, " those are
the things we can't do. And that brings us back to the
same old ideas, sitting on the luggage rack at the back,
or arranging for the car to leave a trail behind it. The
luggage rack isn't a physical impossibility, not in the
way bicycling at forty miles an hour is."

" Unless you promise to give up the luggage rack,"
said Joe, who could be very stubborn when occasion
demanded, " I shall go straight to Mrs. Roberts and
tell her everything. It is all very well to be so grand
and lofty about danger, but it *is* dangerous, and if
your silly necks are broken, Captain will get the
blame. And besides, the first condition the Brister
Gout made was that we shouldn't be seen; and whatever they do in books, in real life you wouldn't have
the ghost of a chance of getting away when they stopped.

You would have precious little chance of getting on when they started, for that matter. You are no fairies."

Philippa snorted again.

" I still think," said Hester, " that a bag of rice, or millet, or grain of some kind could be fixed on somewhere. A long thin bag, with a tiny hole in it, under the rear mudguard or the running-board."

" You have said that eighteen times, but you never say how. Nails? String? Glue? You can't go sticking large sacks haphazard all over a car and expect that the Robertses will be obliging enough not to notice them."

" Better rub the tyres with an onion and track it with our noses," Joe suggested sarcastically. " These tracking games are all very well when you are playing, but in real life they just don't work. If only the car were really like our old Morris," she added with a sigh, " we could trail it for miles by the oil it dropped."

Hester looked up sharply.

" That is a new line. Couldn't you slacken something, nuts or bolts or whatever it is, to make this one leak?"

" I don't know how. And it would take tools we haven't got."

" All the same——" Hester broke off, frowning thoughtfully, and for the remainder of the evening was unusually silent. Her mind had been given the jolt for which she had asked, but when bedtime came the idea she sought still eluded her.

" It is there," she declared, " it is just on the tip of my tongue—a perfectly good sound scheme, only I just can't quite think of it."

" And the worst of it is," Philippa complained, " that time is running on so. The barge may be back at any minute now. I have been expecting it all day, and the more need there is for hurry, the emptier my head feels. A doctor who was giving us first-aid lectures once, told us that the brain looked just like blancmange. I think he must have been right."

For a long time the three girls lay awake, turning from side to side, and more aware than they had been for many nights of the lumps and hollows of the hard ground; but at length Joe and Philippa slipped into a heavy dreamless sleep. In the small dark hours Philippa was roused by a noise, and lifting her head from her pillow saw Hester, a ghostly white figure in the darkness, bending over Joe's bed and shaking her.

" I've got it," she was saying urgently. " Wake up, I am sure I've got it, if you'll just tell me something."

With a sleepy grunt Joe struggled up and sat with her head resting on her knees.

" Don't all cars have a lot of water in them, in the radiator or somewhere?"

" Of course, they do. What an idiotic thing to wake me up about."

" Yes, but doesn't the water sometimes have to be let out?"

" Yes." Although the word was swallowed in a yawn, Joe's voice sounded more alert.

" How?"

" Tap. Under the radiator in a Morris. You just turn it on."

" And if you only turn it a little, the water will just trickle a few drops at a time?"

" Yes, but "—there was no drowsiness now; all three girls were broad awake—" water wouldn't leave any trace. It would dry up too quickly."

Hester, in spite of darkness black as Egypt's night, and heedless of her companions underfoot, did a triumphant dance round the tent pole.

" I've got it!" she cried. " I knew I'd got it."

" Stop being a goat," expostulated Joe, a little breathless from being trampled on. " What is it you have got?"

" Dyes!" shouted Hester, and plumped down on to her bed.

There was an ominous silence, then Joe, very grimly, crawled out from under her blankets.

" Are you going to tell me," she demanded, " that

you have wakened Philippa and me at two in the morning to talk about dyes?"

Hester backed hastily, with arms extended to keep Joe at bay.

" No, listen," she begged. " I'm serious, really I am. Don't you see? We can pour a dye into the radiator, a proper bought dye, not our wishy-washy home-made stuff, some brilliant colour, red, say. It will leave a trail of bright scarlet drops that we can follow easily, at our own speed."

" Bright scarlet——" Philippa, at the other side of the tent, shuddered. " Of all the horrible suggestions! For goodness' sake, Hester, remember that we are three lone, lorn girls all by ourselves in the middle of a dark field surrounded by unknown villains, and don't go talking about trails of bright scarlet drops."

" Well, green then, or blue, or orange. Any colour you like," Hester amended in a flat voice, all her triumph dashed by this cold reception of her plan.

There was a moment's silence, then Joe, getting back into bed, said:

" Don't be a pig, Philippa."

" It's the middle of the night," Philippa excused herself apologetically, " and you were a pig yourself."

" I am feeling slow," Joe agreed. " The beauty of it is only just beginning to dawn. It is a first-rate idea, Hester. We will go into Ventwich in the morning and buy the strongest, brightest colour we can find—a powder will be better than crystals, and we had better make it up in a concentrated solution with as little water as possible so as not to have too much to pour in." She slid under the clothes. " What a relief to have it settled," she concluded, yawning tremendously. " Now we can sleep with easy minds."

Silence fell. There were faint rustlings and whisperings as each girl snuggled down on her palliasse. Philippa's breathing became soft and regular. Joe sighed a long contented sigh. Both were on the verge of sleep when Hester started up again.

" What was that?" she cried breathlessly.

They listened, wide awake in a moment. The tent canvas lifted and swayed in the night wind, but they could hear no other sound.

" It was like a footfall," Hester muttered, pushing aside her blankets, " like soft rubber shoes on grass. I am going out to look."

She reached the tent door, with Joe close at her heels, clutched suddenly at the canvas, and went sprawling forward on hands and knees over something soft and limp which lay in a crumpled heap across the entrance.

" A torch, Philippa," Joe called. " A torch, quick."

Hester picked herself up. A circle of light flashed out upon the heavy folds which had entangled her, and she stared at them, rubbing her elbows ruefully.

She saw a mass of calico, green, and blue, and sickly yellow, and with a cry of recognition she stooped and lifted up one corner to reveal a rakish looking window flap.

" My long lost aunt!" exclaimed Joe, although no aunt ever born could have been of so yellow green a shade. " It is our hide!"

CHAPTER X

The Trailing of the Car

The night was overcast, and a bank of cloud hid the waning moon. Philippa's torch was fading. For a few minutes it cut a wavering wedge of gold through the darkness, then it flickered and went out. The girls, who had set out to scour the field, abandoned their search and groped their way back to the tent. Owing to Hester's fall their unknown visitor had already gained a fair start, and blindfolded as they were by the blackness of the night, they felt that pursuit would be vain. They pushed the hide into a corner and went back to bed, but not to sleep. They were uneasy, and, truth to tell, a little frightened. Philippa's half-joking reminder that they were three lone, lorn girls recurred to each of them, none too pleasantly; and although they said nothing about it, they lay whispering, glad of one another's companionship.

" I am certain it was the Brister Gout," Joe said, as anxious to reassure herself as to encourage Hester and Philippa.

" And I am certain it was the Roberts crew—a hint that Osterhaardt was dealing with us, perhaps."

" Well, if he doesn't deal any more drastically than that, he won't do much harm. How endless this night does feel! What is the time, Pills?"

" Getting on for three. It will be light in a little over an hour."

" Over an hour!" Hester groaned. " It is all very well for you two, but I haven't slept a wink, I have been thinking so hard."

" You have thought to some purpose," Joe told her. " Satisfaction should make you feel like a giant refreshed."

" Well, it doesn't. I don't even feel satisfied. Slips are so common between cups and—I say!"

The dismay in Hester's voice made the other turn involuntarily.

" Do you think we could have been overheard?"

There was a dismal silence, then Joe said " No," but it was a protest rather than a denial. The suggestion seemed only too probable. There was another and longer silence. At last Joe shrugged her shoulders.

" It can't be helped," she said. " If we were overheard, we were overheard, and that's that. All we can do is to carry on and hope for the best. Perhaps it was the Brister Gout, and there may be some message or sign for us on the hide; we'll look directly it gets light—but my goodness! Aren't we duffers. Just imagine us shouting all our plans at the tops of our voices when we know that Mrs. Roberts may come

to look at our tent at any minute. We make me sick!"
Joe pounded her pillow with angry blows and flung
herself back upon it.

At the first faint lifting of dawn they crept shivering
from their beds, and spreading the hide out on the
cold, wet grass, searched every fold. It was Hester
who found the note, pinned under the window flap,
and for a moment they were so relieved that they
said nothing. Then Joe, kneeling by the tent door,
held the paper to the light. The message was in
code, but at the foot a few words had been scribbled
in plain writing. She read them out, softly and
hurriedly.

"Dye plan good. Use dark green or black. Look
like oil and less likely to be noticed."

There was a pause, then Hester said:

"Providence has been looking after us all right
to-night. It is far better luck than we deserve. What
does the first part say, Joe?"

"Get me a pencil. I can't read it straight off."

Without taking her eyes from the message, Joe
stretched out a hand, and after a rapid hunt Hester
put a pencil into it. She transcribed, letter by letter.

"'This'—that means the hide, I suppose—'may
give you away. Don't put it up again. Car will arrive
same place to-day, twelve noon. If you fail, last
chance to-morrow, six morning."

"Twelve," said Philippa soberly. "It doesn't

give us any too much time. Even if we cut prayers and colours and start off directly after breakfast, the first bus doesn't run till nine. And when we come back, there will be the dyes to mix."

" I'll go on Miss Weland's bicycle," Joe said. " If I start about eight I can be home again well before eleven, even though I have to walk up the hill."

" We ought to be hidden in the woods a good bit before twelve," Hester put in. " It would hardly do to be seen trekking down the road with a large jug of black dye. Mrs. Roberts might think we were up to mischief. She has the strangest ideas."

" Don't you be too flippant," said Joe sternly. " We have no reason to feel proud of ourselves so far. Now, we had better get back to bed again and have some rest. We have a hard day's work ahead, and we shall need all the brains we have got, and a few over."

" Just as you like," rejoined Hester, with a cheerful wink at Philippa. " But this is the fourth time you have gone to bed to-night. You must be careful, my dear Joe, or it may become a habit—isn't it astonishing how wet dew is!" Hester felt the legs of her pyjamas which she had neglected to roll up, and made a face of disgust.

" Dew!" echoed Joe, stopping half-way across the tent and turning back. " I wonder——" she hurried outside, but returned a moment later, shaking her head. " I wanted to see if the Brister Gout had left any footprints," she explained, " but she hasn't. Our marks are all over the place, but the Brister Gout must have shuffled. There is nothing but two long straight lines, like the lines we thought had been made by a hedgehog, the first morning we were here."

Although they were able to get two hours of comparatively sound sleep, they felt jaded and far from willing to get up when the time came. The whole benefit of her rest cure, Philippa complained, had been lost. While Hester, after pointing out that as the brain-worker she required a longer period for recuperation than the others, shut her eyes and pretended to fall asleep again. Joe answered both arguments with a wet sponge. Her breakfast, she stated, was to be cooked for her while she put on her tidy uniform, and polished her badges and her shoes, and as usual she got her own way. There was a forceful quality in Joe's compact little person that seldom failed to achieve its purpose.

Out in the fresh morning air Philippa's languor and Hester's overtaxed brains were quickly restored. A stimulating odour of bacon and eggs mingled agreeably with the scent of wet grass. The alarms and excursions of the night were forgotten. The whistle next door, blowing its " Get-up-Guides. Get-up-Guides. Get-up-Guides. Doo-oo ", banished their feeling of isolation; and the thought of the adventure which lay ahead, though it made them nervous, was none the less exhilarating. They saw Joe off from the top of the hill and went back to the camp where they had promised to stay until she returned.

She was away for close upon three hours, and never had Hester or Philippa known hours to pass so slowly. Philippa spring-cleaned the stores tent, partly because it was sadly in need of the attention, and partly because she thought that another message from the Brister Gout might discover itself under the meat safe, in the larder, or poking out from some other unlikely spot. Hester made the beds, tidied the sleeping-tent, rolled the brailing, and finally, having piled bedding and kitbags in three neat heaps round the pole and laid out the disguise frocks with belts, ribbons, and collars ready to put on, let the brailing down again and laced up the tent door so that all could be left at a moment's notice.

At half-past nine they went across to colours and stood, Hester declared, for a whole life-time, while the colour party fumbled with clove hitches and sheet bends. But when they returned to their own field they had still to wait a further three-quarters of an hour before they saw Joe's welcome figure come trudging down from the steading.

" I have had a stroke of luck," were her first words as she reached them, panting a little, and very red in the face. " I have managed to get some liquid stuff from a chemist, so that all we need do is to mix it. It will be far quicker than dissolving powders."

Dropping on her knees she began to unpack her parcel.

"You certainly seem to have bought enough," Hester exclaimed, as one little bottle after another came rolling out.

"That is what the chemist said. But it takes six big cans of water to fill our radiator at home. The colour won't be any too strong by the time it is mixed in. Have you the dixie boiling? We'll pour it straight into the big jug, and tip the bottles in afterwards."

In a few minutes they had brewed a jugful of liquid blacker than the blackest ink which, not daring to set it down on the grass for fear it should upset, each held in turn while the others changed from uniform to cotton frocks.

Then they parted company, Hester and Philippa going down the farm road to the creek to hide their two borrowed bicycles deep in the bracken behind the bushes; while Joe, carrying the jug of dye and an empty basin, went over the fields, across the lane, and into the woods. She went cautiously, keeping under cover of the hedge for the first part of her journey, and slipping through the undergrowth instead of following the beaten path through the woods. She reached the place where the three paths met, and resisting the temptation to loiter in search of fresh car tracks, chose a hiding-place some distance away. She wedged the jug securely between a tree stump and two or three heavy stones, and settled down to wait for the others. They came presently, avoiding as Joe had done, paths and open spaces, and creeping quietly from bush to bush, and tree to tree. For all their caution Joe saw them when they were still far off, and she realized with some dismay that however effectively cotton frocks might disguise them on the high road, in the woods the white printed material betrayed every movement.

She beckoned them to her hiding-place and warned them to keep still. They had not long to wait. Within ten minutes they heard the hum of an engine. It drew steadily nearer, and at length the car came bumping slowly and clumsily up from the lane by the creek. It stopped, backed, turned, and came finally to a standstill with its bonnet pointing almost straight towards the clump of bushes where the girls lay hidden. They crouched low, hardly daring to breathe.

The driver got out and stood glancing sharply about him. He was a small, spare man in grey flannels, with a shabby brown tweed coat, but the girls were too far off to see his face clearly and were, moreover, afraid of peering too hard. Apparently he was satisfied that nobody had seen or heard him, for he closed the door of the car, locked it, and set off towards the Manor; his footsteps, though he trod lightly, echoing between the trees as the twigs snapped beneath his feet. The three waited till the last sounds of his progress had died away, then Joe and Hester crept out. With hands that trembled slightly, Joe unscrewed the radiator cap and peered into the radiator. Then she felt under the car for the tap and drew off two or three basinfuls of rusty water to make room for the dye, emptying the waste water among the roots of the bushes where it would not show. Hester gave the jug of dye a final swirl to make sure that the colouring matter would not sink to the bottom and be wasted, and poured it in, tilting the jug to the last drop. The cap of the radiator was replaced. Joe adjusted the tap beneath to a thin trickle which dripped, she was thankful to observe, into a rut of damp mossy soil. Within five minutes the two girls had rejoined Philippa in their hiding-place.

For a few seconds they remained there, listening intently to the woods around them. They heard nothing save the sleepy noises of a hot noontide, and before another five minutes had passed, they were far down the hill on their way to the creek.

In their second hiding-place, beside the bicycles, their suspense was more prolonged and they found it hard not to fidget. Hester began to grow anxious about quantities. Already their precious dye was trickling away. What if the radiator should run dry before the end of the trail was reached. Joe reassured her.

" I have known ours take six hours to empty in winter, when the tap has been partially blocked up with rust. I am not afraid of its running out too soon, but I am worried about whether it shows. If it all sinks into that rut, we are safe; but if the rut overflows on to the path—well. We can only hope our luck holds. How long have we been here, Philippa? My watch says eleven minutes, but it has been so erratic since I gave it that bang with the mallet that there is no believing a tick it says."

" Eleven minutes is all mine makes it too. It feels like eleven hours."

Another eleven minutes went by, and yet another, before the car appeared. Twice they were roused to readiness, and twice they were disappointed as a baker's van went rattling past them, up the hill and down again. In the end, their quarry almost escaped them unawares, for it was being driven dangerously fast.

" Wait," exclaimed Joe, pulling Hester back as she sprang up to go out into the lane. " Make sure that nobody else is behind."

They heard the car slow down as it turned the corner into the main road, and gather speed again. In a few moments it was out of earshot.

" I am glad we are not trying to follow it itself," Philippa muttered, as she raised her bicycle from its hiding-place in the bracken. " Pretty unpleasant at that speed along such a twisting lane."

" We couldn't have followed," said Hester, walking slowly to and fro, scrutinizing the roadway, " but I hate the empty feeling now that it has gone. I feel as if we had burnt our boats, or missed our chance, or something."

" Any signs of the trail?"

" There are a few wet drops on a stone just down there, but they don't look very black. They will be dry and gone in two minutes under this sun."

" I don't think the dye will mix thoroughly into the radiator until the engine has been running a bit. We shall probably find the marks much blacker later on—if only there are enough of them. Now that she is off, we shall probably wish that I had turned the tap on harder." Joe took her place on the step of Philippa's bicycle, and the trail began.

Their ears told them that the car had turned to the left on reaching the main road; and for over two miles, since there was no other side road, they rode steadily without having to search for tracks. Then the road forked, and they had to dismount. On the ground over which they had just come they found several tiny marks, unnoticeable to the casual eye, but encouragingly black. But beyond the junction not so much as one drop could they find, though they searched for a considerable distance. Then Joe, exploring a narrow and most improbable looking lane, gave a whoop, and a moment later they were off again with

Hester bumping ahead in and out of grassy ruts, and triumphing over the success of her own ingenuity.

The lane led into another which doubled back on its tracks into a third. The third lane emerged on to a by-road which wound interminably and with a wearisome number of cross-roads and side-turnings, between green hedges and fields and ditches. The trail led them north and south, east and west, twisting this way, turning that, with neither rhyme nor reason for its meanderings. At half-past two a hot, hungry, and very thirsty trio stood mopping their faces on a white shadeless highway which led from nowhere to nowhere in the very heart of the Island. The cotton frocks, which had already suffered from contact with moss and bracken and bushes, were streaked with dust in every fold, and clung limply to their wearers. Joe's and Philippa's hands and arms were streaked with more than dust, for a tyre had punctured under its double load, and they had just finished repairing it. Joe, pushing a damp lock of her hair back from her face, left a long smudge of grime on her cheek.

"You are getting that Girl Guide look again," Hester reproved her, wiping it off. "All hot and hardworking. Personally I think this is getting beyond a joke. Does anyone know where we are?"

"Yes," said Joe, pointing to three minute black splashes, "we are on the trail of that car. Come on."

"But what is the use of trailing a car when we don't know where we are or where it is going. We can never find our way back here again, once the trail gets blotted out."

"If we knew where the car was going," said Joe, not unreasonably, "we shouldn't have to follow it to find out. As it is—here, Philippa. Change places again. You have the step."

"I want a rest," said Hester without stirring, "and I want something to eat and drink."

"You can't get either here," retorted Joe, "unless you are a cow or a rabbit. And there is no time to rest. We can buy biscuits at the next tea garden we pass and eat them as we go."

"Talk of slave drivers," muttered Hester; but she had to mount, willy-nilly, for she had no wish to be left behind.

At last the car seemed to tire of its wanderings, and to feel satisfied that it had shaken off all possible pursuers, for the trail, turning into a main road, led straight northwards. The girls followed it to the outskirts of a small town where they dismounted and walked, wheeling their cycles. The little black dots, which had been far from easy to see even on the country roads, were here almost invisible; and every narrow street, side-turning, and courtyard, had to be closely watched. The three had almost reached the market-place in the centre of the town when Joe, lifting her eyes from the pavements in her immediate surroundings and catching sight of a familiar corner from an unfamiliar angle, gave a start.

" Do you see where we are," she exclaimed. " There is the turning to Woolworth's, and there is the car park by the church, and there is the Market Cross away down there on the right. We have been half way round the Island, and have come back to Ventwich."

CHAPTER XI

The Watchers on the Lane

" We have come in from the south. We should have recognized it ten minutes ago if our eyes hadn't been glued to the ground all the time—though goodness knows we have been told often enough to look up as well as down when we were tracking."

" Those wretched little blobs are so hard to see. You can't think of everything at once," Hester complained.

Philippa, who had been reconnoitring the opposite pavement, crossed the street and joined them.

" I haven't found a trace for the last mile. Have you?"

Joe and Hester shook their heads, then Joe said:

" Wait a minute." She vanished into a stationer's shop and came out again with a postcard map of the Island. " There are six roads out of the town," she said, holding it out for the others to see. " I think myself that Ventwich is the end of our trail. I think that all the zig-zagging here, there, and everywhere, was a precaution to throw us off the scent, just in case we should happen to be on it; while the last four miles have been a straight run home. But we can't take anything for granted, so I think our best plan is to ride out a little way along each of those six roads —no, five. We have just come over one of them—and see if we can pick up the trail. It will show up again all right farther out. It is only here that all the traffic of the main street has rubbed it away. But first," she concluded hastily, as Hester's tongue appeared in a most unladylike way and hung down long and pink like that of a panting dog, " we shall go and have some tea."

" What do you intend to do if we draw a blank on all five roads?" inquired Philippa, as they moved off towards their favourite tea shop.

" Explore the town on foot. It shouldn't take more than two or three hours. The place isn't very big, and apart from the Market Square and the High Street, it is fairly quiet. If we find no traces anywhere, we shall have to come back here to-morrow morning, pick the car up as it comes into the town and follow it. But that won't be any too easy. There are six roads, and only three of us and two bicycles."

Refreshed by their meal they resumed the search, and an hour's hunting convinced them that their quarry had not left the town but had gone to earth somewhere in the neighbourhood. They left their bicycles in charge of the car park attendant, and setting out from the market-place, worked their way methodically from street to street, sometimes together, sometimes parting company and meeting again at the end of parallel roads. They divided the ground to be covered into four sections, returning to the Market and starting afresh for each quarter. Foot-sore and a little discouraged, they had for the third time turned their backs on the Square which was dusty and crowded with holiday makers, and were plodding up rather a dreary road of small shops and houses, when Philippa grasped Joe's arm.

A score of yards away, in the door of a little draper's shop, stood a man in a shabby brown tweed coat and grey flannel trousers who glanced from side to side up and down the street, with sharp, nervous movements. Just for a moment the three girls hesitated, then Joe strolled on as if nothing had happened.

" I am going to find some," she declared in an emphatic voice as they drew abreast of the shop. " I am going to find some if I have to try every draper's in the town."

" Find some what?" asked Hester in surprise, but her voice was drowned by the quicker-witted Philippa's.

" You will find plenty, but not at that price. You won't get anything good under one and eleven."

They were past the shop, but Joe answered her argumentatively.

" Nonsense! I have seen a very good quality in one

of the Portsmouth stores at ten-three—quite pretty, too."

"What on earth are you two talking about?" demanded Hester, as she followed them round a corner. "Are you light-headed?"

Joe and Philippa glowered at her, then seizing an arm apiece they hustled her along the street and round another corner.

"Of all the unutterable duffers," muttered Joe, looking back over her shoulder, and pausing for breath.

"Duffer yourself," retorted Hester. "How was I to know you were being clever—good quality in a Portsmouth stores, indeed!"

"I suppose you would have preferred to discuss Mrs. Roberts's size in shoes, or dyes in radiators."

"Would that have been any worse than rushing along as if the five furies were after you? You would have roused the suspicions of a kitten with its eyes shut."

"We were round the corner before we hurried," Joe said, walking on a little uneasily. "He didn't see us—and with any luck he didn't hear you either. I wonder if he belongs to the shop, or if he was only a customer. We must find out."

"He had his hands in his pockets," said Philippa. "I don't know why that should make him look as if he belonged, but it did, and what is more——"

" For goodness' sake don't go drawing any more deductions," Hester interrupted. " They are always wrong."

" And what is more," repeated Philippa with determination, " it seemed to me from the way he was looking up and down the street, that he was expecting somebody. He wasn't just looking, he was peering, as he did in the woods. I shouldn't have been so sure it was he if he hadn't been turning his head in that nervous, jerky way."

" Mm. That is another thing the Chief Scout says: a person's general air and way of moving often betrays them more quickly than their actual appearance. There are two things I should like to do." Joe, having reached the busy corner of the Market Square once more, stopped and gazed through an imposing plate-glass window at a display of linens as if absorbed in them. " I want to get into that shop and make sure, if I can, that it really is his. And I should like to see whether there are any traces of the car outside it."

" It will be easy enough to get in," Philippa said. " You are looking for a good quality at ten-three, and he has heard you say so. But whether he believed you, or whether getting out will be as easy as getting in, is another matter."

" Good quality what?" demanded Hester, who was still a little muddled.

" Lace," said Joe, inspired by the sight of an embroidered tea-cloth in the plate-glass window. "You can spend hours choosing lace; and the longer we are there the better chance we shall have of picking up information. Philippa can wait outside and wander up and down without looking too obviously for tracks; and you can come in with me, Hester—only do, for goodness' sake, keep your wits from wool gathering, and don't say ' what ' to all my red herrings."

" I don't see what herrings have to do with lace," said Hester stolidly. " If you go asking for herrings in a draper's shop, he will think you are mental."

Joe opened her mouth exasperatedly, then shut it again. One could never be quite sure if Hester was really stupid or whether she was just doing it to annoy. Whichever it was, it served a good purpose at the moment, for Joe's exasperation drove away the self-consciousness which she might otherwise have felt upon entering the shop. The question of ownership was settled at once, for the little man stepped back from the door to admit them, and placed a big box of lace upon the counter. But after a perfunctory display of one or two patterns, he called through a glass partition leading into a rear room, and returned to his post in the doorway leaving them to the services of a rather pathetically black-clad little girl, obviously very timid. Joe turned the cards and bundles over one by one, looking at this pattern and that, and all the time darting quick, cautious glances at her surroundings. A shadow darkened the shop door, and she felt rather than saw that a second man had joined the first, and that both were regarding her questioningly. She laid a strip of lace across her wrist.

" This is much the prettiest," she said, holding it out at arm's-length, " but do you think it is wide enough?"

Hester moved closer to her, and together they bent their heads over the box. The little man drew his companion into the shop, and with eyes still fixed on the two girls, began to talk in an undertone. Joe strained her ears, but it was hard to appear absorbed in the laces, to discuss them with Hester, and to listen. After a moment or two, afraid of betraying herself, she gave it up, asked for a yard to be cut from three separate bundles, and stood in silence while her purchases were measured out and tied up. She caught odds and ends of words, but none of them told her anything. " Yes ", " no ", " certain ", " whereabouts ", and then with an inadvertent clearness, " last consignment ". Immediately the conversation dropped to an even lower tone than before, while a quick turn of the little man's head made it plain that he was again watching her.

Joe gathered up her parcel and her change, and slipping an arm through Hester's, turned towards the door.

" I thought of putting an edging round the collar,"

she remarked, drawing a descriptive finger down the neck of her frock, " so the width doesn't matter much for that. And for my other dress, the white organdie, you know it——"

They stepped out into the street and a tiny sigh of relief escaped her, but she continued to talk as they strolled towards the market-place, pausing every now and again to wave a hand over sleeve and skirt. Philippa was waiting for them by the plate-glass window, and they greeted one another with an eager:

" Well?"

Then Joe said quickly. " Not here. Let's get away out of the town."

They collected their bicycles from the car park, mounted rather stiffly after their long day's ride, and set out for home. There was little chance to talk on the main road, but as they dismounted at the foot of the long hill up to camp, they relaxed and looked at one another. Then Joe said:

" Now!"

" I found it," Philippa told her. " There is a mews between the street where the shop is, and the place where you called Hester a duffer. There are passages to it from either street. I went in from the farther one, and pretended to do up my suspender. The car was standing just behind the shop with its blinds drawn. I didn't dare to go close in case anybody should be watching from an upstairs window. What about you?"

Joe gave a little satisfied nod.

"It was his shop, all right; so we have done what the Brister Gout told us to do."

"Did you find out anything more?"

"I am not sure. It just seemed an ordinary shop, with a little of everything, hats and shoes and dusters and silks and satins, cotton-backed satins, nothing grand—except——"

"Except what?" asked Hester, as Joe hesitated. "I looked about me more than you could, because I wasn't supposed to be so interested, and I didn't see any exceptions."

Joe unfastened her little packet of lace and held it out for Philippa to look at.

"It didn't strike me right away," she said. "Some of the stuff was the cheap white imitation you would expect, but some——"

"Real," Philippa pronounced after a close scrutiny. "Very pretty and not by any means cheap. In fact, not a bit like a little mixety-maxety country draper. Now, I wonder what we ought to deduce from that!"

"Talking of deductions," put in Hester, "your last was actually right. The little man was on the look out for a visitor, and he came while we were there. How much did you hear, Joe?"

"Nothing to make head or tail of, except possibly ' last consignment '."

Joe frowned over the words, and for a few minutes

the three girls trundled their machines on in silence. Then Hester gave a sudden exclamation.

" Look here! Didn't the Brister Gout say that if we failed to-day, we would have one more chance to-morrow morning. That sounds to me as if the ' last consignment ', whatever it may be, was going to arrive to-night. What about keeping a watch on the lane?"

Involuntarily all three quickened their slightly lagging footsteps.

" I don't see why we shouldn't," Philippa agreed. " We have done all we were asked to do, and I don't see why we shouldn't be free to carry on for ourselves —only of course we haven't told the Brister Gout yet."

" That's his fault," rejoined Hester. " How can we, till we know who he is and where to find him, or her. Besides, we might see something important, and have much more to tell."

" But——" Joe began, and broke off. Half a dozen objections rose to the tip of her tongue, there to be checked; she had her own share of reasonable human curiosity. She wheeled Miss Weland's bicycle into its place in the farmhouse porch, rejoined the others, and climbed on up the hill in silence.

" But what?" asked Philippa presently.

" If we do watch the lane," Joe said, dismissing her doubts from her mind, " we shall have to make some arrangement for Mrs. Roberts. She is sure to come and look at us again."

"Dummies," said Hester.

Joe shook her head.

"Too quiet. She might get suspicious and switch on a torch."

"We ought somehow to get ourselves settled and hidden before they begin," Philippa said. "You know how we galumph when we try to stalk, especially in the dark."

"Three of us may galumph, but if there were only one——"

"No, you don't," interrupted Hester and Philippa together.

"If you think you are going to slip off by yourself as you did the other morning," Hester added, "you can think again."

"I was only going to suggest"—Joe said meekly—"look here! Hadn't we better turn off through the woods and come up to camp from the farther side. We don't want to be seen crossing the steading dressed like this."

"What were you going to suggest?" demanded Philippa, as they moved under cover of the bushes.

"Well, if I went to bed in the ordinary way," said Joe slowly, "and you two left dummies to hump out your blankets; I could snore and snuffle and yawn as if I were half awake, and Mrs. Roberts wouldn't dare to look too closely into the tent. Then, when she was well away I would slip out and either join you, or else keep a look out on my own farther up the lane."

Philippa and Hester regarded her dubiously. They saw the force of her argument, but they preferred to have Joe with them, both for her sake and their own. All the way home to the field they discussed alternatives, then as usual, gave way. They ate a hasty and not too happy supper, but in the end forgot their fears while getting ready for the night's venture.

Their uniforms, which had hitherto been such a handicap, now proved invaluable. With black stockings drawn over their hands, and collars turned high round their ears, they merged invisibly into the darkness, leaving only the faint white blur of their faces to betray them. A proposal that they should further hide themselves with burnt cork was rejected, since the traces would take several days to wash off and would certainly give rise to unflattering and inquisitive comments in the big camp. A second idea of Hester's, however, met with approval, and they dipped their whole available supply of butter muslin into the rather large bottle of ink which had replaced the one upset by Hester earlier in the week. Tacked together, with holes for eyes, nose, and mouth, this headgear made them look like particularly sinister members of the Ku-klux-klan. But as a disguise it could hardly have been bettered.

" I only hope Captain hasn't chosen to-night for playing extended scouting games in the dark," Philippa exclaimed, as she watched Hester thrust the fringes of her mask under the neck of her uniform and button it securely into place. " You would frighten any of the small fry out of their wits. Whew! It is hot!" She puffed the clinging folds of her own muslin away from her mouth, then stooped to give a final clumsy pat to the kitbag tucked up in her blankets. " I feel as if I had gone back to the days of my pram, and woolly gloves with no fingers. I'll be playing this little pig went to market, to pass the time while we are waiting."

" For goodness' sake don't get chattery," Joe warned her. " The night is so still that your whispers will carry from the barge to the Manor if you once begin. Goodness knows what will happen if you are caught, and your only chance is to sit like graven images without a word or movement, no matter what you see or hear—you had better be going. Take my ground-sheet; it is dark blue and will show up less than yours. And get under cover of the hedge as quickly as you can and keep to it all the way down. No matter how black you are, your silhouettes will show up against the sky if you move about out in the open."

With slightly beating hearts the watchers crept to the tent door, where they hesitated a moment.

" We shall meet you again here, soon after dawn, if you don't join us before," Philippa said, taking a last glance round the tent, at the two beds, hunched, knobbly and empty, and at Joe, propped on her elbows in the third.

Joe gave a little non-committal grunt and slipped down on to her pillow. The two dark figures vanished from the doorway, the soft pad of their footsteps dwindled to silence, and she was alone.

CHAPTER XII

The Watcher at the House

Joe, only half undressed, turned restlessly under the weight of the bedclothes. Even had she been less warmly covered up, the night would have felt unbearably close. The heat and the silence seemed to cut her off from the rest of the world and shut her, a solitary prisoner, into a confined yet defenceless canvas cell. She drew for herself a mental picture of the surrounding fields, and of the two camps. The nearest tent in the larger one, she reminded herself, could not be more than sixty yards away; well within earshot.

That thought was comforting.

She cast a resentful glance at the vague outlines of the beds on either side of her, and wished that they were not so realistically filled. Hester's especially, had reposing upon its pillow a face of pale pink celanese silk stuffed with woven underwear, which roused her to active dislike.

There were moments when she could have sworn

that the pink blob moved, and that the blankets rose and fell with the breathing of their occupant. She turned her back on it, then, finding this more disturbing than ever, fixed it with a stern eye and tried to concentrate her mind upon her own immediate plans.

Apart from satisfying her own curiosity she really hoped, as Hester · had suggested, to glean further information for that mysterious person, the Brister Gout, but she did not see how this could be done by watching the lane. That Mrs. Roberts and her friends would be going up and down with a " consignment " the three girls already knew; but it was unlikely that the consignment would be of such a nature that it could be recognized as it was carried past on a dark night up a yet darker lane heavily overshadowed by trees. If anything were to be seen, the only chance of seeing must surely be at the Manor itself.

Joe wriggled guiltily under her blankets as she thought of Hester and Philippa crouching behind their hedge. Although she was convinced that one person would be far safer than three " galumphing about " as Philippa put it, she did wish that her tent mates had not considered her so brave and unselfish for staying behind.

" Brave! " She leaned across and gave the celanese-faced object in Hester's bed a defiant thwack, and for the second time turned her back on it. The defiance was not all for the celanese face. She knew what its creator would think of her present scheme.

She looked at the luminous dial of her watch. It was close upon half-past twelve, and she wondered how Hester and Philippa were faring, and if they were finding it hard to keep awake. She herself had every sense on the alert, but she found her very sleeplessness tiring, and wished heartily that Mrs. Roberts would pay her expected visit and put an end to this spell of inactivity and suspense. She had looked at her watch at least a dozen times, however, and had foreseen fully as many different possibilities of disaster, before her ears caught a rustling of grass and the faint swish of a skirt. She flung out an arm across her pillow, turned over on to her back and yawned a long and most realistic noisy yawn. The rustling ceased. Joe yawned again, and then in a muttering drowsy voice told herself to be quiet. The triangular patch of doorway darkened, and for a minute that felt an eternity there was absolute silence. Then came the sound of footsteps tiptoeing away.

Joe sat up and listened. The silence and the hot dark night closed in upon her again, and she had an unpleasant feeling of weakness, as if her bones had melted and would give way altogether if she tried to move.

Was Mrs. Roberts satisfied, or had she gone to

fetch a companion, and would the two of them return for a more searching investigation?

Joe looked at her watch for the thirteenth time, and resolutely lay down. She would have patience for another half hour. At length she crept out of bed, donned her uniform, and pulled her inky mask over her head. It clung to her hot face, and, in spite of the holes, hindered her from seeing. She tore the eyeholes bigger and pinned the folds back tightly. Then, after swiftly improvising a face from a vest and a haversack to lie upon her own pillow, she thrust her hands into their stocking gloves and slipped in her turn, a shrouded black phantom, from the tent.

Her plans, as far as she could lay them, had been made, and she moved without hesitation towards the big camp. She crossed to the wood where they gathered fuel and held steadily to the main track till she reached the low grass-clad cliffs at the farther side. Here she turned, and scrambling on hands and knees, made her way over sand and shingle and boulders of stiff clay, till the garden and yew trees of the Manor House loomed through the darkness on her left. Then she paused for breath. The journey, she reckoned, had taken her about three-quarters of an hour. With the half-hour's delay in the tent, there had been ample time for the fetching of at least one load of the mysterious consignment.

Joe straightened her shoulders, weary with stooping, then crouching forward once again, and taking cover where she could find it behind bush and tree, she stole up to the house itself.

She had access to two sides of it. The kitchen and passages were shut off by a wall; and a high hedge of hawthorn and blackthorn enclosed it on the east. But the front of the house, with its rounded porch and tall flat windows, and the long verandah opening to the sea, were both faintly visible in the starlight. At first the whole place seemed deserted. All the windows had blinds, and those to right and left of the porch were shuttered. But presently, between the chinks of one shutter, a light showed faint and flickering, like the light of a moving candle.

Joe slid noiselessly between two clipped clumps of privet at an angle of the wall, where she could keep a watch on drive and garden. She squatted down, preparing to wait, and as she did so, again recalled Hester and Philippa. For more than three hours now they had been behind their hedge, and Joe wondered whether their patience had withstood the strain, or whether Philippa's tongue, or Hester's restless limbs, had betrayed them. As time went on her solicitude gave way to envy. They at least had one another and could keep each other awake. She blinked her eyes and shifted a cramped foot.

Starlight had begun to fade into the deeper darkness

that precedes dawn before her vigil was rewarded. With a suddenness that made her heart beat, the five tall windows in the verandah were edged with gold. Almost immediately there was a creaking of hasps and hinges, and a murmur of voices broke the stillness. At one window the edge of gold broadened to a gap, then closed again, slightly awry.

Trying to feel grateful for this stroke of fortune, yet wishing herself anywhere but where she was, Joe left the shelter of her privet bushes and crept towards the newly opened window. As she did so she heard a man's voice mutter protestingly, and Mrs. Roberts answer:

" Nonsense! It is stifling in here, and who is there to see us from the garden."

Redoubling her caution, Joe mounted the verandah steps and huddled closely into the shadow of the wall. Several people were moving about within, but except for an occasional word or two from Mrs. Roberts their voices were infrequent, and too low to be distinguishable. At first there was almost complete silence. Then came the slam of a door, followed by a tinkle of glasses; then, in a masculine tone, raised a little:

" There. That's better. Now let's have a dekko at the goods."

It was the signal for a series of thuds and rustlings. Joe pressed closer to the window, her fears almost

forgotten in her rising excitement. Where the blind
hung crooked there was a thin crack and she peered
through it, blinking as the light dazzled her. It gave
her a narrow vista of one side of a long table, and of
the space between table and fireplace. Joe, her eyes
growing inured to the glare, drew back and blinked
again.

Table, chairs, floor, and even mantelshelf were
heaped with a blazing mass of colour. Silks and
velvets, satins and brocades, their bales unwrapped by
swiftly appraising hands, flung wide their riches of
blue, crimson, purple and orange, gold and silver and
bronze. A veil of silvery tissue draped a pool of jet
black velvet, to be lost in its turn under a silk shot
with the colours of driftwood flame. To the watcher
at the window the chink of room was like a giant's
paint box, upon the palette of which fresh tubes were
continually splashed by a reckless hand. She gazed,
fascinated, and heedless of time slipping by, minute
by minute.

Behind her there was a faint stirring in the trees,
the first sigh of a world about to waken. A puff of
wind caught the blind of the open window, blew it
suddenly inwards, held it in a swaying curve, and let
it flap down against the low sill.

"What's that?" came in Mrs. Roberts's thin, sharp
voice from across the room.

Joe started back, and in one uneasy glance saw that

the darkness was no longer opaque, but transparent
and tinged with grey. Retreat by the lawn was cut
off, but the verandah still lay black in the heavy
shadow of the overhanging wisteria. She flattened
herself against the wall, her arms outspread to hold
her to the thick gnarled trunk. A patch of brilliant
light fell across the stone flags as the blind was drawn
aside, then she heard the guttural voice of the woman
servant:

" Nix. Nix da."

" Let me see."

There was tread of heavier, firmer footsteps, but
before they could reach the window place the Flemish
woman, who had been peering straight towards the
creeper, gave a lusty shriek, and collapsed in a very
substantial heap upon the sill.

With one bound Joe was over the verandah and
speeding down the path. From the room came an
outburst of confused talk and shouting, but the woman's
bulky figure blocked the window, delaying pursuit for
a score of seconds. Joe raced round the corner of the
house and plunged headlong into the shrubbery,
aware that her only chance lay in getting out of sight.
In front of her rose the black outline of a huge cedar
of Lebanon, its friendly branches sweeping almost to
the ground. Behind, more shouting and the scrunch
of running feet on gravel warned her that she had not
an instant to lose. She flung herself at the lowest

branch and in ten seconds climbed as many feet and fancied herself safe.

"Above eye-level," she muttered to herself desperately. "They won't look above eye-level."

But there was a condition with which she had failed to reckon, a condition which was brought home to her during five agonising minutes of tension, when she watched electric torches seek to and fro, up and down, this way and that, the rounded white arc of their beams travelling everywhere and coming closer with each movement of the sweeping circles. By day the hunter may be limited by his own range of vision, but at night his eyes follow the light he swings in his hand.

The end was inevitable, and it was hastened by Joe's involuntary downward glance when the light fell on the shiny rubber toes of her gum shoes. She clambered to the ground in grim silence, no longer under Mrs. Roberts's contemptuous eyes, looking in the least like a sinister member of the Ku-klux-klan, but only like a sixteen-year-old schoolgirl with a piece of torn and inky butter muslin over her head. In yet grimmer silence she was marched into the house, not to the verandah room, but to the big gloomy hall by the porch, where the door was shut with an unpleasant finality of key and bolt.

She was confronted by her captors. They seemed to be legion, but there were only five. Mrs. Roberts

and her husband; the two men from the shop; and
Osterhaardt. To these there was presently added a
sixth, the Flemish woman, who shuddered and crossed
herself with such obvious aversion that Joe's self
respect was a little restored. It was consoling that to
one person at least she looked more fearsome and less
silly than she felt. But even this crumb of comfort
was quickly reft from her, for Mrs. Roberts's first
words were:

" Take that thing off."

Joe obeyed, hoping that the ink had left no streaks
and smudges on her hot face. Frightened though she
was, she could not keep her mind fixed upon the
plight in which she had landed herself, but found it
wandering off into a comparison between Mrs. Roberts
and herself. Why was she always so dirty and dis-
hevelled, and how was it that Mrs. Roberts, after a
night spent in tramping up and down a muddy lane,
contrived to look as if she had just stepped out of a
bandbox? A second-rate bandbox, thought Joe, so
angrily that she almost spoke the words aloud. She
frowned, and tried to pull herself together to face
this emergency.

" Ah. So it is you. And what are you doing here?"
Joe said nothing.

" Where are the other two?"

Again Joe said nothing. Mrs. Roberts looked at a
clock in the angle of the staircase.

" We are in rather a hurry," she observed. " My husband and I hope to catch the early ferry from Fishbourne this morning, and we have one or two things to arrange first. Where are the others?"

A quarter-past four, and Philippa and Hester were to leave their hedge at dawn. They might be back in the tent, and then again they might not. Joe scowled in her effort to think clearly. Her head felt stupid with weariness. In spite of herself her heart would thump, and her mouth was dry and her tongue felt like cotton wool. She could see no way of diverting suspicion from her companions, while yet implying that she would at once be missed if Mrs. Roberts tried to detain her.

" Where are the others?"

" I don't know," she said at last.

At a sign from Mrs. Roberts, Anna, the woman servant, drew nearer.

" Where are the others?"

" I came up here alone. I left the tent without telling them where I was going."

" Indeed. Why?"

" I was awake when you came to look at us, and I followed you back to see why you had come."

" That," said Mrs. Roberts drily, " was hardly a wise thing to do in the circumstances. I have warned you several times to keep away, you know."

There was silence. The clock on the staircase

ticked placidly. One of the men took a pipe from his pocket and knocked it out against the grate. From outside in the farmyard came the crowing of a cock. Familiar commonplace sounds. Mrs. Roberts's voice was milder than Joe had ever heard it, her words were apparently harmless; yet as the silence lasted Joe felt her knees tremble, and pulled unavailingly at her tunic to hide them.

"Unfortunately for yourself," Mrs. Roberts continued at length, as mildly as ever, "the business you have stumbled into is rather too big for us to allow it to be disorganized by two or three tiresome girls. Anna will have to take care of you—Anna!"

She spoke to the woman servant in rapid French. Her husband and the other men shifted uneasily, eyeing Joe with a mixture of anger and concern; but whatever the scheme put forward, they made no active protest. The cock crowed again, cutting short the conversation. Mrs. Roberts threw back one of the shutters, and the gray light of day dimmed the lamps and made the gloomy hall yet gloomier.

"We must get that stuff shifted to Ventwich," she said, addressing the company in general, and her frankness made one listener's heart sink like a stone. It was plain that what Joe might hear or learn no longer mattered. "There is not much left except this last load, but we shall have to run through the house and make sure we leave no traces. Anna and Oster-

20   (H 21)

haardt will take her "—she glanced at Joe—" down to the barge, and get hold of the other two while we attend to the stuff. Once out at sea——"

She did not finish her sentence, but with a shrug of her shoulders turned towards the verandah room, and left Joe to her fate.

CHAPTER XIII

A Prisoner on the High Seas

The barge rocked gently on the swell of an in-
coming tide, and through the porthole echoed the
sound of lapping water. A fresh wind was blowing
and the waves sparkling in the sunshine, were tipped
with white.

Joe paced to and fro, pausing every few moments
to gaze out at an empty sea and a blank horizon. A
big locker flanked one side of the porthole, and an oil
cooking stove the other. Against the inner wall were
two bunks, and a round wooden table and three chairs
were clamped to the floor in the middle of the cabin.
In cleanliness the cabin vied with the deck and hull
of the barge. Everywhere the unpainted wood was
scrubbed and spotless. The brasswork of the oil
cooker shone like gold. The lower bunk was taut
under a crisply starched blue-and-white cover; and
thick blue-and-white china stood in the deeply socketted
shelves above the stove.

Joe, tramping up and down, saw none of it. Between
chairs and wall there was just space to pass, and she

walked and turned and walked again, with eyes only
for the porthole and for the sea beyond.

Six. Half-past six. Seven.

What had happened to the others? There was a
second cabin with a porthole overlooking the shore,
of which she had caught a glimpse as she was taken
past. Were Hester and Philippa already there,
prisoners like herself? Surely she would have heard
if they had been brought aboard.

Half-past seven.

It was too late now to bring them down the lane.
The whole big camp would be awake and stirring.
Had Osterhaardt failed to find them? Had Mrs.
Roberts after all believed, as Joe had hoped she would
believe, that they were placidly asleep in the tent,
and altogether innocent of Joe's share in the adventures
of the night. Perhaps—the idea came with such a
rush of relief that Joe's knees gave way under her and
she sank down on the chair—perhaps she had simply
been locked into the barge to keep her out of the way
while the whole gang from the Manor House was
making its escape. If this were so, her release would
only be the matter of an hour or two; for after the
Manor House itself, the barge would be the first
place to which Hester and Philippa would lead a
search party.

Joe looked at her watch again. A quarter to eight.
The more she thought over this last idea, the more

probable did it become to her. They would never have dared to wait as late as this if they had really meant to carry her off.

Limp with the reaction from strain, she slipped down, and spreading her arms over the table, rested her head on them. For a second or two she was almost asleep.

She was roused by a throb that shook floor and table, and reverberated in the air outside, and she started up sick with renewed dismay. The vibration was repeated and settled down to a steady thrum. The gentle rocking movement ceased, and beneath the porthole, waves began to surge past in a steady stream. Land slid suddenly into the little circle of sea and horizon, and a moment later she found herself looking across a widening stretch of water to the beach where, a hundred years ago, she and Philippa and Hester had lighted a fire and cooked their supper.

The throbbing stopped and the barge was still again. Feet trampled the deck overhead, and presently she heard footsteps descend the companionway and come down the passage between the two cabins.

Joe rose from her seat and stood, her hands gripping the back of her chair. The cabin swayed, the floor lifting and falling. She shut her eyes to fight the dizziness which threatened to overcome her, and opened them again, hope rising in spite of itself, at the sound of the key in the lock. The door was flung back, and in the doorway she saw Osterhaardt, and behind him, peering over his shoulder, the face of the woman servant Anna.

For a minute that seemed taken from eternity itself there was silence; a silence deepened rather than broken by the lapping of water, and the little wooden sounds of a boat rocked by the tide. Joe's grip on the wooden bar of her chair tightened till her knuckles were white, and she braced her knees against the seat to hide their shaking. Her voice failed her, and as she struggled to speak she remembered with a fresh helplessness that the barrier of language made speech of no avail.

Osterhaardt took a step forward into the cabin, and Joe squared her shoulders and stood erect. From the scanty stock of her schoolgirl French she recalled one word, and she hurled it defiantly:

" Cochon!"

Osterhaardt glared at her.

" If I had time," he exclaimed, in English as good as Joe's own, " you would hear more about yourself in the next ten minutes than you have heard in the whole of the rest of your life."

Joe's defiance crumpled, her jaw dropped, and she sat down very suddenly.

" Oh!" she said in a faint voice. " Oh!"

She stared at the unshaven stubbly chin, at the

dirty red neckerchief, and at the angry blue eyes looking straight into her own.

"Do you realize you've blown the whole show sky high? Didn't I tell you that the one thing that mattered was giving yourselves away?"

Light dawned incredibly.

"You're—you're the Brister Gout!" she cried.

"The what?"

"The Bub-bub——" she choked, and found herself laughing.

Osterhaardt took another step towards her, hesitated, and was elbowed aside.

"Look out, Jerry," interposed a new voice. "Can't you see that the child is at the end of her tether, and no wonder. Go away, crank up the barge or whatever it is you do to start the stupid thing, and leave this to me. I am going to get breakfast, goodness knows we all need it. Here, Joe—you are Joe, aren't you—take the rind off that for me, yes, all of it, Jerry's appetite has to be seen to be believed—go *on*, Jerry, upstairs, or aloft, or whatever you call it. There——"

Kettles were whisked on to the stove, and a packet of bacon was plumped into Joe's lap. She clutched it, her head bent, while she fumbled ashamedly for her pocket handkerchief.

" —that's better. My brother is in the Navy, though you mightn't think it to look at him—commands a gun boat or a torpedo boat or something, and is inclined to think that he can command everything else that comes his way. I have to put him in his proper place now and then. He is home on leave just now, sick leave. Met a Chinese pirate with a knife and he wanted to put him in his proper place too, though the place he thought proper isn't usually called proper in polite circles. My name is Ann, by-the-by, Ann Ashdown."

Joe chopped at her bacon rind, too dazed by the emotions of the past few minutes to take in what was said, yet grateful for the talk that streamed on without putting questions or expecting answers. Presently she ventured to steal a glance at her companion— big, heavy, slatternly as ever, with wisps of hair sticking out from the coil at her neck, and coarse stockings wrinkling down over shapeless clumsy shoes—and yet——

A frying-pan joined the kettles on the stove, and the aroma of sizzling bacon rose in a delicious blue steam. Miss Ashdown bustled about the cabin, rocking the frying-pan with one hand, setting out plates and dishes with the other, plunging into the recesses of the locker for butter and marmalade and milk and bread, and all the time, with a shrewd eye on Joe, keeping up a running flow of conversation.

" There," she said at last, putting a tray laden with crockery on the table, " if you would just finish the frying for me—yes, all those eggs—I'll run up and take the wheel from Jerry while he shaves; he is so much better tempered when he is clean. Then we'll all have breakfast up on deck. You must be dying for a breath of fresh air. There's the teapot, and put the bacon in the oven to keep hot. He won't be long, and he'll give you a hand up with the tray when he is ready."

The barge was well out into the Solent and heading westward under its big red sail when Joe climbed the steep steps to the deck, holding the teapot rather precariously in one hand while she clung to the rope railing with the other. The wind was fresh and cold, and she shivered as a gust caught her, blowing her hair into her eyes. But it was an ordinary shiver. She no longer felt dazed. The humdrum influence of the frying-pan had steadied her; the world had slipped back to its normal friendly ways, and she had slipped with it out of a nightmare too fantastic ever to have been real. She felt all her interest and curiosity waken with redoubled force, and her appetite in this cold salty air, bade fair to outdo even her curiosity.

Ann and Jerry Ashdown were already in the little glass-walled wheel-house labelled " Krootsmann ", above the sleeping-cabins, and Joe could hear Ann's voice from half-way across the deck talking, with breathless indifference to traditional law, to the man at the helm. Joe joined them rather shyly, her newly recovered courage ebbing as she met the grim look which still lingered in the Brister Gout's blue eyes, and returning again when Miss Ashdown pushed her on to a bench, filled her plate with smoking bacon and eggs, and winked at her cheerfully from behind her brother's back.

" And now to business," Miss Ashdown began, as soon as everyone had settled down to their breakfast, " and don't you forget, Jerry Ashdown, that it is my business, so that there is no need for you to lose your temper over it."

She gave Joe another nod, and Joe saw her lips outline the words " proper place ". Jerry Ashdown's scowl vanished for a moment in a grin.

" For sheer gratitude of heart, give me a sister," he exclaimed. " Your business, by all means. And what exactly do you propose to do about it, now that your young friend's finger has played such havoc with your pie?"

Miss Ashdown looked at the clock.

" The Roberts are due in Portsmouth at nine-thirty, and we should make Sandmouth in about fifteen minutes, at the latest. That gives us an hour to get through to your Commissioner friend at Scotland Yard and have them intercepted—that is, if we want them intercepted. But do we?"

" Depends on Joe," said her brother, glancing at Joe interrogatively.

Joe looked startled.

" I—I don't know," she stammered. " They are smugglers, aren't they?"

" You don't say so," commented the Brister Gout drily.

" He means," explained Miss Ashdown, " did you trail the car?"

Still hesitatingly, Joe told of the long ride round the island, and of its end in the little draper's shop which sold such a curious mixture of cheap wares and exquisitely fine French lace. But the discoveries which had seemed so satisfactory at the time, now sounded lame and inconclusive, and although she was disappointed, she was not surprised when her hearers exchanged glances and shook their heads.

" So that's that," said the Brister Gout.

" A Morris, you said, and old," murmured Miss Ashdown. " It would attract less attention, but it certainly wasn't what we hoped. Not that we ever saw—till last night—and then he wasn't there. That woman was really uncommonly clever at keeping us out of the way."

" Sure you trailed the right car?"

" It was the car we found in the woods at twelve o'clock yesterday morning," rejoined Joe a trifle nettled. " And the shop belonged to the little man who was in the hall at the Manor when I was taken in there."

" And it went nowhere else?"

"I don't think so. The black drops were hard to follow, but I don't believe we missed any."

There was a prolonged silence. Then Miss Ashdown sighed.

"The question is, do we rest content with our half loaf, or do we throw our little fishes back and have another try for our whale."

"We are just off Sandmouth pier, so you have about three minutes to make up your mind," her brother told her unhelpfully.

"Do you mean," Joe ventured to ask, "that the Roberts people are only accomplices, and that there is someone bigger behind them?"

"I am sure you read too many shockers," observed Miss Ashdown, "but that is what I do mean. And if we don't catch that bigger someone, it not only means struggling with an impossibly heavy handicap just now, but the whole business will have to be tackled again under less favourable conditions, directly the present scare is over. He will find the profits too high to be foregone at the mere risk of losing an agent or two. On the other hand, if we don't lay hold of the Roberts while we can, if we let them go free as bait, so to speak, I don't yet know how we shall get into touch with them again. The Osterhaardts are dead, I'm afraid. Mrs. Roberts never trusted either of them an inch out of her sight at the best of times, and now there would be all these awkward explanations about Girl Guides—bother! There is the slipway. Jerry! For goodness' sake stop being The Silent Navy and tell me what to do!"

Jerry Ashdown knocked out his pipe and pointed with its stem to the breakfast dishes.

" Take away that clutter," he said, and turned the whole of his attention to rounding the pier and entering the harbour beyond.

The first ferry steamer of the day had just come in from the mainland; such townsfolk and holiday makers as were about were clustered far out at the end of the pier, and the little grey stone harbour was almost deserted. Joe felt a sense of anti-climax as she stepped on to the quay. A big pile of straw-packed crates lay to one side, as they had lain yesterday when she rode by on the trail, as they had lain ten days ago when the Guides first arrived. Old fishing nets hung between the posts, redolent in their tarry fishy smell of the very essence of honest labour. The Harbourmaster's door stood trustfully open, symbolic of his faith in the goodness of man. Over everything, harbour and sea, village and holiday makers, lay a tranquil peace. There was no place here for rogues and vagabonds. The past night became unimaginable, and again fact bore down upon fantasy and denied it existence.

But there was no denying the existence of the barge, or of Jerry Ashdown and his sister. Fantasy triumphed in the very solidity of their fact, and with Jerry's first words, spoken though they were in the most matter-of-fact voice, the placid little quay became a background for drama.

" There is a private call box at the hotel. I am going to ring up Calthorpe at the Yard."

" Then——"

Miss Ashdown and Joe began and stopped simultaneously.

" I don't know," said Jerry, answering their unspoken question. " I'll tell him how things stand, and ask his advice. You had better wait here."

" I think," said Miss Ashdown, looking after her brother's retreating figure, " that I'll take the chance of wiring to my maid to send me down some respectable clothes. We may have to stay on for a day or two, and if I have to meet Chief Constables and things —one never knows—I shan't be a moment."

She set off down the street to the post office, and Joe, left to herself, sat down on a packing-case to wait and to think.

Jerry Ashdown's query as to whether they had followed the right car, although it had rankled, had roused a doubt in her mind which she now felt had been there from the first. Joe frowned as she recalled how widely the imaginary picture Philippa, Hester and she had drawn of that car had diverged from its reality. They had been crestfallen at the time, though never questioning their mistake. Looking back, Joe wished they had questioned a little more, instead of taking the mistake for granted. And yet, the Morris had undoubtedly come up the path by the creek, and had been left at the hiding-place in the woods while its owner went up to the Manor.

She frowned, and then yawned. It was hot sitting on the packing-case in the sun, and she felt drowsy and stupid. People began to drift back from the pier. A large flat-bottomed boat, like an overgrown dinghy, was towed stern foremost to the slipway where it sent waves splashing over the flagstones, leaving them dark and wet and shining. Men in jerseys, half-porter, half-sailor, appeared on the quay and busied themselves with ropes and planks and freight. The Harbour-master came back to his office, and after a moment came out of it again, watch in hand, muttering to himself. Miss Ashdown appeared at the door of the post office, crossed the street to the hotel, and presently reappeared with her brother, walking slowly down the road and, for once, listening instead of talking.

Joe jerked herself upright and slipped to her feet with a guilty feeling of having been asleep at her post. She felt more guilty when Jerry Ashdown, turning from the street on to the quay, broke off in the middle of a sentence. He stared down the slipway, then spun round on his heel.

" Cargo boat is out early the morning, isn't it?" he called to the Harbourmaster. " Thought your first car ferry ran at ten-fifteen."

" And so it will, if he don't look sharp," the Harbourmaster rejoined gruffly, as if speaking to himself rather than in answer to Jerry. He snapped his watch shut, pushed it angrily into his waistcoat pocket, stepped to the top of the slipway, and shouted an order to the men. " Aye, aye, sir," he added in a slightly milder voice, as if suddenly aware of the contrast between Jerry's manner and his appearance. " ten-fifteen is the usual. But this is a special. Mr. Posten ordered it not an hour gone."

Joe felt, rather than saw, Miss Ashdown stiffen suddenly at the name.

" Mr. Posten?" repeated Jerry.

" From over Ventwich way. Comes across regular. But he'll miss her this morning; the passenger boat goes in another three minutes, cargo or no cargo."

He stumped into his office where they heard him opening and shutting drawers, banging things down on his table, and grumbling to himself continuously. He was still grumbling when he stumped out again, slamming the door behind him.

" Thinks he's bought the place, harbour and boats and the whole Southern Railway. But you ain't bought me, me lad. Two minutes you got now, two minutes and off she goes—hie! Steady there! Stand by!"

A big, black shining limousine came sweeping round from the market-place and down the street, low hung, with the long sleek bonnet of a straight eight, and a radiator that glittered in the sun. It drew up for a moment at the top of the slipway, its engine ticking over with an almost inaudible purr that spoke of speed and power held in check. Joe read its name, Delage, on the hub of the rear wheel, and glanced towards its driver, whose broad back looked as sleek and prosperous as the car itself. It nosed cautiously down the slipway, swerving a little as it negotiated the slight curve at the foot, backing to get square to the planks, and finally gliding smoothly into the space left clear for it among the other freight. There was a clank of chains as the gangway was lifted, followed by the thresh of a tug, and the cargo boat slid slowly away from the harbour.

"Your friend?" Joe heard Jerry murmur to his sister.

"My friend—and not one scrap of evidence, not the ghost of a shadow of a scrap, to link him up with all this business—and yet I know—if only——"

Joe stared miserably at the slipway. Was that the "someone big" they were seeking? If only she had never interfered. If only she had not gone up to the Manor last night. If only——

Joe gave a little gasp and, her penitence forgotten, stood, her eyes riveted on the dark wet flags of the slipway. Crossed and re-crossed were the imprints of tyre treads. Four separate distinct wheels, three marked with curves and circles, slightly worn, the fourth new and square, and very sharp. She whirled round.

"That car!" she shouted.

The men on the quay stared, and in a flash the Ashdowns were at her side.

"Quiet, there." Jerry's hand was on her shoulder with a steadying grip. "Yes? That car?"

"It's the one that was in the woods, the one we should have trailed."

"Quietly, child. Go on. How do you know?"

Joe turned to Miss Ashdown, pointing with a finger that shook a little.

"Those three squirly sets—they are French—and the square one is a Dunlop. It has been vulcanized —can you see the smooth patch, there, and there."

For a moment neither brother nor sister moved. Then Jerry took out his pipe and began to fill it.

"Bit tantalizing," he said. "I can try Calthorpe again, but I doubt if he'll act on such a slender chance. only the kid's word for it, and no proof."

"But we have proof!" Joe's voice rose, and sank again at the warning touch on her shoulder. "We took tracking casts in plaster. We have them now—in our tent."

Jerry Ashdown lit his pipe. He held the match till

the flame touched his fingers, then dropped it deliberately into the sea, and looked at Joe with a friendly grin.

"Young woman," he said. " I take back all the things I've thought but not said this morning. Taxi, Ann. Restore Joe to her sorrowing family, and fetch those casts. Our luck has turned."

CHAPTER XIV

The Barge Sails Out

" Well, really, you don't seem to have worried much."

Joe's voice sounded aggrieved. She had slept heavily all the morning and now, at three o'clock, was eating a solitary dinner. She eyed it fastidiously: steak, burnt, tough, and lukewarm, which had been standing on the edge of the fire for over an hour.

" Worried." Hester gave a sniff. " Why should we have worried? Your Brister Gout person left a note saying you would be back about nine. Nothing to worry about."

She, too, eyed the steak. It certainly was not prepossessing. She was touchy about her cooking, and besides, if people wanted their dinner hours after everybody else had finished, what could they expect. She picked up the frying-pan in which the fat had congealed, and stalked off to wash it.

Truth to tell, in spite of the note which the Brister

Gout had contrived to leave, and which they found upon their return from the lane in the small hours of the morning, she and Philippa had been almost distracted with anxiety during Joe's absence. And added to their anxiety about Joe herself, were the very belated qualms of conscience about telling Captain. For the first time they realized how exceedingly difficult explanations, if it came to explanations, would be. Had Joe been a little older and wiser, or even a little less tired, she might have guessed the extent of their feelings by their present extreme crossness. Instead, she compared Hester's indifference with the fears which she herself had endured as much on her companions' behalf as on her own in the cabin of the barge.

" My Brister Gout person, indeed!" she muttered.

She waited till she knew Hester was looking, then scraped the larger half of her steak into the pig-pail, and cut herself a slice of bread and butter. Like the other two, she was suffering from reaction.

Grievances have a way of shutting their cherishers' eyes to other things. Nobody saw the barge come back, and Joe was in the very act of being coldly polite to Philippa over the fire for tea, when all three girls were startled by a lusty:

" Ahoy there!"

Jerry Ashdown vaulted the fence and came striding towards them.

" Ann wants you for a celebration tea," he called. " Cut along, she's waiting for you. I must go up to the Manor, but I won't be five minutes."

The three exchanged sheepish glances, then turned with one accord and ran towards the lane. Proper pride was all very well, but it stood a poor chance against curiosity. As they ran, Joe panted out the story of her morning's adventures, of which Hester and Philippa had heard only disjointed scraps whilst wrapping up the casts for Miss Ashdown, and towards which they had affected an utter lack of interest. They listened now with the pent-up eagerness of the past six hours, and only as they reached the shore did Hester say reproachfully:

" It was horrid of you to leave us out. After doing everything together it did feel as if you had stolen a march on us, and kept the best fun to yourself."

" Fun!" Joe shivered. " Fun! In that cabin! How could I tell things were going to turn out as they did? I never meant to be caught. And anyhow, I was far more worried about you than you seem to have been about me."

" We were nearly sick with worry," declared Philippa roundly. " All we could think of doing was to cook you an exquisite breakfast, just to prove to ourselves how sure we were that you would come back. And you never even looked at it."

" I would look at it now, fast enough, and do more than that," said Joe with a grin, as they crossed the jetty. " Except for a little bit of burnt leather bumping about my inside, I am as empty as a drum—sorry, Hester."

" And a jolly good thing too," was Hester's whispered reply. " Just look!"

They looked, and their spirits rose as only the spirits of hungry youth can rise. Miss Ashdown's ideas of what was proper to a celebration tea seemed to cover the better part of the deck.

Miss Ashdown herself was in the cabin, baking a final batch of scones.

" Popovers," she said, shutting the door of the little oil oven. " You pop them in and you turn them over and there you are. When Jerry is axed and I go bankrupt we mean to start a popover barrow, something like a hot-chestnut man. We shall go round the pit queues on cold winter nights. I shall do the baking, and Jerry will do the selling—popovers and hot dogs. We shall make our fortunes. I am sorry I have not had time to bake more for tea to-day, but we have been rather busy what with one thing and another, so most of the cakes are only bought. You don't mind a big tea, sausages and things, not refined, I know, but we had no time for luncheon, and Jerry's appetite —oh, I told you that before. Just prick those, will you, Joe, yes, all of them—and there is a tin of potato crisps in the locker, Philippa. Hester, if you could hand me that frying-pan, and then run up to see whether Jerry is in sight."

"Was he expecting to find another clue at the Manor? inquired Joe, as Miss Ashdown paused for a moment to manipulate the sausages.

"A what—bless you, no. Only a pipe he left behind this morning. Clue? No, we have finished with clues, I hope."

"Then was—did you——"

"Coming, do you say? Oh! At the foot of the lane —he won't be long then. Wait till we are settled down to tea, then Jerry will tell you the whole story. He was there; went over in a police boat."

The whole story, according to Jerry Ashdown, was quickly told.

"They are holding him," he informed his audience, and fell to upon scones and sausages as if everything had been fully and satisfactorily explained.

"But——" Joe laid down her fork. For all her hunger, sausages at that moment would have choked her.

"But——" echoed Philippa and Hester.

"Calthorpe had rung through by the time the police boat got across, and they searched his car. Found a false bottom. Thought it looked low hung for a limousine. Nothing in it, but an awkward thing to explain, in the circumstances. Police thought it enough to detain him on—have another sausage. Why have you stopped eating?"

" But——" exclaimed all three girls again. So many questions of equal importance were jumbled together in three heads that the heads' owners were for a moment speechless.

" It is his naval upbringing," observed Miss Ashdown, causing her listeners to look, if possible, more bewildered than before. " Précis writing and all that. He concentrates on facts and leaves out the important bits, always has done."

" She means me, not Posten," said Jerry, looking at his sister with a grin. " A clear and concise style is not Ann's strong point. Can't think how she runs her business. She is a partner in a big wholesale firm, imports silks and things. But I dare say you deduced that for yourselves. You are rather hot on deductions, aren't you?"

The girls blushed, and Miss Ashdown gave an indignant snort, while Jerry, still grinning, helped himself to his fourth sausage.

" Well, well! Never mind," he concluded with exasperating kindliness. " All's well that ends well."

" But," cried Hester, her words jostling each other out with a rush. " What we want to know is how it began?"

" Jerry," said Miss Ashdown, " has no more idea of telling a plain straightforward tale than the Hatter. It was simply like this. Posten is managing director

of a rival business which for some time has been selling
its stuff at an impossibly low price. I have had my
suspicions for a long time, but not enough evidence
to take to the police. Then Jerry had this absurd
affair with his Chinaman, and turned up at home
with three months' sick leave on his hands and nothing
to do, and you know the proverb, Satan and all that.
He has always been fond of pottering up and down
the Channel——"

"Again," interrupted Jerry with a twinkle, "she
is alluding to me, and not to—er—er——"

"Pottering," repeated Miss Ashdown firmly, "in
the Channel, and he knows the coast on both sides
like a book. He got on the track of the Roberts people
at a little French port just south of the Belgian frontier,
and when he picked them up again over here I was
sure he was on the right scent. Posten has a big house
at Ventwich, spends most of the summer here and
comes up to town two or three times a week. Mrs.
Roberts had just quarrelled with her skipper (it was
through that that Jerry found her. The man aired his
grievances to anyone who would listen), and Jerry,
who does contrive to get away with the most hare-
brained schemes, hired the barge and the identity of
one of his disreputable friends and applied for the
job as bold as brass. Not that Mrs. Roberts ever
trusted us. It was amazing how she managed to keep
us under her eye day and night. If her husband had

been half as clever as herself we should certainly never have got into touch with you."

" As things have turned out, that would have been a pity," Jerry Ashdown remarked, " but don't run away with the idea that you Guides have been un-mixed blessings. You put the wind up everybody so badly that if it hadn't been for my masterly mis-management of my engines, they would have been off days ago."

" Jerry has a heart of gold," observed Miss Ash-down, " but he conceals it. As a matter of fact it was he who set you on the trail of that car. I was dead against it. I'll admit that. I never have had much use for Guides."

" Not——"

Three faces fell, and the three girls stared at her, taken aback. They occasionally heard grown-ups talk like this, but not, as a rule, nice grown-ups.

" No," pursued Miss Ashdown, placidly. " I was a Scout, myself. Joined Jerry's troop in fact. He was my patrol leader, which is, I dare say, one of the reasons why he orders me about to this day. Never been able to forget it."

" Nobody," said the Brister Gout, " who had coped with Ann in a Scout Troop would be likely to forget it, even after so many years."

" But did you never join the Guides at all?" asked Hester.

"We lived in a remote village on the Norfolk coast, where there were none to join, in those days. Most of the time, too, I was at boarding-school, and there was no Guide Company there either. No one at home or at school ever seemed very interested in the idea of forming one." Miss Ashdown's voice changed a little, and the light went out of her face. "I was just a nicely brought-up feminine girl, aching to do all the wonderful, exciting things Jerry was able to do—you have been very lucky, so few restrictions to hold you back—but I did manage to have some fun, and really I have no regrets. Still," Miss Ashdown's voice changed again, and she chuckled, "I must confess that it warmed the cockles of my heart when Joe flung her unladylike French at our heads this morning, in defiance of two foreign ruffians! If you can't be Scouts, it is evidently better to be Guides than nothing at all. I should like to meet your Captain."

"So should I, but it is a pleasure we shall have to defer," said her brother, looking at his watch and rising from the coil of rope on which he had been seated. "We are due to meet Calthorpe in Portsmouth at seven. I don't want to hurry your young friends, but unless they feel like a short sea trip——"

It was a quiet trio that walked up the lane. The barge was already under way when they reached their field, and the faint chug-chug of its engine stirred the evening silence. They watched it sail down the creek to the sea, and out of sight. They had an odd feeling that they had been away from themselves, and now, as they turned back to their tent, they came home again; home to their own thoughts, their own interests, and their own affairs.

Their little camp wore a friendly look. The grass was cool with early dew, and a pine log smouldering in the fireplace sent up a thin spiral of sweet-scented smoke. They saw the white roof of their store tent dappled with moving shadows from the green oak tree. They saw the dull red and black and smoky gray bricks of their fireplace, and behind it the glittering line of billies, whose tin was turned to silver by the evening sun. And beyond tent and fire and glittering silver, stretched the pale, clear blue of sea and sky. It was pleasant to come home.

" I say!" Philippa, on her knees, tied up a corner of brailing which flapped to and fro in the wind. " We should never have left the tent like this. Look at our things scattered about—and your bedding, Hester, all over the grass. We went off in too much of a hurry."

Joe stirred the pine log, and blew thoughtfully at the charred end.

" Whose turn is it to cook supper?" she asked, as a red spark flickered among the ashes.

" Supper! Joe, you can't want more food now!"

" We shall be hungry before the morning if we don't eat something. Suppose I bake some oatcakes, and we have bannocks and marmalade and cocoa after we are in bed. Get me that tin lid from the wood-pile, Hester. You had better wash it first. I don't believe it has been washed since—since——"